PRAISE FOR CHRISTINE N

The Road She Left Behind

A *WORKING MOTHER* MOST ANTICIPATE
OF SUMMER SELECTION

A *PARADE* BEST BEACH READS O
SUMMER SELECTION

A SHE READS BEST BOOKS OF SUMMER SELECTION

"At the very heart of *The Road She Left Behind* are the powerful lessons of humanity: forgiveness, healing, and letting go, all woven together with the threads that bind family and friends. You will laugh, you will cry, you will root these characters on and miss them profusely when they're gone. I know I do."

—*USA Today* bestselling author Rochelle Weinstein

"Secrets have a way of seeping out, and when they do, they will shatter relationships or bring about healing. In *The Road She Left Behind*, Nolfi has penned a moving story of family, betrayal, and healing."

—Kay Bratt, bestselling author of *Wish Me Home*

Sweet Lake

FINALIST, INTERNATIONAL BOOK AWARDS

"[This book] has such a charming small-town vibe and endearing characters that readers will find themselves falling in love with quirky Sweet Lake and hoping for a series."

—*Booklist*

"In this uplifting and charming story, each room of the inn is filled with friendship, forgiveness, and love."

—*Kirkus Reviews*

The Comfort of Secrets

GOLD MEDAL WINNER, READERS' FAVORITE
AWARDS

"Welcome back to the Wayfair Inn, where discovering secrets and overcoming human frailty are the ingredients for finding love and happiness. Reading Nolfi's *The Comfort of Secrets* feels like coming home."

—Kay Bratt, bestselling author of *Wish Me Home*

The Season of Silver Linings

GOLD MEDAL WINNER, READERS'
FAVORITE AWARDS

FINALIST, INTERNATIONAL BOOK AWARDS

"In *The Season of Silver Linings* we see love on every page. Each novel in the Sweet Lake series offers a special experience for the reader, and the third book may be your favorite yet."

—Grace Greene, *USA Today* bestselling author

Second Chance Grill

FINALIST, PUT YOUR HEART IN A BOOK AWARDS

"Nolfi writes with a richness of heart that is incredibly endearing."

—Renee Fountain, *Book Fetish*

"An emotionally moving contemporary novel about the power that relationships have to transform lives."

—Susan Bethany, Midwest Book Review

Treasure Me

FINALIST, NEXT GENERATION INDIE
BOOK AWARDS

"A riveting read for those who enjoy adventure fiction. Highly recommended."

—Susan Bethany, Midwest Book Review

The Tree of Everlasting Knowledge

"Poignant and powerful, *The Tree of Everlasting Knowledge* is as much a saga of learning how to survive, heal, and forgive as it is a chilling crime story, unforgettable to the very end."

—Margaret Lane, Midwest Book Review

THE
PASSING
STORM

THE
PASSING
STORM

A NOVEL

Christine Nolfi

LAKE UNION
PUBLISHING

Text copyright © 2021 by Christine Nolfi
All rights reserved.

Published by Lake Union Publishing, Seattle

www.apub.com

Amazon, the Amazon logo, and Lake Union Publishing are trademarks of Amazon.com, Inc., or its affiliates.

ISBN-13: 9781542029124
ISBN-10: 1542029120

Cover design by Caroline Teagle Johnson

Printed in the United States of America

In loving memory of Peggy and Mario Nolfi.
And for Barry, always.

Chapter 1

He never worked during school hours. Yet there he was inside the bustling craft emporium, stocking shelves near the front.

Snow whirled through the air, a battering of cold pinpricks on her cheeks. Wiping away the dampness, Rae took hesitant steps toward the shop and peered through the display window. A dark pulse of grief pierced her deeply. Why wasn't he at the high school with the other kids? What right did he have to disregard their unspoken agreement, by putting in hours at noon on a Tuesday?

Rae avoided the shop whenever he worked. Saturdays too, if he was on the schedule. Her office was only three doors down on Chardon Square, and Rae missed the spontaneous stop-ins she'd once taken for granted—especially now, when she needed her closest friend as a bulwark against the sorrow. But she didn't have a better solution to avoid running into Quinn Galecki, other than ensuring they were never in Yuna's Craft Emporium at the same time.

Under normal circumstances, she wouldn't have dropped by this early in the day. Between the art classes and Yuna's current flash sale, the place was particularly busy.

The emporium on the corner of Chardon Square was a treasure chest for the craft enthusiast. Shelves brimmed with bottles of paint and jars of beads for jewelry making. Bolts of fabric vibrated with color as if to steal attention from the tubs of silk flowers displayed in the shop. Near the back of the store, a group of toddlers in plastic smocks and their mothers—in easy-wipe, vinyl aprons—were seated at a long table, finger painting. Older customers looked on, smiling at the tots or winking at their mothers. A happy scene, as warm and welcoming as sunlight.

Rae shivered in the cold air. *Don't go inside.*

Follow the impulse to confront Quinn, and she'd cause a scene. She couldn't trust herself to remain civil if they came face-to-face. On the other hand, Quinn's latest stunt at her property had gone too far. Snooping around the barn, leaving his little art project behind—at seventeen, he was old enough to have some consideration for other people's feelings. And criminal trespass laws, in general.

No, Rae. Just leave.

Stepping out of view, she leaned against the building's icy brick. Quinn retrieved the last of the merchandise from the box at his feet. For a boy nearing manhood, he was too thin, his features too soft. He worked with careful movements, clearly intent on doing a good job. When his extraordinary, long-lashed gaze swept across the colorful yarn he'd arranged on the shelf, a surge of unwanted sympathy welled inside Rae.

Walk away. Come back later. Talk to Yuna after his shift ends.

Cars wound around the square, their tires kicking up snow. Rae's Honda Civic was parked near the Witt Agency, where she'd been lucky to find a spot. She ought to walk back down and climb into the car. Drive home to her father, who assumed she'd taken the entire day off from her job as Witt's office manager. Or call him and explain she'd decided to put in the afternoon at the insurance agency. Bury herself in work to force Quinn from her thoughts.

Good choices, both. Either way, she wouldn't act on an impulse she knew she'd regret.

As Rae tried to get her feet moving away from the building—and without her conscious approval—her hand dipped into her coat pocket.

To brush against the flower's soft silk petals. Heartache surged through her too quickly to fend off. When it passed, she inhaled sharply.

A flash of anger carried her to the shop's door.

Since it was January in northeast Ohio—and a blustery, snowy January at that—a blast of frigid air rushed in behind her. Bursts of snow scattered across two startled women near the display window. Quinn, not far behind them, dropped the empty box he'd just hefted into his arms.

Stepping around it, Rae approached. "I want you to stop," she told him, too loud. Several customers turned around, glaring, and she pretended not to notice. "This morning's stunt was way over the line."

Pausing, she gave him room to apologize. Or at least explain himself, if genuine regret was a bridge too far. He *was* a teenager—kids often chose pride over an admission of wrongdoing.

When he remained silent, frustration bit at her. So did the withering look of a silver-haired matron by a display case of macramé projects. *Busybody.* The altercation was none of her business.

Even so, Rae lowered her voice to an urgent hiss. "Quinn, really—it has to stop. I get that you mean no harm, but . . . it's too much. Do you understand? My dad is getting up there in years, and he's angry every time he finds more footprints near our house. You're upsetting him. And I mean a lot." The trespassing upset her too, which was beside the point. She didn't have twice-yearly appointments with a cardiologist or take statins.

"I'm sorry." Quinn threw his gaze on his feet. "I didn't think it was a big deal."

"Well, it is. A major deal, and it's hurtful. Can't you respect other people's privacy? You can't roam at will over our property. Or traipse through my barn uninvited." Rae cut off, startled. Threads of color bled into Quinn's cheeks, a clear sign of remorse. The reaction stirred the pity she didn't want to feel. "Why aren't you in school?" she demanded.

"We didn't have classes today."

A teacher in-service day? Presumably a truthful statement.

The silver-haired busybody lobbed another glance. "Why don't you leave him alone? He's apologized for going in your barn—as if that's the crime of the century. And he's not obligated to tell *you* if he has school today or not."

The dressing-down injured Rae's pride. A predictable outcome. Her pride often lost against her more impulsive nature. She *was* out of line, confronting Quinn like this.

A voice came from behind—her bestie's.

Today Yuna Onaga-Fraser wore orange Converse high tops and metallic leggings beneath a purple T-shirt. The busy mother and wife of Chardon's mayor could outshine a peacock.

"Rae, what are you discussing with my employee?" she asked pointedly.

"Nothing. I'm done. I've had my say."

"About what, I'm sure I don't want to know." Dousing the rising tension, Yuna stepped between them. "Quinn, are you all right?"

"Yes, ma'am."

"Why don't you run down to the coffee shop and grab something to eat? It's lunchtime—you must be starving. Here." She pressed cash into his hand.

"Sure."

When he bolted out the door, the busybody grunted. "The boy was minding his own business when Miss High-and-Mighty stormed in."

Rae blinked. "I resent that."

Yuna blocked her view of the woman. "Let's all calm down, shall we? Rae, why don't we talk in the back?"

Yuna gave a look that needed no interpretation. The bonds of affection only stretched so far. Argue with customers in your best friend's craft emporium, and those bonds might snap.

Taking the cue, Rae marched past the people in line at the cash register and the table of happy tots to the stockroom.

A shipment of boxes crowded the stockroom's aisle. Farther back, Yuna's desk hid beneath stacks of paperwork. Although February was fast approaching, the bulletin board held a collection of Christmas drawings made by Yuna's five-year-old daughter. Kameko's list for Santa, a jumbled scrawl of wishes, was tacked nearby.

Scanning the child's handiwork, Rae suffered a pang of guilt. Yuna carried enough burdens. Between work, parenting, and marriage, she juggled more than her share. She didn't need theatrics in her store—or more fallout from the grief dominating Rae's life.

The dull ache in Rae's chest had become a constant. The sleepless nights and the surges of anger—the storms of the heart came without warning. They came without providing answers to the questions that battered her in a drumbeat of pain. Yet they didn't justify confronting Quinn inside the shop. She should've found a better way to resolve the matter.

Yuna seated herself in the office chair. "I thought you and Quinn had an understanding—you'd stay out of the shop whenever he works." She began swiveling, left and right.

"I didn't know he was working today. I came by to talk to you. It's important."

"What's the crisis?"

"I found more footprints in the snow."

"Why, because you were hunting for them? If you want to trudge around in ten-degree weather, take up skiing."

Rae folded her arms. "You're supposed to be on my side." A debatable point since Yuna refused to take sides, which hurt. "I wish you'd take this seriously."

"I can't. It's stupid. You're not a hound dog. Tracking footprints across your property has become an obsession."

"Hardly," Rae protested, "and this set is new. I found them today, in the backyard. That's not all I found, after I brought Dad home from his doctor appointment."

5

"You don't have a backyard. You own a forty-acre farm that's going to seed. Why not put the place on the market? Get the house ready to show next month. List in March."

"Don't be ridiculous. I'm not selling my house."

"Your *farm*," Yuna said. "One of my neighbors is planning to sell her bungalow. Three bedrooms, with a yard that doesn't require a tractor to mow. There's a nice fireplace in the living room. And a fabulous kitchen, in case you or your dad ever learn to cook."

The suggestion of change was unwelcome. Rae had experienced too many shocks, too much loss. For months she'd been walking on shifting sands. Longer, if she was honest. Since the last of her teen years, when she'd learned to keep secrets. Throughout her twenties, when those secrets led to unforeseen complications. And now, into the dark, incomprehensible decade of her thirties.

With agitated movements, she unbuttoned her coat. "Mind telling me what's up with the hard sell?" But she didn't remove the garment—the conversation's unexpected turn made her wonder if she should go. "I'm not here to discuss real estate."

"Who gave you the right to set the agenda for all our crazy talks? They happen constantly, in case you haven't noticed." Yuna paused in her swiveling to cast a pointed look. "Give it some thought, Rae. If you move into town, we'll be neighbors. You can bug me in the evenings. *After* I've finished my workday and tucked Kameko into bed."

"You know I can't move."

"No, I don't. It's a free country." With irritation, Yuna shook the black silk of her hair. The glossy strands danced across her shoulders. "You can live wherever you want."

"Dad has owned the property since before I was born." Asking him to leave was out of the question. The dense forest and the rolling acres were etched with memories—for both of them. Only one of those memories was too ghastly to revisit. The rest were sweet and good, and Rae couldn't bear to leave them behind.

"Your father will adapt. You both will."

Heartache tightened Rae's throat. "Stop changing the subject." Her anger flared, a protective shield. She was safe behind it. "Can we get back on point? Quinn's getting careless with the trespassing. Or bold."

"Quinn has lots of interesting qualities. 'Bold' isn't one of them."

"You may want to revise your opinion." Rae dug into her coat pocket. "I found this."

She withdrew a silk daisy like the ones on sale in the front of the store. Artistic flourishes had transformed the silk flower. Gold paint rimmed the petals. Glitter frosted the leaves. Glass beads were strung down the plastic stem. The beads rattled as she shook the offensive object before handing it over.

Yuna twirled the stem between her fingertips. "Give the kid credit. He does nice work."

"His talent is beside the point. I found it inside the barn."

"Wait. Since when does Quinn sneak into the barn?"

Uncertainty washed Rae's stomach with acid. She didn't check the barn regularly. This morning she'd only walked through after finding Quinn's footprints near the building.

"You're not sure if he's gone inside before today?" Yuna pressed.

"I'm not. He doesn't have to worry about expanding his reconnaissance—or startling animals in the barn. We sold them off right after the White Hurricane."

The famous blizzard sixteen years ago remained a grim footnote in Geauga County's history. The unprecedented winter storm was a harrowing experience for everyone who lived through it. For Rae and her father, the White Hurricane was especially tragic—the first in a series of events to irrevocably change their lives.

Yuna's brows lifted. "Where was the flower?"

"Tied with florist's wire to one of the stalls. There's so much junk in the barn, it would've been easy to miss. Quinn must've stopped at my place before coming in to work for you."

"He didn't have school today."

"So I gathered, from our brief conversation. I left the house early with Dad. We were gone for hours. I'm sure Quinn assumed I'd never notice the flower. Well, he was wrong." Pausing, she lifted her accusing gaze. "Hit me with the truth, girlfriend. Are you encouraging him?"

"Of course not!"

"Are you sure? Because I want him to stop inserting himself into my life. I get that he's coming onto my property because he has a lot to sort out. Too much, for a kid his age. He has lousy parents, the kind too selfish to help steer him through the loss. I get that, Yuna—I do. But I can't make it my problem."

"C'mon, Rae. You're blowing this out of proportion."

The bright sting of tears stopped Rae from readying a defense. Better than most people, she knew just how awful Quinn's parents were—once, she'd had the misfortune of crossing the Galeckis' path. Ironically, she'd been the same age Quinn was now, a naive kid without the experience to understand the danger she'd put herself in.

"I see it differently," she tossed back, aware that she couldn't justify her actions without telling Yuna about that night. *Which will never happen. I'll never discuss it with anyone.* Frustrated, she added, "Doesn't Quinn have anything better to do with his free time?"

"We both agree Quinn isn't a bad kid. He's a seventeen-year-old who's been through too much. Does it matter if he walks around the barn?"

"It matters to me—and to my dad. He's retired and spends too much time worrying about the . . . reconnaissance. At least that's how he sees it. If he catches the kid trespassing, he'll blow a fuse. He's *not* Quinn's number one fan."

"Maybe Connor needs to recharge his social life. Whatever happened to his geriatric homeboys? He hardly sees them anymore. At least you have diversions—working too many hours and driving me to distraction. On weekends, you both spend too much time cooped up in the house."

Rae bristled. It was bad enough that Quinn worked part-time at the shop. A definite breach of her friendship with Yuna, although the reason for the act of charity was obvious. Yuna had given Quinn the job last November, a few weeks after his unnerving questioning by the PD. The officers had kept him on the hot seat for hours before releasing him—a grueling ordeal for any kid.

Under normal circumstances, Yuna's charitable instincts were great. Rae also believed in fighting for the underdog. The two women had first grown close while volunteering at Chardon's food bank, nearly a decade ago. The following year, they'd sealed their friendship by cochairing the committee tasked with expanding the local Meals on Wheels program for seniors.

The Galecki boy was different. Not only because of the startling facts Rae continued to resist. Not only due to the PD's report, which she'd tossed into a forgotten drawer. Quinn was off-limits. The reasons were complicated, with roots deep in a seedbed of shame too dreadful to share.

A frigid silence overtook the stockroom. Rae wasn't sure how to break it.

Yuna said, "Tell me what to do to make you feel better. Name it. I'll do whatever you'd like."

The comment broke through Rae's muddled thoughts. Moisture collected at the corners of her eyes. She felt vulnerable and confused. The combination blurred her vision as the office chair groaned to a halt.

Yuna came to her feet. "Should I have a heart-to-heart with Quinn?" On tiptoe, she studied Rae closely. "Persuade him to stop trespassing on your property? It'll open the door to a conversation I don't want to have with him. He's not ready to talk about it, and I'm not either. I'm hurting too, you know."

"I know."

"I'm his employer, not the village priest. It'll weird him out if I meddle in his private life."

Rae took a swipe at her watery nose. "Get real," she muttered, hating the way she fell apart without warning. Her eyes were leaky too, spilling hot rivulets down her face. "Quinn doesn't have a private life. He has school, part-time work, and a future of breaking and entering. He's getting lots of practice, sneaking around my place."

"Stop complaining—and hold still." Yuna was a head shorter, but her maternal instincts were on full display. With soothing movements, she wiped the tears away. When she finished, she asked, "What's the verdict? How do you want me to handle this with Quinn?"

Distracted, Rae combed her fingers through the tumbling lengths of her reddish-gold hair. Did she really want her bestie to have a heart-to-heart with the kid? It didn't seem like a great solution.

As if there *were* a great solution on offer. There wasn't.

"Don't you own a hairbrush?" Yuna asked. With a sudden grin, she twirled a hank of Rae's hair. "Let's schedule an intervention at my salon. Bring smelling salts for my stylist." She wagged the long strands, drawing a howl of protest. "After we revive her, she'll make you look fabulous."

Rae swatted her away. "What's your next suggestion? A fashion overhaul, like metallic leggings on my oak-tree legs? Girlfriend, you're crazy."

"No, I'm the sugar to your spice. That's why you love me." Yuna's expression grew impish. "Do you want ice cream?"

"It's January. Ice cream is a warm-weather treat," Rae said, aware she was being peevish. At home she kept tubs stashed in the freezer. Her father loved banana splits year-round. She peered at the lunch area, a cubbyhole arrangement where Yuna stashed goodies for her staff. "Do you have hot chocolate?" she asked.

"Dixon's has brownies. We'll add a scoop of vanilla on top."

"Like I need a double dose of sugar."

"One dessert—we'll share. Fewer calories, less guilt."

"Forget the fairy wings. You're evil. You know that, right?"

Yuna shrugged. "Should we have Dixon's heat up the brownie?"

Chocolate was Rae's downfall. As was Dixon's, the wine and dessert café on the opposite side of Chardon Square.

Sensing victory, Yuna nodded at the door that led to the alley behind the building. "Let's make a run for it. Leave my staff out front to deal with the customers."

Rae sighed. A quick snack—with or without ice cream—wasn't the worst idea.

Chapter 2

Golden light slanted through the living room. The TV wasn't on. Rae walked through the house, calling for her father.

A cup of coffee sat on the kitchen counter. In the mudroom, Connor's boots and the canvas coat he wore to stroll the property were missing. Those excursions were perfectly safe in warmer months. In winter, when heavy snow and patches of ice dotted the acreage, Rae encouraged her father to wait until she was home to accompany him. For a man in his seventies, Connor was in reasonable shape—but Rae harbored an overprotective streak for her only surviving parent.

As usual, the request had been ignored. Muttering choice words, she hurried out back.

Nearly an acre separated the large, rambling house from the even larger—and thoroughly neglected—barn. During Rae's childhood, the farm had bustled with activity. She recalled downy chicks skittering across her knees in the pasture's soft grass. She'd chased dark-winged moths through the pumpkin patch and the rows of lettuce her mother, Hester, had coaxed into thriving clear into November.

Living off the land had been Hester's dream. While many in her generation traded in their youthful rebellion for the rampant consumerism overtaking the country, she read articles on organic farming while earning a fine arts degree from the University of Pennsylvania. In 1979, armed with a small inheritance and a willing husband, she purchased the tract of land outside Chardon, Ohio. It was her twenty-seventh birthday.

Although she was young, Hester was serious and sensible. Plans for starting a family were put on hold as she and Connor learned animal husbandry and when to plant crops. They hired Amish carpenters from nearby Middlefield to erect their home and the barn. The barn quickly filled with pigs, goats, chickens, and a cow affectionately named Butter. The house underwent several expansions as the couple—like modern-day pioneers—learned to can vegetables and store root crops in makeshift bins. During summer, blackberries grew wild near the forest, and Connor filled baskets with the sweet fruit. Hester preserved jams and baked pies to share with new friends they met in town. By the third year, the Amish were called back to the property. They made further additions to the house, including a small greenhouse Hester quickly put to use.

For most people, the kitchen is the heart of the home. Or, in this case, the kitchen and the adjoining greenhouse.

Hester's grand design was more ambitious. Once the Amish completed the greenhouse, they spent the better part of a sizzling August building a large, A-frame studio.

Hester's studio became the beating heart of the rambling house. Inside, she experimented with sculptural collages she crafted from recycled items. Bits of fabric; pieces of aluminum or bottle caps discovered while driving Geauga County's winding roads; old toys, chipped china, and swatches of embroidery unearthed at garage sales—Hester found imaginative ways to turn castoffs into art. Since her sensible nature came with a thrifty streak, she saw no reason why an hour driving the countryside, or three dollars spent at a garage sale, shouldn't be turned into a tidy profit.

Like his more sensible wife, Connor—who was introverted, witty, and bookish—took eagerly to farm life. Money, and how to earn it, never crossed his mind. He loved the physical labor and the dawn mist rippling across the acres. Living out his days in blue jeans was Connor's idea of heaven.

On drowsy afternoons after finishing chores, he recited Shakespeare's plays for the attentive Hester while she worked in her studio. He read Emerson's *Nature* to the uncomprehending goats during morning feedings. Connor loved music too, and he played Bach and Vivaldi for Butter as the patient cow stood in dignified silence during milking. The feisty pigs, he decided, much preferred rock and roll.

And so, most of her inheritance gone, Hester devised a business plan. Selecting her ten best collages, she booked space at a local craft show. All ten sold within an hour.

Soon after, the owner of a Columbus art gallery began featuring her work. Galleries in Cincinnati and Cleveland followed, and Hester's renown grew. So did her income, and the money was lavished on the farm. By the time of her unexpected death, Hester Langdon was cherished by art lovers throughout Ohio.

The dream she'd worked tirelessly to achieve was now faded and worn.

Regret burdened Rae as she trudged through the snow. She earned a good living as office manager of the Witt Agency, but not enough to cover the upkeep of a forty-acre property. The forest was encroaching on each side of the pasture. Shingles were missing from the barn's roof, carried off by harsh winds. Even the whimsical, magical lighting that had once lit several of the trees between the house and the barn now hung in tattered clumps, many of the bulbs cracked or missing.

Dust spun through the air of the L-shaped barn. Rae strode past the stalls where she'd found the silk flower. Telling her father about Quinn's memento wasn't a great option. Last October, he'd been more distressed by the police department's report than Rae. They were both still navigating dark moments of grief—why upset him unnecessarily?

"Dad, are you here? Hello?"

A short passageway separated the main barn from a small room where Connor, in his heyday, had worked on carpentry projects. A soft clattering reached her ears. Rae quickened her pace. In the bitter month of January, her father rarely visited the shop.

"Dad, it's freakin' cold. If you want to waltz down memory lane, can't it wait until—" A surprised breath escaped her lips. "Why are you cleaning up?" The plywood floor had been swept clean.

Connor grunted. "I was about to ask you the same thing."

"When would I get around to sprucing up your old shop? This week's laundry is still on the agenda. I swear, it breeds when I'm not looking."

"You didn't organize my workbench?"

A niggling sensation carried Rae forward. "Dad, I haven't been in here." On the pegboard, hand tools were neatly hung, the grit from years of disuse wiped away.

"If you didn't clean up, who did?" Her father studied the shelf underneath. "Check this out. Someone dusted off the jars."

The niggling sensation increased as Rae scanned the floor. "I broke one of the jars last summer." She'd forgotten to come back out and pick up the mess. "There were nails all over the place."

"Not anymore." Connor lifted a mason jar, catching sunlight on the lid. "Look here. They've been picked up too. Probably when our mystery maid swept the floor." He smoothed down his silvered beard. "Are you thinking what I'm thinking?"

"Oh, I hope not."

A fizzy silence descended. Rae searched for an explanation. *Any* explanation other than the obvious one.

Connor rocked back on his heels. "The delinquent . . . has he been coming around?"

"Quinn's not a delinquent. A little messed up and definitely a nuisance. He's never been in trouble with the law."

"You haven't answered the question."

"Gosh, your powers of observation never fade."

"Stop fancy-footing. *Your* powers of deception are worthless."

"Yes, Quinn's been upping his game." She explained about the silk flower, adding, "If he was hanging around the barn, he must've decided to clean up the shop."

"Who does that?"

"Quinn, I guess." Yuna's craft store didn't open until ten o'clock, she mused. Had the teen done the cleanup early this morning to avoid being home with his loathsome parents? "He didn't have school today."

"So he dropped by to spruce up my shop?"

"Apparently."

"When I was young, I did my best to avoid helping around the house. A teenage boy who likes domestic chores—that's one for the record books. Most kids his age lean toward graffiti or mucking stuff up. They fly off four-wheelers they're too young to operate or shoot off firecrackers when their neighbors are sleeping."

Rae sighed. "Some of your friends have grandsons from hell. *Those* delinquents aren't a representative sampling of all teenage boys."

Her father weighed the observation, clearly unconvinced. "Has Quinn left anything else around the property?" he asked.

"I haven't looked." There wasn't time in her schedule. If Quinn had littered the pasture with silk flowers and strung trinkets from half the trees in the forest, they'd go undiscovered until spring.

"I'll scout the farm tomorrow. See if he's left other surprises."

The suggestion lifted her brows. "I work late tomorrow. I'd prefer if you didn't roam free. Let's check the property some other day—together. Do your power walk inside tomorrow, five laps around the living room. Follow the 'short leash' rule."

"Stuff it, Rae. Try keeping me on a leash, and I'll string you up by your toenails." Connor's mouth curved wryly. He enjoyed the thrust and parry of their small disagreements more than his daily power walk. "I'm not old. I'm mature. There's a difference."

A predictable retort, and she chuckled. "You left 'mature' ten miles back. You're speeding toward 'ancient.' Mangy cats shed less hair than you. Face it, Dad. You need a leash."

"Go pop a chocolate, Rae. You're sassy when your sugar's low."

"I've already done the sugar buzz, thank you very much. Yuna's treat. We stopped at Dixon's."

Anticipation flashed across Connor's face. "Did you bring anything for me?"

The hopeful query pricked her with guilt. Too often, they resorted to snacking.

"Let's go inside. We'll find something for dinner." Something nutritious, she decided. It was shameful how often she allowed him to throw fries into the microwave or settle for a bowl of cereal for dinner. There hadn't been fresh fruit in the house since October. Since the night their lives were thrown into free fall.

Shadows lengthened in the barn. Rae knew her father wouldn't allow her to take his arm until they reached the threshold and the hard-packed snow. Giving him privacy, she walked ahead. Out of habit, Connor glanced in each of the stalls. He flicked the lights on and off, as if proper illumination mattered in a building they'd largely abandoned.

Rae paced in a lazy circle. Her gaze alighted on the Kubota tractor parked near the wall.

Engine oil dotted the barn's earthen floor. Like Connor's workbench, the grime on the tractor was gone. Every inch of the Kubota's bright-orange surface had been buffed to a high sheen. Breathless, she lifted the hood to check the dipstick.

Connor appeared at her side. "Quinn changed the oil?"

"Yeah."

"He did a fine job, polishing the old girl. I'll bet he changed the filter too. His father is no one's favorite human being, but he is the best mechanic in three counties. Quinn would know to do both." Connor watched her jam the dipstick back into place. "I may need to revise my opinion of the boy."

"Please don't." Her emotions toward Quinn were complicated; her feelings about his parents even more so. If he began doing odd jobs around the farm, it would add to her unease.

"You're the one who said not all teenage boys are delinquents. Maybe Quinn has more good inside than we know."

"I'm sure he does, but I was speaking in general terms." Rae shut the hood. "I didn't mean to put crazy ideas in your head about offering him a job."

"There's a lot around the property in need of fixing." Connor's greedy eyes swept the barn. "A boy his age can do a man's work. I'm too old to handle most of the chores, and you don't have the time."

"Quinn already has a job working part-time for Yuna." Rae patted her father's grizzled cheek. "And I thought you were mature, not old."

"Yuna doesn't have a monopoly on the kid's time. He might be looking for extra work." Connor thumped his fist on the hood. "I'll get going on a to-do list."

"Don't you dare."

Thwarting further discussion, Rae steered him from the barn.

Chapter 3

February sailed in on flirtatiously sunny skies.

The warming temperatures only managed to lower Rae's spirits. She was tired of shoveling snow and wearing enough layers for life on the tundra, but she dreaded the upcoming spring. Then summer, which would serve as a reminder of the loss she had yet to process.

Across the farm's snowy acres, brilliant sunshine revealed patches of green pasture. In town, the brick walkways on Chardon Square were suddenly freed from beneath layers of crunchy ice. Children played in the wide center green while their parents ducked in and out of storefronts.

But Ohio weather is notoriously fickle. By the second week of February, temperatures again plummeted.

On Saturday morning, Rae unpacked groceries as a new round of snow blanketed Geauga County. The forecast called for another three inches by nightfall. If Quinn resumed his unsanctioned visits, his footprints would go undetected.

For the time being, he was staying away. His absence made her hopeful that impulsively confronting him at Yuna's shop—awkward as it had been—was altering his behavior. Nothing more was cleaned inside the barn. New trinkets hadn't been attached to the stalls, and Rae felt confident about putting in extra hours at work. The Witt Agency was hiring two new employees for lead generation. As office manager, Rae had been tasked with training them.

Amid reviewing the training protocol, she tackled a more personal issue. Yuna's remark about Connor's lack of a social life bothered her, and Rae had been working on recharging the friendships he'd put in limbo months ago. The effort was working. As for her own social life, she was still too raw. She had no intention of reviving it anytime soon.

From the living room, her father's smartphone rang.

Connor picked up. A round of hearty laughter followed.

Affection for her father put a smile on her lips. All week long, he'd been in high spirits. At Rae's urging, he went bowling on Tuesday with the men he affectionately referred to as the geriatric squad. Several of his friends came over for lunch on Thursday. Afterward, he called the office twice—once to ask Rae to pick up furniture polish on the way home, then later to announce he'd found his dog-eared copy of *Moby Dick* in a nest of dust bunnies underneath his bed. Connor read late into the night. On Friday, he capped off a full week by finding a new Amazon series to binge-watch.

Not once did Quinn enter the conversation. Rae couldn't help but feel relief.

Rustling through the grocery bag, she placed lettuce and snow peas on the counter. In lieu of a typical weekend shop, she'd spent more time in the fresh produce area than the snack aisle. Resuming the old habit proved more difficult than expected, and she'd felt jittery and anxious while making her selections. She made it back to the car—the groceries spilling across the back seat as she hoisted them inside—before completely breaking down. Burying her face against the steering wheel, she'd sobbed for long minutes.

Connor wandered into the kitchen. "That was Aunt Gracie on the phone. Call her when you have a sec."

Connor's sister, Gracie, and her husband were retired, living in Miami. "Is she okay?" Rae placed fresh bunches of spinach and grapes beside the lettuce.

"She's fine. She wants you to fly down."

"I can't schedule a vacation. Not until later this year." In October her boss, Evelyn Witt, had been more than gracious when she insisted Rae take extended leave. Four weeks, with pay. "If you'd like to visit Aunt Gracie, bring a friend. Any of your homeboys will jump at the chance. Just let me book the flights—an early departure. I'll drop you at the airport before heading to work."

An avocado rolled past the lettuce. "What's with the rabbit food?" Connor wrinkled his nose.

"I found some of her recipes. Last night, when I made the grocery list."

A heaviness fell down upon the room. It came faster and thicker than the snowflakes ticking against the windowpane. Keeping her emotions in check, Rae folded the first grocery bag and began unpacking the next one. The welcome, mindless chore of sorting and putting away.

Her father swept trembling fingers across his receding hairline. "She wrote the recipes down?"

"On cardstock."

"I thought she made them up—flashes of inspiration as she cooked." Connor grimaced. "Not that *I* was inspired by all the vegetables she tossed into her concoctions."

"She was looking out for you, Dad."

"Why did she write them down on cardstock?"

"To make them pretty. They look more like an art project than recipes." A familiar misery welled inside Rae. "You know how creative she was. Experimenting with different mediums, always trying something new. We should frame them."

"Where did you find them?"

Rae nodded toward the cabinetry beside the six-burner stove. "In a bottom drawer, next to the cookie cutters." The sadness pooling between them became oppressive. Hoping to lighten the mood, she added, "Remember Mom's butter cookies? They were heavenly."

"Your mother was a baking machine. Every Sunday afternoon, she'd roll out a new batch. There's nothing better than a warm butter cookie, right from the oven. All that sweetness melting in your mouth."

"Once a month, she made a double batch of the dough to keep in the freezer. I used to sneak into it when she wasn't looking."

Her father smiled. "Me too."

"Pity neither one of us pitched in with the cutting out and baking. Mom could've used the help. Why didn't she ever get after us? I tried to help a few times. I couldn't get the hang of rolling out the dough before it melted."

"You've always been more like me. Too impatient. I guess that's why neither one of us has much knack in the kitchen."

"That doesn't mean we can't learn." Rae layered her voice with false cheer. "The recipes I found aren't complicated. I'm sure we can follow them."

"What if we don't want to follow them?"

"Dad, I get it. Gluten-free breads and tofu stir-fries aren't my thing either, but our diets need an overhaul. Your blood pressure isn't great, and I'm afraid to look at my butt. This summer I'd like to wear a swimsuit without total humiliation."

"Fine. Eat rabbit food while you're down visiting Gracie."

"I'm not going to Florida." Her father reached for the potato chips, the only item she'd purchased from the snack aisle. Playfully Rae slapped his hand away. "Stop pulling me off point. We used to eat the stuff she cooked. Some of it *was* rabbit food, but we didn't complain. She knew we were both seriously inept when it came to respect for the food pyramid. And her meals *were* nutritious. Look at us! We're turning into pudge-muffins."

Grunting, her father patted his belly. "Speak for yourself. My extra padding comes off every spring. If you're giving up bad habits, why punish me? At the risk of being indelicate, there's only so much roughage a man my age can take. I didn't have the heart to tell her. Not when she went all out with those recipes."

"Gosh, you're whiny. Do you need coffee? I'll brew a pot." A caffeine jolt usually made him more pleasant.

"I'll tell you what I need. Reconsider the trip to Florida. You should go." Her father sat down at the table. "I promised Gracie I'd lobby hard. Use every ploy in the parenting guilt-book to make you see reason."

"Why is everyone meddling in my life? First Yuna, and now you. And Gracie, but you put the idea in her head."

"We worry about you."

"I wish you wouldn't."

"You don't sleep. You prowl every night."

"If you hear me, you're not sleeping either."

"I'm not pulling down fifty hours on the job. A change of scenery will do you good."

"I don't need a vacation!"

"Qui n'avance pas, recule."

A French proverb, one of Connor's favorites. *Who does not move forward, recedes.* The proverb meant that life offers us the choice to evolve and accept the changes that inevitably come. Resist those changes, and we devolve into something less—a mere shadow of our true potential.

Weary, Rae leaned against the counter. Why did he expect her to heal? Her life was irrevocably diminished.

"You're missing the bigger point, Dad. I've never moved forward in the right way. I've done everything out of order. The 'carefree twenties' people talk about, finding your soul mate or taking a gap year for self-discovery? My twenties were hard and demanding—and wonderful. There's nothing I'd change about those years. Even on the days it felt like I was walking on hot coals."

"You hardly dated. Young adults are supposed to have fun. Even the ones with lots of grown-up responsibilities."

"I won't pretend I wasn't lonely. The men never stuck around."

"You never gave any of them a hint they *should* stick around. You have more defenses than a porcupine."

The amusing retort made her laugh, even though her heart ached. "Yeah? Well, my defense mechanism is more torqued up now. I'm only thirty-three, but I've dealt with more troubles than lots of women twice my age. I'm road weary. If I didn't have thick skin, I'd crawl into bed and never stop crying. But I don't see how that would solve anything."

"Take some advice, Rae. No one gets through life without dealing with the bad stuff. Death or betrayal, or a financial hit you don't see coming. I've had a few of those . . . I expect you remember. I wasn't myself after we lost your mother, and you grew up too fast. When I consider everything I put you through, I'm ashamed. Right down to my bones. I'm also grateful. You had good reason to hate me, but you never did. I love you for that."

"I know, Dad. I love you too."

"Here's something you don't know. In the seventies, before I met your mother, I went in big for the drug scene. You name it, I tried it at least once. Turned my body into a chemical factory. The only drug I steered clear of was heroin. I was reckless, but not a complete idiot. Anyway, I fell hard for a girl who liked smoking pot and sleeping with my friends. Peace, love, and rock and roll—that girl went in big for spreading the love around. Luckily, she didn't give me the run of unspeakable diseases."

"You . . . *what*?" Rae's jaw fell open.

Never before had they discussed his youthful indiscretions. Her introverted, well-read father was once a wild child?

In an act of contrition, Connor lifted his palms. "Back then, I was just plain stupid." A casual gesture, but she saw the price he paid in sharing deeply held secrets. "I thought if I pretended my girlfriend was faithful, eventually I'd be right. There's nothing more destructive than self-delusion. When she dumped me, it felt like the world ending."

"But you got over her," Rae supplied, wishing he'd end the conversation.

24

"When your mother came on the scene, she knew how to fix everything. Hester screwed my head on straight. Gave my life purpose and taught me how to believe in myself. Those years were special. They were even better once we brought you into the world. We were so busy caring for the farm, and then your mother's art career took off—that close to our forties, we weren't sure she'd get pregnant." Her father hesitated. "You were a little bitty thing when Grandma Langdon had a stroke. Do you remember your grandparents?"

"I'm sorry. I don't."

"The stroke happened the same month we got your grandfather's diagnosis. Colon cancer, too far advanced for medical intervention. I didn't understand loss—the genuine article that drops you to your knees—until my parents died. Two deaths in one season. The point being, I was middle-aged when they passed. I was strong enough to take it."

Rae shut her eyes. *Two deaths.* Her losses, marked by different seasons. The last, too great to bear.

"I'm strong too," she said. "You don't have to worry about me."

"You're my child, Rae. I'd protect you from life's hardships if I could. Don't let grief make you old before you really start living."

～

At two o'clock, Yuna sent a text. She was on her way over.

Rae had just hung up with her aunt. After she declined the invitation to visit Miami, Gracie didn't press. She did extract Rae's promise to call if she needed to talk.

The well-meaning overture left Rae more unsettled. Mostly because she didn't know what to make of her father's impassioned speech. Joining him in the living room, she stared unseeing at the TV. His advice had rattled her. Growing old quickly didn't appeal. Who wanted that? Most days, Rae focused on staying numb. Or she let her temper at life's irritations mask the unpredictable waves of acute sorrow.

Hope and expectation were absent from her life. Did the loss of those virtuous emotions mean she was growing old? Not in a measurable, physical way, but on a deeper level? There was no simple way to regain the verve for life.

A rap sounded at the door.

Yuna appeared in the foyer with her daughter. Shaking the snow from her hair, she shrugged out of her coat. Kameko slipped past, trailing snow into the living room. The five-year-old plopped to the ground and tugged off her boots.

Yuna hung up her coat. "This is pathetic." Approaching, she glanced at the TV. "You're *both* in front of the tube on a beautiful Saturday? Go outside and build a snowman!"

Connor popped a potato chip into his mouth. "Kameko, take your mother home. She wants to build a snowman." After his speech in the kitchen, he'd made off with the bag of chips.

"Mommy can't play outside. She has to go to work."

"That's right, sweetheart. We can't stay long." Yuna snatched the bag. "Pop quiz, Connor. What were your cholesterol numbers on your last blood test?"

"None of your business."

"His numbers weren't great," Rae supplied. She began rising from the couch. Kameko stepped before her, thwarting the movement.

"I'm hot, Auntie Rae."

A puffy snowsuit encased the pipsqueak. She resembled a helium balloon. Unzipping the garment, Rae helped her take a dainty step out.

Connor glared at Yuna. "Mind handing back my chips?"

Rae chuckled. "Give it up, Dad. You know she won't."

With a petulant shake of his head, Connor returned his attention to the TV.

Rae tossed the snowsuit aside. "This is a nice surprise. What's the occasion?"

"Oh, nothing major. I must ask you something."

"What?"

"It's silly, really. This could've waited until next week."

"Well, you're here. What's up?"

Yuna lowered her gaze. Frowning, she noticed the clumps of white melting into the carpet. Retracing her steps, she pulled her boots off in the foyer.

Kameko tugged on Rae's sleeve. "Did you kill them?" she asked.

"Not yet," Rae assured her.

The precocious child blinked suspicious eyes. "Show me."

A trap, and Rae warily sought escape. Yuna's judgments she could take—sometimes. Kameko was a more severe taskmaster.

"Can we schedule a tour with an appointment?" she asked the child. "They aren't receiving guests today."

"I'm a friend."

"Yes, you are. A better friend than me, actually. But they've had a busy morning. You know—soaking up the sun in between snow showers. It's best for everyone involved if you schedule an appointment."

Imagination powered even the most skeptical child. Finally, Kameko accepted the ruse. "What's an 'appointment'?" she asked.

"Like when Mommy takes you to ballet class. You go when the teacher asks to see you. Not whenever you like."

"They aren't busy, like my teacher. Call them." Kameko patted Rae's bottom, searching for her phone. Small children also shunned the personal-boundary rule. "Tell them I'm visiting right away."

Yuna flapped her arms. "Oh, for Pete's sake, Rae. They're plants, not socialites. Take her to the studio!"

Outside the A-frame pyramid of glass, snow fell in whirling sheets. The oak flooring gleamed from a recent mopping. Unlike the attached greenhouse, which was neglected like the barn, the studio held a hint of recent activity.

Rae paused in the center of the generous space. Memories swept through her—some quite recent, too precious and poignant to bear contemplating. She latched on to the older memories from childhood, how she'd hopped up and down to glimpse the collages taking shape as her mother bent over the long art tables; how the damp, verdant scents from the smaller greenhouse were overtaken by the studio's heavy pulse of metallic paints and bitter glue. The drafting table and the art supplies had been sold off long ago. The studio now felt empty and cold. Only a long wooden desk remained, shoved up against the wall.

Dust covered the table's dark surface. The relic was too painful for either Rae or Connor to approach.

Ghosts from the past did not intimidate Kameko. Taking the lead, she dashed forward. Before the pyramid of glass, three plastic tables stood in a bright row with a houseplant on top of each one. The tables were blue, green, and pink: Rae had purchased the toy furniture at a New Year's Day sale. Even if her verve for life was missing, she couldn't resist lavishing gifts on her friend's daughter.

A yellow pail sat beside the tables. A plastic trowel was thrust into the potting soil.

The child scooped up a shovelful of dirt. She threw Rae an accusing look.

"Auntie Rae, they're hurting." Kameko shook a layer of soil around the first plant, a yellowing ivy. She patted it down.

"I did water them, bean sprout."

"When?"

"Last week. Or two weeks ago." Between the new hires at work and concern over Quinn Galecki, she wasn't sure.

"Did you feed them? Mommy says plants get hungry, just like little girls."

"Those plant spikes? I thought I'd wait, let you do it."

Yuna appeared with the toy watering can Rae kept beneath the kitchen sink. She handed it to her daughter. "Sweetheart, give them each a good soaking." She'd also brought along baking sheets to set beneath the houseplants.

With Kameko suitably occupied, Rae steered Yuna out of earshot. "What's going on? You're here, you've got something to say . . . and I'm getting a bad vibe. Like, whatever it is, you don't want to tell me."

"I don't want to upset you."

"Great. That makes me feel better."

Yuna scraped the glossy hair from her brow. "It's about Night on the Square," she said.

Each year the city hosted the June fundraiser; Rae and Yuna usually worked on a committee together. The adults-only event featured drinking and dancing in Chardon Square's center green. Several local restaurants served appetizers and light desserts. As the mayor's wife, Yuna often chaired the committee of her choice. This year's event would fund upgrades for the high school technology department.

Rae cocked her head to the side. "I'm already signed up." She'd done so months ago. "Are you nervous I'll bail on you? I won't. All my other commitments are in the trash bin, but I'll help with the fundraiser. The event is important to you."

"And I appreciate it, Rae. This year, we're handling the publicity. I signed us up this morning."

"Great. I'm ready whenever you are. Should I get design quotes for the graphics?" Searching for her lost verve, Rae added, "The new quick-print shop has opened on Cherry Street. Nice woman, from Shaker Heights. She's having the Witt Agency handle the business insurance. Let's have her bid on the flyers. Keep it local, if possible."

"Sounds great."

"Yeah? Then why do you look nervous?"

Yuna smiled, but the merriment didn't reach her eyes. "Because I am." She clasped Rae's hand, as if to steady her. "The committee has new volunteers. A last-minute thing, and we could use the help. There's extra money in this year's budget for the event. Both of the women have the connections to further our reach."

A terrible intuition drew Rae back. "Who volunteered?"

"Sally Harrow and Katherine Thomerson."

The news kicked the air from Rae's lungs. Sally's daughter and Katherine's were ninth graders at the high school and best friends. The girls were inseparable. Their mothers were part of the loose social group of women active in the PTA and local campaigns benefiting Geauga County. Rae wasn't close to either woman; in the past, their interactions had been cordial at best. Since the tragedy last October, she'd been steering clear of Sally and Katherine, and their popular daughters.

"Rae, I'm sure they volunteered because, well, you've been avoiding them."

"I've been avoiding everyone. Except you." She watched Kameko stroke the spider plant like a favored pet, then kiss a wilting leaf. "And the bean sprout."

"Which is totally understandable, but Sally and Katherine feel terrible. We all do. Avoiding them only makes this worse."

The remark was absurd. From the onset, the situation was beyond repair. When the PD had called Rae that October night, she'd lost everything. Nothing could make it worse.

"I don't care, Yuna. Keep them on the committee. I'll stand aside." A sea swell of emotion pitched through her. Suppressing it, she latched on to her sense of fair play, which ran deep. "I can probably find a way to deal with Sally. She's a reminder I can do without, but she'd have the sense to give me space. I've never blamed her. But if you put me in a room with Katherine, I swear I won't stop screaming."

"Oh, Rae." Pity laced Yuna's voice. "Katherine isn't at fault. Why do you keep blaming her? It was an accident."

Chapter 4

Yuna's car disappeared behind a curtain of snow. With stiff movements, Rae put away Kameko's watering can and the baking sheets.

A sports channel murmured in the living room. Her father lay on the couch, snoring. Rae fetched a blanket and covered him.

The revelation that Sally Harrow and Katherine Thomerson were joining the fundraising committee shook something loose inside Rae—an essential piece of her emotional makeup she'd unwittingly relied upon to hold herself together. Her breaths came fast and shallow. Pressure built in her chest, seeking release.

On autopilot, she went into the mudroom and put on her hiking boots. She was still buttoning her coat when she strode into the weak afternoon light and the relentless snowfall.

In defiance of the weather, birds flitted across the branches of the pine trees. Avoiding the wind's fearsome gusts, they converged on clumps of sunflower seeds she'd thrown down earlier. Squirrels chattered in the bitter air, their tails flicking through the frosted undergrowth. Veering away from the barn, Rae followed their noisy complaints toward the forest. She needed to get far enough from the house to scream until her throat blistered. There was nothing rational about her rage, or reasonable. It spilled over in hot waves.

Walking blindly, she nearly walked into him.

Shock brought her to a standstill. With alarm, she took stock of her surroundings. The gentle incline led to a V-shaped wall of heavy brush. The forest lay beyond. Straying in this direction was a mistake.

Even in summer she avoided this section of the property, and the dreaded tree. Quinn Galecki huddled beneath the tree with his back pressed to the icy trunk. Deep in thought, he appeared deaf to her approach.

The snow was softly burying him. As it had buried her mother sixteen years ago.

The memory of the White Hurricane reared up with devastating clarity. The images came too fast, a vivid horror show. Rae groaned. Bile rose in her throat.

The sound of her distress pulled Quinn from his daydream. "Miz Langdon!" He leaped to his feet, the snow spilling from his shoulders.

Slipping and sliding, he moved in a frantic circle. Rae pressed a hand to her belly. The urge to vomit was strong.

Quinn darted closer, unsure of what to do. "Are you sick?" The wind flapped his coat open. "Did I scare you? Man, you're turning green."

Rae clasped her knees. "Dancing around like a scarecrow isn't helping. Cut it out, okay?" Fending off vertigo, she planted her gaze on her boots. "And zip up your coat. Are you trying to catch pneumonia?"

Obeying, he zipped the parka to his neck. "Are you going to puke? That's no fun."

"Not if I can help it."

"What can I do?"

"About the ulcer I'm brewing? Not much."

"Miz Langdon, I didn't mean to scare you. Honest." He nodded at the forest. "I figured I wasn't bothering anyone out here by myself."

"Stop referring to me as Miz Langdon. We both know I've never been married." A belch popped from her mouth, and she gripped her knees tighter. The wave of nausea passing, she added, "I'm just Rae."

"Got it. Thanks."

The snowfall decreased to a fine misting of white. The air held a faintly metallic scent. A cardinal flew past, a splash of red disappearing into the forest.

Rae straightened. She stiffened when Quinn rushed forward to help. He was tall and slender; strong too. With ease he clasped her arms. No doubt he expected her to drop at any second, and she was silently grateful for the assistance. His hands were large, his fingers gracefully tapered. The hint of a beard shadowed his long, nearly pointed chin.

His eyes seemed much younger. They carried a child's vulnerability. As did his cheeks, blazing pink when he released her.

Rae swatted at the snow collecting on her hair. "What are you doing out here? Of all the stupid . . . are you trying to freeze to death?"

"I'm not cold."

"You're not? Why are your teeth chattering?"

A challenge, and his mouth quirked into a grin. "Okay. I'm cold. My feet are ice cubes."

"I'm not surprised." With dismay, she studied his boots. The leather toe of the left boot was peeling away from the sole. The silver band of duct tape used to repair the mess was coming loose. "You get an A for creativity, but that won't last long," she said, gesturing at the duct tape. "Tell your parents you need new boots."

"Right. Like they'll listen."

"Are you wearing socks?"

"I left the house in a hurry." Quinn lifted a wary hand. "Don't make me explain."

Rae stifled her protective instincts. "I won't." How he dressed for the frigid weather was none of her business. It *was* her business that he was on her property—again—but she let it slide.

Relief scuttled through his gaze. "How's your stomach?"

"So-so."

"Do you really have an ulcer?"

"I hope not."

They fell silent, gauging each other like unwilling combatants. Tension raced across Rae's skin, lifting the hairs on her neck. More threads twined their destinies together than Quinn could possibly imagine. The boy would never learn of their connection. Nor would anyone else.

Not a boy, Rae mused. Quinn was nearly a man. They'd never before engaged in a real conversation. A minor point—the painful questions demanded answers, even if she wasn't prepared to hear the uncomfortable details. Now those questions refused to leave her lips.

Breaking the silence, Quinn patted his roomy parka. "Why did you almost puke when you saw me? I'm not exactly a threat."

The innocent remark hit too close to home. "No, you're not," she agreed in a forced, neutral tone.

"If we got into a dustup, you could take me. Thanks for not kicking my ass."

"Language." Apparently, he assumed humor was the perfect icebreaker. "Swear words are unbecoming, even for a teenager."

"Yes, ma'am."

Quinn gave a jaunty salute. A boy with deplorable parents, but Rae suddenly understood why so many adults in town liked him. There was something quirky and unusual about him. A softness blended with harder, more enduring qualities.

His features were too delicate. Tougher kids probably teased him. It didn't help that his eyes were large, fringed with thick lashes. They sparked with intelligence and compassion—a higher emotion that most people didn't cultivate until they were older, if at all. No wonder Yuna had put him on the craft emporium's payroll. The act of a Good Samaritan, but she'd also glimpsed his better qualities.

A startling discovery: it was easier to hate the idea of a person than the genuine article.

"For the record, you didn't scare me." Rae led him away from the loathsome tree. "You were sitting where I found my mother, after the White Hurricane. It was a long time ago." Needing to change the subject, she scanned the acres. "How did you get out here?"

He motioned toward the forest. "My truck is on the road."

"Not a smart move with the low visibility. There's more snow coming."

"I parked on the berm." Curiosity flitted through his eyes. "I've never heard of the White Hurricane. When did it happen?"

"Sixteen years ago." She sighed. "I'd rather not discuss it."

"No problem." In a bid to appear nonchalant, he pulled up the collar on his parka. "I just don't get why remembering a hurricane almost made you puke. None of my business."

"That's right."

"Some people act weird in bad weather. Emily lives across the street from my parents, and storms make her pee. No joke. I was out grabbing the mail one day when lightning cracked the sky. There was Emily in her driveway, a yellow trickle going down her leg."

"How old is she?"

"Around three, I guess."

"Lots of toddlers are scared of bad weather." Rae gave him a disapproving look. "You didn't make fun of her, did you?"

"No!" Embarrassment flooded Quinn's face. "I'd never tease a little kid. She'll get her act together, eventually."

"She will." They'd reached a hilly section of the property, where the snow was deeper. Climbing at a careful pace, Rae added, "And to be clear, my upset stomach isn't weather-related. It's more complicated."

"If you say so. Storms and such don't bug me either. Most of the time, anyway." He glanced back at the trail they'd left in the snow. "Was your mom sitting under the tree when the storm rolled in? The guy who moved in next door to my parents—he has more tattoos than you can count—he's really into storms. Gets a high from watching them or something. He'll sit on his front stoop with a six-pack in all sorts of weather. Lightning, hail, you name it."

"Your neighbor sounds slightly . . . offbeat."

"But he's nice. Once, he gave me a ride on his Harley. Just around the block." Quinn paused, and she wondered if he planned to describe all the neighbors on his street. As if she were a close friend eager for the details. A suspicion he confirmed by adding, "Want a real example of meanness? You should get a load of Mr. Cox. Yelling at kids for no reason and giving the newspaper lady a hard time. If the newspaper hits the snow instead of his driveway, he's out there bellowing as she drives away. Mrs. Cox packed up and left him about a year ago. What I don't get is . . . why'd she leave without taking Shelby?"

"Who's Shelby?"

"Her rescue dog. Mrs. Cox adopted her from the humane society right around when I started high school. Real cute mutt. Mr. Cox leaves Shelby in the backyard all the time."

"Oh, that's sad."

"Tell me about it. He only lets her in at night, probably to punish Mrs. Cox for leaving. Doesn't make sense, though. She's long gone." A sudden burst of satisfaction lit Quinn's face. "Everything's cool now. I have Mr. Cox's work schedule down. I sneak over to feed Shelby—he's stingy with the kibble. I check her water bowl too."

"You take care of the dog . . . without your neighbor catching on?" The ill-tempered Mr. Cox *was* cruel.

As for Quinn, he wasn't merely quirky. He was also kind. Helpful too. Among his other good deeds, he'd changed the oil in the tractor Rae used in warm-weather months to mow the pasture when the grass reached knee-height. And he'd spruced up her father's shop.

His positive attributes stood in stark contrast to his more serious misjudgments. An issue Rae planned to bring up before they parted ways.

"I hate when people are mean to animals," he was saying. When she smiled in silent agreement, he deftly maneuvered back to the original topic. "The White Hurricane was sixteen years ago? Seems weird for a place like Ohio. I thought hurricanes only happened near the ocean, in places like Texas or Florida."

"The White Hurricane was a blizzard—the storm of the century. More than fifty people died of exposure. Others were trapped in their cars on the highway. In some parts of Geauga County, snowdrifts literally buried houses. It happened in January. I was a senior at the high school when it struck."

"A senior . . . like me."

The remark seemed an effort to find common ground. Rae let it pass.

Recognition broke across Quinn's face. "Wait. I know what you're talking about. Last year, my homeroom teacher told us about the blizzard. She said the snow was piled eight feet high in front of her house. I thought she was exaggerating."

"Believe me, she wasn't."

"Is it true, people were stuck in their homes for days?"

"The lucky ones."

"How long did the blizzard last?"

"Close to three days," Rae said, wading further into the tragic story. "The winds clocked in at eighty miles per hour. Before the storm hit, the temperature was right around freezing. The temps plunged twenty-one degrees in less than an hour."

The peril she described slowed Quinn's pace. "Why was your mother outside in that kind of weather?"

"She wouldn't have been, if my dad wasn't down with the flu. He'd packed himself off to bed that morning, after warning us to stay away. Mom already had the sniffles, but she kept pacing the house. The blizzard came in fast—neither one of us could remember if we'd bolted the barn shut. To make sure the animals were safe."

A sickening wash of memories rolled through Rae. Up ahead, the wall of pine trees hid the house from view. Quinn, riveted by the story, motioned for her to continue.

"The wind was shaking the roof," she told him, "and I volunteered to go out to check on the animals. I should've insisted. Argued, or something."

"You were scared."

"And doing a lousy job of hiding it. Night was coming. We were already in whiteout conditions. And the wind . . . screaming through the eaves like a demon set loose. I've never heard anything like it, before or since. Back then I was fairly bold for a seventeen-year-old. Brave, even. But I'd never been in danger. Not the life-or-death kind. Listening to the wind, I bit my fingernails down until they bled. I wasn't aware of what I'd done until Mom fetched the first aid kit. After she cleaned me up, she told me to stay put."

"Your mom went out alone?"

Rae nodded. "An hour went by, then two. She didn't come back."

"Why didn't you get your dad?"

"I couldn't wake him. His forehead was on fire. Like a hot griddle. That's when I knew I had to go outside to find my mother. So I pulled on my coat and went out."

Quinn ground to a halt. "That's crazy." She swept past, and he picked up his feet to catch up. "If she couldn't get back from the barn, why go after her?"

"There was no way of telling if she'd made it to the barn. You wouldn't believe how fast the wind slammed me against the house. Winds that fast can pick you up off your feet. Toss you around like a rag doll. I made it back inside and switched into my dad's coat. Weighed down the pockets with cans of soup."

"Smart thinking."

"Not quite. I'd walked several paces when something whizzed toward my head. A tree limb or the bird feeder. Whatever it was, it could've knocked me out cold."

She was at a near-jog, the acceleration helping her speed through the story.

"I dove for the ground. When I got back up, I'd lost all sense of direction. We're talking serious whiteout conditions. I was also nearly deaf from the wind's screaming. By some miracle, I heard my father shouting. I crawled back to the house. My dad was delirious with fever, but he knew I was in danger. Somehow, he knew. When I got him to the couch, he didn't fall back to sleep—more like he passed out." A quick intake of breath, and Rae added, "I didn't wake him at dawn, when I decided to go back out. The winds were still high, but manageable. And the daylight helped."

The past blotted out the present. Rae saw herself at seventeen, her muscles burning from long minutes searching the property. Stumbling through the snowdrifts—spotting her mother in the distance. Hester seated beneath the tree, her down coat and immobile features wearing a powdery glaze of white.

The hope Rae clung to morphing into horror. A sob breaking forth as she rested her palm on the frozen, unyielding flesh of Hester's shoulder.

Quinn listened to the rest of the story with the color draining from his face. When she finished, he brushed his knuckles across his eyes. The gesture drew her attention to his hands. They were raw from the cold. Silently Rae chastised herself. On the long trek, they should've traded her gloves back and forth.

"Thanks for telling me the story. Talking about it can't be easy." He caught her staring at his hands and shoved them into his pockets. "Lark never mentioned how her grandmother died. All I knew is that she was gone before Lark was born. We only talked about Hester's art, and how she was famous. Lark wanted to be an artist too." He looked away, embarrassed. "But you knew that, right? Your daughter was nonstop with her dreams. Her favorite topic."

Lark. My sweet, perfect child. Gone forever.

Pain seized Rae. "I never told Lark the full story of how we lost her grandmother. Just the basics."

"Good call, in my opinion. Totally would've freaked her out. Given her nightmares."

They'd reached the barn. Quinn studied the sky. Clouds scuttled past, dark with the threat of more precipitation.

"Thanks again, Miz . . . Rae." He frowned. "Are you okay, walking back the rest of the way?"

The inference being that he was escorting her.

Their cordial interlude didn't erase Quinn's serious lapses in judgment. He'd been trespassing on her property since Lark's funeral last October. The unsanctioned visits were a terrible reminder of the senseless accident on the Thomerson estate. Quinn, the high school senior who'd secretly dated her ninth grader. According to the police report, they'd dated for months before Lark's death.

Anger leaped through Rae, charging the air between them. On its heels came a second emotion that momentarily sickened her.

The change put Quinn on alert. He pivoted toward the forest.

"Oh no you don't." She latched on to his sleeve. "You're coming inside. I have a few questions of my own."

Chapter 5

Rae led her nervous companion through the mudroom. In the kitchen, her father was digging through the fridge, no doubt searching for dinner options.

"Dad, look who dropped by. Lark's old friend—our mystery maid."

His stunned gaze bounced past her, to latch on to Quinn. The fridge's bluish light glowed on his startled features.

She pointed at the table. "Quinn, take a load off."

Connor blurted, "You brought the delinquent into my house?"

"*Our* house, and he's not a delinquent." She gave her father a gentle push toward the table. "He dropped by to answer my questions. Feel free to add a few of your own. Quinn, would you like coffee?"

"I'll pass, but thanks."

"Join us for a cup," Rae suggested. "The pick-me-up will do you good. It's best if you're perky while I grill you."

He darted a glance at her father. "Can I leave?" Connor's silvered brows were lowering, his mouth thinning.

"Move from that chair, and you'll wish you hadn't," she said, closing the fridge.

"Jeez, Miz—Rae. Don't threaten me."

With efficient movements Rae dumped coffee into the machine. A strange euphoria overlaid the heartache that had been her unwanted companion since October. For the first time since Lark's casket was lowered into the ground, she felt alert. Arisen from sorrow's dark slumber.

"Relax, kid. We're just talking."

"I know a threat when I hear one. I'm not stupid."

"No, you're not. If I wanted to threaten you, I'd say something like, 'Quinn, if you were sleeping with my daughter, I'll have to think seriously about doing murder. Because Lark was precious and perfect, and I'll never get over losing her.' Did I say that?"

"Not exactly."

"That's right. I've been known to have a temper, but I'm not a fan of irrational behavior. Doing murder, why, it'd take something serious, like finding out a boy three years older took advantage of my child. Because unbeknownst to me, Lark was sneaking around with you for months. My fourteen-year-old daughter. My innocent child."

"We were just friends!"

The coffee finished brewing. "Define 'friends.' I want to ensure we're communicating." Rae splashed coffee into the mugs, spattering droplets across the counter. "This is awkward for all of us, but I need specifics. Did you lay a hand on my daughter?"

Quinn set his jaw.

A short, stifled growl escaped Connor. "You heard the question. Now, tell us!"

"I've already told you. We didn't like each other that way."

Taking the mug she offered, Connor sat next to the youth. "Okay, hotshot. If everything was on the up-and-up, why didn't Lark bring you around? She brought lots of friends to the house."

"She knew you wouldn't approve. Because I was older than her. She thought . . . well." Quinn wrapped his hands around the mug Rae set before him. He looked frightened, wary, like a cornered animal. But his gaze flashed when it lifted. "She figured you'd think we were messing around. That's what everyone thought at school. Like you must be dating if you're hanging out. Why do people assume a guy always has an agenda? There's nothing wrong with being friends with a girl. Not if you have the same interests."

The same interests. With a start, Rae understood. "Last year . . . were you enrolled in classes at the craft emporium?" Lark had repeatedly taken Yuna's classes for teens. A course on portrait drawing. Other courses, on painting with acrylics and an introduction to sculpture.

"Yeah, we started hanging out during Yuna's classes. Last spring. Yuna let me help around her shop instead of paying for the courses. She knew I couldn't afford them."

"You weren't friends with my daughter before then?"

"Only a little. Whenever I saw Lark on Chardon Square, she was cool. Nicer than most girls. Lots more friendly than the dudes. She never picked on kids, you know?"

"I'd hope not," Connor grumbled. "We raised her better than that."

"We did," Rae softly agreed.

Quinn began to add something else. Instead, he hesitated. The tension melted from his features. The change in his demeanor from defensive to delighted was abrupt, confusing. Like daylight breaking on a cold midnight.

Smiling, he pushed his coffee aside. When he reached for the art stacked beside the napkin holder, Rae's breath snagged.

Gingerly, he slid one of Lark's recipes near. The cardstock was flamboyantly decorated. Two recipes were listed, the ingredients in different colors. The border surrounding them was a vibrant blend of mixed media—bits of glitter, old buttons, and tiny stars Lark had painted in blue and gold. The heavy cardstock seemed a lifeline, and Quinn held on tight.

"Avocado toast and blueberry quinoa." Despite the perspiration slicking his brow, he laughed. "I taught Lark these recipes. She loved them."

Connor grunted. "I didn't. Like eating birdseed and slimy crap on toast. When did avocados win the popularity contest? They're worse than quinoa."

Rae shushed him. "Quinn, how did you teach Lark the recipes? Were you in my house?"

"Only when you and Mr. Langdon weren't around! Me and Lark cooked stuff together. That's all we did—cook, eat, and get out."

A child's answer, desperate and silly. Too genuine to mask lies.

Whatever the specifics of their relationship, it hadn't been sexual. Apparently, her father had reached the same conclusion. With frustration Connor fell back in his chair. Beneath the lengthening silence, Quinn tapped his feet. The thunk of one boot hitting the floor, then the other. A prisoner awaiting the verdict of two bewildered judges.

Connor noticed the duct tape coming loose from Quinn's boot. "That's one fine mess, son."

"Tell me about it."

"Why don't you buy new boots?"

"Money's tight. The insurance on my truck comes due soon."

"You pay your own insurance? That's responsible."

"I pay my own everything." Quinn shrugged. "That's the rule."

The remark stirred the suspicion Connor wasn't ready to dispel. "You work part-time for Rae's friend," he said. "Those wages can't amount to much. How do you pay for everything?"

"Side jobs for people I know. Not all dudes my age sit around playing video games. Most of those games are too violent anyway. I'd rather be doing something useful." With a dash of pride, Quinn added, "I've got skills. I've learned how to fix lots of stuff."

Connor's expression shifted. "Your mighty maid routine in the barn was nice. What do I owe you for the cleanup?"

"Nothing, sir. It was my pleasure."

The remark's sincerity eased the tension-filled air.

Rae exchanged a thoughtful glance with her father. She could almost hear his thoughts: *A teenage boy with a penchant for cooking, tidying up, and home repairs? Not a delinquent.*

Quinn's gaze darted between them, gauging their reaction. Sympathy for the teen welled in Rae alongside a second, more bittersweet emotion. Daring a longer glance, she fell upon the similarity that drew her interest like a bee to honey. Something in Quinn's expression was reminiscent of Lark, before adolescence made her stubborn and too persistent. Lark at seven or eight, when she'd exhibited a wide-eyed need for approval.

Connor glanced at the clock. "It's almost dinnertime. What were you doing outside?"

"Oh, just thinking about Lark. I miss her, you know? I miss talking to her."

"I do too."

Freed of their censure, Quinn took another recipe from the stack. His fingers glided across the border of yellow daisies Lark had embroidered, then carefully glued in place. A lump formed in Rae's throat. Her father was affected too, his eyes gaining a damp sheen.

"Lark found this recipe online," Quinn said. "Not my favorite. I don't like brussels sprouts. Even if you mix in caramelized onion."

Memories, some of them sweet, embraced Rae. On many nights, her daughter had made dinner. Afterward Lark had often spent long hours in Hester's old studio finishing homework or working on craft projects, a DO NOT DISTURB sign tacked on the door.

Some nights, however, she'd battled with Rae. During her final months, they'd argued constantly. A never-ending tug-of-war, with no winner.

The memory lodged despair in the center of Rae's chest. Pushing it away, she appraised Quinn. "You enjoy cooking." It was a talent she'd never picked up.

"I'd like to go to culinary school."

"Is that your plan, after high school?"

"Oh, I don't have a plan. Not exactly. But I'd like to go someday."

Money, she suspected, was the real issue. She couldn't imagine people like Quinn's parents setting aside funds to ensure their son's future. "You'll make a good living as a chef."

"I hope so."

Her mothering instincts, dormant since Lark's death, rose suddenly to life. "When I found you by the forest, you looked lost in thought. Did you need to talk to Lark? Today, especially?"

"She was going to make me a cake. She'd been promising for months. A *beet* cake. Kind of a joke, but not really. She had a recipe for chocolate cake made with beets. It sounds totally disgusting, but she swore I'd like it."

The response was surprising. Lark had promised to . . . bake him a cake? One she'd planned to make before death erased her plans.

Rae's heart lurched. "Quinn, is today your birthday?"

He drummed his fingers on the table. "The big one-eight." Defiance flickered in his eyes. "It's official. I'm all grown up."

The defiance fled as his expression fell. The change came too fast, and Rae feared he'd cry. A humiliating outcome for a teenage boy.

"Some birthday, huh?" he said. "My parents kicked me out of the house."

Chapter 6

Outside the studio's pyramid of glass, the moon played tag with fast-moving clouds. A smattering of white swirled through the air. Rae watched the snow's descent with her thoughts leaping and turning.

Throughout dinner, a nervous Quinn had talked nonstop about Lark. In between, he plowed through leftovers she dug from the fridge. Macaroni and cheese, lunch meat, a cucumber she hastily sliced—his bottomless appetite left the worrisome impression that he rarely ate a decent meal. When dinner ended, Quinn helped with the dishes before loping after Connor to the living room. They were deep into male bonding over Cleveland's upcoming baseball season when Rae slipped out.

Confusion vaulted through her. For months, she'd wanted to believe Quinn was a bad kid. Preferred believing it over the proof she'd witnessed directly—of a bashful boy who worked diligently at the craft emporium, and whose grief over the loss of her daughter was tangible and deep.

The police report of the events surrounding Lark's death had stated they were secretly dating. Add in the reputation of Quinn's parents, and Rae had assumed the worst. Even Yuna's ready defense of the teen wasn't enough to sway her.

Yet the real Quinn bore no resemblance to her worst fears. In many ways, he was emotionally younger than the daughter she'd lost. Less mature, less confident. A teenager perched on the edge of adulthood—a kid who snuck around feeding the neighbor's dog. A vivid conversationalist who spilled out stories with a lonely child's enthusiasm.

A surprising logic underpinned his friendship with Lark. There was more to it, of course. Since reading the PD's report last October, Rae had resisted the truth: destiny had played a role. Her late daughter and Quinn were kindred souls. If they'd grown up in a large city, odds were they never would've met and discovered their natural affinity. In Chardon, with a population in the thousands—not the tens of thousands—they'd been given a few brief months to learn just how much they had in common.

The circumstance was both heartening and unsettling. Heartening mostly, Rae decided—Lark had left an indelible mark on her bashful friend. The confidence inherited from her grandmother Hester, the streak of bravado—Lark had possessed the same fire, the same generous spirit. She'd warmed everyone caught in her orbit.

Perhaps Quinn, most of all.

From the driveway, an engine rumbled before cutting off. Quinn, pulling his truck in from the road.

The soft padding of footfalls down the hallway. Two voices, mixing briefly. A door clicking shut.

The moon slipped behind the clouds.

"He's all set."

Shadows enveloped the studio. Her father waded through them.

"He's in the guest bedroom?" she asked.

"Camped out with his homework. Doubt he'll get very far with the trig. The kid looks exhausted." Connor arched a brow. She was seated on the floor beside Kameko's plastic tables and lovingly tended plants. "Do you want a chair?" He flicked on a lamp. "My joints hurt just looking at you."

"I'm fine." She eyed the bottle of Johnnie Walker and the two glasses he carried. "You're breaking out the Scotch?" Other than holidays, they rarely imbibed.

"We both need a drink."

He peered over his shoulder. His uneasy gaze landed on Lark's wooden desk and office chair, which they'd pushed up against the wall. Rae had purchased the chair one short week before the funeral. The chair—and a gift card for supplies from Yuna's Craft Emporium—had been a fumbling attempt to forge a cease-fire with her daughter.

"It's okay, Dad. Grab the chair."

"You don't think she'll care?"

She'll care, as if Lark were still roosting in her bedroom, painting her toenails three shades of green and breaking the family bylaws with late-night Zoom chats with her girlfriends. Laughing like a donkey near midnight. Laughing harder when her grandfather revved past the bounds of arthritis and sprinted down the hallway to pound on her door. Leaving butterscotch candies on his love-worn edition of *The Complete Shakespeare* the next morning to apologize for her antics. Lark skipping down the farm's long, curving driveway to the school bus as the driver blared the horn.

"Lark's in heaven," Rae said. "Get the chair—she won't mind. We can't talk in the living room. Our voices might carry." They'd had enough trouble persuading Quinn to spend the night. Despite the frigid temps, he'd been serious about sleeping in his truck.

Connor fetched the chair. She filled both glasses with Scotch.

She took a generous sip. "Did he call his parents?" Fire sluiced down her throat, and she grimaced.

"No need. They left tonight. Vacation in Atlanta."

"They threw Quinn out, *then* left on vacation?"

"According to Quinn, his parents got a nice payout on a lottery ticket—they tossed the kid a birthday card with fifty bucks inside, then told him to move out."

"How long are they gone?"

"Ten days. They're visiting a fellow mechanic who retired to Atlanta. The man worked with Mik Galecki at the auto dealership. It's anyone's guess how they sobered up enough to walk through airport security."

"The assholes."

Connor withered her with a look. "Language." He brushed the sparse hair from his forehead. "Why is cruelty easy for some people? I've heard rumors about Quinn's parents same as everybody. Lots of nasty scuttlebutt. Still, I never thought they'd stoop to throwing their kid out. On his birthday, of all days."

Rae latched her restless gaze on the wall of glass. Snowflakes pelted the ground outside. Dread came trundling up her gut as she recalled the one instance when she'd unintentionally tangled with Mik and Penny Galecki. Out of habit, she avoided the couple. The reasons were dark and complicated—and unknown to her father.

After a moment she said, "I'm not remotely surprised. Mik has a solid work history, but everyone knows his temper is unpredictable. Throwing wrenches at the younger mechanics, giving them a hard time—I heard he's not allowed near the dealership's clients now because he's so testy." Mik was the lead mechanic at Marks Auto Dealership, a muscular bear of a man. "Penny isn't much better. She can't hold down a job for more than ten minutes."

"And she gets into barroom brawls with other women. Who does that? If you ask me, Penny has a drinking problem."

"Dad, both of the Galeckis are alcoholics. Their idea of a good time is sitting around in bars. As for Quinn, I assumed . . ." Remorse prevented her from completing the thought.

"That the apple doesn't fall far from the tree? I thought the same—he was just like his parents. A hell-raising delinquent. A piece of trash, luring my granddaughter into situations a fourteen-year-old had no business contemplating." Pity etched Connor's features. "Here's a fun fact. The boy hiding out in our guest bedroom can make a crème brûlée. He walked me through the steps."

Once, Rae had attempted a basic American pot roast. "Quinn's into French cuisine?" She'd served up rawhide.

"There's a YouTube show on French cooking he watches. Most boys his age double-dare each other into filming dumb stunts for YouTube. Quinn's torqued up about next week's show, the basics of cheese soufflé. I should get him a gift card from Williams Sonoma for tidying up the barn. Buy him a set of whisks or something." Connor frowned. "What right did we have to judge him?"

"Save your shame, Dad. I'm doing enough penance for both of us. I feel terrible in about ten different ways." She declined to add their assumptions reflected poorly on Lark's memory. As if the terrible boy they'd imagined could've secured the friendship of the bright, beautiful girl who'd stood at the center of their lives.

"I'll tell you this much. I know what my granddaughter would expect us to do."

Rae glimpsed the path laid out before them. "Lark would want us to do right by Quinn." Would a benevolent hand guide them past the dangers?

"Are you ready to make it official?"

On all major issues they voted. With Lark no longer alive to play tiebreaker, they arrived at too many stalemates.

Not this time.

"We can't leave Quinn out on a limb." Rae wiggled her fingers in the air. The fear she'd find a way to manage—cowardice went against the grain. "Even if he wanted his parents to reconsider, I'd attempt to talk him out of going back. The situation's not healthy. Family Services has short-term foster homes, but they'd struggle to find an emergency placement for a teenager who'll graduate from high school soon. It's more likely Quinn would land in a group home." The prospect didn't bear contemplating.

"If we ask him to stay, he'll accept. The boy hungers for a homelife. We can't make this sound like charity, though. He's got his pride."

Rae hadn't been much older than Quinn when she became a mother. Still, she'd learned quickly that even as a toddler, Lark wanted to perform big-girl chores. Helping to pick up toys in the living room or fold dish towels. Later, she'd helped Connor with vacuuming and dusting as Rae's advancement at the Witt Agency demanded longer hours.

Regardless of age, pitching in gave a child a sense of belonging and purpose.

"Give Quinn a list of weekly chores," Rae suggested, "to let him know we rely on him. It'll boost his confidence."

"I'll talk to him in the morning." Connor swirled his drink, studied the amber liquid. "How will this play out, when his parents get back from Atlanta? Will they care that we're putting their son up?"

The reservation in his voice sent a chill through her. The Galeckis loved a good fight. They didn't need a reason.

"They *did* throw him out, and he is of age." Uneasy, she reconsidered. "We should factor in their cruelty. Did they expect Quinn to live in his car until they returned from Atlanta? Then come back home?"

"I wish I knew. They don't view him like a son, that's for sure. More like someone they can kick around. That's my basic takeaway from our conversation tonight."

"What else did you discuss? You were in the living room for a long time."

"His homelife for a few minutes. Seemed like too hard a topic. I didn't want to press. School, a little. Mostly we talked about Lark. He misses her something awful. I believe our bold girl was his only real friend." Considering, her father took a sip of his drink. "Until Quinn started yammering on about her, I hadn't noticed how much we avoid talking about Lark. Treating anything related to her as off-limits. What's wrong with us?"

"It's only been a few months. We're still in shock."

"We're doing a lousy job of honoring her memory."

A distinct possibility, and Rae's shoulders sagged. The grief over losing her beloved daughter was vast, an ocean of uncharted depths she could easily drown in.

"Don't underestimate the shock," she insisted. "I dropped her off at a slumber party the weekend before Halloween. Three hours later, the police called. I was texting Lark, worried when she didn't respond. It's sheer luck I heard the landline. You'd fallen asleep in front of the TV. Everything happened so quickly . . ."

"We lost your mother the same way, when you were in high school. Too fast. There wasn't time to prepare."

Her mother's death sixteen years ago *had* been an upheaval. An earthquake severing Rae's childhood from the hard changes that came like successive blows.

So many hard, scarring blows. The fog of depression falling over her father after the White Hurricane took her mother. Rae's acts of defiance, with their unforeseen consequences. The humiliation she felt, just a few months later, when she graduated from high school without Connor in attendance and her pregnancy still a secret. How the startling changes to her body, later that summer, forced her to reveal the pregnancy to her father. Connor's anger surfacing from the depths of his depression when she refused to name the man responsible for her condition.

You're not having this baby alone, Rae! We both know who's the father—don't try to stop me from making him own up for what he's done.

Dad—no. This is my baby. Don't you dare interfere.

The arguments didn't last long: Rae threatened to leave Ohio. If Connor followed through on his plan to seek out the culprit, she'd go. He didn't want to lose his daughter, or the unexpected grandchild growing heavy in her belly.

Then Lark's birth, near the end of that year. The gloom from Hester's death broken by a newborn's cries. The demands of the tiny, wriggling life galvanized Connor, who regained his emotional footing.

He became less introverted and fiercely devoted to his daughter and new grandchild. And Rae found new meaning in her shattered life.

"It was hard when we lost Mom," Rae said, "but at least she enjoyed a long life. Not long enough, but she had us, and years of touring galleries."

"Your mother still had time left to live."

"I didn't believe I'd survive losing her. Then I got Lark."

"She made everything worthwhile."

"Yes, but she wasn't here long before she was taken from me. Dad, I lost my child," Rae said, the bitterness thick in her voice. "I hate everyone who took her away from me. Her stupid little girlfriends and Katherine Thomerson—I hate the whole dreadful series of events."

"The anger's not healthy, Rae. It's tearing you up." Gentling the criticism, her father rested his palm on her shoulder. His tenderness nearly pulled a sob from her throat. She was swallowing it down when he added, "You have to get past it. Lark's death was an accident. A rotten, heartbreaking accident. No one's to blame."

"I can't change how I feel. Why did Katherine leave the house after the slumber party began?"

"She wasn't gone long. It's not like she let Stella invite her friends over and then left for hours."

"Running an errand was stupid and self-centered. She left a house full of adolescent girls racing around. Lark never should've died. What's safer than a sleepover with a bunch of girls staying up late, giggling? Only *my* daughter ended the night in the morgue. Not that I've let myself off the hook. Far from it."

Disapproval thinned her father's mouth. "We've been over this too many times. We *both* knew Lark wanted to skip the party. She wouldn't give the reason. A falling-out with one of the other girls, or an argument—she wouldn't explain."

"I encouraged her to attend. You didn't."

Broken, she recalled the text Lark sent minutes before her death. A cry for help.

An accusation.

Should've stayed home.

On her shoulder, Connor's fingers tightened. "What about grief counseling? I can make a few calls."

"For you, maybe. Not for me. I'm getting through this in my own way. I'm not ready to deal with the sorrow. Only in small doses. Let too much in, and I'll never find my way out." Rae laughed, the sound hollow even to her own ears. "I'm sure of one thing. Having Quinn staying in our guest bedroom is Lark's final payback. Her way of getting in the last word."

You have your secrets, Mom.

Surprise! I have a few of my own.

"Waging battle was never her intention, Rae. You *do* keep secrets. I've always respected your privacy. I held out hope you'd explain someday. Even if you didn't, I thought you'd have the good sense to fill Lark in."

"She asked the hard questions too soon. I wasn't ready . . ."

"The decision was never yours. Lark decided when she was ready. She needed answers."

There was no refuting the claim. A child without a father listed on her birth certificate would eventually have questions.

Chapter 7

True to her father's prediction, Quinn accepted the invitation to stay.

The arrangement pleased Connor, which the teen instinctively grasped. Rae's emotions were mixed. Much as she wished to help Quinn, he brought to mind the daughter she'd lost, and the tangled threads of a past buried long ago.

On Sunday, when he left the farm to collect more of his belongings from his parents' house, Rae felt a jolt of inappropriate relief. The reaction was small-minded and selfish. No matter the ghosts Quinn awoke in her memories, he was a boy in need. She resolved to do better. Later, when his truck rumbled into the driveway, Rae donned an expression of false cheer. Greeting him at the door, she gave him a house key.

On Monday, she left for work early and stayed late. She returned home past seven o'clock. She found Connor forgoing his normal TV regimen to help Quinn with homework. Dinner had been made and rested neatly wrapped on the stove.

Braised chicken with a side of rice noodles tossed with sautéed vegetables. A delicious meal.

As Rae delayed leaving the Witt Agency on Tuesday, she wondered what new surprises awaited her at home. Another beautifully prepared meal? Her father, brushing up on his math skills to help Quinn with his trig? They shared a natural affinity, and their instant rapport was heartwarming to behold. From the bits and pieces Connor had shared with her over the years, Rae knew he'd once been insecure and bashful like Quinn. The self-assured, opinionated man he'd become didn't fully take shape until Hester's death and Lark's birth forced him to muster inner resources she doubted her father had known he possessed. The strength he displayed clearly appealed to Quinn, and their interactions were seamless, comfortable.

Why couldn't *she* get with the program? Every time she interacted with Quinn, she caught herself using her most distant—and formal—business voice. The one reserved for frantic clients experiencing personal or property loss.

Her boss stuck her head into Rae's office. "Working late two nights in a row?"

Slightly older than Rae's father, Evelyn Witt sported permanent smile lines and a calm demeanor no matter the crisis. Tall, willowy, and single, she'd spent the better part of her professional career building the Witt Agency. Rae adored her.

"Oh, I'm leaving soon." Rae closed the file on her computer. "I just wanted to review the next part of the training protocol for the new employees."

"It's nearly eight o'clock." Evelyn pursed her lips. "Is there a problem with our new hires?"

"Not at all. They're doing great."

"How's everything at home?"

A diplomatic question, the subtext easy to detect. *How are you and Connor managing since your daughter's passing?*

In the months since Lark's death, Evelyn had posed similar questions, a delicate gauging of Rae's emotional state. For a woman who'd never stepped off the career track for marriage or children, her sensitivity to the cataclysmic loss in Rae's life was reassuring.

"We're doing fine, Evelyn. Really." Although she'd never confided in her mentor, Rae found herself adding, "We have a . . . houseguest. I'm not sure how long he's staying with us."

"A friend of your dad's?"

"No. He's a local boy, a senior at the high school. He needed somewhere to stay until he graduates."

"And you've taken him in?" When Rae nodded, the kindness that came easily for Evelyn flowed across her features. Entering the small office, she sat in the chair tucked against the wall. "Well, then. I suppose you're having a full-circle moment."

"What do you mean?"

The question was barely out when Rae chuckled with understanding. The autumn after *she'd* graduated from high school, she'd been waddling through the grocery store, miserable in the third trimester of her pregnancy when Evelyn—whom she'd never met before—walked up and offered her business card. *If you're looking for a job after the baby comes, please let me know. I'm sure we can work something out.* When Rae called several months after Lark's birth, Evelyn started her out part-time, as an assistant to the insurance agents.

During her first week on the job, Rae had discovered the reason for the charitable deed: a mixed-media collage by Hester Langdon hung on the wall of Evelyn's brightly colored office.

"I guess it's my turn to help out a kid in need," Rae agreed, "but I'm floundering. He was friends with Lark . . . actually, he was the boy that found her that night. Quinn Galecki."

"Good heavens, that can't be easy. How is Connor handling this?"

"Better than I am. No one will ever replace his granddaughter's place in his heart, but he's really taken to Quinn. And the feeling is mutual." Embarrassed suddenly, Rae laughed. "It'll all work out, right?"

"In time, I'm sure it will." Evelyn rose, nodded at the door. "I was closing up. Would you like to walk out together?" A playful light entered her soft brown eyes. "Or would you prefer to hide out at the office alone for another hour or so?"

~

On Wednesdays, the Witt Agency closed at four o'clock. Dashing across Chardon's snow-bedecked center green, Rae looked forward to meeting Yuna at Dixon's wine and dessert café for an hour of girl talk. Yuna wasn't yet apprised of Quinn's new living arrangements. The surprising turn of events would lead to good-natured teasing. Something along the lines of how Rae's brash exterior hid the sweeter qualities of her chewy, nougat center.

She was scanning the dessert menu when her phone buzzed.

"I have to cancel," Yuna said in a rush. "Kameko's babysitter is down with a cold, and the high school called off cheerleading practice. The coach is also out sick. Want to guess where the cheerleaders are hanging out? We're already busy—I don't need a bunch of girls rooting through merchandise without making a purchase. If that's not bad enough, a delivery arrived early. Twenty boxes." A pregnant pause, then, "Why didn't you tell me?"

It was hard keeping up. "Tell you what?"

"About Quinn moving in with you and your dad. I'm proud you've grown a brain. I'm also peeved you didn't share the news."

"Hey, I was planning to fill you in when we met up today for an afternoon snack." Rae frowned. "Wait. How did you find out? Quinn doesn't work for you until next weekend." The conscientious teen had shared his work schedule with Connor.

"Your new houseguest told me. Quinn's unpacking the delivery as we speak. He's the one kid on the planet who picks up when his boss calls with an emergency." Another pause, this one more tentative. "So . . . Quinn said it's okay for Kameko to stay at your place this afternoon. Seeing as how my babysitter is down for the count. He's good with kids."

The remark's subtext stung. Rae wasn't first choice for stand-in babysitter.

"No worries, Yuna. We'll take good care of Kameko." A competitive note colored her voice. "*Both* of us."

"I owe you one, girlfriend." A clattering in the background, followed by wild giggling—Kameko's. "It's mayhem over here."

Rae slid out of the booth. "On my way."

All manner of chaos was raining down on Yuna's Craft Emporium. The gaggle of cheerleaders talked at a deafening volume, clattering through jars of trinkets for jewelry making, their jaws moving faster than their hands. They blithely ignored the trinkets skittering across the floor.

Behind them, two women argued over the last stalk of silk iris in stock. On the other side of the craft emporium, trembling Mrs. Ogilvy—her gaze frantic behind thick bifocals—attempted to escape the waves of quilting fabric gripping her ankles. She'd unwisely pulled the bolt down from a shelf without assistance.

At the cash register, customers formed an impatient line. Both of Yuna's employees were preoccupied. The tall brunette raced to Mrs. Ogilvy's rescue. The slender college student sprinted to the back of the shop, where a toddler was lobbing balls of yarn over his head. The colorful projectiles flew past his mother. Oblivious, she flipped through a book on knitting.

Kameko banged into Rae's knees. "Tag—you're it!"

Pivoting, the five-year-old launched off the toes of her sneakers. She dove beneath a table, a length of toilet paper fluttering out from beneath her dress. It rendered the high-dexterity move less impressive.

Rae peered beneath the table. "Come out, please. I'm not crawling in after you."

"No."

"We can't play in your mommy's store. There's too much stuff we could knock over. When we get to my house, you can run around nonstop."

"I want to play now."

On bended knee, she studied Kameko's flushed cheeks and overly bright eyes. "How many juice boxes have you torn through?" The sugar would explain her buzzy rebellion, and too much liquid, the toilet paper trailing out of her tights. "I'm guessing you've exceeded the daily limit."

Chortling, Kameko scampered out of reach. One of the cheerleaders, cackling like a hyena, shouted encouragement.

Her compatriots joined in. Rae, tossing her dignity aside, dropped onto all fours. Ducking beneath the table, she latched on to an ankle. "Game over, bean sprout. We're taking a stroll to the bathroom." She dragged her quarry out. "You have unfinished business."

"No, no, *no!*"

Rae slung the child over her shoulder. Tiny fists pounded her back, a series of teeny wasp's stings. A high-pitched shriek followed. It vibrated through Rae's molars like a jackhammer.

"Jeez, Kameko—enough! We can't play in the store, and we *are* going to the bathroom."

The flailing halted. "Someone, save me!"

The cheerleaders' laughter swallowed the plea.

The wasp's stings resumed. They were accompanied by the added bonus of thrashing legs. Kameko's feet whipped past Rae's nose. She clamped down on the child's yellow sneakers. What the kid lacked in size, she made up for in fury.

An unhappy situation for a stand-in babysitter, especially a subpar one. Rae turned in a desperate circle. Where was Yuna?

She spotted her at the back of the shop. Palms raised, Yuna was fending off complaints from a disgruntled customer. The fashionably dressed blonde—loaded down with a basket of art supplies—wagged an impatient hand toward the line at the cash register. She got in Yuna's face, her complaints rising in pitch. Yuna looked ready to weep.

Rae's nostrils flared. Her tolerance for bullies was precisely zero.

She charged forward. At the sudden movement, Kameko dug pointy elbows into her neck. Her cherub's face bobbing, she tried to assess what the fuss was about.

The blonde was better clued in. Sensing danger, she whirled around. Her startled gaze shot from Rae's wriggling prey to the fluttering tail of toilet paper.

Rae skidded to a halt. "Is there a problem?"

The woman angled her neck. "What business is it of yours?"

"Don't press my buttons, lady. You want service? Wait your turn like everyone else."

Yuna's mouth lifted in a watery smile. "Rae, it's all right." She *was* ready to weep.

"No, it's not." On her shoulder, Kameko stilled. No doubt Rae's defense of her beleaguered mother pleased her. "Lady, get in line. I'm not letting you hassle my friend."

"Well, I can't wait. I have an appointment."

"Which you'll miss, unless you stop complaining."

An impasse, and the woman tottered on her heels.

"Did you hear me?" Rae stepped closer—a vivid, animated presence. "Get moving!"

The woman's jaw loosened. Snapping it shut, she rushed to the back of the line.

At her fast retreat, Kameko released a grateful breath. She patted Rae's back.

Yuna gripped her skull. "Bestie, you're a lifesaver." She flashed a warning finger at her daughter. "Stop running around and behave for Auntie Rae." She sprinted to the cash register.

In the bathroom, Kameko let Rae peel down her tights and remove the offending toilet paper. They both washed their hands.

"Auntie Rae, why was the lady shouting at Mommy?"

"Some people get impatient, bean sprout."

"What's 'impatient'?"

"They don't like taking turns. They always want to be first."

"That's silly." Kameko bounced on her toes. Growing still, she glanced longingly at the bathroom stall. "Can I go again?"

"Don't let me stop you." Rae hesitated. "Do you need help?" At five, Kameko juggled babyish behavior with fierce independence.

"I'm okay." The stall banged shut. Humming punctuated the short interlude. Then she said, "Quinn told Mommy I can stay with him and Mr. Connor."

"And me," Rae offered. More juice boxes were out of the question, and she searched for an activity sure to raise her ranking in the child's affections. "Want to water the houseplants? We'll feed them too."

"You didn't kill them?"

"Give me a break. You watered them last weekend. I promise, they're thriving."

"What's 'thriving'?"

Sorrow brushed across Rae's lips unbidden, swift. She mustered the courage to breathe it in. "It means we're taking good care of Lark's houseplants."

"Are we allowed to talk about Lark now? Mommy said we shouldn't."

A kindness—Yuna understood the dangerous terrain of grieving. Rae had yet to begin the journey in a meaningful way. But their unspoken agreement was forged by adults; Kameko had been affected too. Banishing Lark from conversation made no sense to her. From a five-year-old's perspective, Lark had gone away. She wasn't gone forever.

No wonder Kameko worried about Rae killing the plants. She'd killed off all mention of her daughter. A thoughtless choice. We breathe life into our memories by celebrating those loved ones in conversation.

Rae said, "We can talk about Lark whenever you want."

Inside the stall, silence bloomed. At length Kameko said, "Why didn't Lark take her plants when she went to heaven? She loved them."

"She wanted you to take care of them."

"Can I visit Lark? I miss her."

The question pierced Rae. "I'm sorry, bean sprout. You can't see Lark until *you* go to heaven. Not for a long, long time."

The toilet flushed. "Can Daddy see Lark's plants when he picks me up?"

"That's a great idea."

"Daddy likes plants. He grows pretty flowers for Mommy when the snow goes away." From beneath the stall, Kameko's feet shuffled about. Grunting, she tugged up her tights. "Can I play tag with Quinn? Or color pictures with Mr. Connor? Mommy said he'll be happy to color pictures with me."

"Whatever you'd like," Rae said brightly, concealing the hurt. Even her father rated higher in Kameko's affections than she did. "When is Daddy coming for you?"

"Oh, I don't know." Kameko scampered to the sink. "Later?"

Under normal circumstances, Yuna wouldn't ask Connor to aid in a babysitting intervention. With Quinn's help, he'd manage. Which begged the question—why hadn't she asked Rae instead?

The answer came immediately. This wasn't really about Connor. Prior to her death, Lark was Yuna's go-to babysitter in a pinch. Quinn wasn't much older. A teenager was a livelier companion for a small child than any adult.

Rae turned on the tap. "It doesn't matter when Daddy picks you up. We'll have fun until he comes for you."

Kameko took the paper towel Rae handed over and set it by the sink. She proceeded to flap her hands through the air. A game, and she was having fun. "What am I having for dinner? Can I have a snack too?"

"If we get out of your mother's hair, you can have whatever you want." *Except juice boxes.*

In the stockroom, most of the new merchandise was unpacked. Quinn was placing the last packages of floral wire on a shelf.

Rae glanced back at the shop, where Yuna swiftly rang up sales. "So . . ." She returned her attention to Quinn. "Looks like we're both on babysitting patrol."

"Should I have asked you first? I figured since you and Yuna are friends . . ."

"You did great. It was nice of you to bail her out." The standoffish behavior wasn't doing either of them any favors, and she lightened her tone. "Hey, do you mind if I take Kameko in my car? I keep her old car seat in the trunk."

"Actually, that works better. There's something I have to take care of." Quinn seemed reluctant to elaborate. "Can I meet you back at the house?"

"Sure."

Refusing to pry, she zipped Kameko into her snowsuit. Together, the trio went out.

A brisk wind blew across Chardon Square. Quinn's truck was parked in front of the craft emporium. He was about to climb in when Rae stopped him.

The front tires were nearly bald. Leaving Kameko at the curb, she walked around the truck. The back tires were passable. Not much tread left, but they'd get through the winter.

"Change of plans, Quinn." She pulled out her phone and dialed Rudy's on Route 6. "We're taking your truck in for new tires. The ones in front are shot."

"I can't afford new tires."

"Well, I can." He began to object, and she cut in. "No arguing. Follow me to Rudy's and drive carefully."

Chapter 8

Hurrying out of Rudy's Tires, Rae climbed into her Honda Civic.

In the back seat, Kameko withdrew a sparkly wand from her backpack. As they pulled out of the lot, she waved it at the service technician beside Quinn's truck. For his part, Quinn resembled a boy separated from a favorite toy. He stared forlornly out the passenger-side window.

Pulling onto Route 6, Rae merged with the afternoon traffic. "You'll have your wheels back first thing tomorrow," she assured him.

"You don't mind driving me in?"

"It's on my way to work."

Quinn studied his hands. He began picking at a ragged nail. "How much were the tires?" He'd stayed with Kameko while Rae went inside.

"Not much. Rudy gave me a discount." A lie. She'd purchased expensive, all-weather tires. Although Quinn was responsible, he was still a young driver. She'd sleep better knowing he was safe on Geauga County's icy roads. "It's not a big deal. Stop worrying about it."

"I'll pay you back."

"Aren't you planning on culinary school someday? Save your money."

"Then let me do something in trade."

"Fine. Work it out with my dad. But fair warning. His to-do list is a mile long."

Kameko, bored, twitched in the car seat. "Can we play tag?" She bobbed the wand near Quinn's ear.

From over his shoulder, he grinned. "When we get to the house? I guess." The grin fading, he cleared his throat. "I still have to make a stop. It's important."

Unease centered in Rae. After the conversation with Kameko regarding Lark and heaven, her emotions were too close to the surface—barely skin-deep. She wasn't prepared for new surprises. The day was unusual enough. If not for babysitting duty, she'd gladly don boots once she returned home to hike the farm until her emotions settled.

"Are we picking up more of your belongings?" She reminded herself that the Galeckis were still vacationing in Atlanta. Whatever else today offered, there'd be no confrontation.

"I cleared out my stuff last weekend, but I do need to stop on my parents' street." Quinn rubbed his lips together. He looked embarrassed, although she couldn't imagine why. "It'll only take five minutes."

Accepting the cryptic response, Rae followed his directions to a residential area northeast of Chardon Square—a poorer area of town, with the houses standing in tight rows. Before the garage of a cramped white dwelling, a garbage can was overturned. The contents spilled across the snow. Farther down, a black shutter hung askew on a faded-blue house.

Curiosity edged past her unease. Which place belonged to Mik and Penny? She slowed the car to a crawl.

Her knowledge of the Galeckis' current life was restricted to rumors about Mik's testy behavior at Marks Auto and the drunken fights Penny waged with other women in local bars. Penny was reputed to have a work history involving multiple firings. She never held a job for long. Before their son entered Rae's life, her interest in the couple's personal life had been nonexistent. Quinn's eyes, pinned on the road, gave no indication which dwelling was his childhood home.

At his feet, his book bag groaned with textbooks. Hoisting it onto his lap, he rummaged around inside. The crinkling of plastic, and he stuffed a bag into his parka. A stealth move, and tension pinged through Rae. What was in the bag? Was the kid dealing drugs?

Immediately she discarded the thought.

Each morning, Quinn made the bed in her guest room with military precision. He cleaned every dish he used—and most of Connor's too. At bedtime, he brushed his teeth for a good two minutes, then wiped down the bathroom sink. Last night, he found the glass cleaner in the cupboard below and polished the mirror.

Stalking his movements wasn't admirable, but he *was* bunking at her place.

Halfway down the street, he instructed her to pull over.

Cold air rushed in when Quinn opened his door. "Be right back." His eyes lifting, he began stepping out. "Shit." He pulled his foot back inside.

With her wand, Kameko bonked him on the head. "Bad word!"

"Sorry."

The wind ruffling his hair, he shut the door. Frowning, he peered through the windshield. He sighed. Rubbed his hands down his jeans and sighed again.

While he worked out the mystery dilemma, Rae assessed his jeans. Tears were forming in the worn fabric at his knees. He needed sturdier jeans to carry him through the rest of winter. His parka, the cuffs tattered and the collar fraying, had also seen better days. At least he'd added a fresh strip of duct tape to his left boot to keep the sole in place.

She was pondering online shopping when he said, "I'll go around back. That's the best move. You know, because he's home. He won't notice if I sneak around the side of the garage." Wrapping up the puzzling monologue, he gave her a look of apology. "Do you mind parking near the end of the street? We can't stay here. If he sees us, we're toast."

"Quinn, what's going on? *Who* are you worried will see you?"

The words were barely out when Rae's attention strayed to the gray house to her right. A beige sedan was parked in the driveway. Past the sedan, a frightfully thin dog paced behind a chain-link fence.

The dog was part terrier, with a pointed snout and sleek haunches that seemed undersized for its long, curling tail. With a start, she recalled her conversation with Quinn when she found him beneath the dreaded tree on the day he'd turned eighteen. The snow spilling from his shoulders. His nervous chatter about the neighbors on the street. Including a bit about a woman who'd left her grumpy husband last year.

The woman left her dog behind.

Indignation broke past Rae's self-control. "You're worried Mr. Grouchy Pants will catch you feeding his dog?" The temps were below freezing, the sun dipping below the rooftops.

"His name is Mr. Cox. And, yeah, he's grumpy." Quinn rolled his shoulders. He was an edgy bantamweight, scared to enter the ring. "I don't like tangling with him."

"No problem. Let me. Giving you a hard time for feeding his dog— I'll give him a piece of my mind."

"What?"

A better idea surfaced. A deliciously perfect solution. Yanking the keys from the ignition, she got out.

"Auntie Rae!" Kameko's wand battered the window.

"*Shhh!*" Quickly, she unstrapped the child from the car seat. "No talking, bean sprout. We have to be quiet."

Clueing in to her intentions, Quinn leaped from the car. He darted around the hood.

"Rae, we can't just walk up the drive and feed Shelby." He took Kameko's free hand, his worried gaze landing on the front stoop. "Mr. Cox isn't usually home this early. If he catches us, he'll come out. You don't want to see his temper."

"Like I care if he has a temper. I have one too. A big one."

Kameko dropped her voice to a whisper. "You do," she agreed. Her eyes sparkled. "See? I'm being quiet as mice."

Quinn patted her head. "Good job." He leaned toward Rae, his expression surprisingly mature. "Get back in the car. I can't let you give Mr. Cox a piece of your mind. If he blows his stack, I'll . . ."

"You'll what?"

"I'll have to defend you."

A gallant impulse, and she nearly laughed. Which would injure Quinn's budding manhood, so she composed herself instead.

"I appreciate the gesture, but I don't need your help. I'm not scared of your grumpy neighbor." A more upsetting thought intruded. "If he's home, why isn't the dog inside? Who leaves a dog outside in February?"

Despair slumped Quinn's shoulders. "Mr. Grumpy Pants."

"Well, that settles it."

"Settles *what*?"

"Whether I'm in the mood to be a Good Samaritan or a horse thief. Ride on, cowboy." She thrust out her hand. "Give me the bag. I'll feed the dog. Her name is Shelby?"

"Yes, and *I'll* feed her."

When they walked up the driveway, Shelby yipped. A small, soft noise—the dog was edgier than Quinn. Tail wagging, she trotted closer to the fence.

Quinn opened the plastic bag. Crouching down, he went nose-to-nose with the mutt. A private greeting between man and dog, and the way he steered his kibble-laden fingers through the chain link was heartbreaking and sweet, the patient endeavor of a loyal friend. Shelby gobbled up every crumb. Mud flecked the dog's fur; she was shivering from the cold.

Rae took a gander at the fenced-in backyard. It was depressingly empty. No shrubs, no trees. There wasn't a doghouse for shelter. A water bowl hugged the fence, a glazing of ice on top.

Her temper flared. "Saddle up, cowpokes. We're doing this."

Quinn looked up. "What are we doing?"

Ignoring the query, she released Kameko's hand. Stepping back, she studied the fence. Five feet tall or thereabouts. *I've got this.*

"I'm going over," she informed him. "Let's call this a rescue operation."

Rae carried more pounds than she liked, but she was strong. Luckily, she also preferred sensible flats. With ease she climbed over, dropping down on the other side. The obedient dog sat at attention, her tail thumping the ground.

Quinn palmed his forehead. "I'm not sure if you're crazy, or you've just become my personal hero."

"I vote for the latter." She reached out to him. "Let's wrap this up. Give me the bag."

Alarm streaked his features as he handed over the remainder of the kibble. Rae dumped it on the snow. Even during a rescue operation, there was time to feed a starving dog.

Shelby made quick work of the meal.

"Good girl." Rae smoothed her hand down the dog's back. The shivering beast smelled oily and damp. Shelby was good-natured, and Rae encouraged her closer; the dog dipped her snout and snuffled in search of more food. Rae hoisted her into her arms.

At the ready, Quinn hung over the fence. After they transferred the dog, she climbed back over. They put Shelby and the joyous Kameko in the back seat, then got in.

"Auntie Rae, are we stealing her?" Kameko ruffled the dog's ears. "Can I keep her?"

"Yes. No," Rae said, wading into a moral dilemma. She flipped the car's heat to high.

The glee faded from Quinn's eyes. "We *are* stealing her. There'll be repercussions."

"Don't be a pessimist." She preferred to believe they'd hightail it out of Dodge without problems.

"Rae, get real. What are we supposed to do if Mr. Cox sees us somewhere with his dog? It's not like Chardon's a big town. And two wrongs don't make a right."

"Good point." Another decision confronted her, this one thornier. She got back out. "Stay here."

Ascending the front steps, she donned her game face. Ringing the doorbell was the sensible choice. Her temper, however, was past simmer.

She pounded instead.

Mr. Cox flung open the door. "What are you, a lunatic?" He wore a ratty bathrobe and a dour expression. "Why are you pounding on my door?"

A bottle of beer dangled from his fingers. In the background, a sports channel blared. The despicable Mr. Cox was a barrel-chested man. The calves peeking out from beneath his robe were hairier than his neglected mutt.

On the positive side, he was a good head shorter than Rae. An advantage if reasoning failed.

She said, "I'm taking the dog."

"What dog? *My* dog?" He took a swig of his beer. "Get off my steps, lady."

"Fine. I'm leaving—with Shelby."

Ire flashed across his face. His attention swung to the curb and Rae's car. In the back seat, Kameko—hugging the dog—was chortling.

Cox pushed open the door.

Rae shoved him back. "I'll pay. Is fifty enough? It'll keep you in brewskis for a month." When he stared at her, dumbfounded, she added, "You're not coming outside and scaring the kids. Try it, and I'm taking you down. And I don't mean 'taking you down to the police station for animal endangerment.' I'm taking you down personally. I hope you're ready to face-plant, because I'm an ace at self-defense. And seeing how you've treated the dog, I'm clean out of patience."

"Cool down, lady. Who said anything about scaring the kids?"

"Do we have a deal?"

Greed lit his eyes. "Do you have seventy-five? Cash, no checks."

"Done."

She dashed to the car for her purse.

~

When they got to the house, Rae left a disgruntled Kameko in her father's care. The five-year-old seemed aware that there was more high drama afoot and was visibly upset she'd miss out on the fun. After Connor steered her toward the living room, Rae fetched the watering can from beneath the kitchen sink. Then she ushered Quinn and the dog into the guest bathroom.

"What are we doing now?" Quinn asked her.

Rae waved her hand before her nose. "This really can't wait. I've smelled garbage cans with a nicer stink than this dog."

"We're giving Shelby a bath?"

"Assuming she'll let us." Rae turned on the faucet.

While she fetched shampoo from the cupboard, Quinn tugged off his boots. He rolled his jeans up on his shins. With devoted eyes Shelby watched, her tail nervously thumping the floor. The soft, cooing sound he made was sweet and unexpected. The dog quieted. Gently he picked her up and placed her in the water.

Rae eyed his malnourished companion. "Don't let her jump out, okay?" A slippery, skittish dog could harm herself.

Perched on the edge of the bathtub, he gave a hasty thumbs-up. There was no telling how the muddy dog would react to an impromptu bath and grooming.

Their concerns were quickly put to rest. Leaning against Quinn's knees, Shelby lapped at the rising water. After she drank her fill, she licked the side of his face.

He laughed. "I guess she's into bath time."

"Thank goodness. I'd rather not chase a wet dog around the guest bathroom."

Rae squirted a thick line of shampoo down Shelby's back. Quinn helped work a frothy lather through the dog's coat. The crisp scent of orange blossoms spiked the air.

"Was this Lark's shampoo?" His expression grew wistful. "It's familiar."

His tone was gentle, soothing. As if to calm her, as he'd done with Shelby.

"The shampoo was Lark's favorite," she admitted, glad suddenly to venture into topics she'd avoided. Doing so brought a measure of relief as heartening as Quinn's tender handling of the dog. "My daughter bought it online from a botanical site. One of her favorite places to shop." Lark had been an adolescent detective, unearthing spa-quality products and making too many charges on Rae's credit cards. "I'm nearly out of shampoo, and my dad's brand is a no-go. Too spicy for a sweet girl like Shelby."

"It's nice."

"I can't bring myself to throw away her toiletries. Even her toothbrush and ten different types of body wash. It's all beneath the sink. As if she might reappear one day and give me a hard time if I've thrown anything out."

The reverie was too personal—why was she rambling on? Quinn missed Lark too. She didn't want to burden him.

In a lighter tone, she added, "I hate to see the toiletries go to waste. Use whatever you like."

"You don't mind?"

"If Lark's shampoo is okay for your dog, who cares if you splurge? She'd want you to."

The offer seemed to please him. As did the phrase "your dog." With a burst of joy, Quinn built the lather on Shelby's back into foamy peaks.

His soggy companion—standing agreeably in four inches of water, her belly full for perhaps the first time in months—watched him work with docile curiosity.

Leaning in, he lathered Shelby's legs. "I've never had a pet before." The dog's sloppy pink tongue flicked out, grazing his cheek.

"Not true. You've been taking care of Shelby for months. In my book, she's been your pet for a while."

"How much does a vet cost? Can I wait until summer to take her? After graduation, I'll work full-time."

"You'll need those wages to save up for culinary school. And, no, the vet can't wait. Let's set up a time when my dad can go with you. His schedule is looser than mine. Besides, I have a bad feeling Shelby's overdue for a visit. Let me cover the cost."

"Okay, but only if—"

"I know," Rae said, cutting him off. She smiled. "You'll swap work in trade." Quinn's desire not to take advantage was admirable, but there were more important concerns. Like giving him a chance to finish growing up. "Ask my dad for a list of chores you can tackle—and please space them out. You graduate from high school in June. Build in time to study for those final exams."

"I will."

"Good."

"You're really great, Rae."

"I don't know about that."

"Really—I appreciate everything you've done for me." Quinn reached for the watering can. He poured a gentle stream over Shelby's head, taking care not to get shampoo in her eyes. "Watching you in action was amazing. Taking on Mr. Cox, rescuing Shelby . . . You're a superhero." He darted a bashful glance. "Totally awesome how you took charge of the situation."

"Stop with the flattery. It'll go to my head."

"You *are* nice. Everyone on the street knew Mr. Cox didn't treat Shelby right. They never got involved. You're braver than anyone."

"Hardly."

"I wish Lark could've seen you in action. I bet she would've changed her opinion of you."

The comment dropped between them, unchecked. An error, and clearly unintentional.

"Oh man. Rae, I didn't mean . . ." Splotches of red crept up Quinn's neck.

Struck deep, she briefly closed her eyes. Had Lark complained about her constantly? Described her as the worst sort of parent? Their relationship *had* been on shaky ground.

"Don't apologize. You're right. Lark didn't have a high opinion of me. Not toward the end." Weary, Rae let the water out of the tub. "Our debates were awfully heated."

"About the things she wanted to know?"

At sea, Rae nodded. "About the facts she *deserved* to know. I kept them from her. A foolish decision, and now she's gone. I'd give anything for the chance to set things right."

"I'm sure you had good reason for not telling her about the guy."

A starkly accurate remark—it floated in the air, unbound. They were speaking in generalities. Yet Quinn seemed cognizant of the facts. As if he was familiar with the painful topic that had damaged her relationship with her precious daughter.

The guy.

With dismay, Rae searched for an adequate response. She doubted one existed. How much did Quinn know about the substance of her arguments with Lark? Too much, apparently. The irony was remarkable, disturbing. Of all the people Lark might have confided in—any of her girlfriends, or Yuna or her grandfather—she'd chosen Quinn. The sweet, immature boy whom fate had guided into her life.

The last of the water gurgled down the drain. It lent Rae the perfect excuse to step back, giving Quinn room to finish with the dog. Her knees felt wobbly. Wiping the distress from her features, she leaned against the counter.

The air crackled with the emotional charge from unanswered questions. Quinn pretended not to notice. Hoisting Shelby from the tub, he set about drying her.

Rae tried to catch his gaze. "Quinn, did my daughter tell you *why* we were fighting?"

The flush on his neck bled into his cheeks.

"I'm not mad, just curious."

Kneeling beside the dog, he risked a glance. "She told me everything." With nervous movements, he fluffed Shelby's fur. "About her dad, I mean. She thought it wasn't fair, how you wouldn't tell her who he was."

"There was a reason for holding back the information. A very good reason."

"Did Lark understand?"

Frustration surged through her. Lark had viewed her refusal to reveal the facts as a betrayal. Each attempt to make her understand failed miserably. Their conversations had followed a dismal trajectory. Lark's demands for information about her father were followed by Rae's evasive responses—clumsy attempts to shield her from the ugly truth. Then pleas for Lark to wait until she was older before demanding answers. Each debate ended in shouting.

Stop asking me to wait! Who is he, Mom? I have a right to know my father.

When her fury met with silence, Lark would storm out.

The memory left a bitter taste in Rae's mouth. "None of my explanations held water with my daughter," she said. "Lark was mature for her age. Still, she was only fourteen. Not old enough to hear . . . all of it. I know that sounds cruel—it's natural for a child to want a full understanding of her parentage—but my first instinct was to protect her."

"She didn't see it that way." Quinn instinctively took her side.

"Kids tend to oversimplify the choices adults make." As he was doing now, sticking up for the friend he'd lost. He was also young, untested. Innocent to the murky choices grown-ups made in a world that wasn't black and white. At a loss for a better way to explain, she added, "Life is complicated."

"What if she wanted to know her dad because . . ." His voice trailing off, Quinn blushed to the roots of his hairline.

"Go on," she prodded.

"Like, maybe she hoped you'd start dating her dad again."

Rae's mind reeled. "Is that what she thought?"

Quinn backpedaled fast. "I'm not sure. It's just a guess." Tossing aside the wet towel, he grabbed another. His dog flopped to the floor as the towel sped across her back. "Lark never gave me lots of details about her motives. She was awfully touchy whenever we talked about her dad. I do think, though . . . she hoped you and the guy would end up together."

The irony was mind-boggling. Leave it to her daughter to romanticize the most difficult era of Rae's life.

The shocking loss of her mother during the White Hurricane. Connor's descent into depression. Rae's corresponding fear that she'd virtually become an orphan. How her anger and confusion led to full-out rebellion.

A rebellion, she saw now with heartbreaking clarity, that led directly to her pregnancy.

None of which Lark knew. With nothing to go on, she'd romanticized the story.

Connor, Yuna—practically everyone in Chardon—finally came to a more practical conclusion. In her last months of high school, Rae was acting out. Taking risks. The pregnancy was the result of a one-night stand. Shame was reason enough not to list the man's name on Lark's birth certificate.

Sorrow wove through her as she asked, "Did Lark talk about her dad often?"

A tentative query. Quinn handled it with care.

Nodding, he said, "She told me she felt like half a person, not knowing who he was. She didn't understand why you kept him a secret. Even if she couldn't get you two back together, she didn't see why she should lose out."

"She wanted a relationship with him."

Ducking his head, Quinn took his time drying the panting dog's legs, coasting the towel across each paw. "She had a point, Rae. Even if grown-ups hate each other, their kid shouldn't lose out. Don't you agree?"

A knock on the door spared her from answering. In a fog, she found Kameko waiting with a bright smile.

The five-year-old swayed eagerly from side to side. "Is Shelby pretty now?" Her longing gaze fell on the dog. "Can she come out and play?"

Chapter 9

After the revelations about Lark, Quinn seemed determined to correct any missteps he'd made.

Despite Rae's assurances he'd done nothing wrong, he insisted on making dinner, whipping up a vegetable frittata and a side of hash browns. Kameko—announcing Quinn would sit beside her—daintily helped set the table. She folded the napkins into perfect triangles while Rae fetched the dishes. The excitable Shelby trotted back and forth, her snout capturing the marvelous scents raining down from the stove.

When Quinn brought the platters to the table, the malnourished dog wisely lingered near Kameko. In the space of an hour, she'd become the mutt's greatest admirer.

The adults feigned indifference as most of the food mysteriously dropped from her plate. Her furry coconspirator made short work of it.

Dinner ended with a spontaneous round of applause for their ingenious chef. The praise took Quinn off guard.

Amid the clapping he rose from his chair. The familiar blush crept across his skin as he took a stiff bow. Yet even a kid with little experience with praise learns fast. Rummaging through the cupboards, Quinn announced he'd bake something for dessert.

While he placed ingredients on the counter, Rae noticed his dog rooting around inside his book bag. Beneath the heavy textbooks, a handful of dog food was scattered across the bottom of the bag.

Shelby—tongue lolling and ears cocked—seemed agreeable to another meal. Rae chopped up small chunks of cheese. Connor fetched the peanut butter. The dog plowed through the savory mixture.

By the time the doorbell rang, and Rae ushered Yuna inside, a celebratory air had filled the living room.

On the floor, Kameko—having stolen one of Connor's athletic socks from the laundry basket—played tug-of-war with Shelby. Her peals of laughter resounded through the room. From the couch, Connor cheered her on. Quinn did the same, in between polishing off mouthfuls of the leftover hash browns that had been growing cold on the coffee table.

Taking in the lively scene, Yuna said, "I'll give you credit, Rae. When you make a change, you don't settle for half measures."

"You know me. Go big or go home." Rae helped her out of her coat. "I thought your hubby was picking up Kameko. Did Chardon's dedicated mayor get hung up?"

"His meeting started late. I won't see Kipp until later tonight." More laughter rang out. Yuna glanced affectionately at her daughter. Kameko rolled onto her belly and nuzzled Shelby's neck. "Is the dog Quinn's? She has a sweet temperament."

"Can we discuss Shelby in a sec? There's something I need to tell you." Rae plunged forward before second thoughts intruded. "I've changed my mind about Night on the Square."

"You'll help with the fundraiser?" Yuna smiled broadly. "What made you reconsider?"

There was no simple explanation. Rescuing Shelby from Mr. Cox had brightened Rae's outlook. Quinn's revelations about Lark were less cheerful news. Still, he'd lent insight into Lark's secret hopes and wishes. Rae was grateful for the knowledge. Together, the two events seemed a turning point: Rae often felt immobilized by grief, but her life *was* moving forward.

In fits and starts.

She was no longer stuck in place. Even if her verve for life slumbered beneath frosty layers of sorrow, she was beginning to feel, well, hopeful.

None of which she could describe at the moment. Kameko leaped up, and her eager playmate barked. Connor balled up the sock and pitched it neatly. Child and dog raced after.

Rae said, "It's not right to bail on the June event. I made you a promise, Yuna. Count me in as your second-in-command." She inhaled a fortifying breath. "I do have one condition."

With expectation, Yuna stared at her.

"I'm not attending the committee meetings. I'll do the PR legwork and report to you directly."

"You're not ready to see Katherine Thomerson or Sally Harrow?"

"It's too soon." The women were a stark reminder of Lark's death. Rae didn't trust herself to keep it together if forced to spend any amount of time with either woman. "I'll keep you posted if I change my mind."

"That's fine." Yuna followed her into the kitchen. "Thanks for reconsidering. We have a million tasks ahead of us. I'd be lost without your help."

"Let's get started this week." Rae began to add something else. Instead, she frowned. "Don't you teach a class tonight? Kameko's more than welcome to stay. I'll drop her off later."

"The knitting class is canceled. There must be a bug going around. Two of the women are down with colds." The sweet fragrance of cinnamon wafted through the air, and Yuna spied the loaf of banana bread cooling on the stove. "Since when do you bake?"

"Since never. Quinn made the bread."

"Did he use one of . . . ?"

"Lark's recipes? He did." Rae smiled with reassurance. "It's all right. With Quinn around, my daughter is no longer a taboo subject. He talks about her all the time." She declined to add that he was also a surprising repository for Lark's hidden longings, which highlighted Rae's failures as a parent. She hadn't supplied what Lark needed most—the truth about her father.

Regret slowed Rae's movements as she poured coffee. "Quinn found Lark's gluten-free flour in the freezer. He tossed a mashed avocado into the batter. Don't tell my father. Connor hates avocados."

"For Connor's heart health?"

"Yes. Since Quinn moved in, we're eating a more balanced diet."

"When he has time, ask him to make Lark's chocolate-zucchini bread. Two loaves. I'll pay for one." Yuna tipped her head to the side, her expression thoughtful. "Actually, the chocolate-zucchini bread is Quinn's recipe. He gave it to Lark."

Rae's eyes misted. "I thought she found the recipe in one of my mother's old cookbooks."

"No, he gave it to her sometime last year."

"I guess I shouldn't be surprised. All my assumptions about Quinn were mistaken. On the surface, he's nothing like my daughter. Bashful, unsure. Underneath, it's a different story."

Yuna brushed gentle fingers across the furrow deepening in Rae's brow. "They had a lot in common," she said. "They were good for each other."

"How much did you know about their friendship?"

The question lowered Yuna's eyes. Putting her on the spot wasn't fair. Yet after the conversation with Quinn, it was clear Lark had kept too much hidden from view.

Guilt seared Rae. A child does not come naturally to deception. The art is learned through example.

Like mother, like daughter.

Running from the thought, she cut a slice of banana bread. She set the plate before Yuna, a peace offering. "After you hired Quinn last autumn," she prodded, "did he mention Lark?"

"All the time."

"I understand why you didn't tell me. Quinn was trespassing on my property."

"He was."

"And I'd become obsessed with his behavior. As if he'd committed a crime. Making him the central focus helped me avoid thinking about the accident, and how I'd lost my precious daughter." The familiar grief welled as she opened the silverware drawer. Placing a fork beside the plate, she briefly caught Yuna's gaze. "I never gave you the chance to speak up. I'm not even sure why you've put up with my behavior."

"Simple. Because I love you, Rae."

"I love you too."

"You hold yourself to a high standard. Which I admire. But you *have* been through a hard time."

"That doesn't justify making Quinn an easy target. I'm ashamed of myself."

"Don't be. The police report backed up your worst suspicions. The PD shouldn't have assumed the kids were dating. They jumped to conclusions." Seating herself at the table, Yuna poked at the banana bread with her fork. The weight of her thoughts curved her spine. "If it's any comfort, my husband thought I'd let you down. After I hired Quinn, we argued constantly."

"Why were you arguing with Kipp?"

"Quinn would come into work and talk nonstop about his friendship with Lark. No doubt he was having trouble dealing with the loss. Talking about her seemed to help. All the late-night Zoom chats, and how they were sneaking around together after school."

Yet another revelation in a day rife with them. "Lark was skipping her after-school activities?" She'd had no idea.

"And sometimes they secretly got together before the new school year began."

"Quinn told us about how he'd struck up a friendship with my daughter . . . but he left a lot out." More details than she'd imagined.

"Even if you hadn't been furious about him roaming your property, I wouldn't have told you everything I knew. We're best friends, but I felt a responsibility to Quinn too." Anguished, Yuna looked up quickly. "How do you break a confidence if you're the only adult a boy can trust?"

Her desire to protect the lonely youth put something sweet in Rae's chest. A brighter emotion to sit beside the grief.

"You don't," she said. "A child's trust is sacred. You did the right thing."

A muddy silence fell between them.

As it lengthened, she imagined Quinn trudging across Chardon Square last fall, his grief fresh over Lark's death. The safe haven that the craft emporium represented. Yuna's welcoming smile as she ushered him in; the tea kettle whistling as she prepared hot chocolate in the stockroom's makeshift kitchen, where she kept treats for her staff. Did her kindness release the burden of memories Quinn yearned to share?

He'd unburdened himself with the knowledge that someone was actually listening.

Now Rae wondered: What other secrets did Quinn place in Yuna's care?

Apprehension carried her to the table. "Lark was the only person Quinn relied on, until you hired him. He knew he could trust you. What else did he talk about, aside from my daughter?" Taking Yuna's hand, she squeezed her cold fingers. "It's okay. Tell me. I care about Quinn too. His safety is my primary concern."

A flicker of relief crossed Yuna's features, an indication that she *did* want to talk this out. Then apprehension colored her words as she confided, "He came into work one day with a bruise on his arm. A handprint. It was large, turning purple—I couldn't pretend I hadn't seen. There was no choice but to ask him about it."

"You mean, his dad . . . ?"

A tremor shook Yuna. Shot through Rae too. What other cruelty had Quinn endured at the hands of his father?

Yuna said, "The Galeckis were drinking, per the usual. When they began fighting, Quinn tried to break it up. Mik backhanded him. Then he dragged Quinn to his bedroom. Ordered him to stay inside."

The description chilled Rae. "Quinn stayed in his room while Mik and Penny . . . abused each other?"

"That's what he used to do. Frankly, I'm worried Quinn spent most of his childhood cowering in his bedroom while his parents fought. Not anymore."

"What do you mean?"

Yuna's eyes flashed. "Last spring, your ingenious daughter came up with a solution. Whenever his parents fought, she told Quinn to lock his bedroom door and turn on the music. Then climb out his bedroom window." Dispensing with the fork, Yuna tore off a chunk of banana bread. She chewed with gusto, the anger in her gaze melding with a sudden flash of triumph. "Quinn never stayed out past midnight, and the Galeckis were none the wiser."

Love for her daughter edged past Rae's worry. "Ten points for Lark."

"She deserves a gold medal." Tearing off another chunk of bread, Yuna eagerly stuffed it into her mouth. She stared heavenward, mumbling, "We love you, baby."

"When you found the handprint on his arm . . . after Quinn snuck out of his parents' house, where did he go?"

"To the movies. He didn't come back home until the lights were off in his parents' bedroom."

"The poor kid."

"Before we lost your daughter . . . you *do* know where he'd crash."

The pieces tumbled into place. "My house."

"Right."

"All the times Connor stalked down the hallway to silence Lark's wild cackling—Quinn was in the bedroom with her. He climbed in through her bedroom window. The house never quieted down until midnight."

The curfew that Lark, ever sensible, set for Quinn. She would've ensured he drove home before he was too sleepy to get behind the wheel.

From the living room, Kameko's laughter rang out. Barking followed. Someone applauded—Connor or Quinn.

Yuna said, "So tell me about the dog. Quinn never mentioned having a pet."

"He didn't, until this afternoon."

"Gosh, Rae. Free room and board, plus a new dog. You're vying for Woman of the Year. When did you visit the humane society?"

"I didn't." She explained about Mr. Cox's maltreatment of Shelby and the seventy-five dollars she'd paid to save the dog. Wrapping up, she added, "Rescuing Shelby was a real emotional boost. There's too much ugliness in the world. It's not every day you get to make a difference."

"You *do* look good. The first time in months."

"And now I'm wondering . . ."

"What?"

Deep in thought, she rose. On the counter, the coffee she'd poured had grown cold. Rinsing out the cups, Rae unlocked yet another secret.

"C'mon." She gestured toward the hallway. "I have a hunch. There's something we need to check out."

They retreated down the hallway, away from the barking and the scampering of feet. Kameko chasing the dog or the other way around; a heavier thud, probably Quinn, hopping up from the couch to join in. If they were teaching Shelby new tricks, hopefully the living room's furnishings would survive the lesson.

At the door to Lark's bedroom, Rae asked, "Last year, when Quinn and Lark first took one of your classes together, did they seem to connect fast?"

Yuna nodded. "I'm not sure why, though. Quinn never explained."

"I know the reason." Playfully she flicked Yuna's nose, drawing a laugh. "Quinn told my daughter about Shelby's plight, and they bonded instantly. Last year—when Mr. Cox's wife walked out."

"She left the dog behind?"

"Exactly. Now I'm wondering if a timid kid like Quinn would've braved his neighbor's wrath to feed a starving dog. I'm sure he wanted to. I'm not convinced he would've mustered up the courage on his own."

Understanding lit Yuna's features. "Or was he inspired by a teenager with more bravado?"

They found the answer inside a bedroom painted spring green. An outlandish border of hand-painted, neon-yellow daisies banded the ceiling. The bed was still rumpled. Just as Lark had left it in October, before leaving for the slumber party at Stella Thomerson's house.

The faintest hint of orange blossoms floated in the air. Rae swallowed down her grief. She chose instead to celebrate her daughter's ingenuity. It had bolstered Quinn when his homelife was a war zone—and lent him the courage to feed a starving dog.

And, surely, the *means* to feed Shelby.

Plastic storage containers were stacked beside Lark's chest of drawers. They contained all manner of art supplies. The second container down, however, wore a film of dark splotches across the rim. Fingerprints.

Wedging the container out, Rae placed it on the floor.

Ten pounds of dog food met her gaze. There was also a selfie. Appraising the photo, Rae's breath caught—her daughter, crouched before the chain-link fence. At her side, the image of Quinn was cut off; only a sliver of his jeans and his worn boots were visible.

On the other side of the fence, the dog poked her nose through the chain link to nuzzle Lark's ear.

Chapter 10

Shelby's tail thumped the floor, an anxious metronome as Quinn walked past.

Climbing into bed, he drew the sheet to his chin. Next came the blanket. The plush fabric was a sensory delight as he pulled it over his chest. Each night he performed the same ritual, folding the comforter across his waist and smoothing out the wrinkles. There were four pillows on the queen-size bed; he chose a different one each night. All four were marvels, fat and airy. Not one smelled of mold.

Shelby followed his every move with alert, eager devotion. A luxurious silence enveloped the house.

"C'mon, girl," he whispered.

With canine befuddlement she dipped her head.

"It's okay. We're safe." He patted the mattress. "Jump up."

Snuggling with a human, in a human's bed, was an indulgence beyond the dog's experience. Hindquarters quivering, she approached. Her damp nose snuffled across Quinn's knuckles. Whining, she trotted back to the center of the rug.

"Shelby, we're not sleeping on the floor." Quinn sat up, unhappy to have disturbed the perfectly arranged bed. He knew he should fetch the dog, but his toes were so warm.

The container of dog food sat before the nightstand. Why wasn't Lark's mother angry? The reason evaded him.

Not ten minutes ago, he'd come out of the bathroom with Shelby trotting behind. Rae was waiting by the guest bedroom door, the container hefted in her arms. Perspiration sprouted on his brow. Since coming to live at her place, he hadn't thought to mention the stash of dog chow hidden in Lark's room. Or to reveal that Lark, in the months before her death, was Shelby's main benefactor. She'd bought most of the ten-pound bags of chow from her seemingly bottomless allowance. Lately, he'd been skipping lunch at school to cover the cost.

All of which totaled up to an awkward tally.

Rae deserved a full accounting days ago. Or he could've told her today. After Yuna let Kameko kiss the panting dog for the umpteenth time and finally carried her to the car. Once Connor wandered off to read. There'd been a good five minutes in there to confess. *If only.*

Between rescuing Shelby, bathing her, and making dinner, coming clean was the last thing on Quinn's mind.

Now he was found out.

What Rae did next was perplexing. Miraculous, even. It ranked up there with one of his teachers switching a Friday test to the next week.

She handed over the container. Without a word of reprimand. Patting Shelby on the head, she bid him good night.

Remembering, Quinn felt a surge of relief.

Leaning sideways out of the bed, he flipped open the container. He scooped out a handful of chow. On the comforter he built a tidy mound of savory bits.

Shelby's ears perked.

They both knew better than to skip a meal. If food was available, you dug in.

"C'mon, girl. Jump up!"

She bounded onto the bed. The dog chow vanished. Sitting at attention—a tricky feat, on a mattress—Shelby flicked out her tongue. Just once.

"I can't feed you more. You'll need to go out, and it's bedtime." Gently he pushed her onto her side. No further encouragement was necessary. With an elaborate sigh, the dog fit her compact body against his legs. A rare sense of contentment filled Quinn.

He wanted to curve the arc of time, bend it back to when he was eight years old. Before his parents fought day and night. Only they wouldn't be his parents—Rae would. She'd do fine with double duty because her dad liked to help out, and Connor was cool for an old guy. She'd do great. Quinn would call this bedroom his own; every night, Shelby would share his bed. Lark, sleeping down the hall, would be his bossy little sister.

This fantasy led to an obvious and terrible conclusion. He'd gladly trade in his parents. Tell the universe he was picking a different card, leaving Mik and Penny in the deck.

No question about it. He'd make the switch in an instant.

Shame pricked Quinn. What decent kid dreamed about trading in his parents? He loved them both. At least he loved them most days. When Mik came home from Marks Auto and Penny got back from her latest job, and they just drank beer. On the nights when they chose the hard stuff, they weren't likeable at all. By the third drink, they became different people.

From what Quinn could tell, Rae and her dad weren't drinkers. They even kept milk in the house. Low-fat, but it was better than nothing.

At his side, the sleeping dog twitched. Shelby's paws began paddling the air as she chased something in her sleep. Quinn wanted to sink into dreams too. He stared at the ceiling instead. In the silence enveloping the house, it was hard to fend off the thoughts crowding his head.

Or the guilt stinging his heart.

Rae and Connor were good people. They never yelled. They didn't care if he grabbed a snack from the fridge. They were generous too. He was getting new tires for his truck, and Rae was letting him keep Shelby.

How was he reciprocating their kindness? By breaking a cardinal rule for houseguests, and teenagers in general.

Never lie to adults. Never lie directly, or through acts of omission. *His* lies were stark, and far-reaching.

About his parents, and who'd ordered him to leave.

About Lark and her dad.

And the police. They still didn't have the facts straight about Lark's death.

None of which Quinn—focused on self-preservation—dared tell Rae. Open his mouth, and she'd throw him out. Leave him with no options. He'd end up living on the streets.

Chilled by his mountain of lies, Quinn burrowed deep beneath the blankets. Keeping secrets—and betraying Rae—was wrong. And the only way to stay safe.

On the windowpane, snowflakes ticked a heavy rhythm. Shelby yipped in her sleep. Throwing off the blanket, Quinn gave her a pat. He steered his feet to the floor.

Then he watched the snowfall increase to a blinding sheet of white.

Chapter 11

Swirls of snow collected on the steeply pitched roof of the Tudor mansion. A virtual castle of stone and stucco, the grand house lay seven minutes east of Chardon Square.

At five o'clock on the dot, Griffin Marks pulled into the drive. With satisfaction he noted his sister's Ford Explorer was already parked in his parents' driveway. He'd hoped to arrive early to speak with Sally privately. With luck, he'd find an opportunity before dinner. Although they were both now in their thirties, he continued to solicit his sister's advice as if they were still children, and Sally, two years older and constant like the seasons, was still required to help Griffin solve his thorniest problems.

The indecision was wearing him down.

Although it was Tuesday, family dinners at his parents' house were now common. Two or three times a week, lately.

Some nights his mother, Winnie, pulled out all the stops, arranging fresh flowers and setting the dining room table. On more casual nights, they ate buffet-style. They filled their plates in the kitchen and carried them into the walnut-paneled family room, where the disembodied heads of his father's hunting trophies—a 22-point buck and four less mature whitetail—observed the festivities from doleful glass eyes. On those nights, they played Scrabble or Monopoly with the intention of allowing the only child in their midst to win every game.

His niece, Jackie.

Unlike his mother and his sister—not to mention his spineless brother-in-law and thoroughly unbending father—Griffin believed it was time to bring in professional help. Jackie's condition was worsening. With each passing week, she slipped further away. Granted, none of the unfortunate girls who'd been at the slumber party last fall were taking Lark's death well.

And why would they? From conversations with his niece, Griffin knew the upsetting details. Katherine Thomerson had nearly called off her daughter's slumber party. Sometimes winter came early to northeast Ohio, but no one expected five inches of snowfall the week before Halloween. Stella pleaded to keep her plans, and her mother relented.

Once everyone had arrived, Katherine left to run an errand. As the girls watched a movie in the darkened basement, Lark went upstairs alone. She walked outside, slipped on ice, and fell into the empty in-ground pool.

Lark pitched eight feet down. A quick and horrible death.

Pandemonium ensued after Katherine returned from her errand. Spotting young Quinn Galecki climbing over her brick wall, she began screaming nonstop. The commotion brought girls racing up from the basement. They cowered behind the family room's picture window as Quinn clambered down the steel ladder into the empty pool.

From their vantage point, snow glittered beneath the spotlights. A fine etching of ice crept across the brick wall and the slate stonework. The gleam of black vinyl covering the outdoor furniture, and the pool— a dark, gaping mouth in the center.

Katherine halted at the pool's edge. As her shrieks rose to fever pitch, Stella backed away from the picture window. She dashed to her bedroom. The door shut with a crack of sound. Another girl fainted, collapsing to the floor unnoticed. The rest of the girls clung together in a whimpering, sobbing mass.

All of them, except Griffin's niece.

Breaking off from the others, Jackie went outside. Nothing proves a girl's mettle like her response to calamity.

Taking care to avoid the icy patches, Jackie trod to the pool's edge. She pressed a calming hand to Katherine's back. The screaming ceased. Turning away, Katherine fled from the pool's edge and the scene below. Only then did Jackie allow her fearful gaze to alight on Quinn.

Eight feet down, in an inch of murky water, he cradled Lark. While sobbing uncontrollably.

Pulling out her phone, Jackie dialed 911.

Ever since that night, most of the girls cried easily. They dropped out of school activities. No longer did they socialize in a large, boisterous crowd. The shock of what they'd witnessed drove them apart.

And Jackie was a shadow of her former self.

Christmas Day had offered the final proof. Griffin and his family were clustered around his parents' elegantly decorated ten-foot spruce. They were about to open presents when Jackie shuffled out of the guest bathroom with her long, chestnut hair cut into short, jagged clumps.

By January, her weight loss became noticeable. She began missing too much school. Jackie complained of stomachaches. She slept at odd hours and for lengthy periods. Sally took her daughter to the pediatrician and a gastroenterologist. She taught Jackie meditation and started her on yoga. Sugar was banished from her diet, and Sally filled a cupboard with herbal teas.

Nothing worked.

To Griffin's mind, the solution was obvious.

His niece wouldn't improve without the guidance of an experienced child psychologist. Jackie needed help processing the senseless death of her friend. Since no one in his family agreed—at least, not publicly—he'd stopped broaching the subject. Even if he got Sally on board, her husband would veto the idea. Trenton never put a toe out of line with Griffin's father.

The hard-edged and successful Everett Marks viewed psychology as a pseudoscience for the simpleminded.

In the grand foyer, light from the chandelier sparkled across the stone flooring. The low thump of music floated down the staircase. Curious, Griffin went upstairs to investigate. The quiet second floor smelled of lemon furniture polish and lavender; he climbed another flight of stairs to the beautifully appointed attic his mother called her own. The large, rectangular space was swathed in feminine accoutrements, from the floral wallpaper to the overstuffed chintz upholstery. Apparently, Griffin's niece had selected the music playing softly from the built-in speakers: *Abbey Road*. Recently the ninth grader had discovered the Beatles' iconic music.

At the attic's far end, a white table nested beneath the eaves. Winnie sat beside her granddaughter.

Her silvered head lifted. "Griffin! I didn't expect to see you for another hour."

"I left work early." He owned Design Mark, the website design firm across the street from his father's car dealership not far from Chardon Square. "I was hoping to chat with Sally before dinner."

"About what?"

Brow arching, he leveled her with a glance. *None of your business.*

"Ah. I see," she said brightly. She'd always taken pride in the close relationship between her two children. Changing the subject, she asked, "Did you land the winery?"

"The one in Geneva? Not yet. They're waiting for another quote from an outfit in Shaker Heights. I should have an answer by next week." He hesitated. "Am I interrupting?"

"Of course not. Come see what we're doing." She waved him closer. "Your father and Trenton are still at the dealership. We'll eat at six thirty."

"Beef bourguignon?" He'd caught the mouthwatering scent on his way upstairs.

"Compliments of your sister. She's in the kitchen, finishing up."

Cartons surrounded the table. Inside were neatly organized white packets of photos. The more recent additions Winnie had downloaded and made into glossies. She despised the ephemeral nature of selfies and social media; every month or two, she ordered physical copies of the best snaps from her phone. Winnie also loved crafts, everything from needlework and quilting to paint-by-number pictures she completed and then stored away.

Apparently, she was now devising a new project to occupy her granddaughter. Since Lark's funeral, she'd led Jackie through a variety of crafts. Winnie held the unshakable belief that with enough busywork, her granddaughter would regain her sunny temperament.

Sidestepping the boxes, Griffin appraised his niece. Jackie was bent over a leather album, a group of photos by her elbow. Her disturbingly chopped hair stuck up every which way. Faint shadows rimmed her eyes. Her skin was unnaturally pale, as if she hadn't glimpsed sunlight in days.

When he rested his palm on her shoulder, she barely stirred. "How are you, kiddo?"

"Okay, I guess."

"Did you go to school today?"

"Grandma let me stay with her."

"I was glad for the company," Winnie put in. Her instinct to protect her only grandchild was fierce.

"Mom, she can't keep skipping school. Tenth grade begins soon. The coursework gets harder."

"How you exaggerate. It's only February. Jackie won't finish this term for another four months."

Jackie's eyes lifted. "I'll go to school tomorrow, Uncle Griffin. I'll keep up with the work."

"I have your word?"

"Sure." Putting the debate to rest, she nodded at the images before her. "Which one do you like? I can't decide."

From the looks of it, she was filling the album in chronological order, from her birth to the present day. Griffin sifted through the photos, taken when she was in elementary school. Jackie posing in a purple mermaid costume for Halloween. Playing basketball with a group of other girls. His niece seated on the front lawn before the Thomerson mansion, her arm slung around Stella Thomerson's neck.

In the background, Lark was a flash of movement, cartwheeling across the field of green.

"This one." Taking care to keep pity from his voice, Griffin handed over the photo. On closer inspection, he saw that many of the photos caught Lark in the background—moving, laughing, spinning in circles. None featured her in the foreground.

His mother said, "You'll get an album too, Griffin. Jackie is making one for each of us."

"Sounds like a big project."

"It'll give us something to do until the weather thaws. This endless winter—what I'd give to see daffodils springing up in my flower beds."

"Me too," Jackie said. "I'm tired of all the snow."

Winnie gave her a quick hug. "We'll muddle through, dearest heart." Drawing back, she withdrew a packet from the carton at her feet. She sent Griffin a mischievous glance. "Care to waltz down memory lane?"

"Is that an actual or a metaphorical question?"

"Actual. This box contains your visual history, all thirty-three years."

"What about Sally?"

"Oh, I have all her photographs in another box—everything from her first baby pictures to a recent anniversary photo with Trenton. Pulling together your sister's visual heritage was easy, but I am missing a chunk from *your* twenties. Before we get started on your album, let me skim through your smartphone. We should include a few snaps of Boston."

"Whenever you'd like."

After college, Griffin had started his career as an account executive at a graphics firm in Boston. He'd intended to put down roots on that coast. The money was good, and he dated a girl at the firm. When the relationship didn't pan out, his parents began dropping hints about the business possibilities back home. Geauga County was thriving.

Two years ago, his father made an unexpected offer. The deed to the two-story brick building across the street from Marks Auto would transfer to Griffin if he cut ties in Boston and returned to Ohio. The building now housed Design Mark. The move had been a good one, and Griffin enjoyed being his own boss. With a staff of seven, he was building a client list across the Great Lakes region.

Opening the packet, Winnie spread the photos out. "Oh, Griffin—look. This was taken when you set Bubbles free. Weren't you the cutest thing?"

The shot captured him at age six. There was his distinctive egg-shaped head and broad nose, a growing potato in the center of his cheerful face. A fluffy tuft of brown hair covered his forehead; his receding hairline wouldn't kick in until his twenties. His mother had taken the photo as he held Bubbles the goldfish by his wriggling tail above the swirling toilet bowl.

"Enough with this torture," he joked. "Put it away."

"Don't be fussy. You were adorable."

Winnie's memory was selective and Teflon-coated. "Why didn't you *stop* me from setting Bubbles free?" An instant after she'd trained the camera on him and the toilet bowl flushed, he'd become a blubbering mass of tears. "It wasn't like I'd thought the plan out. Wasn't Bubbles's safety more important than recording the moment for posterity?"

"Don't be peevish. *I* didn't think the moment out either."

"Obviously."

"Cheer up. After you freed Bubbles into the sewer system, he may have grown to massive size. Perhaps he's become a king of the sea. Neptune, with fins."

"Are you striving for a *ha-ha* moment? Don't take your routine on the road just yet."

His niece gave a sleepy glance. "Who's Bubbles?" She yawned theatrically.

"Your uncle's first pet. A goldfish he foolishly returned to the wild. We tried a bird next, with the same result."

Griffin recalled the stealthy deed he'd performed at daybreak. "Setting a bird free seemed logical." He'd always been an early riser. If his sister had awoken before he crept outside, she would've intervened.

His mother feigned insult. "I'll have you know that ridiculous conure didn't come cheap."

"I didn't want a conure. I asked for a dog. Repeatedly. It's every boy's dream." An unfulfilled yearning. His mother would never sanction a pet large enough to track mud into her showcase of a home.

"You're all grown up now. You want a dog? Buy one."

"I'll take it under consideration."

"You do that." Smiling like a game show host, Winnie reached back into the carton. "Shall we try again?"

Out came another packet. The snapshots were taken during the halcyon year before the White Hurricane schooled him in heartbreak.

His niece set her album aside. "Uncle Griffin, isn't this Lark's mom? What's she doing with Grandpa's rifle?"

The warmth of fond memories took Griffin unwillingly. The image was one of his favorites, of Rae sitting in a field of tall grass. The original nature girl with sunlight pooling around her knees. The heavy ropes of her unkempt hair danced in the breeze like golden-tipped streams of fire. The snapshot was taken during their junior year. Griffin recalled the weather had been brisk; his father's plaid hunting jacket hung from Rae's shoulders.

In her lap: Everett's Weatherby bolt-action rifle. A powerful weapon, and not one for amateurs.

"Grandpa used to take us hunting," he told his niece.

Jackie frowned. "You don't like to hunt."

Rae hadn't either, and neither Griffin's mother nor his sister would go anywhere near a firearm.

Even today, Everett's fascination with blood sports made Griffin queasy. Back then, he'd tagged along for the sheer joy of watching Rae hone the skill of marksmanship. Her prowess made her a favored pet of Griffin's father. She'd refused to kill wildlife. But she'd been a natural, with stunning, pinpoint accuracy.

From thirty paces off, she could nail a yellowing leaf on a maple tree. Rocks, tin cans, stuffed animals Griffin stole from Sally's closet and jokingly strung from trees—Rae never missed the mark.

Winnie studied the image. "Jackie, your grandfather taught Rae to shoot. He'd boast to everyone about her nonexistent learning curve. She had an amazing talent right from the start. Grandpa adored her. Rae was such a bright, fearless girl. Nothing at all like your mother at that age, or Uncle Griffin. They were both more . . . introspective."

"We were wimps," Griffin added dryly.

A grin flickered on Jackie's mouth. "You were not!" A positive display of emotion, her first in months.

The change wasn't lost on his mother. Beneath her encouraging glance, he found another photo of Rae.

"Wondering how I came by my friendship with Lark's mom?" He slid the photo before her. "When *your* mom and I were growing up, Grandpa made some good investments. He did so well, he became a serious player in Geauga County. He amassed more wealth than Midas, but he refused to put us in private school. There was a private academy in Chagrin Falls—I'm not sure how she managed it, but Sally got all the information. She even got her hands on the application forms."

"Who cares about private school? Sounds boring."

"Your mother thought otherwise. Sally begged to go. She was two grades ahead of me, and I always followed her lead. Private school sounded like a good deal."

"Why?"

"When Grandpa bought up the land to build the car dealership, he put a small factory out of business. A couple of retail establishments too." His father's tactics had been nothing short of ruthless. "Unfortunately, we went through the grades with lots of kids whose parents lost those jobs. We were picked on a lot." On several depressing occasions, Griffin was beaten up by older boys. A detail too humiliating to share.

"*I* go to public school," Jackie countered. "No one picks on me."

"It's different now, kiddo. Those jobs disappeared. Then Grandpa opened the dealership and created new jobs. No one remembers the factory now, or those other businesses."

"When kids gave you a hard time . . . Rae stuck up for you?"

"And she stuck up for your mother. I first met Rae with her dukes up, in the middle of the playground. Two girls were hassling Sally, and she intervened. Told them they'd both get a fat lip if they didn't back off." Despite his discomfiture with the conversation's turn, Griffin caught himself smiling. "After that, I sat beside Rae in every class. From second grade all the way through high school."

"In high school, Rae was your girlfriend. Right?"

Discussing their earlier camaraderie was simpler. "We were friends, mostly. We'd been friends for a long time by then." The passion that flared between them near the end of their junior year had been a mistake.

Jackie's gaze was a searchlight trained on his face. "But Rae became your girlfriend," she persisted. "Until you went to college. Wasn't she?"

He nodded.

It was a reprieve when his curious niece switched topics. "When you were a kid, before you were friends with Rae, why did she stick up for Mom? Kids don't usually defend someone they don't know."

"That's simple," Winnie put in. "Rae knew what it was like to be different. Her family wasn't prosperous like ours, but she also stuck out like a sore thumb. She dressed like a farmer—the poor dear was utterly lacking in fashion sense. People thought her parents were hippies, growing heaven-knows-what on their farm and serenading the pigs. The strangest couple. From a mile off, you could hear music blaring from the barn. Rae's father would tell anyone willing to listen the musical preferences of his pigs and goats. He's still a bit of an odd sort." This was too harsh, given the family's recent loss. Swiftly Winnie backpedaled. "It doesn't matter now. We must keep the Langdons in our prayers. They're undergoing a difficult time."

The oblique reference to Lark's death stole the glimmer in Jackie's eyes. She stared blankly at the table.

The gloom ebbing around her brought Griffin to a decision. He needed his older sister's counsel on a private matter, but asking Sally for advice would have to wait.

He pulled up a chair. "We have an hour before dinner." A curtain of grief shrouded his niece, and he spiked his voice with enthusiasm. "If I dig out my baby pictures, do you promise not to laugh? Let's get started on my album."

The curtain parted briefly. "All right," Jackie agreed.

Chapter 12

The white Colonial was dark. Cutting the engine, Griffin surveyed the other houses on his street. All were aglow, the parents inside helping their children finish homework or watching TV. The older couples, he imagined, were quietly chatting or spending a few solitary hours reading.

Griffin liked being single. He liked it less at night. There was no one to share his day with, or to cuddle with on the couch. He missed intimacy, of course, but not the heavy expectations. At times, he was convinced he'd never find a woman he clicked with on all levels—intellectually, physically, and emotionally.

Maybe he should get a dog. A lumbering husky or an energetic retriever to greet him at the end of the day. His office was only ten minutes away—he'd drop in at lunchtime for a quick game of fetch.

The night was still young. On the drive back from his parents' house, the Cavaliers had beaten the Pelicans in the game's final seconds. Before dinner and after, there hadn't been a way to catch his sister alone. He considered calling Sally but dismissed the idea. A difficult conversation was best handled in person.

He was skimming email on his laptop when she appeared at the living room's threshold. For a tall woman, Sally possessed the stealth of a cat.

"Don't you knock?" he teased, glad to see her. He set the laptop aside.

"Since when does anyone in the Marks family knock? Dad insists we have keys to each other's houses. One of his many quirks."

"We should rebel."

"You first." Sally laughed. "I'm used to Dad handing down edicts from on high. He's been doing it all my life. All your life too."

Opening the liquor cabinet, she assessed the bottles on the wine rack. Selecting a merlot, she eyed him questioningly. He nodded.

As Sally poured, he said, "Is this surprise visit of the psychic variety? Your timing is perfect. I need your advice."

With affection she studied him. Physically they were similar. The same bland Marks features and generous height. Still, his sister was by far more attractive. Sally's innate kindness shone through. Her common sense was unfailing. She was better at facing problems head-on. Even during the Boston years, Griffin had solicited her advice long-distance.

"I can't speak to my psychic abilities, but there are two reasons why I'm here." She handed him a glass. "For starters, I needed to drop off paperwork at Yuna's house."

"For the June event in Chardon Square?" His sister enjoyed social activities, working on the school's PTO and for local organizations.

"I'm on the committee for Night on the Square. I promised Yuna I'd get information and bids from local restaurants. We're discussing menu options."

Yuna's family lived next door. "She's running the event?"

"Oh, you know how she is. Yuna prefers to keep everything democratic—Chardon's original diplomat—but she's in charge."

"What's the other reason for your visit?"

In response, she lovingly pressed her finger to his chest. As she'd done when he was five or fifteen.

"You tell me, baby brother. You weren't yourself at dinner. You hardly spoke. What's bothering you?"

The conversation was months overdue. Floundering, he wondered why he didn't go to Sally immediately. Or later, once it became clear he was being drawn into a complicated situation.

There was no simple way to begin. At a loss, he said, "I knew Lark. We met not long before she died."

Sally's lips pursed. "How is that possible? You've done everything in your power to avoid Rae and her family."

Only once did Griffin break the self-imposed rule; there was no reason to enlighten his sister. At Lark's memorial service, Sally and her family sat in a pew near the front. He stood in the rear of the somber church, drowning in a sea of emotion he didn't dare analyze. From his vantage point, only the fire-burst of Rae's hair was visible in the crowd of mourners.

Dismissing the reverie, he said, "Believe me, I didn't go out of my way to meet Rae's daughter. Far from it."

"Where did you meet?"

"At my firm." When disbelief flooded his sister's face, he calmly added, "Lark used to come by. Fairly often, toward the end. Please don't quiz your daughter about the visits—I doubt Jackie knew anything about it. Lark always came in alone."

The wineglass paused midway to his sister's mouth. "Why was Lark popping into Design Mark? What interest did she have in the company?"

"She was researching the gig economy for a school report. She needed background on website design and the educational requirements for a career in graphic design. Or so she said."

"And this was . . . ?"

"The visits began in early September. Lark ducked into my office when my assistant wasn't at her desk. She launched into an introduction, as if I didn't know who she was."

"That's gutsy."

"You're telling me. I didn't have that much gumption until I began my career."

Sally kicked off her shoes. "Having a paycheck on the line will teach anyone a thing or two about chutzpah. I'm glad you found yours." She swung her feet onto the coffee table.

"It took practice to hone the skill set. But not for Lark. She was perfectly at ease. She breezed into my office like she owned the place." Discussing this was difficult, and Griffin set his wineglass aside. "It seemed perfectly innocent. A kid doing research for school and needing information. In retrospect, she must've planned the whole thing out."

"From a ninth grader's perspective, website design *is* cool. All those big-screen monitors and the design programs—nirvana for an adolescent."

"She *was* fascinated with the tech."

Sally regarded him with concern. "What was it like, meeting Rae's daughter?"

"Difficult," he admitted. "Don't get me wrong—I don't bear Rae ill will. Whatever her reasons for breaking off our relationship back in high school, it no longer matters. Still, I didn't relish having a face-to-face with her daughter." At sea, he lowered his elbows to his knees. Rehashing old hurts wasn't productive. He'd abandoned speculation about Rae's motives years ago. "Seeing Lark in the flesh . . . I was struck by how much she resembled her grandmother Hester. The same doll face and light-blonde hair. The same fascination with art. Her personality was another matter."

With understanding, Sally nodded. "She had Rae's boldness, the same self-confidence." She took a reflexive sip of her wine. "Why didn't that trait come through from our parents? I mean, *look* at Mom and Dad. No one ever pushes them around. Why are we both . . . milquetoasts?"

A much-needed moment of levity, and Griffin smiled. "I can't believe you're asking. If either of us was born with confidence, Dad excised it with surgical precision."

"Remember Dad's grilling sessions?"

"I try not to."

"Even over small decisions, we'd have to explain ourselves." Sally gave a mock shiver. "I hated those sessions. Why couldn't Dad let us wing it?"

"He's too controlling. I grew up believing my first impulse was always the wrong one. A logical conclusion since the great and infallible Everett Marks was sure to question any choice I made." Letting the topic go, Griffin succumbed to the pull of curiosity. "There's something about Rae I don't get," he said, breezing past the instinct to protect his emotions.

"Which is?"

"How does a woman with enough guts to climb the Himalayas become the office manager for an insurance agency? It's not a career I'd describe as colorful. When we were kids, Rae was fearless."

Sally gave the query serious consideration. "My opinion? Insurance represents safety. Having a baby right out of high school, and Connor's depression—Rae needed to anchor herself. What better than a career in risk avoidance?"

"Avoiding risk doesn't sound like a draw for a woman like Rae."

"Little brother, you haven't spoken to her since high school. She changed in her twenties. When Lark was a baby, Rae went through a phase where she seemed afraid of her own shadow. Walking by on the street, she avoided eye contact. If someone called out in greeting, she pretended not to hear. Eventually she came out of her shell and regained some of her spunk. But not right away."

The description was pitiful and sad. "She took her mother's death hard," Griffin said, aware her daughter's passing was an even greater blow. An unimaginable loss for any loving parent. "It would explain the changes in Rae's behavior."

"No, there was more to it. Another disappointment, something else that left her feeling beaten down. It seemed like one day she was graduating from high school and the next, she was pushing a baby carriage down the grocery aisles. Perhaps the gossip wore her down. Some of it was awfully cruel once her pregnancy began to show." Sally picked at imaginary lint on her sweater. The memory clearly saddened her. "Whatever the cause, it took a long time for her to get past. Not that you were here to witness her worst years, Griffin. You left for college, then moved to Boston. You never looked back."

There was no denying the assessment. During college and later, when he lived on the coast, Griffin only flew in for the occasional holiday. He never stayed in Ohio for longer than the weekend. Never asked for news about Rae. The shock of her pregnancy was best carried in private. An agony, but he'd refused to ask Sally for updates on Rae and her child.

Retrieving his wineglass, he said, "Raising a child alone couldn't have been easy. All I'm saying is that I didn't expect Rae to settle for a dull career."

His sister gave a disapproving glance. "Look who's being critical. All through childhood, you were a pushover for anything with four legs and fur. I was convinced you'd become a vet. And where did you land? Griffin, you have zero artistic talent."

"Yet I spend my life dealing with graphic designers and pitching website design."

"Exactly. People rarely end up where you expect." Softening the criticism, Sally added, "I am sure of one thing. Rae's mother influenced you. Hester Langdon might not be the primary reason you chose an art career, but she did have an impact."

A suspicion he shared. Where Everett had made Griffin feel inadequate, the Langdons had encouraged him to thrive. Beneath their gentle influence, he came to appreciate creativity.

"I admired Rae's mother, and Connor," he admitted. "Hanging out at their farm was light-years easier than our homelife. They never had an agenda, never cared about the plans Rae or I made for college, or what we'd study. Even after my friendship with Rae became something more, they treated me like a son."

"They thought you *would* become their son. After you and Rae fell for each other and you were both accepted to Ohio University, it seemed like a done deal. Everyone presumed you'd get engaged freshman year of college. If the White Hurricane hadn't taken Rae's mother, I'm sure you would have."

"Most high school sweethearts don't stick through college, Sally. There's too much opportunity to stray."

"Are you admitting to lots of extracurricular pursuits at Ohio University? My tenderhearted brother on the prowl? Spare me the details. I'm sure I don't want to hear them—except tell me you kept your promise."

"I never broke it."

Worry edged Sally's features as she canvassed his face. "I've always wondered." Then relief smoothed the lines on her brow. "I'm glad you didn't do something foolish."

Griffin was moved by her impulse to protect him. At times, they disagreed fiercely. Not often, and he was thankful to have a sister who kept his best interests at heart.

Rising, she refilled her glass. "For the record, I wasn't a saint in college either. Don't tell my husband. Trenton still believes I walk on water."

"Your secrets are safe."

"For now, at least. Remind me to check the photographic record before Mom and Jackie start working on my album. I have a feeling there are snaps from Oberlin I should destroy."

"Better get crackin'."

Rejoining him on the couch, she asked, "Last fall, how often did Lark visit Design Mark?"

"Right up to the week of the slumber party. She came in just a few days before."

"Oh, Griffin. You saw Lark the week she died? Why didn't you tell me any of this sooner?"

A suitable answer refused to materialize. He felt sick then, unmoored. Like he'd felt that January when the White Hurricane's first salvos of beating wind and pelting snow caught him driving home from a part-time job at his father's dealership, and his car hydroplaned. The tires skidding, nearly hurtling him off the road. The snow suddenly blinding. The wild staccato of his pulse beating in his ears as he fought to keep the wheels on the road.

Or later, how he felt when power was restored to a shocked and battered northeast Ohio. Learning of Rae's failed attempt to rescue her mother, and Hester freezing to death.

And in March: how the tragedy kicked the bottom out of his world. Rae breaking off their romance with icy resolve and without explanation. Wrecking their plans to attend Ohio University together. Leaving him too heartbroken to stay in Chardon for more than a few days after they graduated in June.

Bookcases lined the living room's back wall. Approaching, Griffin hesitated before the only shelf devoid of books. A box, too beautiful for competition with dusty tomes, sat alone on the shelf. A keepsake intricately and lovingly designed.

Hewn of cherrywood, the whimsical treasure chest was the approximate size and depth of a shoebox. Beneath layers of golden lacquer, rivers of crushed glass flowed across the top. A mythic, miniature shoreline sprinkled with conical horn-snail shells and wisps of embroidery thread. More lacquer encased the four sides, where a variety of tiny antique buttons formed a loosely geometric design.

Griffin kept the box in plain sight. A physical reminder—a misguided act of contrition. He knew his inaction sixteen years ago damned him. As did his missteps with Rae during that year.

His voice, unlike his heart, was calm when he spoke again.

"The last time Lark stopped by, she brought this with her." Placing the box on the coffee table, he steeled himself for what would come next.

Leaning forward, Sally expelled a soft breath.

Chapter 13

"This belonged to Lark?"

Sally placed the keepsake on her lap. With awe she traced her fingers across the bumps and grooves of the lacquered top.

"Originally it was Rae's," Griffin explained. "I don't believe she meant for her daughter to find it."

Sally was barely listening. "This is one of Hester's pieces. Good heavens, the workmanship is gorgeous."

"Connor made the box to Hester's specifications. She spent weeks on the detail work, setting in the crushed glass and the shells, adding layers of shellac. She finished when Rae and I were in sixth grade. It was one of Rae's most cherished possessions. She kept it on her bedroom dresser all through high school."

"Griffin, did Lark give this to you?"

At last, he captured his sister's attention. "Not intentionally. The last time she came in—the week of the slumber party—she was visibly nervous. Unfortunately, she picked the wrong day to drop by. The guy we sent out to grab lunch was in a fender bender, and a client's website was down. Everyone on staff was bickering, and I was late for a meeting in the conference room. Lark's timing couldn't have been worse."

The details earned him a look of censure. "Please tell me you did *not* lose your cool with a fourteen-year-old. You know how sensitive girls are at that age."

"No, I didn't. Lark was so nervous, I knew that whatever the reason for the visit, we wouldn't be chatting about the gig economy or school reports. It was serious. I asked if she'd mind coming back in an hour and we'd talk then."

On his feet now, Griffin began pacing. Trying to outrun the guilt dogging his heels. Why didn't he clue into Lark's distress weeks earlier? The surprise appearances. The giddy laughter masking a young girl's self-doubt. The trivial chatter concealing the questions she feared asking. Why didn't he *see*?

Lack of parenting experience didn't absolve him. His niece was Lark's age. Jackie was part girl, part woman, a bubbling cauldron of emotion. Lark had been no different. What had it cost her to confront him?

Glass clinked as Sally poured the last of the merlot for herself. Padding to the liquor cabinet, she fetched the Jack Daniels and a shot glass.

She watched him drink. "Another?" She looked ready to pour one for herself.

"I'm fine." He resumed pacing as she returned to the couch.

She slid the box near. "I'm afraid to ask what's inside." She inhaled a tremulous breath. "When you told Lark to come back later, what happened?"

"She opened her book bag and put the box on my desk. She looked ready to cry." He grimaced. "I'll give her credit. She got the whole speech out. How it was the happiest day of her life when she found the box in her mother's attic. How much she'd wanted the missing pieces of her life. How grateful she was to finally have them." Heartache threatened to steal Griffin's composure, but he plowed on. "She was burying the lede—not that it mattered by then. I knew what she was trying to ask. Because I knew what she'd found inside the box."

A potent silence fell between them. Sorrow inked Sally's gaze. Then doubt thinned her lips. Griffin caught the reaction a split second before she washed her face clean of emotion.

A silent accusation, but he brushed it aside. What right did he have to take offense? This wasn't about him or his feelings. It was about Rae and her daughter. About finding an honorable resolution.

The weight of what would come next made Griffin weary. The past he'd worked hard to expunge from memory, exposed.

"Go on," he urged, "see what's inside."

"Griffin, if you'd rather I—"

"Go on, Sally. Look."

The invitation crowded her face with doubt. Then the lid creaked open.

The contents charted a boy's affections. One by one, his sister placed the items on the coffee table. A bracelet woven from long grass. A bird's nest, old and crisp as kindling. A glass vial with pebbles inside. A clumsy drawing of a girl with flame-colored hair, and the graying skin of a baseball. Just the skin: the baseball's core was missing.

Her nose wrinkling, Sally held up the soiled cowhide.

"Connor gave it to us as a joke," he explained. "When we were kids, Rae and I pitched a lot of rounds. One summer, we wore the ball out."

"I remember."

"You do?"

His sister's eyes misted. "You wanted to play pro ball. Rae decided if you were heading to the major leagues, she'd go too."

They'd been eight or nine. Too young to grasp life's limitations. "We figured we'd play on the same team."

"No one had the heart to tell you otherwise." She sighed. "You and Rae were inseparable. I was a little jealous."

"That was stupid. Why didn't you hang around with us? We wouldn't have minded."

His sister regarded him as if he'd grown a tail. "Who's being stupid? You wanted Rae all to yourself. The chemistry was there from the beginning—even before either of you were old enough to understand. You brought out the best in each other. Tempered each other too."

"Rae became a little less impulsive, and I came out of my shell."

"I guess, on a different level, I wasn't jealous. More like . . . relieved. After all the bullying from other boys at school, you'd found a friend who liked you for exactly who you were."

Her expression shifting, Sally returned her attention to the box. She withdrew a series of photos. All were close-ups from high school, a visual representation of the dangers of love.

Pausing, she frowned. "What else is in here?"

When he remained silent, she removed the love letter he'd feverishly penned right after Rae broke up with him and said to stay out of her life—permanently. He'd never received a response.

The letter rustled open.

Sally averted her gaze. "Should I stop? This must be excruciating for you."

Griffin poured himself another shot. *Excruciating? Not even close.* The alcohol wasn't strong enough to dull the pain.

"Go on. Lark's already been through the contents. You need to see what she found."

More love letters drifted onto the coffee table. Sally handled them with the care one took with sacred objects. Next, the silver locket he'd given Rae on her seventeenth birthday. Then a Valentine card, crumpled and worn.

All of it, the map of a young man's heart.

Looking away, he got back on track. "After Lark put the keepsake on my desk, my assistant came in. The client waiting in the conference room was furious about the delay—I only left for a minute. When I returned, Lark was gone."

"But she left the box?"

"To ensure I'd go through the contents. I didn't have her phone number."

"You didn't feel right calling Rae."

"What was I supposed to say? 'Rae, your daughter was in my office. She wants to know if I'm her father.'" He sank to the couch, his emotions in flux. Now he wondered if he should've called Rae and tackled the issue head-on. Insisted she talk to him. Unsure, he added, "I didn't open the damn thing until the week after Lark's funeral."

"You have to return this to Rae. You mentioned Lark took it from the attic. Which means Rae has no idea it's missing."

"I figured you'd do the honors. Drive over to the farm, play intermediary."

"No!" The contents were quickly put back, the lid snapping shut. "Griffin, I've never been close to Rae. Our daughters were friends, and sometimes we volunteered for the same committees. That's all. Since the slumber party, she's been missing from the social scene. I'm sure she won't have anything to do with me. I'm sorry—this is one problem I can't solve."

Frustrated, he rubbed his palms across his face. "So I need to contact Rae?"

"That's not a good idea either. She's had enough upsets. She doesn't need you reappearing in her life." Sally tapped a polished nail against her wineglass. "Talk to Yuna. She lives next door—get her advice on what to do. Yuna knows Rae better than anyone. If you're lucky, she'll offer to return the keepsake."

A course of action he'd already mulled over and discarded. "I was hoping not to drag Yuna into this." He preferred to avoid another retelling of his brief acquaintance with Lark.

Sally regarded him with disbelief. "Get your head out of the clouds, little brother. Dragging Yuna in is the *only* option."

~

On Thursday Rae strode into the craft emporium's stockroom. "One order of pad thai, no bean sprouts or shrimp, with extra chicken." She held up the bag. "Normally you love bean sprouts and shrimp, but who am I to complain if you need a change of pace?"

Yuna cleared a space on her cluttered desk. "You're a lifesaver. I have a class in thirty minutes. I haven't eaten since breakfast."

"It wasn't an inconvenience. I promised Dad and Quinn I'd bring dinner home—a guilt move on my part. Quinn has been cooking nearly every night. Am I taking advantage of my talented houseguest?"

"Oh please. Quinn likes to cook. Doing his bit helps him fit into your household."

"True, and he's never had Thai. He's in for a treat."

"Never? That's just sad."

"From what he's told us, his parents rarely took him out. Burger joints or pancakes. Nothing fancier."

Quinn's parents were deadbeats. Better to relegate them to the past—she'd help Quinn move toward a better future. He was fitting into their homelife well, and quickly becoming her father's sidekick.

In a lighter tone, she veered to another topic. "Want to guess who I ran into this morning? It was great."

The bag rustled open. "Not Katherine Thomerson or Sally Harrow, I presume. Since you're still avoiding them, you must mean someone else."

"Don't push, Yuna. Just because we're besties doesn't mean we have to like the same people. I can't interact with any of the women whose daughters were at the slumber party. I just can't. Every time I see one of them, I'm reminded of how I lost Lark. I just want to move on."

"You *are* moving on. Look how you've opened your heart to Quinn. Change is hard, Rae. Even when it's uncomfortable, you have to keep putting one foot in front of the next."

"I am doing that—with Quinn." *In more ways than you understand.* "It's enough."

Sheltering him gave Rae an unexpected means of making peace with the girl she'd once been. A girl that Yuna—although she'd been

117

in the same grade, back in school—hadn't known well. Yuna had been much more popular.

"Can't you bend a little?" Yuna looked exasperated. "Sally's not bad. She never has a mean word to say about anyone. You should give her a chance."

"The truth? She'd irritate me less if she weren't so tight with Katherine—and Katherine I can do without."

"Are you sure you're not misplacing your animosity?"

"What do you mean?"

"C'mon, Rae. Sally's and Katherine's daughters have been close since they were little . . . and Lark was on the outside. The friend they let tag along. They never fully brought her into their private circle. As if she wasn't good enough."

The baldly honest remark was delivered with affection. It was meant to enlighten—not injure Rae with a reminder of how the other girls had treated Lark as second-best. Besides, Yuna spoke the truth: Jackie and Stella never considered Lark an equal.

"The way they treated my daughter was never right," she agreed. "But, honestly, I've never liked Katherine. She's catty and superficial. You must achieve a certain net worth before she'll consider adding you to her posse. Haven't you ever noticed? All she does is shop and primp."

"She's bored, Rae. She didn't take her divorce well."

The remark stirred the pity Rae didn't want to feel. Two years ago, Katherine's husband, a surgeon at the Cleveland Clinic, ran off with one of his nurses. He'd been a lousy father before that. Rae couldn't recall a time when he'd shown up for a school activity. Not once. Stella hadn't been a true-blue friend to Lark, but the kid had deserved better. The ink was barely dry on Katherine's divorce before the fortyish divorcée was back on the hunt for a new husband. There were women convinced they couldn't function without a man. They viewed single life as a demotion in status.

In balance, however, the family's personal issues didn't matter.

"Can we get something straight?" Rae folded her arms. "On the night of the slumber party, Katherine shouldn't have left the house. Not even for an errand."

"I agree."

"I'll always wonder if Lark would be alive. If Katherine had stayed home, Lark wouldn't have gone outside and slipped on ice."

"I get it. I didn't mean to upset you." Leaping up from her chair, Yuna wrapped her arms around Rae. "I love you. I only want you to—"

"Put my life back together."

"Because you deserve happiness."

"Whatever."

"Cheer up. You'll get there." Hugging tighter, Yuna rested her head against the lapels of Rae's coat. "Do you love me?"

"Not when you lay on this much sugar." Grinning, Rae struggled out of her arms. She shook the tension from her neck as Yuna returned to her chair. Reconsidering, she added, "I *do* like your kooky side. You're never boring."

"Spontaneity is my secret sauce."

Yuna opened her carton of Thai. It seemed odd when she took a hesitant sniff. She was crazy for the stuff. Rae was about to ask if there was a problem with the carryout when Yuna spoke again.

"Don't keep me in suspense. Who did you see this morning?"

"I had two seconds of face time with the deplorable Mr. Cox." Rae chuckled. "The best two seconds of my day, so far."

"The man you paid to free Quinn's dog?"

"The one and only. Cox strolled into the drugstore. I was picking up a scrip for my dad on my way to work."

"Rae, you won the battle. The dog is safe. There's no reason to pick a fight with Mr. Cox."

"I didn't! He took one look at me and darted into the shampoo aisle. Knocked over a display case and kept on moving. There were bottles of shampoo rolling across the floor, but he never looked back." She chortled. "He couldn't escape fast enough."

Yuna picked up her fork. "Putting the fear of God into the average man. You must be proud."

"Watching him hightail it *did* feel good."

"I'm sure." Yuna gestured at Rae's briefcase. "You have the quotes?"

In between training the new employees at the Witt Agency, Rae was making progress for the June event, Night on the Square.

"All done. Quotes for brochures, posters, flyers—you name it. Three of the quotes are from printers here in the county. One is from Mentor. A larger outfit, and their prices are competitive." She handed over a sheaf of papers. "The final decision is yours."

"One task down, but we have a million other considerations. We still need a theme for the event. So far, no one on the committee has come up with a compelling idea. I'm tired of themes around moonlight and flowers."

"Older couples like the traditional fare. Anything that stinks of romance. It draws them like flies."

"Your cynicism is *not* your best attribute. But you're right. We need a change." Considering, Yuna began swiveling her office chair, side to side. "We should come up with a theme to draw more younger people. Besides, lots of singles attend. You go every year."

"Only because you insist." Rae didn't mind playing third wheel at Yuna's table, and the food was always good. "If you're aiming to draw in more singles, come up with activities other than dancing."

Yuna looked intrigued. "Like what?"

"I don't know . . . what about gambling? We can set up a mini casino at one end of the square, with the dance floor at the other end. If people want to go stag, they'll have options."

"That isn't the worst idea in the world."

"Gee, thanks."

Yuna dipped her fork into the carton. "Will you reconsider attending the planning meetings? Sit down, give your input—when the meetings wrap up, you can hightail it out like Mr. Cox. I promise no one will care. You don't have to stick around and chat with Katherine or Sally, or anyone else."

The tension returned to Rae's neck. "Sometimes you're a pain."

Yuna batted her eyes. "This is me begging." Pointing at her face, she added a charmingly fake smile. "Please. Change your mind. Just this once, for me."

Intuition lifted the hairs on the back of Rae's neck. Yuna cajoled and bribed with chocolate. She nudged Rae toward difficult choices. Sometimes she was relentless, but she didn't beg.

A woman had to draw the line somewhere.

On closer inspection, fatigue rimmed Yuna's eyes. Exhaustion, or something more worrisome?

Anxiety surged through Rae. "What aren't you telling me? Yuna, are you ill?"

"Don't be silly. I'm great. It's just that, well . . ."

"What?"

"It's nothing." Yuna shrugged. The cheerful expression fled her features, and she suddenly appeared troubled. "I mean, it's nothing bad. Don't jump to conclusions."

"Why the mystery, then? You're scaring me."

"I'm not trying to scare you. I need you at the meetings, that's all. No one has volunteered to lead the committee. I'll get stuck with the honors."

Rae laughed. "What else is new?"

The same process occurred each year. Yuna insisted she wasn't taking charge of the effort. The other volunteers waited her out. Over time, she became the de facto leader.

"I can't handle everything. I need your help."

"Gosh, Yuna. Thanks for the guilt trip."

"Is it working?" Yuna held out the fork, twined with savory noodles. "Want a bite? I'll share."

"No."

In her coat pocket, Rae's phone buzzed. She scanned her father's impatient text:

Will hell freeze before U bring dinner?

"Let's talk later," she said. "I have to go."

Chapter 14

At home, the living room was empty. Rae set the carryout on the kitchen counter.

"Dad? Quinn?"

From the hallway, she detected the click of nails on hardwood. Her arrival had alerted the family's new four-legged member.

Shelby trotted in from wherever she'd been sleeping. Quinn's bed, or Rae's—lately the adventurous mutt roamed free, seeking out the coziest places in the house. Whenever the dog chased critters in dreamland, she slept belly up, her paws twitching and pedaling the air. The mutt's voracious appetite was less amusing. A half-eaten snack left on a table or the counter was likely to disappear.

Shelby's hunger was matched only by her stealth.

"Hey, girl." She ruffled the dog's ears. "Where is everyone?"

Wherever her father and Quinn had gone, they'd left the kitchen immaculate. The cabinets were scrubbed down and buffed to a high gleam. The spotless floor smelled delightfully of geraniums. Last week, Quinn suggested that Rae add the all-natural cleaning product to the grocery list.

Like the kitchen, the adjacent greenhouse was also spotless. There wasn't a smidgen of mold on the glass panes. Junk that had been collecting against the walls for years—boxes of knickknacks, forgotten sporting equipment, and crates of old power tools—was cleared away.

Returning to the kitchen, Rae detected a clatter from below.

At the bottom of the basement stairwell, which led to a warren of musty rooms, her father was sealing a trash bag. He tossed the bag next to the others by the wall.

"What's this?" She brushed a cobweb from his hair. "Getting a jump start on spring cleaning? You're making great progress."

"Thank Quinn. Spending the afternoon doing chores was his idea. Completely messed up my napping schedule. I was about to camp out on the couch when he came in from school. He noticed the chore list I'd been putting together. I'd left it on the kitchen table."

The teen despised feeling like a charity case. Rae wished he'd accept their help with less fuss.

"How long is the list?" she asked.

"Two pages. I'd hoped we'd begin soon, maybe by the weekend. I didn't expect him to get moving this fast." Rubbing his back, Connor added, "The kid's worried about paying us back. Or he wants to prove he can pull his own weight and isn't looking for a free ride. Either way, he hasn't stopped moving since he got home."

"Dad, he's our guest, not an indentured servant. Don't let him go overboard. If he's exhausted, how will he finish his homework tonight?" Rae peered through the gloom. "Where is he?"

"In one of the storage rooms. We were finishing up, and he decided to look around." Leaning close, her father lowered his voice. "Lately the boy's edgy. Have you noticed?"

"Not really. You see him more than I do. I haven't spent much time with Quinn since we sprang his dog from prison." Between work and duties for Night on the Square, her days were full. "At the moment, I'm more concerned about Yuna."

"What's wrong with Yuna?"

"She insists she's fine. I don't believe her."

"What are you saying? Yuna's dealing with a health issue she refuses to discuss?"

"I sure get that impression. If my best friend has a major health concern, would she hide it from me?" Rae didn't want to entertain the notion. Yuna wasn't just a friend. They were as tight as sisters—the inseparable kind. "There's something going on, some reason she's putting me on a guilt trip."

"Don't let your imagination run away with you. Who takes better care of herself than Yuna? I've never seen her eat so much as one potato chip. She's got a real love affair with fresh fruits and vegetables. She'll outlive the rest of us." Her father eyed her closely. "What's the guilt trip about?"

"Night on the Square. She wants me at the committee meetings, helping to make the weekly decisions and playing the role of her sidekick. A big ask. I'm totally not interested."

"Your cowardly lion routine is getting old." Connor lifted his shoulders. "No offense."

"What's that supposed to mean?"

"Stop wandering alone in the wilderness. I know you miss Lark—I miss her too. Which is beside the point. The grieving is hard, I get it. But you can't stop living. Lark wouldn't want that."

"Probably not."

"You're in your prime, kiddo. Do you have any idea how fast middle age comes? Like a bullet train roaring down the tracks." Her father sized her up in a manner indicating he found her lacking. A lost cause because she wasn't having enough fun.

His silvered brows lowered. "Rae, I want to ask you something."

A funny feeling warned her where this was going. "Oh, I wish you wouldn't."

"Get ready, because I'm asking." He paused for effect. "When was the last time you enjoyed the pleasures of romance?"

She opened her mouth, then closed it again. *Too long.*

With ill-concealed pity, her father shook his head. "It'll do you good, to get out more. What's the harm in trying?"

"Gosh, I don't know. Because I wouldn't know where to begin?"

"Fair enough." The admission that she'd even consider his advice put merriment on his features. "What about a dating site? Fill out your profile and see what happens. If you're nervous about dipping your toe in the water, keep me posted. I'll help by throwing you into the deep end. Yuna will help too."

"I'm not ready for the deep end. With or without a life preserver."

"Yes, you are. Which is why Yuna's guilt-tripping you. It's easier than kicking you in the keister. Although I'm sure she'd like to do that too."

Insult and amusement vied for prominence in Rae's heart. An improvement over the months of sadness, she decided.

"Thanks for being on my side," she sputtered. "I can always count on you."

"Guess again. I'm on Yuna's side."

"My, you're in a salty mood." She gestured toward the stairwell. "Want to fire off more insults, or dig into Thai? Dinner's getting cold."

"I'm famished, but dinner can wait a sec." Connor peered through the basement's shadows, apparently to ensure Quinn was out of earshot. "Are Quinn's parents back from Atlanta?"

"I don't know, Dad. It's not like I keep tabs on their whereabouts." She preferred not to let the Galeckis invade her thoughts. They were damaged, cruel people. It was best for everyone involved if they left Quinn alone. "Does it matter?"

"It would sure explain why Quinn's edgy. Have you noticed him avoiding eye contact sometimes when you're talking to him? I'll tell you what that means—he's hiding something."

Considering, Rae toyed with a lock of her unruly hair. There *were* moments when Quinn seemed unable to look at her directly. Just this morning, while filling her travel mug for the drive into work, she'd asked breezy questions about school. A typical morning greeting before heading out. Quinn's attention remained glued on his cereal bowl.

Children—and teenagers—avoided eye contact for a variety of reasons. Guilt over a secret infraction. Nerves regarding an upcoming test at school. Or worry over a falling-out with friends. From what she could tell, Quinn didn't have friends at the high school. There were no tests this week.

Which left the other possibilities her father seemed to imply. Did Quinn feel guilty for reasons undisclosed? Or worried?

Probably worried. His parents threw him out. It doesn't mean they'll stop giving him a hard time. If I were in his place, I'd worry about Mik and Penny making my life miserable too.

His parents refused to support him. It didn't mean they'd stop the emotional abuse. Rae sensed they viewed him more like a possession, one they were in the habit of mistreating. A conclusion that made her both angry and heartsick.

"It's like there's something he wants to tell us," Connor said, clueing in to her private speculations. "He can't bring himself to pipe up. I can't help but wonder if his parents are having second thoughts about kicking him out. Remember what Quinn told us? They were drinking the night of his birthday, getting ready to hop a plane to Atlanta. People say the stupidest things when they're under the influence."

"I don't care. Mik and Penny threw him out. What he does is no longer their business." Concern edged through Rae. "Have they been in touch with Quinn?"

"Who knows? I'd check his text messages, but I don't have the password. I've tried snooping when he taps in the code. No luck so far."

"Dad!"

The conversation abruptly ended. From deep in the basement's dusty bowels, Quinn shouted, "Connor, check this out!"

Her father bounced a thumb toward the rooms in back. "You first," he advised. "See if you can encourage the kid to open up. Getting him to talk might take the feminine touch."

"Don't get your hopes up. If he doesn't want to talk, I can't pry his secrets loose."

"There's a first time for everything."

"I suppose."

Relenting, she went ahead, her nose itching in the dusty air. In the last room, Quinn was crouching amid a group of boxes that were instantly recognizable.

Rae's breath caught. Delight sifted through her.

Beaming, Quinn held up a string of lights. "Look what I found!" If worry about his parents' return from Atlanta was bothering him, the discovery quelled the emotion.

Flipping open another box, he inspected the bundles of industrial-grade lighting. Each string was neatly wound. Crinkly tissue paper separated the layers. All the boxes were the same, packed tight with strings of lights.

"Oh, Quinn. You found my mother's last art project. Wow—this brings back memories." Good ones, and she savored them.

"There's enough here to decorate fifty Christmas trees. They all look brand new."

"They *are* new." She crouched beside him. "These aren't for Christmas. We keep the holiday decorations in the studio closet, upstairs."

"What are they?"

The fond memories warmed Rae. "My mother's final inspiration. An art project she never got the chance to finish. It was amazing, how much time she spent on the design."

"I thought Lark's grandmother worked with mixed media. Like the picture hanging in your family room."

"Usually, but this was an exception. I can't recall why she got it into her head to create a lighting display. Once the inspiration struck, it's all she thought about."

"When was this?"

"The autumn before the White Hurricane. Mom began stringing lights between the house and the barn, but only on the lowest branches. She wasn't crazy about heights. It was the beginning of my senior year of high school. It looked so pretty, we all decided to pitch in. We had fun working on the project."

A soft lump of regret formed in Rae's throat. Griffin had also helped, she recalled. On the nights when he didn't man the customer service desk of his father's dealership, he'd worked until dusk, climbing high into the trees—his body stronger than Rae's and faster, and it seemed he'd bump into the sky. Griffin had strung lights from the highest branches as she clung to lower branches, not entirely certain she trusted her balance, and as Hester shouted warnings from below. Rae's father had worked on the second tree in an amusing, silent competition with Griffin. Rae's mother had planned to hire a man in town to string the lights on the treetops, but Griffin—eager to see the final result—had started work on the project immediately. Connor had quickly joined in.

Dismissing the memory, she said, "My mother designed an elaborate color scheme to cover every tree between the house and the barn. It would've been lovely if she'd finished. There are nineteen trees separating the distance. She planned to decorate every one of them."

Quinn's eyes rounded. "Talk about a major job. Your barn is half an acre from the house."

"Just about. My father hired an electrician to trench cabling across the entire span. *That* part of the project was completed."

"Where did she get lights in so many colors? I've never seen anything like this in the stores."

"She knew a hotelier in Philadelphia. He put her in touch with a manufacturer. The lights were designed to her specifications."

"They're beautiful."

"I've always been partial to this combination." Rae held up a string for his inspection. The thumb-size bulbs were a series of silver, violet, and the prettiest spring green. Some of the bulbs were oval, and others were shaped liked stars. "And these," she added, retrieving a strand in varying shades of blue.

"How do you choose a favorite? I like them all."

"You just choose. Whatever strikes your fancy."

Pulling another box close, she rustled through the layers of tissue. Before the White Hurricane, all the lighting had been laid out near a wall in Hester's studio, ready for installation. They didn't get far with the project. When the first snowflakes dusted the acres in November, work came to a halt. Hester spent the holiday season rearranging the sequence of lights, updating her schematic with each change.

Sixteen years later, the lights were still in pristine condition. There wasn't dust in any of the boxes. Absently Rae wondered when her father had packed away the lighting. Busywork, for the days when he'd kept his depression at bay.

Breaking the silence, she said, "It's been so long . . . I can't recall where the lights were actually made," she told Quinn.

"Germany." Connor appeared in the doorway. "The company is still around. They make hand-painted glass ornaments. They got out of the lighting business. Too much competition from Asia."

Rae straightened. "It would've been gorgeous, if Mom had finished." Then she told Quinn, "Some of the lights are still up outside—they're on the trees nearest the house. I don't know if they still work."

Surprise lifted Quinn's brows. "Don't you turn them on?"

"Frankly, we forgot about them." Rae searched her memories. "We stopped turning them on around the time Lark enrolled in her first pottery class. She was in second grade. After that, our lives were busy."

Connor leaned against the doorjamb. "I never understood why you let her choose pottery. Dumbest move in the annals of parenting. Why didn't we buy Lark a block of Play-Doh and call it a day?"

"Dad, you're a font of wisdom—*after* the fact. Why didn't you chime in at the time? I lobbied to sign her up for a class in cartoon drawing. When Lark argued for the pottery class, you egged her on."

"I was her grandfather. It was my job to spoil her."

"Yeah, and I should've assigned you to laundry duty. Getting the clay out of Lark's clothes was a major PITA. I threw out several of her T-shirts before the sessions ended." To Quinn she said, "Life went into warp speed once Lark discovered activities. My daughter never sat still. The original busy bee."

"Like me," Quinn volunteered. The pleasure on Rae's features was infectious, and he smiled. "I like to keep busy. It's one of the things I had in common with Lark."

On any other day, the remark would've given Rae pause. Like the first streak of lightning announcing the incoming storm. Signaling the need to take cover.

Today, however, the past—and its secrets—were far from mind.

A buoyancy overtook Rae's mood. As did a dawning awareness. For the first time since the funeral, she was discussing Lark easily. Without the sharp sting of regret or the hard pull of grief.

With only affection.

Quinn bounced on his heels. "Can we go outside? See if the lights work? They must look incredible at night."

A rumble erupted from Connor's stomach. "Let's eat first."

Chapter 15

The trees slumbered in winter hiatus. Bare-armed, they were unable to hide the damage.

Lengths of electrical wiring drooped from the branches. Nearest the house, a string tapped aimlessly against its tree trunk, dislodged by high winds or busy squirrels. The second tree was a taller maple. Rae anxiously peered up at the limbs. In the past, she never stopped for long to study the lighting that represented her mother's final burst of creativity. Doing so was too difficult.

Her heart fell. "They're in worse shape than I'd realized." Many of the oval- and star-shaped lights were broken.

"They do look bad," Quinn agreed, disappointed.

"I feel awful. I don't know how many times I've walked by without noticing."

"You forgot about them, that's all."

They'd come outside through the mudroom. Most of the snow had melted, thanks to last night's rain. Her father, still near the house, was shoveling the last of the slush from the walk.

Rae gestured toward the deck. "See the switch, near the sliding glass doors?" she asked Quinn. "Go ahead and try them."

Nothing happened. Connor, walking past, muttered choice words. There was no missing that Rae's disappointment paled beside his.

On the third tree, a cord hung limply. Connor reached up and hooked it back into place. "Forgive me, Hester." He regarded the moon riding above the cloudless night. "You spent weeks mapping out your twinkly lights. You never got a chance to finish, but they sure were pretty. I'm a shit for letting your inspiration go to seed."

"Language." Rae patted his back. "Mom understands. Life got in the way."

"Your mother put a lot of thought into the design. All those different hues. Like fireflies leading from the house to the barn. All that trouble, and for what? We should've noticed they were falling apart. If Hester were here, she'd pitch a fit."

In silent agreement, Rae winced. Her mother's temper hadn't flared often. Only when her art was the point of contention. She'd imposed strict rules governing when her family was permitted inside the studio. The only time Rae broke the rule—out of boredom on a lazy summer day—she'd touched a sculptural collage in progress. Her mother had blown sky-high.

If they couldn't get around to repairing the lights, Hester would've preferred they were taken down.

"Sorry, Mom." Rae sent an apologetic glance at the moon. "We screwed up."

From the back deck, Quinn said, "We should fix them." He kept flipping the switch, as if repeated attempts would produce a better outcome. "We've got lots of supplies in the basement. More than enough. Connor, do you know how they're supposed to go up? If you don't, let's wing it."

"There's no need—I have my wife's schematic. She was a perfectionist. The design is as detailed as an architectural rendering." Connor chuckled. "Hester was also big on overkill. It's a wonder she didn't sketch in leaves on the trees."

Quinn hurried down the steps. "Where's the schematic?"

"In my nightstand."

"That's great! Maybe when we finish, I can bring a friend over to see them."

Friend? What friend? Rae exchanged a curious glance with her father. Not once since moving in had the boy mentioned anyone from school.

"Who is he?" she asked, happy to learn her daughter hadn't been his only companion. Given all the stress in his life, he could use a buddy.

"Not a guy . . . Ava. We're not really friends. Not yet anyway. She's in eleventh grade. Sometimes she says hi when I see her between classes. She's always nice when she sees me."

The explanation seemed to test the limits of Quinn's ability to discuss the issue, and he blushed to his hairline. From the looks of it, he had a serious crush on a girl at school. It was such a sweetly normal dilemma that Rae nearly laughed out loud.

Connor looked equally pleased. "You like Ava?" he asked bluntly.

Quinn's Adam's apple bobbed in his throat. He managed to nod.

"What are you waiting for? Ask her out!"

"Oh, I can't do that."

"Why not?"

Rae swatted her father. "Dad, what is it with you today?" Encouraging her to try a dating site, and now badgering their clearly embarrassed houseguest about asking out a girl at school—maybe Connor was the one who needed to kick-start his romantic life. A notion that *did* make her laugh out loud as she added, "He didn't ask your advice on how to handle the situation. And Quinn, if she's greeting you in the hallways, that constitutes friendship in my book. Do you ever stop when you see Ava, just to share small talk? I'm sure she'd enjoy talking to you."

"It's too hard, at school. You know . . . finding a way to strike up a conversation. There's not much time between classes."

"What about at the coffee shop on Chardon Square?" After school, the place was usually filled with teenagers—especially the older kids. College students too. "If you see Ava hanging out there, it might be easier to chat. Less pressure, and you don't have to worry about running late for your next class."

He brightened. "That's what I've been thinking. Maybe I'll run into her at the coffee shop, and it'll make everything simpler."

Connor rolled his eyes. "Don't overthink your strategy, Quinn. It'll just make you more nervous when you *do* talk to her. Trust me on this. When I was your age, I was just as bashful. Seeing a pretty girl . . . why, my first impulse was to run in the opposite direction."

The disclosure spilled relief across his features. "Tell me about it!" He studied Connor with interest. "You were bashful once? Man, I never would've guessed."

"I grew out of it. Meeting Rae's mother helped. Having the right woman at my side was more good fortune than I deserved. Hester was the love of my life."

For a fleeting moment, sadness flickered in her father's gaze. Rae understood the parts he was leaving out: Connor hadn't fully come into his own until *after* her mother's death, when Lark was born. When he'd needed to take control of his depression and help Rae manage their lives. The worst of times break some people; her father, however, found his inner strength. He went on medication to ease the darkest periods of depression and threw himself wholeheartedly into helping raise his granddaughter.

Letting the subject go, Connor sniffed the air. "Winter *is* wrapping up. I doubt we'll have more snow."

"How can you tell?" Quinn asked.

"Experience, son."

"Then we can get started on the lights. It'll be fun."

"Forget about fun," Rae put in. "I'd love to see the lights finished too, but I can't have my father climbing a ladder in the middle of winter. Or any other time, for that matter."

"But he said that spring's coming. It's almost March first. It's practically spring already."

As if the date mattered. "Quinn, this is northeast Ohio. Five more feet of snow might fall before Julius Caesar gets a warning on March fifteenth."

"Who's he?"

Connor palmed his forehead. "She's referring to one of Shakespeare's plays," he explained. He planted his frosty regard on Rae. "FYI, it's none of your business if I climb a ladder, or take up rock climbing, if it tickles my fancy. Get the pecking order straight—I'm your father. You want to push someone around, pick on Quinn. I'll do whatever I want."

"Dad, I have two words for you: hip replacement." She challenged his frosty regard with narrowing eyes. "There are some activities one avoids after a certain age. Can you even remember the last time you climbed a ladder?"

"Go pop a chocolate, Rae."

Quinn went a little green. "Mr. Nixon at the high school got a hip replacement. He teaches history classes. He walks with a cane now." He hesitated. "Connor, you should listen to her. She's only looking out for you."

"Go on, hotshot. Take her side."

"I'm not taking sides."

"You should," Rae insisted, glad he'd spoken up. "In our family, we vote on serious matters. It's the rule."

The word "family" latched Quinn's gaze to hers. Searching, probing, his eyes brimmed with questions and uncertainty. They also held doubt and fear—or panic. It was hard to tell, and the intensity of his gaze made Rae aware that her father was right. Quinn rarely looked at them directly. Rarely for longer than a moment.

He threw his attention on his feet.

"We've got odd numbers here," she announced, moved by the questions she'd glimpsed in his eyes, the hope. But the fleeting panic she'd sensed roused her mothering instincts. Did Quinn have secrets? Was he in some sort of trouble? Pushing aside the thought, she added, "I'm looking for two-to-one. Quinn, are you with me?"

The challenge stirred his latent maturity. Shoulders straight, he managed to look at her again.

"Here's what we'll do," he decided. "I won't let your dad near a ladder. Not until the temps stay above freezing."

"You won't let him near one *at all*. No exceptions." When her father began to protest, she lifted a warning hand. "I mean it, Dad. If you don't agree, I'm putting the lights into storage. Or donating them to the charity of your choice. Either way, you won't have them anymore."

A fissure of irritation shook through Connor. "Fine. I'll stay on terra firma."

"Thank you. Quinn, please keep an eye on him."

"Will do." A childlike eagerness slipped into his voice. "When can we get started?"

~

By the following Saturday, her father and Quinn were making progress. Balancing on tree limbs with no apparent fear of heights, Quinn wielded wire cutters to remove the damaged lights. On the ground, Connor salvaged the few oval- and star-shaped bulbs that had survived years of neglect. The weather lent a hand, warming enough to melt the last traces of snow.

Leaving them to their work, Rae drove into Chardon Square. Her boss, Evelyn Witt, was preparing for a much-needed vacation in the Bahamas. Until her return, Rae was in charge. Although Rae rarely came in on Saturdays, Evelyn requested she stop by to discuss her additional duties.

Near lunchtime, Rae's phone chimed as she left Evelyn's office. "What's up?" It was Yuna.

"Are you in town?"

"Heading back to my office now." Earlier in the week, she'd mentioned Evelyn's vacation.

"I was hoping to catch you." Relief colored Yuna's voice. "What do you have planned today?"

"Not much. A quick stop at Dixon's for a snack, and grocery shopping. Then I'm spending a relaxing Saturday night digging through laundry. With a teenager in the house, I need a snow shovel. Quinn would help fold, but he has a trig exam next week. He'll be holed up in my guest bedroom tonight, studying."

"A trig exam . . . that explains why he didn't come into work today."

Reaching into her file cabinet, Rae paused. "Was he supposed to?"

"Yes, but it's fine. There wasn't much for him to do. I didn't have any merchandise deliveries this week."

"If Quinn was scheduled, shouldn't he have come in regardless?" The words were barely out when she realized *why* he hadn't gone in.

"It was surprising that he didn't call to explain."

"Yuna, my father must've outbid you." Rae explained about the project to complete Hester's lighting. Summing up, she added, "I'll tell my dad not to ask Quinn for help on days he's scheduled to work for you. No matter what he's willing to pay."

"More than I can afford, I'm sure. But don't badger your dad. It's sweet that he's hanging around with Quinn. It's good for both of them." After a long pause, Yuna said, "Rae, did you get a chance to come up with more ideas for Night on the Square? We're getting together at the library at one o'clock." The library was located directly across the square from the Witt Agency, not far from Dixon's wine and dessert café. "I'd like to present a list of themes at today's meeting."

Rae was glad for the heads-up—she'd skip grabbing a snack at Dixon's. Since the funeral, she'd managed to avoid Katherine. Twice she'd nearly bumped into Sally at the grocery store. She'd quickly steered her cart into a checkout line.

On her computer, she located the file. "I only have some themes so far. I'm not finished."

"Can you drop off what you have?"

Rae detected fatigue in Yuna's voice. Transmitting the file was simpler, but it wouldn't hurt to check in and ensure her friend was okay.

"I'll see you in a minute," she promised.

The break in the weather had brought customers in droves to the craft emporium. The cash register sang happily. The four employees were busy, but not overly so. After months of slate-colored skies and constant snowfall, everyone seemed sunny like the weather.

The sole exception? Yuna.

Replenishing stock near the front, she appeared wan and listless. In lieu of her normally eccentric clothes—metallic leggings paired with a bold T-shirt or one of her gauzy pixie tops—she wore loose jeans and an old cable-knit sweater. An outfit more at home in Rae's closet, sensible and boring.

"I hate mysteries," Rae said by way of greeting. "You were trying to tell me something the other day. Now I'm officially concerned." Yuna wasn't wearing makeup either. Not even lip gloss, as if she'd rolled out of bed and marched straight to work. "Do you need to see a doctor? Let's go—I'll drive."

"There's no need. I've seen a doctor."

"What was the diagnosis?"

"It's great. A happy-happy diagnosis," Yuna said in a dull monotone that was decidedly unhappy. She surveyed the busy store. "Let's not talk here."

Taking the lead, Rae beat her to the stockroom. Anxiety steered her all the way to the back. At the employee lunch table, she plunked down.

Yuna quickly dispensed with the mystery. "I'm pregnant." She took the seat opposite. "I've known for some time."

Unexpectedly, the news carried the scent of Lark's newborn skin. How Rae couldn't resist pressing her nose against her daughter's soft belly after she bathed her. The earthy connection they'd forged, mother and child.

Then her stomach did a painful flip. "Why didn't you tell me? Is there a problem with the pregnancy?"

"Everything's fine." Yuna plucked at her ratty sweater. Discovering a yarn coming loose, she tugged at it. "I meant to tell you the other day. I'm excited, but I'm also . . . oh, I don't know. I suppose Kipp is right— I've been dreading this conversation. I wasn't sure how to tell you."

"Because of Lark?" Rae swallowed around the lump in her throat. Then she cast a jaundiced glance at the unraveling hem. "Stop picking at your clothes and look at me." When Yuna's dark, worried gaze lifted, she smiled. "I'm thrilled for you and Kipp. Over-the-moon delighted. A baby is happy news."

"You're not upset?"

"Don't be ridiculous. Why wouldn't I be happy about my bestie's pregnancy?"

Without warning, sorrow flooded her. Refusing to let it pull her under, Rae flopped her hands onto the table. She wiggled her fingers.

Taking the cue, Yuna reached across. Their hands caught and held. Their bond was powerful, like the one Rae had lost with her daughter.

Gratitude swept through her, banishing the last of the despair. "Do me a favor," she said.

"Anything."

"Stop tiptoeing around my feelings. I'm managing. Some days are easier than others. The bad days? I muddle through. They aren't as frequent now." Yuna eyed her with suspicion, and she quickly added, "I promise—I'm doing fine. Even if I weren't, it wouldn't change my feelings about your pregnancy. You're my closest, dearest friend. I want nothing but good things for you. A baby! I know how much you've wanted a little brother or sister for Kameko."

Yuna returned her hands to her lap. "That's true," she murmured, "but I hate the timing. It just feels wrong."

"Stop it. Grieving for Lark doesn't mean I can't feel happiness for you . . . and pity, if you're having morning sickness like the last time. How are you faring?"

"Not great. Spices, perfumes—I'm never sure what will set me off. When Kipp made burgers last night, I fled to the bathroom. He fed Kameko in record time, then took her to the movies. The sound of Mama retching may scar her for life."

"Count on it. *I'm* scarred from your last go-round. In the annals of pregnancy, you stand as the unchallenged Vomit Queen."

"Take my crown. I don't want it." Yuna grew thoughtful. "Why do they call it 'morning sickness' when the nausea strikes at all hours?"

"A man devised the term, I'm sure. Some guy in a lab coat with no firsthand experience with menses or the complete humiliation of a gynecological exam." Rae winced. "Or the delightful ordeal of labor."

"Let's kill him."

Pregnancy, she mused, altered Yuna's even-keeled personality in fascinating ways. During her second trimester with Kameko, her staff had banished her to the stockroom, as Yuna couldn't wait on customers without yelling at them. By the third trimester, Kipp was sleeping on the couch. He'd grown tired of his wife's late-night complaints that if he really loved her, he'd cut a hole in the mattress, allowing her to drop her belly through. By then, Kameko was doing the merengue on her bladder every ten minutes.

"Rein in those hormones. We're not doing murder." Rae glanced at her phone. "It's almost one o'clock. The witching hour for the Night on the Square meeting."

"Change of plans. I'm not going. Listening to everyone squabble . . . I'll hurl on the table."

"Who'll run the show if you're absent?"

Yuna's head fell back, her dejected gaze settling on the ceiling. "His name is Mayhem," she joked. "He'll destroy all my work."

"I'm glad pregnancy hasn't stolen your sense of humor," Rae said, coming to a decision. "And you can cheer up now—I'll escort you. I'd rather eat dirt, but you're in no shape to go alone. If you're a no-show, there *will* be pandemonium."

"You'll come with me? You're serious?"

"Don't look surprised." Rae fished around in her purse. "You knew my loyalty would override my objections." Finding the tin of mints, she slid them across the table. "If you feel the urge to rush out of the room, I'll take over. The rest of the time, I'm playing Minion Rush on my phone. Don't sit us anywhere near Katherine."

~

Chatter swirled through the conference room. Rae counted twelve participants, two men and ten women. Half of the faces were unfamiliar. At the head of the table, Katherine and Sally were already seated. Deep in conversation, they seemed oblivious to the noise around them.

Rae led Yuna to the other end.

One of the men, an athletic chiropractor who'd recently moved to Chardon, kicked off the meeting. Should they hire a big band ensemble like last year, or opt for a DJ? The chiropractor had done his homework well. The quotes he handed out fluttered around the table.

A lively conversation ensued. Apparently queasy, Yuna popped a mint into her mouth. She appeared relieved the others weren't asking her to weigh in.

"Do the meditative breathing," Rae suggested. It was helpful during Yuna's last pregnancy. "Deep breaths, slowly. That's right."

"Who's wearing perfume?"

"Every woman in here, except me." Rae pretended to read the quote, passed on by the woman to her right.

"I want to kill them too."

"Next time, send a memo. No perfume at the meetings."

Near the center of the table, a man with bifocals perched on his nose raised his voice. He began talking over the others, listing the merits of an ensemble band. He began debating with the chiropractor who, evidently, was vying for a DJ. Rae considered dozing off.

The hairs on the back of her neck lifted. Someone was watching her.

Startled, she ranged her attention down the table. To Katherine, staring at her with contempt.

Cutting off the exchange, she leaned toward Yuna's ear. "I have a problem," she whispered.

"What's wrong?"

"Check out Katherine. The way she's looking at me."

Yuna hazarded a glance. "What do you expect?" Beneath the table, she kicked lightly at Rae's foot. "You haven't been exactly friendly. Learn to get as well as you give, sister."

"Whose side are you on?"

"Wait. She's whispering to Sally. Whatever they're discussing, Sally looks upset."

"They're talking about me."

"You don't know that."

"Call it a gut feeling."

With her eyes planted on her lap, Rae tensed. The others were beginning to notice the short bursts of whispered conversation between her and Yuna.

"Can I leave?" Rae couldn't banish the quaver from her voice. "I'll just sneak out."

The mutual protection society between close friends was ironclad, and Yuna's mouth thinned. "No need. Just hold tight for a minute."

Around the table, the debate began to cool down. One of the women collected the quotes on music options. Breaking in, Yuna took charge. No one complained; everyone knew she was their de facto leader.

"I'll notify you with the date and time of our next meeting. Thank you, everyone." And with that, they were finished. Beating everyone to the door, she led Rae out.

The sun played tag with fast-moving clouds. Crossing traffic, they ran into the center green and darted around the side of the courthouse. They halted in the shadows. The moment's stress caught them both, and they were suddenly laughing.

In between bouts of laughter, Yuna tried to catch her breath. "I shouldn't have been flip when you noticed Katherine staring," she said between gulps of air. "You *have* been giving her the cold shoulder, but she should understand the reasons."

"I half expected her to pull a voodoo doll from her purse and start jabbing pins into it."

"She wouldn't dare—not with me around."

"Thanks." Sobering, Rae pulled in a calming breath. "She did look totally peeved. I guess I assumed . . . oh, I don't know." She pressed a palm to her forehead. "I just assumed she didn't care what I thought, one way or the other."

"Perhaps it's time for you to consider that she might be hurting too. Questioning what it cost, for her to run that errand on the night of the slumber party."

The observation made Rae's eyes burn. "Maybe," she agreed.

"Well, I pity Sally—whatever Katherine whispered to her, it wasn't good. What do you think she said? Sally looked ready to faint."

"I don't know, or care."

Rae suffered a twinge of pity for Sally, who'd clearly been distressed. During childhood, Griffin's older sister had been kind to her. Distant—and a little bossy where her brother was concerned—but Sally had always meant well.

Yuna said, "No more meetings, okay? You're officially off the hook. From now on, you report to me."

"What about your tummy?"

"I'll take my chances at the meetings." Yuna smoothed a hank of Rae's unruly hair back in place. "Should I give Katherine fair warning? Smooth the way, in case you run into her on Chardon Square? I'd hate to lose her help on the committee, but her behavior was incredibly rude."

"No! I don't trust your fluctuating hormones. You won't stop at a civilized reprimand. You'll bite." She flicked Yuna's nose, drawing a laugh. "Let's not blow this out of proportion. Katherine's opinion of me is the least of my worries."

"Perhaps it's best if you stay away from her."

"As if I need a warning." Rae thought of something else. "Are you low on saltines or melba toast?" During Yuna's last pregnancy, they were her go-to foods. "I'm on my way to the grocery store. I'll grab whatever you need."

"No worries—Kipp has already stocked me up. His way of apologizing for grilling burgers. He knows how they upset my tummy."

"Poor guy. If he's on an almost-vegetarian diet like the last time, it'll kill him."

"He'll survive." Yuna glanced across the traffic at her shop. "I'll talk to you later."

With a wave, she sprinted across the street. She disappeared inside the craft emporium.

Rae's car was parked before the Witt Agency. The car keys jingling from her fingertips, she paused on the driver's side. Frustrated, she dug deeper in her purse. Where was the grocery list? She couldn't recall if she'd grabbed it before leaving the house.

"Rae Langdon!"

The voice—female, angry—came from the center green. Shielding her eyes from the sun's glare, Rae looked back toward the courthouse. With horror, she spotted the woman.

Her keys jangled to the ground.

Chapter 16

Cars screeched to a halt. Striding across the street, Penny Galecki tacked her furious gaze on Rae.

Quinn's mother was . . . incongruous. The tight-fitting leather jacket showed off a youthful build. Her well-toned body stood in stark contrast to the wrinkles marring her face after years of smoking and drinking. Frequently Penny changed her hair color. Today her cropped tresses were jet-black. They matched the disturbing, thumb-size pitchfork tattooed on her neck.

"Don't move! We're having words, sister."

Breathless, Rae searched the ground for her keys. Scooping them up, she attempted to rouse her temper. With horror, she realized she couldn't marshal her defenses.

Time leaped backward, jarring Rae with images. The security lights surrounding the empty post office. The shadows draping the section of the lot farther off, where she'd parked. A couple approaching, arguing about their son. Penny's voice rising in pitch, drawing Rae's drunken appraisal.

The memory sickened Rae. She felt winded, off-balance.

"Is it true?" Penny backed her against the car. "My son is living at your place?"

"Yes, he is."

Her response, barely audible, left a scent—like blood on a wounded animal. She was easy prey, and Penny knew it.

"How long's he been staying there?"

Confusion spilled through Rae. Then disbelief. "Since you and Mik left for vacation," she sputtered, wondering if the furious woman before her had assumed Quinn was living in his truck.

"Well, the party's over. Tell Quinn to get home, and I mean today. The little brat doesn't have my permission to stay at your place."

Little brat.

The remark stirred the memory Rae wanted desperately to suppress. *Little brat*—what Penny had called her son on that terrible night. When Quinn was a small child left unsupervised in an apartment while his negligent parents were out drinking.

Anger darted through Rae. Quinn was no longer a defenseless child. He wasn't trapped in a home short on love and heavy on abuse. Despite all the bad examples he'd received, he was nothing like his parents. Each night Quinn dutifully completed his homework. When he climbed into bed, he sang charming lullabies to his malnourished dog.

"Penny, you can't tell Quinn what to do."

"Yes, I can. I'm his mother. He's my kid, not yours."

"That isn't the point." The effort to meet Penny's gaze proved impossible. Her large eyes, fringed with thick lashes, were disturbingly similar to her son's. Yet they were set in a face carved by hard living.

The same face that had once haunted Rae. For years after the last bleak months of high school, when Rae was grieving, broken, and pregnant, she'd been unable to eradicate Penny from her mind.

"I don't think you're hearing me. Quinn is my son. You've got no right to be moving him into your house." Penny's lip curled. "What do you want with a boy his age? Are you into something kinky, Rae? Is he sharing your bed?"

The lewd suggestion hung between them like a foul stench. Dignifying it with a response was out of the question.

Cars streamed past. A young couple, walking arm in arm past the Witt Agency, quickened their pace. They were eager to escape the dangerous atmosphere brewing between the two women.

Rae said, "My father checked with an attorney for clarification on Quinn's rights." A retired attorney—one of Connor's friends on the geezer squad—but there was no reason to elaborate. "You can't tell Quinn what to do. An eighteen-year-old can choose to leave home prior to completing high school. Quinn has no obligation to you. He has a new home. I suggest you deal with it."

"What gives you the right to mess with my family?" Lightning quick, Penny shoved her. A hard jab to the shoulder that jolted Rae's pulse.

She fell against the car. Instinct warned her not to react. Do so, and Penny *would* punch her.

"I'm not interfering." The cold rush of fear made Rae's muscles loose. She steadied herself. "You told Quinn to move out. He needed somewhere to stay. As an adult, he's perfectly within his rights."

"I'd never throw my son out." Her predatory instincts were on full display as Penny curled her fists. "Who told you that—Quinn? He's a liar."

The denial was stunning. Had Quinn . . . fabricated the story? Pretended he'd been thrown out because he was sick of living with his heavy-drinking, combative parents? Rae blinked with confusion.

Penny raised her fist. "You'd better keep something in mind. You've got no business interfering. Do you need a lesson in why you shouldn't mess with another woman's family? Is that what you want?"

From behind, a man cleared his throat.

David Greer, the new account executive, stepped out of the Witt Agency. Close to Rae in age, David smiled readily and talked incessantly about his wife and two daughters.

He wasn't smiling now.

"Rae, is this woman bothering you?"

Penny flashed a venomous glance. She stepped back.

With her middle finger raised, she marched off.

Chapter 17

Only three of the large-screen monitors glowed with activity on Design Mark's ground floor.

On Saturdays most of the staff worked remotely, if they worked at all. Freedom of choice brought higher creativity. Griffin encouraged the staff to build their own schedules. The only exception? When clients were on premise. In the age of teleconferencing, those in-person meetings took place less frequently.

The business-casual dress code didn't extend to Saturdays. Two of the graphic designers who'd come in today wore jeans and ball caps. The third, Tabby Jones, was hunched over her keyboard in flannel pajama bottoms and a neon-green *Little Mermaid* top, a souvenir from a recent trip to SoCal. No one acknowledged the boss striding past. Fingers streaming across keyboards, they were locked in concentration.

The second floor rested in silence. The conference room smelled of pepperoni; Griffin threw out the day-old pizza box left on the table.

The reception area was orderly, like his large, sparsely furnished office.

With the building's refurb, the old plaster had been removed from the outer wall to reveal the red brick used to erect the building in 1887. The new bank of windows overlooked the street and his father's car dealership, which was partially hidden in warmer months, when the century-old maple trees leafed out. Griffin had chosen sleek Danish furniture, including a long white leather couch for impromptu meetings with the staff. No personal mementos graced the office. The only exception was a silver-framed photo on his desk of him with Sally and Jackie at last year's Geauga County Fair.

If Design Mark resembled a frat house most days, Griffin didn't mind. He drew the line at his personal space.

He was finishing a call when his sister swept in.

He did a doubletake. Sally's features were stiff with rage. An uncommon sight. By nature, both of the Marks siblings were even-tempered. He could only recall a handful of times when he'd seen his sister upset.

"Last year, how often did you take Lark to Dixon's?" Sally demanded.

Warily, Griffin placed the phone in the cradle. "Does it matter?"

"Obviously. You didn't tell me."

Brows lifting, he searched for a reply. Taking Lark out for ice cream had been a kind gesture, nothing more.

His bafflement merely increased his sister's anger. "Why didn't you mention it when you showed me Rae's keepsake? Griffin, we talked for more than an hour. We covered a lot of ground. You had ample time to fill me in."

"It wasn't relevant," he snapped. "Why do you believe it is now?"

"Because an innocent man doesn't hide the facts."

The strange accusation warned there was more here than was obvious. *What am I missing?* Sally marched back and forth before his desk. Agitation spilled off her in waves.

"I took Lark to Dixon's twice," he said with care. "How is that a crime?"

"I guess it depends on how much you knew. Were you completely in the dark? Griffin, you took her to Dixon's on Wednesdays." Sally regarded him as if he was a fool. "If you weren't keeping secrets, then Katherine is correct."

Mention of Katherine sent anger flashing through him. They'd stopped dating months ago—not long before Lark's tragic death. Sometime in early October. The relationship was never serious.

"Sally, what are you trying to say?" With misgivings, he grasped the real issue. He never should've agreed to take Katherine out in the first place.

"Katherine believes Lark used you as bait. She used you, and you had no idea why."

"My personal life is none of her business." For emphasis, he came to his feet. He didn't relish arguing with his sister. Yet he refused to allow her best friend to meddle in his affairs. "I don't care what she's told you, or why she's suddenly focused on Lark. Or me, for that matter. You're overstepping here, sis."

"Am I? Katherine is convinced it was no coincidence that you dumped her after Lark began coming around. A reasonable conclusion, isn't it?"

"Sally, that's ridiculous."

"You might want to change your assessment. She overheard Lark bragging about you to Stella the week of the slumber party. When she picked the girls up from my house. They were walking to the car, and Lark was bragging up a storm. The driver-side window was open. She didn't know Katherine was listening."

The revelation doused him like ice water. "Lark discussed me with Stella?" Weakly, he sat back down.

"In great detail, apparently. About what good friends you were. How you'd take her out on Wednesdays and let her order whatever she liked. Were you blind to Lark's ulterior motives? Baby brother, you're a master at sticking your head in the sand. Even so, I have trouble believing you're that myopic."

The attacks came too fast. "Why would Lark use me as bait?" he demanded, frustrated by his inability to form an adequate defense.

"You *are* blind." She planted her hands on his desk. "Dixon's," she emphasized, "on Wednesday afternoons."

Griffin tensed. A dark foreboding crept through him. Whatever critical information he'd missed, he didn't want to hear it now.

A conviction that held no importance to Sally.

"Rae meets with Yuna at Dixon's," she spelled out. "Every Wednesday afternoon like clockwork." When he looked at her, speechless, her eyes narrowed. "You never bumped into Rae when you took Lark there?"

"No. Never."

It was sheer, stupid luck. How would he have explained, if he *had* run into her?

"I'm sure Lark was disappointed. Given all the bragging she was doing to Katherine's daughter. Apparently, Lark was playing matchmaker."

"She . . . what?"

"She planned to fix you back up with Rae. Don't you get it? So the three of you could live happily ever after." Sally gave a short, mirthless laugh. "Griffin, you *are* dense. Manipulated by a ninth grader, and you didn't have a clue. Would you have caught on before she picked out the date for you to marry her mother? Before she ordered a big white cake?"

Stunned, he fell back in his chair. "I didn't know," he murmured. Nor could he recall who first mentioned the outings. Had he offered to take Lark to Dixon's, or had the suggestion been hers?

He didn't keep tabs on Rae's schedule. He didn't keep tabs *on Rae*. Until her daughter began coming around, he'd studiously barred her from his thoughts.

Lark, however, would've known her mother's schedule.

"Griffin, we've always been able to trust each other. Last summer, I encouraged you to ask Katherine out because she's a dear friend, and you both seemed lonely. You've hardly done anything but work since moving back to town, and she's dated some real duds since her divorce.

I was hoping . . . oh, it doesn't matter. Fixing you up was incredibly dumb. What was I thinking?"

Wheeling from the desk, his sister marched to the bank of windows. Cars came and went from their father's dealership. The hum of activity was a million miles away. It was utterly detached from the pain leaking into the office.

"Sis, I never asked you to set me up with Katherine." When she refused to turn around, he scrubbed his palms across his cheeks. "We only dated a few months. We didn't have enough in common." *Anything* in common.

"Your opinion, not hers. From the start, Katherine felt differently. She's in love with you, Griffin." From over her shoulder, Sally glanced at him swiftly. Her eyes were dark, accusing. "I don't like seeing her torn up. We've been tight for years. She's important to me."

"I never meant to hurt her."

"Well, you did."

"I'm sorry. It was never my intention."

The apology provoked an unexpected reaction. A tremor shuddered down his sister's back. When she turned to regard him, her eyes were blank slates.

"I don't believe you," she said. "I've loved you all my life, but I've never really known you." She wheeled back to the desk. "Who were you to Lark? The truth, baby brother."

A thunderous silence overtook the room. It lasted long enough for the shame and the confusion to pull Griffin under, a treacherous undertow dragging him out to sea. He knew the most grievous wounds were inflicted carelessly. How much injury had he caused when Rae shut him out of her life—and he'd reciprocated by shutting her out of his heart?

Lark's hidden agenda hardly mattered. Given all she'd discovered—his love letters to Rae, the photos—why wouldn't she devise a plan to put him back in her mother's path? The dreams Lark had constructed were fragile—spun glass.

He'd abetted her in spinning each one.

In agony, he grasped his grave mistake. He'd taken Lark to Dixon's to fulfill a secret wish sealed beneath the seabed of his emotions. As Lark slid into the booth across from him and proceeded to enthrall him with giddy laughter and a young girl's nonstop, effervescent chatter, he'd allowed his thoughts to veer onto the reckless ground of fantasy.

This is my daughter. The perfect child Rae and I brought into the world.

Sally's fist hammered the desk. Pulled from the reverie, Griffin flinched.

"Answer me!" Revulsion glazed her features. "In high school, why did Rae break up with you?"

He set his jaw, too heartsick to respond.

"You got her pregnant. You refused to own up to what you'd done. Were you afraid to tell Dad? You didn't have the courage?" Tears brimmed in Sally's eyes. They glistened with pain and the awful conviction that her brother was a dishonorable man. "He loved you and he loved Rae, but he never would've forgiven you for knocking her up. For having Lark before he'd groomed you to take over the dealership."

"Back off, Sally," he growled. "What happened between me and Rae is none of your business."

Even the closest siblings harbored resentments. Fault lines existed in every relationship. Griffin sensed they were approaching one in theirs.

"I never wanted the dealership," he added. "That was *your* dream."

"I'm not a man. My dreams never mattered."

"How is that my problem? Dad was too sexist to put a woman in charge. Not my fault." Cruelty wasn't Griffin's normal play, but he'd tired of the attacks. They struck too deep. He needed to strike back. "Cheer up, Sally. You had the sense to marry right. Trenton will let Dad lead him around by the nose until you both inherit Marks Auto. When you do, push your sniveling husband aside and take over."

"Go to hell."

Pride stopped him from responding immediately. She was his sister, his blood, and they'd taken this too far. There wasn't anyone he valued more. She was nearing the door when he called out, the apology still forming on his lips.

Too late. In the doorway, Sally delivered a parting shot.

"The next time you're on the prowl, stay away from my friends."

Chapter 18

On the east end of Chardon Square, kids talked over each other inside the coffee shop. The place was a hole-in-the-wall, and a favored hangout for just about everyone at the high school with a driver's license and spare time. Weaving through the crowd, Quinn reached the counter.

Ordering a latte, he took stock of the pretty girls. With the wad of cash from Rae's dad, he'd bought new boots. He'd left his crappy parka in the truck and had put on a clean shirt.

There were more girls outside, some with boyfriends. Nervously scanning the faces, he found the girl from the junior class he was looking for. Remembering the advice from Rae and Connor, he told himself to relax. Talking to Ava would be easier if his heart stopped thumping so hard and he got rid of the jitters. *Play it cool.*

Quinn didn't have much experience talking to girls other than Lark, and she'd been more like a kid sister who'd gladly filled the long silences and had liked cooking as much as he did. She'd also loved Shelby and helping him out when his parents acted crazy. Suddenly he missed her more than anything. How she'd crack a joke when he was scared or feeling bad. If she were here right now, she'd tell him to stop stalling and go over to speak with Ava.

Confident and easygoing, Ava wasn't very tall. He liked her long brown hair and big eyes. Sauntering near, he pretended to check something on his phone.

"Hey, Quinn." Her lips curved, revealing white teeth.

She was making this easy, and he broke out a grin. "Hey."

"Nice boots. New?"

He patted the cash in his pocket. "Splurge day. I helped my grandpa this morning. Gramps pays good—I guess you could say he spoils me," Quinn said, falling into the story he'd been telling himself since coming to live with Rae and her dad. Stupid dreams, mostly, but now he almost believed them.

"What were you doing to help your grandpa?"

"Stuff around the yard. It's still pretty cold, but we got a lot done." He thought about saying they were hanging lights in the trees, but he worried that would sound like they were putting up Christmas decorations at the end of February. Instead he added, "We worked all morning—really wore Grandpa out. He's home, taking a nap. He was supposed to go bowling with his crew, but he was too wiped out."

Ava's smile widened. "Your grandpa lives with you?"

"He moved in with us last month. We gave him the spare bedroom." More lies, but he couldn't seem to stop. The way Ava was looking at him, with her eyes full of interest, made him feel great. "My mom said it's okay. She likes having someone new in the house. They've always been close."

"You're lucky—none of my grandparents live nearby. Mom's are in Cincinnati, and Dad's moved to Oklahoma. My grandma's company relocated her. An HR job." Finishing her coffee, Ava pitched the cup into the trash can. She looked at him expectantly.

"Want something else?"

Her friends were giggling as he held open the door and Ava strolled inside. She wanted a lemon bar. He ordered two.

They were licking the sticky icing from their fingers when she asked, "Which one's your favorite? Of your grandparents?"

Quinn's phone vibrated, and he nearly fell out of his role. He didn't know much about his real grandparents. Both of his mom's parents had done time in prison; he assumed they were dead. He hoped his paternal grandfather *was* dead. Mik's stories of how he'd been treated as a kid seemed worse than the beatings he'd given Quinn over the years.

Ava nudged him from his thoughts. "You don't have a favorite grandparent? That's okay."

"There's just the one. He's great, though. Gives me advice but never pushes. Helps me learn new stuff. If I had ten grandparents, he'd still rate as the best."

They talked outside the coffee shop until the sun dipped below the courthouse. Ava's girlfriends began checking their phones.

When he couldn't draw up the nerve to ask for her number, she gave him an out. "See you at school." She rejoined her friends. "Be good."

He grinned. "You too."

Climbing into his truck, Quinn savored the high emotion. The trig homework would take all night, but tomorrow he'd practice what to say when he ran into Ava on Monday. How to ask for her number. See if she wanted to meet next week.

His phone vibrated. It was his mom bugging him—again.

Pulling the phone from his pocket, he resolved to delete the texts. What would it cost to get a new phone? With all the extra work for Connor, the expense was doable. Then Penny couldn't reach him.

He was about to swipe "Delete." A twinge in his stomach persuaded him to open the text.

Don't answer. See if I care. I talked to Rae. Get home, asshole.

Quinn reread the text as the bottom fell out of his world.

Chapter 19

Rattled by the confrontation with Penny, Rae skipped the grocery store. She drove straight home.

She blew into the house like a woman on fire. The door banged against the wall. With a gargled shout, her sleeping father rolled off the couch.

"Dad!"

Grunting, Rae hauled the coffee table back. Freed of the constraint, Connor rolled fully onto his back. His bleary gaze pinioned hers.

"What's wrong with you?" He swatted her away. Wincing, he rubbed his elbow, which had taken the brunt of the fall. "You scared the daylights out of me."

In breathless spurts—and after repeated apologies—she explained about the run-in on Chardon Square. By the time they reached the kitchen, where her father promptly steered her into a chair, concern had replaced his irritation.

Tufts of coarse hair stuck up from her father's skull. He looked like the victim of an electrocution as he limped to the stove.

"What's your poison?" He held up a box of chamomile tea and the Scotch.

"Tea, definitely."

"You're sure you don't need something stronger?"

"The tea will soothe my nerves." She anxiously watched him fill the teapot. "I'm sorry I woke you, Dad."

"Stop apologizing. You gave me a start, that's all."

"How's the elbow?"

He examined the tender flesh. "Not bad."

Shelby padded into the room. The wily mutt was like a heat-seeking missile, homing in on the kitchen whenever humans clattered about. The dog nosed the back of Connor's legs, a none-too-subtle hint, before planting herself obediently in the center of the floor.

"Good thing Quinn's dog was asleep on his bed." Connor tossed a biscuit that Shelby neatly caught. "Sometimes she sleeps right beneath me when I nap on the couch."

"That would've been a disaster."

"You're telling me." Her father was about to add something else when his phone chirped. After withdrawing it from his pocket, he read quickly. "Here we go," he announced.

"A text from Quinn?"

"He's on his way back—says he'll be here soon. I have a feeling he knows his mother confronted you on the square."

Her father made the tea, then poured a small glass of Scotch for himself. The clock ticked an impatient rhythm as they nursed their drinks.

At length, Rae said, "Why would Quinn lie about his parents throwing him out? I believed every word of it."

"He's young. Kids are prone to all sorts of foolishness."

"Something doesn't add up," Rae insisted, angry and worried about what they were tangled up in. A disagreement between a teenage boy and his parents—two unpredictable adults whom no one in Chardon liked to cross. *I don't want to cross Mik and Penny either.* She'd made that mistake once, back in high school. Not long after the White Hurricane.

Connor frowned. "What do you mean?"

"The day I found Quinn near the forest, he couldn't have known we'd invite him to stay."

"So he made up the story about his parents throwing him out while we were grilling him?"

"I don't know. Would a teenager have the presence of mind to invent a story that elaborate under duress? It feels like a stretch. It's not like he could've known we'd roll out the red carpet and move him into the spare bedroom."

A puzzle, and Connor tapped his fingers against his glass. "You're forgetting one thing."

"Which is?"

"We didn't know Quinn, but he knew all about us—from Lark. He knew we were good people. Caring. Not the sort to throw a teenager out. Especially if he didn't want to go home."

"He was planning to spend the night in his truck," she recalled. That portion of Quinn's tale seemed authentic. "Was he planning to run away while his parents were vacationing in Atlanta? Then he bumped into me near the forest, and inspiration struck?"

"Lots of teenagers dream about running away." Sadness drifted through Connor's eyes. "You did, at that age."

The solemn observation pierced Rae. After the White Hurricane took Hester, Connor had seemed unreachable. Too depressed to recognize that he'd left Rae to singlehandedly keep their homelife from completely falling apart. She *had* wanted to run—to escape the sudden adult responsibilities she was too young to shoulder.

"Dad, that was different." With gentle reassurance, she squeezed his hand. "I never would've run away after we lost Mom. Our lives were turned upside down . . . I was just scared."

Pain skimmed across his features. "You had good reason. I let my depression get awfully bad. I should've—"

"Don't." Impulsively, Rae pressed a kiss to his forehead. "It was a long time ago. It no longer matters. Besides, we have more important concerns." She glanced at the clock. "Quinn will be here any minute. I have no idea what we should say to him."

"Let him talk first. Explain why he lied about his parents throwing him out. Maybe Quinn didn't know he had options about where to live—the boy didn't understand his rights until we met with Lloyd over at the bowling alley." A member of the geezer squad, Lloyd Washington was a retired attorney.

"That's true."

"The kid assumed he was obligated to live with his parents until graduation. It's an interesting loophole in Ohio law—parents must support a child until age nineteen if the child hasn't yet finished high school. However, an eighteen-year-old can elect to move out."

"Which I attempted to explain to Penny Galecki." Rae swallowed down the metallic taste in her mouth. Even now, adrenaline from the encounter raced through her. "I really thought she'd hit me. The look in her eye was unnerving. Like there's something missing inside."

A muscle in Connor's jaw twitched. "A spark of humanity," he supplied. "I'm concerned Mik doesn't have one either."

"He doesn't."

"We should buy a gun. Remember when you and Griffin were young, and his dad took you hunting? Everett swore you were a natural. You'd breeze through the classes in firearm safety. Maybe I would too."

Rae looked at him, aghast. Her father—who'd protested against the Vietnam War, a sworn pacifist—was implying they needed . . . protection from Penny and Mik Galecki?

A chill ran through her. That was the implication. Because they *were* dangerous. Impulsive. They were both heavy drinkers—and too much liquor brought out the worst in people. It made them unpredictable, prone to reckless behavior.

As I well know.

Shame crashed through Rae, bringing with it the dark memory from high school. She understood the awful mistakes one made when under the influence.

"We're not bringing firearms into the house." Taking a hasty sip of her tea, she focused her thoughts on the matter at hand. "I hate guns. And when I was in high school, I hated those hunting trips with Everett Marks. Griffin did too. We only tagged along to sneak in some alone time. Easy enough to do once Everett started tracking a deer." Winding anxious fingers through her long hair, she noticed the jagged ends. She was in desperate need of a trim. A normal, ordinary thought, and it made her feel better. "We'll look into a home security system, if you'd like."

"They're expensive. My Honda's on its last leg, and our food bill's exploding." He patted the dog, who was patiently resting her head on his leg. A biscuit appeared from his pocket. "It's a toss-up who eats more—our new houseguest or his furry friend."

"Let's not rush into anything. We'll shop around for an affordable system."

"Sounds like a plan."

The familiar rumble of Quinn's truck came up the drive. The engine cut off. Rae exchanged a glance with her father.

The clock ticked, the minutes passing. Finishing his drink, Connor poured another.

Rae dropped her voice to whisper. "Why doesn't he come inside?"

"He knows he's in trouble."

"What, he's got a crystal ball in the truck? I hope he doesn't get frostbite reading the signs." On an intake of breath, she stumbled across a more probable reason. "Penny called or sent him a text. She filled him in about our encounter on Chardon Square."

"That's my guess. Now he's stewing in his car."

"Should I fetch him?"

163

"Leave him be. This is his decision. He's got to decide whether to take a child's way out or act like a man. First off, he'll weigh the merits of heading for the hills. Driving all the way to California, or some such nonsense."

The possibility made Rae's stomach lurch.

No matter how much she dreaded another confrontation with Penny—or, worse still, with Mik—having Quinn run off didn't bear contemplating. The skinny youth was beginning to gain weight. He was a genuine help to Connor. He pitched in around the house and insisted on paying for Shelby's dog food. Some nights, when he thought Rae was asleep, he sang to his dog. Quietly, in a lilting whisper—silly, nonsense songs. The sort one sang to a toddler.

Shelby, entranced by the serenade, contributed amusing yips and full-throated yowls to the chorus.

The Galeckis were a threat. She'd take her chances to protect Quinn.

At last, heavy footfalls approached from the living room. Relief spilled through Rae. Then consternation. Quinn halted in the hallway, just a few feet away. She detected a scattered mumbling of words.

Was Quinn praying?

Connor rolled his eyes. Prayer or not, there were limits to his patience.

"Get in here, son! We're waiting."

From the doorway, Quinn dredged up the classic teenage response. "I can explain everything."

"And pigs can fly." Connor stabbed a finger at a chair. "Let's take this one step at a time."

Once Quinn was seated, Rae jumped in. "Why did you lie to us? You led us to believe your parents had thrown you out of the house."

"It was only a half lie. My mom told me to move out. She said if I didn't, I'd catch hell when she got back from Atlanta. She was getting drunk, but I knew she wasn't kidding around. She, um . . ." Embarrassed, Quinn hung his head.

"What?"

"She had me by the neck when she spelled it out."

Disgust pinged through Rae, stirring her tender, mothering instincts. "Where was your father while this transpired?"

"In the bedroom, packing for the trip."

"Mik left for the airport without knowing Penny told you to move out?"

"She warned I'd get a walloping if I told him."

"So Mik doesn't know she threw you out. He thinks this was all your idea. He assumes you took advantage of their trip to Atlanta to clear out—and avoid setting him off."

Connor shifted in his chair. "Penny's stirred up one fine hornet's nest," he muttered. "I'll bet Mik's furious."

Quinn shrugged out of his parka. "I suppose she'd put together a story to tell him when they got back. About me going to live with friends, or something." His gaze was still downcast, the color rising in his cheeks. Discussing this was clearly a humiliating experience for the kid. "She gets really pissed off when she drinks too much. I wasn't going to argue with her."

The sentiment was understandable. This afternoon, Rae hadn't wanted to argue with Penny either. She'd been frightened. A shameful response. When Penny pushed her back against the car, she should've clocked her, and good.

With confusion, Connor scratched his head. "If Penny wanted you to move out, why's she gunning for you to come home now?"

"Lots of reasons. Coq au vin, mostly."

Rae frowned. How did the kid's mastery of French cooking figure in?

Her father was faster on the uptake. "Your dad likes when you make dinner?"

"Oh yeah." Quinn grew animated. "I get along with him a whole lot better when I cook stuff he likes. Coq au vin is his favorite. I've also got a venison bourguignon I make during hunting season. Dad loves to hunt. When school's not in session and I'm not working, I make French bread and desserts too. The more he eats, the less he drinks."

Sympathy filled the webwork of lines comprising Connor's face. "How long have you been cooking for him?" Reaching into his pocket, he slid a biscuit down the table.

Murmuring thanks, Quinn gave the treat to his dog. "Oh, since I was eight or nine. A lady who used to live on our street taught me the basics."

"That was sweet of her."

"She was old. She missed cooking for her husband. He'd died. One day when my parents were fighting, she found me sitting at the picnic table in her yard. I thought she'd get mad. She didn't—she invited me inside." Remembering, he coasted thoughtful fingers across Shelby's back, smoothing down the fur. "After that, I started checking out food shows on YouTube. My dad is less of a bear when I make dinner. I think it soaks up the booze."

"You're a smart young man," her father said.

Rae asked, "What about Penny? Does she cook?" Apparently, a macho guy like Mik never went near a stove.

"She thinks she does. Mostly she burns stuff in a skillet." A trace of fear swept through Quinn's eyes. "My parents have some scary go-rounds about Mom's cooking. She'll get dinner started, then walk away. Start watching TV or make a drink. Lots of times the kitchen reeks of smoke before she remembers what she's doing. Really pisses Dad off. The rest of the time, he makes fun of her. Teases her about her lousy cooking or mocks her when she goes heavy with the makeup to try to look younger."

Rae felt sick. "Does your Dad make fun of you too?"

"All the time," Quinn replied with indifference, as if verbal abuse was commonplace in most homes. "Dad says I'm more of a girl than Mom. He'll ask if he should get me a girlie apron to finish my transformation into a chick. I just keep my mouth shut when he starts in."

A gratifying trace of pride blotted out the fear. "What does he know? Lots of men cook."

"Including some of the world's greatest chefs," Connor added. "Your dad is a dumbbell. No offense."

Quinn laughed. "None taken."

Rae finished her tea. "Well, now I understand why Penny was ramped up today. They got back from vacation, and Mik wasn't happy the French chef had moved out."

"I'm sorry about my mother."

"Forget it. I can take care of myself." It wasn't entirely true, where Penny was concerned. She resolved to prepare for the next standoff—which seemed inevitable. Switching topics, Rae asked, "Why did it take so long for your dad to notice your absence? They must've returned from Atlanta days ago."

"I'm not sure. Somehow my mom got him believing I was still around."

Connor grunted. "She's a dumbbell too. Probably stuffed your bed with pillows. Figured she'd fool your dad forever."

"Could be." Quinn gripped the table's edge, then began drumming his fingers. "Should I move out? You know, because my parents want me back?"

"Hell no."

Rae cast a warning glance. "Dad—language." To Quinn she said, "I can't promise your parents won't keep demanding you return home. But the choice isn't theirs to make. Quinn, you're a legal adult. This is your decision. We're glad you're living with us, and we want you to stay." For emphasis, she paused. Locating the steady, serious tone she'd once used to steer her late daughter in the right direction, she added, "Will you do me a favor?"

"Sure."

"Trust matters in relationships. That means you don't hold back or lie. You should've told us immediately that your mother—not *both* of your parents—made you move out. The specifics wouldn't have mattered to me or my father. We still would've offered you a place to stay." She looked at him closely. "Do you understand? I'm not trying to come down on you. I'm just explaining the rules of the road in the Langdon house."

Quinn swallowed. "I get it."

"Good." She hesitated. "Is there anything else you'd like to tell me?"

Unaccountably, his gaze skittered away. Rae's heart sank. She was wondering how to press when he caught the error. Quinn pulled his attention back to her.

"We're good, Rae," he said too quickly. "We've covered everything."

～

Nightfall dropped the temperature to near freezing.

Grass crunched beneath Rae's boots. Swinging the flashlight in a loose arc, she strode past the barn.

The air smelled boggy and damp from winter's thaw. Small pools of water dotted the pasture, the last remnants from the snowdrifts that had blanketed the acres. A hawk swooped through the approaching night. Its dark wings caught a downdraft as it sped toward the forest.

Slowing her pace, Rae sorted her jumbled thoughts.

She feared she wasn't finished with Penny and Mik. In one form or another, they'd reappear. They'd continue to badger Quinn, putting at risk the fragile equilibrium she'd brought to his life. They wouldn't stop there. Mik and Penny were like seventeen-year locusts, once dormant and now deadly. Burrowing up from the past to destroy everything in their path.

They'd devastated the emotional terrain of Rae's life once before. On a dreadful March night, two months after the White Hurricane had upended her world.

Would they do so again?

Normally Rae wasn't a fatalist. Yet their reappearance in her life felt preordained. Like an error that destiny insisted she repeat until she'd learned a critical lesson.

Grimly, she halted in the pasture. *What is the lesson?*

She'd worked hard to bury the past's mistakes. To seal them over and move on. Even though she'd lost her precious daughter, Rae knew she'd built a good life. She loved her job and cherished her friendship with Yuna. Her father was now getting on in years, but he was thankfully in good health. Having Quinn around had put a spring in Connor's step.

It had been years since she'd been haunted by thoughts of Quinn's parents. Bedeviled by the memory, which she'd relived countless times in her unwelcome sleep. The nightmares hadn't stopped until Lark's toddler years, when Rae's job at the Witt Agency went from part- to full-time. The combination of long work hours and motherhood proved an unexpected remedy. Each night she'd fallen into bed exhausted, welcoming the dreamless sleep.

Quinn's arrival into her life hadn't stirred those private demons. Hadn't punched through Rae's subconscious to start the nightmares once again. Would the encounter with Penny?

I can't get trapped in the past. I must stay sharp.

A necessity, she decided. The battles with Penny and Mik weren't over.

Chapter 20

For days, Griffin immersed himself in the monotony of work.

He trudged into Design Mark at dawn. Often, he stayed until midnight. His assistant joked he should sell his house and live in his office.

In between meetings, he attempted to reach Sally. His sister refused to pick up. The sincere apologies Griffin left on voice mail, he suspected, were summarily deleted.

For two siblings so close, the break in diplomatic relations was a first.

Griffin took full ownership of the mess. Last weekend, when Sally had appeared in his office, hurling accusations like well-aimed darts, he shouldn't have become defensive. It should've been obvious she was upset about more than Katherine's revelations concerning Lark. Or because Katherine still harbored feelings that Griffin couldn't return.

His sister's anger ran deeper.

Sally believed he'd broken a key element of *their* relationship: trust. Which he'd done through his inability to give her the full, unvarnished truth. Why hadn't he mentioned taking Lark to Dixon's for ice cream? Had embarrassment kept him silent? Playing a shadow game, he'd offered some facts while hiding others.

Now Sally viewed everything he'd told her as suspect.

By Thursday night, it became clear the standoff might last indefinitely. The prospect spurred Griffin out of Design Mark. What choice was there but to drive over to Sally's house? When two adults disagree, nothing beats in-person negotiations. A face-to-face would soothe his sister's ruffled feathers. Griffin was prepared to eat crow, if it came to it.

On the first knock, the door opened a crack. His brother-in-law looked agitated.

"I don't know what you've done, pal." Trenton spoke at barely a whisper. "Your sister is hotter than Death Valley. She's more dangerous than extreme weather. She's like the volcano that erupted in . . . which country was it? Somewhere in Asia."

A query not worth exploring. "I get it, Trenton. May I speak with her?"

"No."

"No?" Griffin polished his tone to a brittle sheen. "May I ask why?"

"Like you don't know."

"Okay, I know. I'd still like to come in. I need to apologize."

"You're wasting your time."

"Let me be the judge." His irritation flared. "Back up, man. I'm coming in to talk to my sister."

"No way." Trenton cast a nervous glance behind him. "If I let you in, she'll strip my ego naked and dip it in bleach. I'm not that strong. Go away."

The door clicked shut.

The rejection deflated Griffin, and he trudged back to his car. He returned to Design Mark to stew in a broth of self-pity and remorse.

The self-pity was especially hazardous. It led him down the blind roads and rocky paths to that last, unfortunate year at Chardon High. A smarter man would avoid such a journey. He wouldn't poke around the undergrowth of his memories to examine the most painful events.

But the sting of Sally's darts was still fresh.

And so, Griffin paced the empty halls of Design Mark with the memory of his former self dogging his heels. The sweaty dope whose only redeeming quality—a full head of hair—was now in full retreat. The awkward boy who'd been hopelessly in love with Rae Langdon.

Griffin meant what he'd told Sally: he bore Rae no ill will. Since moving back to Ohio, he'd only glimpsed her from a distance—not once making the attempt to approach and strike up conversation. Besides, she'd been a girl when she'd broken his heart. What sense was there in despising the woman she'd become?

We are each many people in a lifetime. We slip through versions of ourselves, no more staying in place than a fast-moving river. Rae wasn't the girl she'd once been. Nor was he, thankfully, still an inept teenager. The harm they'd done to each other long ago seemed like the errors of two people Griffin didn't know at all.

At dinnertime on Sunday, Griffin ended the pity party. He abandoned the office. He went home, took a shower, and made a salad for dinner. Trenton was correct—Sally needed to cool down. There was no sense putting in more calls. Griffin could, however, act on the advice she'd offered the day he'd shown her the lacquered box.

Ask Yuna to return the keepsake to its rightful owner. With luck, she'd agree to handle delivery. Toting the thing next door, however, was presumptuous.

Odds weren't great that Yuna would jump at the chance to get involved. Why would she? Lark had taken the box from Rae's attic without her mother's consent. Rae didn't know it was missing. How the thing had landed in Griffin's possession—and the thorny implications—were sure to upset Rae.

Set on a course of action, Griffin pulled out his smartphone. He snapped a photo of the precious object.

A boxwood hedge separated the yards. With grim resignation, he walked around. He was still working out what to say when the door swung open to reveal . . . no one.

He looked down.

His favorite mini human was dressed in flannel pajamas. "Mommy threw up—twice!" Kameko pinched her nose dramatically. "Smelly!"

Griffin aped her expression of disgust. "Yuck."

"Want to come in?"

Not on your life. "If she's sick, I should come back later."

Latching on to his wrist, Kameko made a pouty face. "Don't go! Mommy's not sick."

"But you said—"

"The baby is mean when Mommy smells burgers. Me and Daddy like burgers." Her face fell. "We can't eat them anymore. The baby won't let us."

Baby? What baby? He wondered if his arrival had disturbed the child's fantasy play.

Toys were strewn across the living room. A cornucopia of plastic animals and talking books. There wasn't a doll in sight.

"He jumps on Mommy's tummy. Like this." Kameko hopped up and down to demonstrate. Then her expression grew earnest. "Griffin, do you make burgers?"

"Sure. Sometimes."

"I'll come over and eat one. Maybe tomorrow. Don't tell the teeny baby."

"Good plan," he murmured, following her to the kitchen.

Did she mean her mother was pregnant? It would explain the teeny baby's unpleasant behavior, not to mention Yuna's distress. He'd lived next door long enough for Kipp to regale him with tales of Yuna's morning sickness when she'd been pregnant with Kameko. Each story came with a colorful and amusingly gruesome title. "Life with the Hurl Master" or Griffin's personal favorite, "Vicious Stops on the Vomit Train." The stories were never told when Yuna was within earshot.

"Mommy, Daddy—look who's here! I told Griffin about the mean baby!"

The atmosphere in the kitchen was testy. At the table, Yuna sat in a miserable silence. She was flicking saltines past the napkin holder like poker chips. Kipp, hovering nearby, looked ready to bolt.

Griffin appraised the subdued couple. "Are we celebrating or sitting shiva?" he asked.

"Hey, pal." Kipp pulled a cold one from the fridge. "We're celebrating. Yuna's pregnant."

"Congratulations to you both. A baby is happy news." Accepting the beer, Griffin frowned. "Aren't you joining me?"

"Naw." Kipp patted his middle. "Yuna says my abs are starting to resemble blubber. If her hormones get much worse, I'm worried she'll buy a harpoon. But enough with the small talk. I'm going to be a daddy—again!" He raised his bottled water. "To my sperm. May they always swim fast and free."

Yuna gave him a jaundiced look. "Language—your daughter is in the room. As for 'swimming free,' if they do, you're in trouble."

"It's just a toast!"

"Whatever." She smiled weakly at Kameko. "Daddy's goofy tonight. Mostly because he's excited about the teeny baby. Don't listen to him."

"Okay, Mommy." Kameko obediently stuck her fingers in her ears.

"*I'm* sitting shiva," Yuna informed Griffin. To Kipp, she said, "I promised to marry you on one condition. We split all family chores fifty-fifty. I'm thrilled about the baby, but it's *your* turn to gestate. I'm so done with morning sickness."

"Whoa, sweetheart. Some duties are outside my jurisdiction—like the laws of nature."

"Amend the law," Yuna sulked. She regarded Kameko, fingers still dutifully stuck in her ears. Gently she removed them. "Sweetheart, can you go upstairs and brush your teeth? Daddy will be in soon to read you a story."

"Can I have a snack first?"

"No. You had cookies after dinner. Go on."

Her dimpled chin jutting out, Kameko glared at her mother's tummy. *"Mean baby,"* she hissed. She stomped off.

Her tempestuous departure left a heavy silence. Griffin cleared his throat.

"Listen, I'm catching you at a bad time," he said to no one in particular. "My issue pales in comparison to your happy news. Really great news—congratulations again. How 'bout I touch base this weekend? I'll call."

Female intuition was a strange phenomenon; Yuna knew he meant *her*.

"Sit." With her toe, she nudged a chair out from the table. "You look upset."

"I am, I suppose."

"Your car hasn't been in your driveway all week. Were you out of town?"

"No, just living at my office. Burying myself in work. It's the manly way to deal with tough problems." He pushed the beer away. "Or avoid them. Which is why I need a favor. I hate to ask."

"It's fine, Griffin. I'm always here for you."

"I know you are. I appreciate your friendship."

Turning to Kipp, she glared. "Why are *you* still here?" Evidently her sympathy didn't extend to her husband.

Kipp drew himself up tall. "Because Griffin's upset," he volleyed back, "and I'll gladly discuss anything not related to vomit or marital equality. I've sworn off red meat and have thrown out my favorite sriracha sauce. I'm dealing with your mood swings. What more do you want from me?" When she remained silent, he landed a palm on Griffin's shoulder. "Spill—we're here for you."

Glad to get on with it, Griffin pulled out his phone and found the image. To Yuna, he said, "I need you to return this to Rae." He slid the phone before her.

"What is it?"

"A keepsake Hester made when Rae was in elementary school. It was special to Rae when she was growing up. I have it."

Running through the story about Lark's visits was no picnic. Griffin kept it short and sweet. There was no reason to mention the box's humiliating contents—knowing Yuna, she'd never look inside. Her sense of propriety ran deep.

A minor consolation. By the end of the telling, her jaw hung loose.

Kipp's reaction was the opposite. He looked entertained. Any man in trouble, other than himself—*that* was a joyride he was happy to take.

He snatched the beer Griffin hadn't touched. "That's some story, man." Taking a swig, he eagerly pulled up a chair. "Rae's daughter was dropping by your office repeatedly?"

"I thought she was working on a school report."

"She had you fooled."

"Obviously."

"One question. Why would Lark, may she rest in peace, get it in her head that you were her father?" Kipp fought the grin quirking his lips. "Don't take this the wrong way, pal. Lark was way too pretty. If your DNA got in the boxing ring, Rae's won the match. Lark didn't look anything like you."

At the good-natured teasing, pain rushed through Griffin. He recalled the shocking phone call from his sister during his first semester at Ohio University. Learning that Rae—whom he hadn't seen since their graduation from high school—was pregnant. How the gossips in Chardon were chattering that he was the deadbeat father.

How the news of Rae's condition gutted him.

Yuna threw a saltine at Kipp's head. "Kipp, baby-making turns you into an idiot. I'm *not* looking forward to another five months of your juvenile behavior." Her eyes flashed. "Griffin was childhood friends with Rae. I know I've mentioned it—can't you remember anything? What I didn't tell you was that they dated in high school."

"They did?"

"That's right. Over time, their childhood friendship had evolved into something deeper. They broke up near the end of their senior year."

"Ah. Now it all makes sense."

"Go." She pointed toward the hallway and the stairwell beyond. "*Your* daughter is waiting for you to read her a bedtime story."

Chapter 21

As Kipp left the room, Griffin released a pent-up breath. He was glad for the privacy. He wanted to finish this quickly.

With interest Yuna studied the image on his phone. "Hester made this? It's incredible. I'm surprised Rae never mentioned it. Of course, we hardly knew each other in high school. We didn't become close until our twenties. By then, she must've packed the keepsake away."

The casual remark injured Griffin's pride. Was he surprised Yuna was unfamiliar with the keepsake? It seemed natural for Rae to pack away the box and all reminders of him. She went on with her life without a backward glance. Reason enough to feel a sense of injury, he decided.

By comparison, it took him years to get over her. A secret he'd never shared, not even with Sally.

Tamping down the reaction, he asked, "Will you return it for me?" He reminded himself of how much Rae had lost during the White Hurricane. Recently, she'd lost even more.

Yuna set the phone down. "I'll pick it up from you soon. I can't promise when I'll take it to Rae. In a week or two."

"Why the delay?" None of his business, but he was curious.

"She's dealing with enough at the moment. The run-in with Penny Galecki last weekend, and now that woman's totally crazy behavior. Whenever Penny drives through the square and spots Rae, she yells obscenities. She must be gunning her car in the bank's parking lot, waiting to drive by when Rae steps out of the insurance agency."

The frazzled monologue put Griffin on alert. "Mik Galecki's wife, right?"

Yuna nodded. "Yesterday when Rae went in early to open the Witt Agency, there was garbage dumped across the entryway. I'm talking about a whole can of trash. Evelyn wanted to put in a call to Chief Johnson at the police department, and Kipp encouraged her to do so. Rae vetoed the idea. She thinks it's best to ignore Penny's antics in hopes she'll stop. I'm not convinced she will."

"What's Penny's interest in Rae?"

"Quinn's been living at Rae's house. He's staying until he completes high school. Longer, probably."

Griffin tensed. *Rae has taken in Mik's son?*

He was still absorbing the news as Yuna retold how Lark and Quinn became friends. Two kids hitting it off during art classes at the craft emporium.

Mik's position at Marks Auto was longstanding—Griffin had first met Quinn when he was a fearful-eyed toddler allowed free rein in the mechanic's bay by his irresponsible father. Had Quinn found safety, thanks to Rae? The idea of him finally catching a break was gratifying. Given the turbulent nature of his childhood, the solitude of farm life would do him good.

The potential consequences for Rae, however, were chilling.

Drawing from the reverie, he heard Yuna say, "Quinn doesn't know the half of what his mother's been doing. Rae believes it's best to keep him out of the loop. We're guessing Penny's lost another job. She has nothing better to do than hassle Rae."

"Or she's concerned about her husband's wrath, if Quinn doesn't come home. Mik's worked for my dad for decades—the other mechanics treat him with wary respect. He's territorial by nature. Even more so when it comes to his family. As for Penny, she never wanted a child in the first place."

Yuna lowered a protective hand to her belly. "She didn't want Quinn?"

"Her relationship with Mik wasn't serious. They'd only dated a few weeks when she got pregnant." Searching his memories, Griffin added, "I was around fourteen when Penny told him she was getting an abortion. She walked into the service bay at Marks Auto and made her announcement in front of the staff. Demanded Mik pay for the abortion—said she wanted the cash immediately. From what I heard, the public argument really knocked Mik down a notch. I'm sure he was humiliated. After they'd finished the shouting match and Penny walked off, one of the younger mechanics foolishly made a wisecrack. Mik read him the riot act, complete with f-bombs—he was screaming so loud, customers in the showroom were able to hear."

"Your dad didn't fire him?"

"I think he would've if he didn't know Mik had a baby on the way. From my dad's perspective, it wasn't right to put a man out of work under those circumstances. But he *did* tell Mik to tone down the gutter talk, or he would lose his job." When Yuna looked at him, aghast, he added, "Save your outrage. Me, Sally, my mother—at one time or another, we've all begged my father to dump Mik. We probably shouldn't have pushed. Everett Marks doesn't like anyone telling him what to do. And Mik's a talented mechanic, especially with refurb work on classics, like Chief Johnson's '68 Camaro. He's a failure as a human being, but the guy was born with a gift."

"Having a talent doesn't give you the right to act out." Sighing, Yuna let it go. "How did Mik talk Penny into keeping the baby?"

"A day or so later, he went into my dad's office and demanded a raise. Said he was getting married. My dad increased his salary on the spot. He also—delicately, mind you—asked if Mik would prefer to have the child placed in an adoptive home. My dad assured him that private inquiries would be made, at no expense."

Yuna's eyes widened with amazement. "How do you know all of this?"

"My mother." Griffin's affection for his mother merged with disgust that she'd needed to get involved with such an upsetting situation. "She was visiting the dealership on the day Penny marched in with her plans to get an abortion. Arranging a private adoption was her idea. Pity it didn't work out. After Mik and Penny married, there were several interventions by Job and Family Services."

"Why?"

"People in their apartment building were putting in calls about a toddler being left alone. That's when my mother got seriously involved. She found a day care facility for Quinn and tried to take Penny under her wing. When that didn't work out, she badgered my dad about giving Mik a big Christmas bonus. She'd found an affordable house in town for the couple. She hoped putting down roots would make Quinn's childhood easier."

"God bless Winnie," Yuna murmured. Although her eyes were damp, she smiled. "I've always liked your mother. She treats all of your dad's employees like family."

"She does . . . but it didn't make much difference. Not with Penny. She's never had anything but loathing for Quinn."

"What about Mik? Did he ever care about his son?"

"He gave parenting a shot when he was younger. Now? From my vantage point, it's a safe bet the guy's an alcoholic. He doesn't care about anything but the next drink. Penny encourages his worst traits, and now their son is living at Rae's place. There's nothing about the situation that leaves me feeling warm and fuzzy inside."

"But Quinn is doing so well! When he comes into work at my shop, he actually smiles. Talks nonstop about Connor and all the projects they're doing together. He's more distant with Rae—he *is* a teenage boy, and they don't have much in common—but you can tell he's blossoming. Getting a real sense of belonging, living with them."

"I'm sure he is."

"Won't his parents see that eventually? Leave him alone, and let him finish growing up in a home that's stable and safe?" Yuna seemed unable to glimpse the harder truths. "It's more than they've been willing to give him."

"I doubt they'll see it that way."

The air grew taut as Griffin inspected his thoughts. He felt impotent, powerless. Rae was no longer part of his life. How to protect her? He didn't relish discussing the larger issues with Yuna, of all people, in the early stages of pregnancy, battling nausea. Under different circumstances, he'd never draw her into this. The concern brewing inside him brought him to an uneasy decision.

"Promise me something." He leaned in for emphasis. "Keep an eye out for Mik. I'm not worried about Penny—she has low impulse control, but she doesn't usually get too far out of line. Not unless she's getting blitzed in one of the local bars and starts arguing with another woman. But if Mik contacts Rae—if he so much as sends a threatening text—I want a full report. If he shows up at the Witt Agency, or you catch wind he's threatening Quinn—call immediately. I'll take it from there."

"What are you saying?" Yuna shrank back. "I know Mik's been abusive to Quinn. Penny has been too. The bad stuff that happens in some families . . . it's unimaginable. But Rae isn't a part of that."

"No, she's not." Griffin couldn't halt the urgency in his voice. "It won't matter."

"She doesn't know Mik any better than I do!"

"Forget logic, Yuna. It doesn't apply to broken people."

"Why should Mik care at all? He should be grateful Quinn has somewhere nice to stay, free room and board in a house with adults who really like him—no, more than that. Rae and Connor are invested in his welfare. They want to help him succeed in life, in all the ways that matter. It's like he's become a member of their family."

Yuna cut off suddenly. Her gaze darkened with fear as it clung to his, seeking reassurance, needing a guarantee impossible to give.

"Griffin, be straight with me. Do you think Mik poses a danger to Rae?"

Unease stole into Griffin's bones.

Yes.

Deftly, he hid the unease behind a look of reassurance. "No harm will come to Rae," he promised. "Just keep me informed."

Chapter 22

A long, hot shower was normally a weekend luxury.

Rae didn't care. She took her time washing her long reddish-gold hair, savoring the therapeutic pounding of water droplets on her back.

Would more headaches spoil the new week?

Rae was tired of feeling like a criminal. She'd spent the better part of last week sprinting down the alley behind the Witt Agency for quick visits to Yuna's shop, or to grab lunch at a nearby restaurant. An indignity, to be sure. There'd been no better option to avoid the flurry of obscenities pitched from Penny's car each time she drove by.

At least Penny couldn't dump more trash in front of the Witt Agency. Her days of risk-free vandalism were over. The nearby shop owners and businesses were now keeping an eye out. With tax season approaching, several of the overworked employees at the accounting firm were arriving for work at dawn. Later in the day, the owners of the antique shop took turns patrolling the street.

If Quinn's mother planned more foolishness, she'd have to haul herself from bed before sunup. There was little chance a woman into late-night partying could pull off an early-bird routine.

Confident the new workweek would prove calmer, Rae took her time dressing and drying her hair. Out of habit, she reached for a scrunchie—usually she pulled her unruly tresses into a loose ponytail for the office. Tossing the scrunchie aside, she let her hair tumble past her shoulders. She felt good. There'd be no public shaming this week.

At just past seven thirty, she left her bedroom with a bounce in her step. An early start today—her boss, Evelyn, was back from vacation. Rae planned to catch up on paperwork before their ten o'clock meeting. Connor's bedroom door was still closed; his rumbling snores drifted out as she walked past.

Quinn was at the kitchen table, staring off into space. His book bag leaned against the chair, zipped up and ready for the school day. Shelby, nosing around her food bowl, gobbled down the last chunks of kibble.

Rae turned on the coffeepot. "Aren't you having breakfast?" There wasn't even a glass of juice before him.

"I'm not hungry."

"You're sure? I can make toast."

"Don't bother."

Normally Quinn ate a hearty breakfast. If Connor woke early, lending Quinn an excuse to whip up a meal, a dozen eggs and half a pound of bacon could disappear from the fridge. Not to mention half a bag of potatoes, and most of the pancake mix. A teenager's pride is a fragile thing, and Connor—grizzled and time tested like an old-fashioned stopwatch—was a skilled thespian. Playing his role convincingly, he pretended to need a large breakfast to start the day.

It was all the encouragement Quinn required to begin grabbing skillets and cooking supplies.

Once the platters were filled and Connor changed his mind—complaining about how he hated to see all the good eats go to waste—Quinn dug in. He'd consume enough calories to put the average person into a food coma.

He never skipped breakfast altogether. "You look tired," Rae said, concerned. "Did you get enough sleep?" Sometimes he stayed up late studying.

"I'm okay." He gave her a cursory glance. "Your hair looks nice."

Giving her head a playful shake, she hoped to draw a smile. "We all need to let our hair down sometimes." When no reaction was forthcoming, she ditched the humor. "Any tests this week?" she asked.

"Nothing major." He watched Shelby trot out of the kitchen, no doubt to doze on his still-warm bed. "Just a few quizzes."

"That's good."

He pulled out his car keys. "I guess." He stuffed them back into his coat pocket.

On the parenting highway, his indecision signaled distress. Was there something he needed to discuss? He was also back to his old trick of avoiding eye contact. Another bad sign.

Worried, Rae turned off the coffeepot. Filling her travel mug, she searched for a new conversation starter. Whatever troubled him, he appeared in no hurry to open up. Leaving for work wasn't an option until she got to the bottom of it. How to proceed was the real issue. They didn't have a natural rapport. Without Connor to provide the essential chemistry, many of their interactions were stilted or brief.

"Should I pick up dinner on my way home?" Opening the fridge, she pretended to hunt for a breakfast option. "Do you want pizza tonight? Or I can bring home Thai. You liked it, the last time."

"Why would you get takeout?" Quinn glanced at her peevishly. "I cook on Mondays. I'm making rosemary chicken patties and garlic potatoes. Connor's helping me."

"Sounds heavenly." She closed the fridge. "You know, we appreciate all the great meals. Before you moved in, we lived on lunch meat and frozen entrées. But you're under no obligation to pull kitchen duty. If you have to study or aren't in the mood to cook, just give me a call. I'll pick something up."

"The recipes are easy. It won't take long."

"How's it going with the decorative lights?" She'd been too busy to check. "My dad says you're making great progress."

Quinn reached for his book bag, then reversed the motion. "Great," he said with exactly no enthusiasm. In another worrisome habit, he began picking at his nails. "We're on the fourth tree now. We'll have all the lights strung this afternoon. We might get started on the fifth tree, if the weather holds. Connor thinks it might rain later on."

"The forecast doesn't call for rain until tonight. Only a twenty percent chance."

"Whatever."

A snippy response, and totally *not* Quinn's style. "Do you need lunch money?" she asked, determined to get him talking. There was a chance bribery would soften up the churlish teen.

His eyes flashed. "Why would you give me lunch money? I'm not your kid."

"I'm feeling generous this morning," Rae tossed back, thinking, *Hit the brakes. Trouble ahead.* Speeding up instead, she asked, "Any new text messages from your mother? I'm hoping Penny had better things to do than badger you all weekend." A touchy subject, but Quinn was already peevish.

"I took Connor's advice and blocked her. He got pretty mad when I showed him the texts." Dots of blood appeared on Quinn's pinkie as he tore the nail too close to the skin. "He said a grown-up shouldn't talk filth, especially to her own kid."

The self-inflicted injury made Rae wince. "I agree. Parents should treat their children with love and respect."

"Someone should tell my mom. I hate her stupid texts. She knows more cuss words than anyone on the planet."

"Tell me about it. I googled a few of the unfamiliar ones."

"Me too." Quinn hesitated. "I also blocked my dad."

A trill of fear swept through her. "You did?" Blocking Mik was like throwing down a gauntlet. There *would* be repercussions.

"I figured, what the heck. No guts, no glory. That's what Connor says when I get hung up on decisions. The glory feels like a reach, though."

Her heart went out to him. "Finding courage is never easy, Quinn. What matters is that you make the attempt."

"Yeah. Learn to stand up for myself."

"You will, in time." Rae's pulse jumped as she struggled for a placid tone. "Don't let anyone stand in your way."

Quinn rubbed his temples, as if dispelling a disturbing thought. "My dad will be angry when he figures out why he can't reach me."

"Just remember what I told you. The choice on where to live is legally yours. Mik has no power over you."

"He won't see it that way."

"Maybe not, but you're more than welcome to stay here."

This didn't sound nearly as positive as she'd like. Pausing, Rae dug deep for the right words. Quinn was learning to stand up for himself. She refused to let him down.

She caught his gaze. "I want you to stay, Quinn. You're doing well in my home, and I like having you around. The last months have been hard . . . You've been an incredible help. More than you imagine. Plus, my father adores you. He seems ten years younger since you moved in."

It was too much affection too fast. Quinn looked pained, too distraught to respond. Silently Rae chastised herself. His emotions were a delicate ballet. She was still learning the steps.

She picked up her briefcase. "I guess I'll head out." The urge to embrace him was powerful. To give physical proof to her desire to stand by him. Rae warded off the impulse. "If there's anything else you'd like to discuss, I don't have to—"

"No. I'm good."

"Sure. Well, have a great day at school."

"Okay."

"I'll see you tonight," she added, stalling.

Quinn's expression churned, and she knew there was something more. Another problem he seemed incapable of sharing.

With misgivings, she pivoted away.

"Wait." Quinn bit at his lower lip. "Rae, there's something I've been meaning to talk to you about. I shouldn't have waited this long. A dumb move, on my part."

"Sure. I'm all ears."

"It's about Lark . . . what she was doing without telling you. I suppose she would've filled you in, eventually. I don't want you to get mad, finding out now."

The oxygen left the room. A new, darker element rushed in.

"I won't be angry, promise." She dredged up an encouraging smile. "What is it?"

"It's about the stuff you wouldn't tell her. The things you and Lark fought about." A darting glance, this one anxious. "You know—about her dad."

The moisture fled Rae's mouth. "You mean, how she wanted to know who he was?"

Past tense, and Quinn frowned. "Who the guy *is*," he said, correcting the error. "Lark *did* know him. She knew him well. Sometimes they spent time together, on Wednesdays."

Chapter 23

Outside, tires screamed.

Dropping his briefcase, Griffin sprinted to the window. Two stories below, a blue Honda Civic swerved past the dealership. Jumping the curb, it clipped an empty flower planter near Design Mark's entryway. The car screeched to a halt.

There wasn't time to process what was happening. Within seconds Rae was up the stairwell and marching into his office. An easy maneuver; his staff wasn't in yet.

"Griffin! You sneaky, manipulative—" She bit back an oath. "What's wrong with you? Who gave you permission to associate with my daughter?"

Bafflement held Griffin like a vise. Of all the potential interactions he'd imagined having with Rae when they eventually ran into each other, he never could've predicted this full-on assault. Scrambling for the right words, he managed to fake an air of composure.

"Slow down, Rae," he said. "Why don't you let me—"

"Don't tell me what to do! We're not in high school anymore. You're not my boyfriend. Even when you were, I didn't let you order me around."

"Listen, I can see you're upset."

"I'm not upset. I'm livid! I can't begin to comprehend what excuse you think will get you out of this. Of all the devious, backhanded stunts. Lark was visiting Design Mark *for weeks*? Why didn't you put her on the payroll, Griffin? Ask her to drop her after-school activities to schlep coffee for your staff? No one in their right mind lets a ninth grader roam their place of employment, not without checking with the girl's mother . . ."

Getting in a word proved impossible. Better to let her vent until she ran out of steam.

As she railed, Griffin found himself evaluating her. Despite the grievous losses she'd endured, the years had been kind to Rae. Her eyes were more striking than he remembered, a dusky forest green. Her hair was appealingly long. The riot of reddish-gold locks cascaded past her shoulders. She was disturbingly attractive—and nearly intimidating, given her height.

The silly conviction he'd forged in high school captured his thoughts.

If Vikings ruled the world, Rae would be their queen.

"Stop zoning out!" She came forward. "Your daydreaming always drove me crazy. You'd zone out whenever I was upset. Like you were picking up radio frequencies from Mars."

Or sending an SOS.

"I'm listening." He gestured toward the window. "You're shouting loud enough for everyone at the dealership to hear you. Mind turning down the volume?"

"All right." Her voice dropped to an acceptable level. Her eyes narrowed. "Are you aware a child Lark's age is impressionable?"

"I am."

"Did you know my daughter was badgering me nonstop? All those demands for the name of her father. After years of raising her in blissful tranquility, we were suddenly having a million stupid arguments. And no wonder. Lark had you in the background, egging her on. It's appalling how you encouraged my daughter."

"Calm down," he snapped. "I can't talk to you when you're like this."

"I wouldn't *be* like this, if it weren't for your scheming."

"Rae, sit down. Let's talk this out like reasonable adults."

"Last warning, Griffin. Stop telling me what to do."

She was coming at him too fast, overrunning his defenses. Apparently Yuna had returned the keepsake faster than anticipated, to poor results. Which was baffling. Yuna had indicated she'd wait a couple of weeks before playing delivery boy. Even more curious: she'd returned the box without giving him the heads-up he was sure she would provide.

None of which mattered now.

Griffin rocked back on his heels. "I didn't encourage Lark," he said, determined not to let Rae throw him off-balance. It was her special talent. But he was older now, with skills of his own. "You're implying I devised a master plan to strike up a friendship with her. Nothing could be further from the truth. Lark approached me. Not the other way around."

"So it's her fault? That's big of you. And how would you character-ize repeated visits between a girl and the man she's picked out for her father? If that isn't encouragement, what is?" A low growl of frustration escaped Rae. "My daughter cooks up a lottery, and you're the winning ticket. It would be funny if it wasn't tragic."

A low blow, but he took it in stride. "Rae, I didn't understand what was going on. Not immediately."

"You're pleading . . . stupidity? *That's* your excuse?"

Another blow, and his anger sparked. "It's the only one I have."

"Griffin, I worked hard to raise Lark. I put her front and center in every decision I made. She was everything to me. She didn't need you jumping in, pretending you were eager and available to play the role of father. She had me and a grandfather who adored her. She was fine.

More than fine—Lark was smart and confident and capable. She didn't need you."

"I never said she did."

It was galling how Rae wouldn't accept a modicum of blame. As if she bore no responsibility at all. Why keep his love letters in the first place? Or the tokens he'd given her in childhood—if they meant nothing to Rae, why keep them at all? By holding on to the remnants of their long-dead affection, she'd guided Lark into his world.

"You weren't meant to be part of her life, Griffin. What right did you have to confuse her?"

Straddling anger and remorse, Griffin chose the dangerous emotion. They were arguing about a child they'd both loved. A child neither of them would have the joy of watching grow into womanhood. Whatever promise lay buried in the cold ground, Griffin knew he'd never stop grieving. Rae wouldn't either.

The facts made him angrier. With the anger came a surge of male pride, sharpening his thoughts to a diamond's edge.

"I didn't confuse Lark," he growled. "Why didn't you tell her what she needed to know? Spare her the wild goose chase?"

"It's none of your business."

"All evidence to the contrary. You storm into my office after sixteen years, and suddenly I'm responsible for whatever problems you had with your daughter. She was a teenager, Rae. Old enough to hear the facts. Why didn't you supply them? Were you afraid Lark wouldn't take it well, once she learned you made some incredibly reckless choices when you were young?"

The salvos hit the mark. Rae flinched as if his words had struck her like a physical blow. When her expression nearly crumbled, self-loathing coursed through him. He was responding from a place of pain, like a defensive child.

Like a fool.

But he'd forgotten Rae's inner strength, the emotional reserves she brought to bear in times of crisis. Rallying, she dodged his questions to pose one of her own.

"Was this a form of payback?" she asked. "Use my daughter to hurt me? Great job, Griffin. It worked."

"What are you talking about?"

"I broke your heart, and you've been waiting to return the favor. I never explained, when I ended our relationship."

"No, you didn't. You wouldn't take my calls. You avoided me at school." When she left the graduation ceremony, he'd spent the day in a stunned malaise.

"And those unanswered questions have festered inside you ever since. What do you want from me—an apology? You're pathetic. Less than a man, if you'd manipulate a child to nurse old wounds."

The assault broke something inside him. A thread of composure Griffin hadn't known was fraying.

"Why did you name her Lark?" he demanded.

The silence was deafening. Stepping too close, Griffin invaded her space.

"Of all the names you could've chosen, why Lark?" With the advantage of height, he pinioned her gaze. "If you have more children, will you use *all* the names we chose? Is Adam next, or Penn? Remind me, Rae. We planned to have two boys, two girls—the perfect combination. What was the name we picked for our second daughter? I can't recall."

Why was he dragging her down this path? Reminding her of the best moments of their youth—reminding himself of the halcyon days when he'd loved her unconditionally? The plans they'd made for college and a family. A fog of confusion overtook him. He was intentionally hurting her. Shame rushed over him in scalding waves.

Stricken, she searched his face. "You've changed, Griffin. I didn't know you were cruel." She inhaled a shuddering breath. "What happened to you?"

The soft rebuke cleared the fog. Only then did Griffin realize he'd miscalculated. They were talking past each other. Like two actors, blind to each other's script.

Rae didn't know about the keepsake. Yuna had *not* returned it. Rae had learned of his acquaintance with her daughter in some other way. But how?

Griffin found the answer. *Quinn told her.*

Sick-hearted, he tore his gaze away. "I'm not cruel."

"No?"

"I'm stupid. It's not an excuse. I'm just stating the facts."

A tear wended down her cheek. She was too proud to brush it away.

"I won't ask you to forgive me. I have no right to question the choices you made. I know that."

The admission softened her the slightest degree. "No, you don't."

"I should've contacted you the first time Lark stopped in. Letting it go on without telling you . . . I'm sorry."

She folded her arms.

"There *is* something I'm not clear on." He hesitated. "You don't owe me an explanation, of course."

Her brows lowered. "Obviously," she muttered.

"Please, Rae."

"What do you want to know?"

"When did Lark tell Quinn about her decision to find her father?"

A weary silence overtook the room. Rae scanned the floor, as if weighing the limits of her kindness. They both knew she owed him nothing.

"Lark told Quinn last September," she said at last. "They were in the high school library. Lark was bragging about how she'd solved the mystery of her missing father. As if the man responsible for half her genome was accidentally misplaced."

"She gave Quinn my name?"

"But nothing else. She wouldn't explain how she'd found you."

"And you're not sure how she did it." A statement, not a question. Rae had given the confirmation Griffin needed: she didn't know Lark had found the box.

"They *were* in the library," she murmured, speaking more to herself than to him.

She was sifting for clues in a puzzle Griffin had already solved.

Rae added, "I suppose Lark found our high school yearbook in the archives. That would make sense."

"And she was planning to contact every boy in our graduating class?" he asked, playing along. Rae was supplying more detail than requested, lowering her guard. It was thrilling when her expression became loose and vulnerable.

"That's right. Lark's creative fairy tale, to find the father waiting to claim her. Naturally you made the top of the list, Griffin. You're, well . . . mysterious." Fleeting amusement crossed her features, then disappeared. "You had to know my daughter. Sometimes she was too smart. Tenacious. And she loved mysteries."

I did know her.

"Why mysterious?" he asked gently.

Chapter 24

"Because you moved away, to Boston," Rae heard herself say. "That would've been enough to impress Lark."

"I've been called a lot of things in my time. Mysterious isn't one of them," Griffin said.

His modesty, coming on the heels of their argument, softened Rae. "Most of the men in our graduating class never left the area," she explained. "They attended nearby colleges or married early. The pharmacist, the mail carrier—Lark knew most of them. Quinn told me . . . never mind." She'd already said too much.

"What did he tell you?"

She cast a furtive glance toward the reception area outside his office. Someone had arrived. A drawer squeaked open. With a diplomatic thud, a cabinet was shut. The sharp scent of coffee reached her nose. Bits of conversation followed.

Rae's stomach tumbled. If she'd stormed into Design Mark five minutes later, she would've humiliated herself in front of the entire staff. Given the tight-knit quality of Chardon and the marvels of social media, it wouldn't have taken long for half the town to learn about it.

What am I doing here?

She remembered his question about Quinn. "It's not important."

"I can't stand the suspense." Griffin offered an engaging smile. No doubt the one he used to close the deal with a prospective client. "C'mon. Tell me."

It was also, she realized, the smile he'd used when they were younger to win her over to his way of thinking. Or to get himself out of hot water if she was irritated by something he'd done. The way he was looking at her brought back the easy rapport they'd once enjoyed.

An unsettling development.

Relenting, she said, "According to Quinn, my daughter planned to fix my relationship with her father. Patch up a broken romance."

"She was naive," he supplied.

Sadness ebbed through the moment's enchantment. "She had nothing to go on, so she built a fairy tale. She assumed once she found her father, everything else would fall into place. At that age, we were just as naive."

"We were."

"It's the danger of innocence. You can't account for the ugliness in the world. Not if you've never experienced it firsthand."

"Ugliness . . . I guess that sums up my own memories." Griffin palmed his forehead. "I'll never understand that year. Everything the White Hurricane destroyed. I carried my regrets for a long time, Rae. I suppose that's why I moved to Boston. I didn't want to spend the rest of my life reliving the past."

"There's no reason you should."

"It's no way to live."

"And yet you've returned."

She'd never thought to wonder why. She'd so thoroughly excised Griffin from her life, it was almost as if he'd never existed.

"Why *did* you come back?"

"The simple answer? Security." He waved a hand to encompass the office. "My father gave me the building, free and clear. If I'm being truthful, however, I missed Ohio. Walking the forests, apple cider in

October—it's quieter here." He stopped then, clearly aware he'd revealed too much. In a formal tone, he added, "Rae, I hope you'll accept my condolences on your loss. I'm deeply sorry. If there's ever anything you need, I'm here. If it's not asking too much, I hope someday we can become friends."

"Thank you."

A muscle in his jaw twitched. "About Lark, her fairy tale . . ." For a long moment he paused, the hesitation on his features ill-concealed. Finally he added, "Talk to Yuna. She'll fill in the missing pieces."

The suggestion took Rae off guard. Yuna could no more divine Lark's motivations than predict the future. If she'd had an inkling of Lark's plan, she would've spoken up months ago.

Griffin held up a palm. "For once, don't argue. Talk to her."

Then his mouth tightened. Which made his tenderness more alarming when he brushed a lock of hair from her cheek. Taking his time, smoothing the strands over her shoulder. The subtle notes of his cologne whirled between them.

His hand fell to his side.

His navy blazer was beautifully cut. The silk tie at his throat expertly knotted. Freed of the anger, Rae saw him fully. Not as the boy who'd accompanied her through childhood and then adolescence. Or as the eager youth who'd taught her French kissing and the pleasures of foreplay.

She saw the man Griffin was now: tall, muscular, comfortable in his own skin. Lines etched the sides of his mouth. His hairline was beginning to recede. Only his grayish-blue eyes, tranquil as a lake, were familiar.

With cool patience he accepted her appraisal. Which made Rae feel foolish.

Her dignity in tatters, she promised to speak with Yuna.

~

Dry potting soil covered the steps outside Design Mark. It crunched underfoot as Rae paused, brows puckering.

Inches away, her car was parked at a crazy angle. With a start, she recalled jumping the curb and leaping out.

What is wrong with me?

An empty flower planter was wedged beneath the bumper. Mortified, she gripped the sides and heaved it out. Driving to Griffin's firm in a state of fury was bad enough. What was she doing, vandalizing the premises?

It's no different than Penny dumping garbage before the Witt Agency.

She lugged the damaged container to the steps. She'd write an apology note. Tuck a check inside, to replace the planter.

A voice came from across the street.

"Rae Langdon!"

From the shadow of the dealership's service bay, Quinn's father strode out.

Panic rooted her to the spot. She'd assumed any future run-in would happen with Penny. Mik Galecki was a more formidable opponent.

He was tall, like Griffin. The similarities ended there. There was something combative in Mik's square face, something off-center in his eyes—like a walking grenade with the safety clip detached.

"What did you tell my son?" He reached her before she could react. "He's not taking our calls."

"For good reason," Rae said. "Quinn doesn't want to talk to you, or Penny."

The matter-of-fact tone was a ruse. It masked the fear bubbling inside her. Mik was momentarily taken aback.

Then rage broke across his features. "Tell him to get home, and I mean today."

"No."

"This isn't a request. You got that?"

A buzzing started in her ears. She was acutely aware of Mik curling his fist.

Bile rose in Rae's throat. "Don't threaten me." She managed to put steel in her spine. "Your wife threw Quinn out. He's not coming back."

"He's not your son. He's mine."

"Get out of my way."

When she attempted to dart around him, Mik blocked her path. "Who do you think you are? Do you think you're better than me? You can't have my son."

"He doesn't belong to you, or anyone." She cast a desperate glance toward the dealership. There was no one outside to come to her aid. "Now, I'm asking you nicely. Please back off."

From the corner of her eye, Rae caught movement. *Griffin.* He swept past her like a bullet.

He shoved Mik back. "Are you threatening Rae?"

He shoved again, harder, and Mik took a hard step off the curb. Mik looked around wildly. Like Rae, he hadn't seen Griffin sprint outside.

"Listen closely, Mik." Griffin stepped into the street to face him. "You can't threaten Rae—ever. Am I making myself understood?"

"Get out of my face. You're not my boss."

A challenge, and Griffin took it up readily. "No, but my father is," he growled. "You're done, Mik. Do yourself a favor and start looking for a new job. I promise you, he *will* fire you."

The warning shuddered fury across Mik's shoulders. He looked ready to deck Griffin. Yet he seemed aware that he was no longer the more dangerous man. Griffin, slow to anger, gave off a menacing air. Rae could nearly taste it.

Mik could too.

Without daring a reply, he strode back to the dealership.

Chapter 25

From the kitchen table, Rae watched the sun dip behind the barn's roofline. Shadows lengthened toward the house, and the trees where Quinn and Connor worked.

The weather was cooperating. It seemed the only positive development in an upsetting day.

Across the table, Yuna peered over the rim of her cup and out the window. Quinn was high in the sixth tree, a long string of lighting slung over his arm. From the ground, Connor shouted directions.

Yuna lowered her peppermint tea. "It's amazing how quickly they're putting up the lights."

"They were only planning to work on the fourth tree today. Maybe the fifth."

"At this rate, they'll finish soon. I can't wait to see the final result."

"It'll be gorgeous," Rae murmured.

Holding her breath, she watched Quinn climb higher. He was having fun, his features animated, his movements fluid and easy. Like a kid discovering new talents and the confidence that came along with them. He planted his feet on a thick branch. Grinning, he gave Connor a thumbs-up.

"You look like a worried mommy bear," Yuna teased. "Quinn has great balance. He climbs to the top shelves in my storage room without batting an eye. Relax."

"I'm concerned he's overdoing it to make me feel better." She recalled their conversation this morning. "He knew I was upset when he told me about Lark's visits with Griffin. The way I lit out of the house in a fury . . . what if I scared him? It's not like he needs more anxiety." She sighed. "Not that I do either."

"That's not the only reason Quinn's working hard. You've been good to him. This is his way of thanking you."

"I suppose."

"Will you tell him about the altercation with Mik?"

"Absolutely not. He's already scared of his father. More so now that he's blocked his calls. Telling him that Mik's livid about the living arrangements . . . Nope. Not a great idea. I *did* check with the high school principal."

"You called the high school again? The principal won't let Penny or Mik on school grounds. Quinn's a legal adult. They can't barge into the high school and insist on seeing him."

Which Rae understood, but she'd been desperate for more reassurance. The look on Mik's face when he'd confronted her this morning—she'd been frightened. For her own safety, of course. Once she'd arrived at work, she began to understand how much danger Mik posed to his son. What would set off his temper next?

Breaking into her thoughts, Yuna said, "Quinn has stopped parking in front of the craft emporium when he works. I didn't notice right away."

A wise choice, in Rae's estimation. "He's parking in the alley behind the buildings?"

"Yes, and doing his best to avoid his parents." Despite the gravity of the situation, Yuna chuckled. "I told him you'd been using the alley to avoid Penny. That might've given him the incentive to park there. Whatever works, right?"

"Has Penny been around Chardon Square? Please tell me she hasn't."

"Not that I've seen. With you and Quinn both staying out of sight, maybe she's stopped driving in circles around the square. Or she's landed a new job. With any luck, it's a job in Mentor or Willoughby—miles away from Chardon. She can only go so long without pulling down a paycheck."

"She'll need the money—Griffin made it clear he'll talk to his father. Mik's job is gone."

"Threatening a woman in broad daylight—Mik *should* lose his job. And I'm thrilled Griffin took him on. Probably the first time anyone in town has ever stood up to him. What I'd give to have watched."

"He did more than stand up to Mik. I thought they'd come to blows. It was awful."

"The outcome was good. Griffin came to the rescue."

"If you're trying to make me feel better, forget it. Griffin rode in like a white knight *after* I rammed my car into the planter outside his firm. Oh, and barged into his office screaming. I wouldn't let him get a word in edgewise. Then I blamed him for a situation he did *not* set in motion. What's wrong with me?"

Yuna appeared torn between pity and a bad case of giggles. "Did you chew him out?" For a best friend, she rated top of the class. But the situation was *not* funny.

"Yes, I did," Rae admitted. Knowing that her dumber moves tickled Yuna's funny bone managed to increase her discomfort. Mostly because she never should've stormed into Griffin's office in the first place. A smarter woman would've thought it all out first. "Don't put me on the hot seat. I'm not going there."

"You don't have a choice. My life has been reduced to morning sickness and my five-year-old complaining about the 'mean baby.' As if a feisty embryo is responsible for the removal of red meat from my household." Yuna batted her lashes. "C'mon—dish. If I can't live vicariously through you, what have I got?"

"Thanks, Yuna. Like I'm not embarrassed enough."

Walking on glass was preferable to divulging the details. That was the problem with anger. After it hoisted your common sense out the window, it made you behave badly.

"I won't stop teasing until you give up the goods. What did you say to Griffin?"

"I made a complete fool of myself. He, on the other hand, was nothing but decent. He even helped me into my car after he sent Mik packing. As if I hadn't just read him the riot act. And the way he handled Mik . . . Yuna, I wasn't even aware Griffin *had* a temper. When we were young, he never got mad. The biggest rise you'd get out of him was irritation. I thought he was born without the trait that makes someone like me behave stupidly."

The impish glee faded from Yuna's features. "Don't be too hard on yourself. Yes, you can be impulsive. But you didn't know Lark had found the keepsake. Or that she'd given it to Griffin. If anyone should take the fall, it's me. I should've returned the box right after Griffin gave it to me."

"Why didn't you?"

"It seemed best to wait before dropping another bomb on your head. With Penny dumping garbage in front of your office and shouting cuss words whenever she drove by . . ."

"It wasn't right to hit me up with more bad news?"

"If I'd known Quinn was keeping secrets—and would come clean this morning—I wouldn't have delayed."

Yuna's attention strayed to the center of the table.

The lacquered box caught the sun's golden light. The tiny rivers of glass sparkled.

Drawing the box near, Rae smoothed her palm across the pleasingly glossy surface. "Lark must've found it last summer." She dimly recalled a sweltering August day—rushing to leave for the office—and Lark trudging out in her pajamas, moody and needing a project to occupy the hours. "Near the end of summer, Lark was incredibly bored.

I suggested she spend the day organizing her bedroom for the upcoming school year. Or help Connor with chores around the house. Later, she called me at work—she'd been rummaging around in the attic. I assumed she was sorting through some of my mother's old things. My dad wasn't with her. If he'd gone up to keep her company, he would've recognized the box."

"And told her to get your permission before taking it," Yuna supplied.

"I'm sure she began devising a plan to contact Griffin soon after."

"You know, this might explain why Katherine has been less than kind toward you. From her perspective, she has good reason."

"Such as?"

"Rae, she was dating Griffin."

The news came as a surprise. "When?"

"Last year."

"How long were they dating?"

"I'm not sure exactly. Not long. But if Lark was bragging to Quinn that she'd found her father, what if she also told Katherine's daughter, Stella? Or Griffin's niece?"

Lark was gone, but Rae's instinct to protect her daughter remained fully intact. "Even if she was bragging to the other girls, why would it matter? Yes, Lark was friends with Stella and Jackie, and she may have told them. But they treated her like a second-class friend. Why would they care if she was bragging?"

"Think about it. If Lark told them while Griffin and Katherine *were* dating, it might've irked Stella. She's a nice enough girl, but she's the Queen Bee."

"All that Thomerson wealth—she's not used to having competition."

Yuna nodded. "If Lark announced that Griffin was her father . . . it probably didn't go down well. Stella wouldn't have liked another girl boasting about the man dating her mother. It might've embarrassed her."

Dazed, Rae fell back in her chair. "Lark didn't want to attend the slumber party," she murmured. She looked up suddenly. "I knew she was on the outs with one of her girlfriends."

"Lark wouldn't tell you who she was fighting with?"

The question made Rae shake her head with bemusement. "Wait until Kameko reaches adolescence. There's lots of stuff your teenage daughter won't share. You'll do your best to dredge up the intel on all sorts of issues, but you'll get nowhere fast."

Yuna rolled her eyes. "Gosh, I can't wait."

"All I knew was that Lark had a falling-out with one of the girls. A disagreement over who-knows-what. Girls that age have the silliest battles."

"And the way I heard it, Katherine wasn't happy when Griffin broke it off." Yuna's shoulders lifted in a show of unease. "Last year, when I heard they were going out . . . should I have told you?"

"Of course not," Rae said too quickly. Regret feathered through her, along with the rush of "what if" questions she'd learned to suppress. Pushing them away, she added, "My relationship with Griffin ended in high school. Months before we graduated. I'm not even sure when he left for Ohio University—fast, is what I heard eventually. I guess he spent the summer working down in Athens before starting classes in the fall."

"You're sure it doesn't matter?"

"Yuna, I last dated Griffin sixteen years ago. We're different people now. This morning I humiliated myself in front of a man who's basically a stranger. I'm sure he thinks I'm rude and obnoxious." She picked up her coffee, her emotions in flux—about Griffin, but even more so, Lark. Was it possible she'd argued with Stella over Griffin? The thought made her unexpectedly sad. "I am a dope. This morning I accused him of encouraging my daughter. He hadn't, obviously. When Lark first showed up in his office, it must've thrown him."

Yuna's lips pursed. The question she was too courteous to ask floated between them.

Was Lark correct? Was Griffin her father?

She'd never pose the question. For good reason—she was Rae's dearest friend. Their bond was airtight. And she understood: if Rae had wanted to share the name missing on her daughter's birth certificate, she would've done so before now.

Instead, Yuna appraised the lacquered box with palpable respect. "I didn't open it. Griffin wasn't keen about discussing the contents. I can tell you aren't either."

"No, I'm not." Rae took a meager sip of her coffee. "I *do* need to apologize to Griffin."

How did one compose an apology that was years overdue? It seemed an impossible task.

"Leave it for now. Griffin won't think less of you. For whatever the reason, you've both gone out of your way to avoid each other. What happened this morning doesn't change anything." Yuna offered a comforting smile. "You're both good people. Lark's fairy tale no longer matters. It's best to move on."

"You're right."

"I usually am."

Rae swallowed around the lump in her throat. "Have I told you today that I love you?"

"You have not." Affection brimmed on Yuna's features. "And I love you too."

"How's your tummy? I left mouthwash in the guest bathroom, just in case."

Yuna lifted her cup. "The peppermint tea is doing the trick." She'd brought along her laptop. Flipping it open, she added, "Kameko's play date lasts another hour. Since we've both knocked off work early, want to tackle another item for the June fundraiser? We still haven't decided on a theme."

~

On the second floor of Marks Auto, his father's private area was a hawk's nest overseeing the activity below.

The sales staff, the office staff, the service reps—all were relegated to cubbyholes on the main floor. What those offices lacked in size, they made up for in privacy. They weren't visible from above.

With two carryout bags in his fist, Griffin strode from the elevator.

The balcony outside his father's office ran a good length above the showroom below, where a select group of new-model cars and trucks gleamed beneath spotlights. At the circular customer service desk, a young couple was flipping through a Marks Auto brochure on financing options. Near the back of the showroom, behind a nine-foot partition, part of the cafeteria was also visible. Though employees were required to punch in and out for lunch, it hardly mattered. No one lingered for long, not with the boss able to spy from above.

Griffin checked his phone. It was twelve on the dot. *Perfect.*

Mik entered the lunchroom. After three days of this cat-and-mouse game, the mechanic was no longer caught unawares.

His angry gaze lifted to the balcony. Loathing narrowed Griffin's eyes.

The staring match lasted for eight seconds before Mik surrendered. Two seconds longer than yesterday, Griffin mused.

Frowning, Mik strode to the cafeteria's vending machines. He dug cash from his pocket.

From his office, Everett finished barking into the phone. "How long are you going to keep this up?" he shouted.

Griffin strolled inside.

"You tell me, Dad—he's still here, and you and I had an understanding." When his father refused to pick up on the comment, Griffin paused before the mahogany desk. He held up the larger of the two carryout bags. "I brought you turkey on rye. If I keep bringing you steak sandwiches, Mom will get after me. There's also a side of fries. And a fruit cup, if you're feeling adventurous."

With irritation his father appraised the bag dropped before his nose. Everett was a large bull of a man, with a potbelly and a ferocious intellect. He liked appearing in the showroom unannounced to watch his minions scatter.

"You don't need to bring me lunch, short stuff. I have a staff at my beck and call."

Short stuff. At seventy, Everett stood six foot four. Age had stolen an inch of his height.

Griffin was six two.

"It's my pleasure," he said, ignoring the bait.

"You've been working across the street for two years now. We never 'do lunch.'" Everett scratched the white thatch of hair rimming his temples. "Why is that?"

"You know why, Dad. If we make this a habit, I'll get hooked on antacids. I'm a man in my prime. I shouldn't have to deal with heartburn."

"You come over for family dinners. I don't see you popping antacids."

"That's different. You ease off the gas when Mom's around."

Superiority glossed Everett's smile. "You may have a point." He waved a benevolent hand. "Take a seat."

Three chairs were arranged before the desk. Hard-backed, steel—they resembled prisoners lined up before a firing squad.

Griffin tossed his bagged lunch on the nearest one. "Hold that thought," he murmured, falling upon inspiration. A new tactic.

Just to keep things interesting with Mik.

At the balcony, he watched the mechanic tear open a bag of peanuts. Earbuds stuck in his big, square head, his foot tapping along. Griffin drilled him with a hard stare. Mik looked around, starting suddenly when he encountered Griffin's expression.

Nuts scattered across the floor.

Everett shouted, "Stop badgering him! I told you I'd talk to him, and I did!"

Griffin came back inside. "I didn't ask you to talk to him. I want Mik fired." Rustling the bag open, he withdrew his lunch.

Dodging the remark, his father landed his competitive gaze on the container. "What'd you get for yourself?"

"A salad, with ahi tuna."

"Lettuce is a side dish. A man needs a hearty lunch."

"And how long have you been taking statins?" When his father shrugged, Griffin switched topics. "What did you tell Mik?" For three days now, he'd been unsuccessful at prying the details loose.

"You first. Why was Rae at your firm on Monday? You never explained. Are you designing a website for the Witt Agency?"

"No."

Everett smirked. "I know that, short stuff. I called Evelyn Witt to check."

"Then why'd you ask?"

"To see you squirm, I suppose." With relish, his father bit into the turkey on rye. "The way I hear it, Rae almost rammed the building. The girl who left you in the dust back in high school, aiming her car like a bullet—craziest story I've heard in weeks. Why was she fired up?"

"It's complicated, Dad."

"Does this complication involve your sister?"

"The two issues are mildly related."

Griffin speared a chunk of tuna. It was maddening how his father took every conversation hostage.

"According to your mother, Sally's not speaking to you. Winnie said that's why you missed our last family dinner."

How to mend the relationship with his sister still eluded Griffin. Yet after Monday's events, the falling-out with Sally seemed a minor issue.

Getting back on point, he said, "Let me make this clear. Mik was out of control when he confronted Rae in front of Design Mark. If I hadn't intervened, he would've struck her. Dad, I'm a mature adult. I know when a man is a threat. Give him a severance package, then kick him to the curb."

"He was mouthing off. Which is bad, I agree."

Finishing his sandwich, Everett balled up the wrapper. He wasn't used to anyone telling him what to do. He'd spent a lifetime calling the shots, with no one second-guessing his decisions. But three days of Griffin's hardball lobbying was wearing him down.

Sensing an opening, Griffin pressed harder. "Mik has a drinking problem. His wife does too. Their homelife is a powder keg, and they aren't happy about Quinn moving out. You *do* remember Quinn, don't you? The little boy who used to spend every Saturday in the service bay because Mik dragged him to work? That kid should've been in Little League or horsing around on a playground. You remember, Dad. Mom used to show up at the dealership every Saturday to feed Quinn home-cooked meals and work on his reading skills."

His father picked at his fries. "I remember." Falling back in his chair, he began rocking.

"Quinn lives with Rae now. He's been at her place since February."

"That's why Mik's angry?"

"Correct."

The chair stopped rocking. Evidently, hearing the whole story gave him pause. Griffin wondered if he'd made a mistake, burying the lede. He should've told his father at the outset about Quinn moving into Rae's place—if only to make him take seriously the threat Mik posed. He hadn't because the boy's living arrangements shouldn't matter. The way Mik had threatened Rae was reason enough to fire him.

The chair groaned as Everett set it back in motion, his expression cooling. Inexplicably, he sent the conversation in a new direction.

"Son, you've always been a disappointment. I've made my peace with it. I doubt you have a clue how much you've passed up, turning down the job as my second-in-command. Marks Auto is worth millions. The most profitable dealership in Geauga County, bar none. In plain English, I can't make you assume control of my life's work when I retire."

The words were a blade, cutting Griffin to the quick.

But he managed to chuckle. "Not even if you beg."

"Have it your way, smart-ass. I'll leave the dealership to your sister and Trenton—who closes three sales a month, if he's lucky. But you're my son, Griffin. You have an obligation to carry on my name. You can't do that by starting up again with Rae. She crushed your heart under her boot when she was a kid."

"Drop it, Dad."

Everett wasn't listening; from his standpoint, his expectations were all that mattered. "Rae took off and had a baby on the fly," he continued, "then dumped that guy too. Oh, there were people who wondered about her pregnancy, especially when she began to show that summer, after your high school graduation. But don't you worry, Griffin. People knew Everett Marks raised his son right. Everyone in town knew my son would never stick a toe out of line. The Marks family, why, we're upstanding people. I'm a pillar of the community."

In anguish, Griffin briefly closed his eyes. He suddenly understood why he'd stopped dating Katherine in a hurry. She'd reminded him of Everett. Outward facing, concerned only with her image. Focused solely on how the world viewed her.

His father wasn't finished. "I loved Rae back then," he admitted. "It still tickles me, how a girl could heft a rifle and pick off a target every time. I looked forward to the babies she'd give you. Figured someday I'd have a grandson in the marines or heading a SWAT team. But Rae Langdon is flighty. Take my advice, Griffin. Set your sights elsewhere."

There was nothing in the monologue worth dignifying. Checking his anger, Griffin came to his feet.

"Listen close, Dad. I'm going to spell it out. Mik isn't finished with Rae or Quinn. Are you willing to gamble their safety?" Striding around the desk, he towered over his father. "Fire Mik. No one else in the county will take him on—everyone knows he's not worth it. Let Mik go, and he'll move someplace else."

A chill descended between them. Welcoming it, Griffin kept his attention trained on his father. He'd had enough. If Everett made the wrong decision, they were done, over. He'd walk out of his life for good.

A prospect his father clearly sensed as he rubbed his chin with swift, agitated movements. "All right," he muttered.

"Mik's gone?"

"At the end of his shift." Everett snapped up his wrist, checked his watch. "In three hours."

"Do yourself a favor. Don't tell him until he's clocked out."

Without awaiting a reply, Griffin walked out.

Chapter 26

Teenagers flooded into the corridor. The school day was over.

Letting the crowd carry him forward, Quinn scanned the sea of faces. When his gaze alighted on a swish of long brown hair near the lockers, his heart lifted.

"Hey, Ava."

She twirled the lock. "Hey! I was hoping to see you."

"Here I am."

Pulling open her locker, she hoisted out her book bag. "We're still meeting, right?"

"Five o'clock?"

She smiled. "I'll be there."

Most days when Quinn worked at Yuna's Craft Emporium, he had a standing date to meet Ava at the coffee shop on Chardon Square. Not a date, exactly. More like chilling over a latte in hopes it would lead to something better. Ava showed up after cheerleading practice. Or she walked up to the coffee shop from her home on North Street. When she did, she sent a text and Quinn took a twenty-minute break from stocking shelves. Usually he'd find Yuna grinning at him as he pulled on his coat and dashed into the alley.

He bounced on the toes of his new boots. "Should I carry that?" he asked, nodding at her book bag. He wasn't sure if Ava was his girlfriend or not. He did want to prove he was a gentleman—in case she wasn't sure. "I don't mind. I'll carry it for you to the school bus."

"I'm good." She slung the bag over her shoulder. "Walk me out?"

"Sure."

They merged with the students flowing toward Chardon High's entryway.

Quinn was nearly a head taller. Doing his best, he shielded Ava from kids knocking elbows and shoving their way outside. He tried to think up words to say.

When teenagers dated, they were supposed to talk. Only he wasn't sure of the right topics. The noise level was deafening, and big crowds made him nervous. Ava didn't seem to mind that he was tongue-tied. He was *always* tongue-tied.

At the coffee shop, she carried the conversation. He listened. The arrangement was better than perfect.

When they reached the doors, Ava took his hand. Just for a second, long enough to give his fingers an affectionate squeeze.

She dashed outside.

Kids pushed and shouted. Quinn walked slowly, a stone in a fast-moving river. Only he was rushing or floating inside in a way no one could see. He was lighter than air. He watched Ava climb into the school bus, her glossy hair swinging across her back.

If he didn't get a move on, he'd be late for work. But he couldn't make his feet move fast. Not with his fingers tingling with warmth. Wending his way to the parking lot, Quinn studied his hand. Ava had touched him. Did it mean she was his girlfriend?

Engines revved as kids shouted to their friends. Some of the teenagers walked diagonally through the lot, past the cars, talking loudly and swinging tennis rackets. The tennis courts sat in a grassy bowl of acreage not far from the school complex. The kids looked eager to bat around a few balls even if winter wasn't really over. Far behind the lot, a thick buffer of fir trees formed a green necklace. Quinn paused to take it all in.

The view was incredible, the trees emerald green and the birds chirping and the air smelling sweet. The sun was almost too bright; Quinn shut his eyes a moment as the pain lanced him like a blade, slicing through the happiness, bringing with it a sense of foreboding.

The good stuff never lasts. Something bad will happen. It always does.

A girl skirted past, running to her car. A cloud of blue exhaust seared Quinn's nose as more cars rumbled to life and sped from the lot. Teenagers like him, on their way to afternoon jobs or to meet with friends. Only they weren't like him. Their parents weren't drunks; no one ever hit them.

"Galecki, move!"

A palm landed on his back, shoving Quinn forward. The air whooshed from his lungs, and he nearly fell. Ben Dolan, the school's quarterback, strode past with a satisfied grin.

Fear raced through Quinn as Ben walked away. He felt small then, insignificant. Almost too frightened to move.

When the last of the cars disappeared, he climbed into his truck.

~

On Friday, Rae cleared off her desk at four o'clock. Yesterday and on Tuesday, she'd worked through the dinner hour. Both days provided a diversion from worry over Quinn's parents, or reliving the embarrassment of her behavior at Griffin's firm on Monday.

Leaving early posed no problem. Rae grabbed her purse. Slipping out to the alley, she climbed into her car.

The workweek was over. No one on the Square—not Yuna, the other shop owners, or any of the professionals in the various firms—had glimpsed Penny's car circling Chardon Square. Five days running.

An optimistic trend. Rae prayed it would hold.

Pulling out of the alley, she considered stopping at the drugstore. She didn't own stationery. Buy a blank card to compose an apology note to Griffin? She had no idea what to write. She couldn't, however, drop a check in the mail for the damaged planter without an accompanying note. It would be rude. She'd already embarrassed herself thoroughly.

Her phone buzzed. She put her father on speaker.

"Are you still at the office?" He sounded excited.

"Just left. Stopping at the drugstore. I'll be home afterward."

"Can the drugstore wait? Make the trip in the morning?"

"Sure. Why?" She hesitated. "Should I pick up dinner?" This morning Quinn had left for school early; she wasn't sure if he was cooking tonight.

"Already taken care of," Connor assured her. "I'm having Italian delivered. Veal parmesan, ravioli—the works. Did you know the only Italian food Quinn's eaten is pizza? That must be some sort of crime."

In Rae's book, it was. She loved Italian. "I thought he was into all things French," she joked.

"When *he* cooks. Quinn's ready to branch out, and we're celebrating."

"What's the occasion?"

"We've got half the lights strung. Actually, a little more than that—we stopped about a third of an acre from the house. Then we went ahead and started work on the lights near the barn. To get an idea of what the final result will look like. It's something to see, Rae. Hurry on home."

Clearing the traffic on the square, Rae accelerated. "Oh, Dad—that's wonderful!" Bringing her late mother's last artistic creation to life meant a lot to him.

Moisture gathered in her eyes.

It means a lot to me too.

A light drizzle pelted the windshield. Turning into the farm's winding driveway, Rae sighed. There was little chance the recent, unseasonably warm temps would continue. The maple tree on the front lawn was still without buds; the slate walkway leading to the front steps wore a sheen of dampness. Like many people in northeast Ohio, she watched Canada's weather in March. Lake Erie was the shallowest of the Great Lakes, and late-winter storms that blew southward often brought more unwanted snow.

No wonder Connor was using every spare minute to work on Hester's design. He'd been grousing all week: his earlier prediction was off. Winter hadn't finished pummeling the town just yet.

There was no one in the house. From out back, Shelby's rapid-fire barking cut off suddenly. The dog was in the middle of a game of fetch, Rae mused, placing her purse and briefcase on the couch. As she wended her way through the kitchen and then the mudroom, the raucous barking resumed.

Streaking past the barn, Shelby caught a tennis ball. Rae stepped outside.

And gasped.

The trees seemed adorned with thousands of colorful fireflies. The tiny bulbs, in a variety of shapes, emitted light at different levels—some with sharp brilliance, others with a deeper, milder glow. Rae's thoughts tripped back to the summer before her mother died. The countless days Hester spent working and reworking her design, throwing out one schematic and then another; her eyes flashing when Rae or Connor teased that she was obsessing over a silly lighting display. Who cared how they strung it all up?

Now the reason for Hester's diligence was breathtaking to behold. On the trees nearest the house, swirling waves of purple found their counterpoint in moon-shaped swatches of gold. The fifth tree away stood in contrast, blazing in shades of blue. Half an acre past, the barn stood untouched, still shedding paint chips, but it was easy to imagine the structure brought back to life with a new coat of red paint. The trees midway across the expanse were dark, but the majestic oak and the two shorter maples near the barn were ablaze in shades of silver, green, and a surprisingly compatible rose-tinted hue.

She watched her father walk toward the barn. Connor paused. Shelby dropped the ball at his feet. Scooping it up, he tossed it toward the pasture.

Quinn appeared from behind the third tree. "Rae!"

She hadn't noticed him, fiddling with the lighting winding around the trunk.

Approaching, he smiled. "What do you think?"

"Oh, Quinn . . . this is the most . . ."

"The most . . . what?"

Anticipating a compliment, he rocked back on his heels. Quinn didn't have much experience with confidence, or ego-boosting moments. He was eager to learn.

Rae glanced at the steel-colored clouds. Icy bits of rain pelted her face. She didn't care.

Mom, are you seeing this? It's beautiful!

Puzzlement stole Quinn's bravado. "Are you . . . crying?"

Overcome, Rae pressed a palm to her mouth. *Lark, are you with Grandma? Are you seeing this, baby girl? Aren't the lights pretty?*

"Wow. You are crying." Blushing, he looked away. "I didn't know you were a crier. I mean, you're kind of tough for a lady. No—that's not what I meant. I just didn't think you did the weepy thing. At least not often."

His knowledge of pure joy was limited. Or nonexistent.

Eyes welling, Rae pulled him into her arms.

"You sweet, beautiful young man." She landed a smacking kiss on his lightly stubbled cheek. He wasn't sure how to react, and she laughed through her tears. Without giving him time to figure it out, she cupped his face and kissed his other, blushing cheek. "Quinn, this is the best gift—ever! Thank you. Really. The last months have been so hard, I've been so down—" She broke off, laughing again. Then she was crying, harder now, as she hugged him mightily. "You are simply the best. I love you."

"I can't breathe, Rae. Let go."

"Oh. Sorry." She released him from her affectionate hold.

"No problem." His shoulders inched toward his ears. "I love you too . . . if it's okay to say."

"Of course it is." Unable to resist, she pinched his cheek. "You are the best!"

Shelby barked.

The sound broke the sweet interlude.

Connor reached them. "The lights look great, don't they?" He caught a whiff of the tenderness passing between his daughter and their young houseguest. "This looks like a Kodak moment. Aw, Rae—your nose is all runny. You're not going to cry, are you?"

"Too late," Quinn said. "She's already gone there." He regarded them both with confusion. "What's a Kodak moment?"

~

They ate a ridiculous amount of Italian food. Quinn's dog, doing her part, sampled veal and sausage and greedily accepted a bowl of ravioli. Rae wasn't sure if red sauce was healthy for a dog, so she rinsed the pasta first.

As they were finishing up, Shelby flopped down in the center of the kitchen and dozed on her back. Her paws twitched. She resembled a beached whale with fur.

"Well, I'm done." Connor gestured at the empty platters strewn across the table. "You two clean up. My knees are on fire. I need to soak these old bones in Epsom salts."

Wrinkling his nose, Quinn leaned toward Rae. "What's he talking about?" he whispered.

"Soaking in a bath."

"Got it," he murmured as Connor shuffled past. "Sleep tight."

Connor gave a thumbs-up.

221

When he was gone, they shared a companionable silence. Their first. Privately, Rae wondered why she hadn't displayed physical affection weeks ago. She was a mother; she understood the power of touch. Children needed words of encouragement, but they thrived most when they were supplied with the basic human need of the shelter of an adult's arms.

Granted, Quinn wasn't a child. Legally, he'd reached adulthood. Yet she doubted he'd received much nurturing. When was the last time Mik or Penny had hugged him? Their disheartening abuses were painful to consider, a dark terrain Rae preferred not to visit. Were there other, kinder moments?

Quinn said, "Do you mind helping me clean up?"

A trace of nerves rimmed the comment. He was already ferrying dishes to the sink.

Rae scraped back her chair. "Do you have homework? I can take care of this."

Opening the dishwasher, he darted a glance. "It's Friday, Rae. I have all weekend to study." He peered out the window at the darkness. "Connor says we'll get snow tonight. We won't be able to work on the rest of the lights."

"Are you scheduled at the craft emporium tomorrow?"

"Yeah." Moving past, he fetched more dishes. "I meant on Sunday. That's when I was hoping to work on the lights. It'll look cool, once we finish." A spoon skittered off the platter he carried.

When he returned to the sink, she stared at him pointedly. "Quinn, what's the matter? Five minutes ago, you were perfectly relaxed. Now you seem nervous."

"I am." Setting the platter on the counter, he inhaled a deep breath. "Can I ask you something?"

"Always and anytime. I'm here for you. I hope you know that by now."

His gaze dropped to his feet. Which kicked in her mothering instincts as she neared.

"There's nothing you can tell me about Lark that will upset me," she said evenly.

"That's not true. You were really mad when I told you about Griffin."

"And I was wrong."

"You were?"

"I shouldn't have lit out of the house the way I did. Quinn, even grown-ups misbehave at one time or another. I'm not talking about the really bad things grown-ups can do, like getting drunk, or—" Rae ground to a halt. Emotion welled up quickly. Finding her footing, she pressed her hand to his cheek. "Or when they behave really badly, like when they hurt a child. That should never happen."

When her hand fell away, Quinn's Adam's apple bobbed in his throat.

"I'm talking about regular-variety, dumb stuff," she added. "Grown-ups should know to think before they react. Most of the time we do. The point I'm trying to make is that you can tell me anything, and not worry that I'll get mad or upset. I want you to confide in me. You *are* a fine young man, and I'm on your side."

"What we need to talk about . . . it's about the night Lark died. I guess you know why I went over to the Thomersons'. I knew I probably wouldn't see Lark, but she needed moral support."

"I know," she murmured, "my daughter had been thinking about skipping the party." It was easy to imagine Quinn pacing outside Katherine's elegant property, sending Lark comforting text messages.

"Yeah, but there's something else."

"Go on."

"Rae, the police got it wrong. I don't mean they messed up their conclusions exactly. Or maybe that is what I mean." He blew out a frustrated breath. "I'm not sure."

Shock held Rae transfixed. *What did the police get wrong?*

The dog rolled onto her side. She yipped in her sleep.

A diversion, and Quinn took it readily. He skirted past her, clearly needing distance before continuing. Lowering to his knees, he began stroking his dog. Long, even strokes. Calming Shelby as she slept. Calming himself.

"You know about the first part," he said, "when I climbed over the wall surrounding Mrs. Thomerson's pool. The police got that right. I climbed over in a hurry. I tore my jeans on those prickly bushes."

The brick wall enclosing Katherine's pool area was seven feet tall. "The holly bushes," Rae supplied. The PD's report had given the details. Quinn scrambled onto the holly bushes to grab hold of the wall's top edge. Then he'd gone over.

"Holly bushes—right. That's what they're called. Anyway, the first officer showed up. Young guy, not much older than me."

"Officer Collins." A new recruit, only three months on the job.

"That's his name. I was still in the pool with Lark. I didn't want to leave her there. Not even when Officer Collins ordered me out. I told him to go away, just leave me alone. There was lots of commotion—the girls screaming from inside the house, and Mrs. Thomerson kept pacing around the pool, slipping. It was all keeping Officer Collins awfully busy." Quinn hesitated before adding, "I was crying pretty hard."

At her sides Rae clenched her fists, her nails digging into her flesh. "I can imagine," she whispered, trying hard not to.

"I was scared. I didn't believe Lark was dead." Quinn brushed a shaky hand across his eyes. "Sometimes I still don't."

An ache tore through Rae. "Me either," she agreed.

"I don't know how much time passed before the other guys showed up. I remember yelling at them, making them angry. They climbed down the steel ladder into the pool. They had to drag me out. I didn't want to leave Lark down there alone."

Rae pushed away the image. "The other guys . . . you mean the other police officers?"

Nodding, Quinn pulled his knees to his chest. The telling was hard on him.

"The first guy—Officer Collins—he put me in his cruiser. I was talking real fast by then. Telling him I only trespassed because I'd heard Lark on the other side. I heard her shouting and knew something was wrong. I guess I was in shock. Plus, I didn't know about my Mirabelle. No. Mara—"

"Your Miranda rights?"

Again, Quinn nodded. "Collins drove me to the station. He was being smug. Like he'd solved the case right there. He gestured to a lady detective, and they took me into a room. Accused me of killing Lark. Pushing her into the pool after a lover's quarrel. They kept asking the same questions, over and over. Hoping to trip me up and get a different answer. I was really scared by then."

This part Rae knew well. An interrogation mishandled. A minor grilled without a shred of evidence of wrongdoing. By sheer luck, the night-shift receptionist—arriving about ninety minutes into Quinn's interrogation—was the daughter of Theresa Russo, Chardon High's principal. After receiving a call from her daughter and hurrying to the precinct, Theresa demanded a halt to the interrogation.

Quinn's parents never arrived to stand by their son. Predictably, they were out making the rounds of the bars. From what Rae had gleaned from Theresa since Quinn had moved in with her, the Galeckis didn't get around to returning the PD's calls until the following morning. By then, Quinn was holed up in his bedroom on a chilly Sunday morning, the damage done.

"You were scared," Rae prodded, "and you wanted to go home. You didn't want to tell Officer Collins and the lady detective anything else. You were afraid they wouldn't believe you."

"And they'd never let me go home. Maybe put me in jail, even."

"Quinn, it's okay. You didn't do anything wrong. You tried to save my daughter." In agony, Rae pulled in a quick breath. "What did you forget to tell the officers?"

On the floor, Quinn began rocking. Like a small child, overwhelmed.

"Rae, I didn't climb over the wall *only* because I heard Lark shout. That's what the police wrote up in the report. I climbed over because I heard Lark *arguing*."

"She was . . . are you sure?"

"I'm positive. She was fighting with another girl. Their voices carried—it was easy to hear them. I just couldn't hear what they were yelling about. They were talking fast, shouting at each other. Whatever they were mad about, it was bad."

Quinn stopped rocking so quickly, Rae flinched. The moisture evaporated from her mouth.

Don't tell me the rest. A trapdoor opened beneath her world, revealing a truth too dark to contemplate. Too dark to endure.

Quinn's eyes misted as they found hers. "There was another girl there," he insisted, "someone else who'd gone to the slumber party. I'm not implying someone pushed Lark in, but she wasn't alone when she fell. I just thought you should know."

Rae paled.

That was exactly what he meant.

Chapter 27

Rae stared unseeing at the TV.

Quinn was in his bedroom.

After finishing the story, he'd appeared physically ill. Traumatized by the memory. Rocking on the floor, his arms tight around his knees. Secrets were corrosive, especially when they were bottled up for too long. Rae knew this from bitter experience—her own secrets had weakened her relationship with her late daughter and tested her father's love and his patience as he reluctantly learned to live with them. Quinn, however, felt somehow complicit in her daughter's death. As if he could've stopped an argument between two girls from leading to tragedy.

Masking her shock at everything he'd described, she'd thanked him for sharing the true events surrounding Lark's death. Then she helped him to his feet.

Hugging Quinn gently, his lean body slack in her arms, she proffered reassurance. *I'm glad you told me. Really grateful. Now put that night out of mind. Quinn—it's not your fault. You did great. You did all that you could when you heard the girls fighting. Lark was your friend, and you climbed over the wall to try to help her out. There's nothing more you could've done.*

A flurry of reassurances; he remained silent through them all, his gaze unable to meet hers when she released him. Head bowed, he'd trudged down the hallway with Shelby on his heels.

Now turmoil seared Rae's thoughts.

Last October, eight teenagers had attended the slumber party. They formed Stella Thomerson's crew of popular girls. Most of the girls were casual acquaintances of Lark's. She hadn't known most of them well enough to be at odds regarding anything of importance. Certainly nothing so earth-shattering as to lead to a shouting match outside on a snowy autumn night. In the popular crowd, Lark was an outlier. A second-tier friend, a tagalong.

She'd been surprised that Stella had invited her at all.

Wheeling her thoughts back to Monday, Rae dissected the conversation with Yuna, when she'd stopped by in the early afternoon while Quinn and Connor were hanging the decorative lights. Rae picked through everything they'd discussed with the thoroughness of a detective sifting through clues. How she'd described making a fool of herself at Griffin's firm that morning. How the conversation veered to Lark as Yuna launched a further shock when she placed the keepsake—which Rae had assumed was forgotten, a relic hidden in her attic—on the table between them. And then described Lark's plan.

Rae, if Lark was bragging that Griffin was her father . . . it probably didn't go down well with Stella.

Was Lark quarreling with Stella that night? Having an argument that became so heated, they took it outside? Of the popular girls, Stella was the Queen Bee. The others did her bidding whenever she liked. She was also more reserved than some of her friends—not the sort to engage in a shouting match. At least not in Rae's experience. In all the years she'd known Katherine's daughter, she couldn't recall a time she'd witnessed Stella even bicker with one of the other girls.

Rae turned and tested the possibilities racing through her mind, rearranging them like the pieces of a Rubik's Cube. Perhaps Stella held back. If she was furious with Lark, she could've asked one of the other girls to do the dirty work. Argue with Lark outside, without witnesses.

Any one of them would've jumped at the chance. A way to earn brownie points with the Queen Bee.

The quiet descending upon the house felt oppressive. Her stomach in knots, Rae flicked off the TV. A gust of wind rattled against the windows before hurrying off, allowing the silence to flood back in.

Sifting for clues secondhand would never uncover the truth. All Rae had was a trail of pure conjecture based on the events Quinn had described. There was only one reliable fact: Lark was gone, her life cut short in the most tragic way. There was no proof she'd been fighting with Stella—or anyone else, for that matter. *Over Griffin, of all things.* Because Griffin was dating Katherine at the time, and Stella may have reacted badly to Lark's boasts.

Am I the one who's overreacting?

Assuming Lark had argued with one of the other teens, it probably meant nothing. They fought, and then the other girl went back inside. Lark stayed outside, dangerously near the icy, empty pool—alone.

Or did she?

Snatching up her smartphone, Rae thumbed through the texts. Her daughter's final message leaped onto the screen.

Should've stayed home.

After sending the text, Lark slipped on ice and fell into the pool. *Or someone pushed her in.*

Dread gripped Rae's throat. How would she ever know for sure?

Grimly, she sighed. There was only one way. She needed to talk to each of the girls who'd attended the party. Sit them down, one by one, then compare each of their stories. Yuna could help her contact each of the families—Yuna got along with everyone in town and had better diplomatic skills than Rae. They could begin by contacting the girls in Stella's posse, and leave the call to Katherine for last. If Stella was behind Lark's accident—directly or indirectly—it made sense to talk to the others first.

Rae's heart sank. All the girls were loyal to each other—and to Stella especially. If they'd lied as a group to the PD on the night of Lark's death, what chance was there of garnering the truth now? They'd simply lie again.

I need an inducement, something to pry one of the girls loose from the others. Something to encourage one of them to stand apart and substantiate Quinn's version of events.

The solution was suddenly obvious. Groaning, Rae hid her face in her palms.

I need Griffin's help. Lowering her hands into her lap, she drew a steadying breath. There really was no other option.

Griffin's niece, Jackie, had not only attended the party, she was Stella's best friend. If Griffin could impress upon Jackie the seriousness of the situation, she'd do the right thing. Perhaps not immediately. But Rae was confident he'd get his niece to open up. Jackie *would* verify the true version of events. Which would leave Rae—if the worst-case was the actual scenario—dealing with a more awful situation than she'd bargained for.

Don't even go there. The worst-case scenario is only a remote possibility. Very remote, and not worth considering. Stella and the others were typical fourteen-year-old girls, with their love of fashion and the latest music and their catty disagreements. A little spoiled and certainly indulged by the parents who loved them—Rae had been no different when it came to Lark's wants, and her needs—but every one of the girls was grounded by a core of decency. Good kids, all. Not one of them would've intentionally harmed Lark. It was unthinkable.

"Want to watch a movie?"

Flinching, she looked up. Her father padded to the couch. Connor wore flannel pajamas with a green plaid robe sashed tightly around his waist.

Despite the tension balled up inside her, Rae dredged up a smile. "I thought you'd gone to bed."

"I might sleep on the couch . . . if I can fall asleep. I've got a fire in my belly, and I'm not talking about ambition."

"Too much dinner tonight?" she asked, glad to engage in a reassuringly normal chat.

"Why'd you let me eat all that Italian food?"

"Too much garlic never agrees with you." Grabbing the throw, she pressed it around his knees. "I should've remembered."

"Too much everything. My insides are on fire." He glanced toward the hallway. "Where's Quinn? I thought he was out here, watching TV with you."

"He went to his room. Best guess, he's studying." At least she hoped he was. Quinn also needed a reassuringly normal task, something to take his mind off tonight's disturbing conversation.

"I wonder if he'd like to play cards."

"What?" Blinking, Rae focused her attention on her father.

"I might be more comfortable sitting at the kitchen table."

"If the indigestion's bad, it'll help to sit in a straight-back chair. Should I get something for your stomach?"

"I pop too many pills. I should know better, eating all that spicy food."

"What's done is done."

"Why don't we play a few hands of poker? I'll turn on Hester's twinkly lights—we can see them from the kitchen. I'm sure I can persuade Quinn to join us. It'll keep me occupied, until my stomach settles down."

Rae found she wasn't listening. With a start, she came to a decision. It was after nine o'clock, but this couldn't wait. She needed to speak with Griffin immediately. He'd talk to his niece and put Rae's worries to rest. *He'll confirm nothing untoward happened to Lark.*

"What do you say?" Connor looked at her expectantly. "Are you up to a game of poker?"

"Dad, I'm going out. I need to get the ball rolling on this, or *I'll* never sleep. I need to know for sure—I *do* know for sure," she added breathlessly, hopeful and sick-hearted all in the same instance. "There's a perfectly innocent explanation, even if it doesn't look that way. But I need confirmation. The rock-solid kind."

"What are you babbling about?"

"I won't be gone long." She started for the foyer, then stopped when she noticed his hand pressed to his tummy. He did look uncomfortable. "Would you like ginger tea to settle your stomach? It'll help. I'll make you a cup, before I go."

Connor pulled the throw off his lap. "I'll make it myself. It'll do me good to move around." With mild exasperation he watched her pull on her coat. "What's the hurry? You look . . . agitated."

"That's putting it mildly."

"What did I miss?" He watched her fingers dart up the coat, buttoning quickly. "Are you going to Yuna's?"

"Not exactly," she said.

~

If the Cleveland Cavaliers had materialized on his front porch, Griffin couldn't have been more surprised. Not even if they'd piled inside the house to raid the fridge for brewskis.

Arms crossed, fists tucked into the armpits of her coat, Rae attempted a smile.

Griffin didn't step out to join her. He *did* open the door a fraction more. Her appearance rendered him mute.

A minor setback. Rae, predictably, grabbed the conversational reins.

"Winter's back." She cocked her head at the snow, falling in sloppy patches across his yard. "I guess my dad is right. Spring is still a way off. What I'd give for short sleeves and hot weather. Did it snow much in Boston?"

"Sometimes," he replied, dragging his voice out of hiding.

"I've never been on the East Coast. Well, either coast. Come to think of it, I've never been much of anywhere. Vacationing in Cincinnati probably doesn't count."

"You should visit."

She studied him with intense, nervous interest. "Where?"

"The coast. Either one. They're both nice."

"Do you have a preference?"

Griffin blinked. *What is this strange phenomenon?* Rae was making . . . small talk. An art she'd never practiced, much less mastered. He was considering lending an assist when her green eyes rounded.

"Oh crap," she blurted. "It's Friday."

"Yes."

"Friday *night*."

"An astute observation."

"Popping by like this is rude. Completely." She glanced at her car, disappearing beneath a layer of white. Her sheepish gaze swung back to him. "Barging in on a Friday night—*date night*. Totally my bad."

Amused, Griffin leaned against the door jamb. "I thought Saturday was date night."

"I'm not sure." Rae shrugged.

"Don't you date?" Prying was impolite, but she *had* appeared at his place uninvited.

She huffed out a breath. "Hardly." Her eyes darted away from his. "At least not since dinosaurs roamed the earth."

This pleased him. "You should get out more."

"You sound like my father," she tossed back, irritation creeping into her voice. "Listen, I'm sorry for dropping by—it's important. If you prefer, I'll come back at a less inconvenient time. Although I do need to talk to you. I'd rather not push this off to another day." She cleared her throat. "Are you . . . entertaining guests?"

She peered around his waist. Apparently to confirm that a harem of naked women wasn't cavorting in his living room.

This also pleased him, inordinately so.

He gave himself a mental kick in the keister. In matters concerning Rae, he wasn't used to having the upper hand. It was no reason to fall for her bumbling charm offensive.

Still, putting her at ease was the better part of valor. He'd never before seen her this nervous.

"I don't want your money," he said, guessing at her reason for the visit. "The planter you mowed down in front of my office isn't a family heirloom. Imitation terra-cotta—all plastic. I'll pick up a new one for next to nothing. Your road rage is forgiven."

"Yuna told you I planned to send a check? That was a private conversation!"

"Yuna told Kipp. He blabbed."

"Kipp spilled?" For a marvelous instant, the worry left Rae's features, and a grin lit her face. "The monster."

"Don't be too hard on him. Dealing with his wife's hormonal swings is testing his mettle."

Trashing on mutual friends was an icebreaker, and he sensed her relief. As if she needed a lighthearted interlude before launching into the true reason for stopping by.

"Kipp's a lightweight," she said. "Yuna can bend his mettle even when she's not pregnant."

"Yeah, and he's practically living at my house. Mostly because Kameko has been knocking on my door. She's the bigger carnivore."

"Weird, isn't it? For a little kid, she can chow down the protein."

This new, anxiety-riddled version of Rae was fetching. What did she need to discuss? The fact that she'd appeared unexpectedly was an opportunity.

Seizing it, he swung the door wide. "Why don't you come in?"

"Thanks."

Helping her out of her coat, he discovered a faded green T-shirt underneath. It was emblazoned with orange lettering. I'M NOT SHOUT-ING. I'M IRISH. A castoff from her father's closet? On closer inspection, she hadn't brushed her long and wonderfully untamed hair. Apparently, she'd jumped into her car and driven over, accompanied by nothing more than a bad case of nerves.

Which meant Rae's guard wasn't up. *For once.* What were the odds it would ever happen again?

Giving her space, Griffin rooted himself in the center of the living room.

"Rae, let me go first." He resisted the urge to begin pacing. Allow Rae to detect that they were *both* nervous, and he'd lose the upper hand. "There's something I have to say."

"Can it wait? What I need to discuss is more important."

A debatable conclusion, but Griffin let it slide. She'd always been stubborn and a little bossy.

"I have to get this off my chest," he admitted. Since Monday, he'd been silently composing the speech.

"Go ahead."

"You tend to act first and think later. I'm the opposite. I take my time, think things through."

"You know how you feel *before* you act. That's no big secret. You're the tortoise, and I'm the hare." She tipped her head to the side. "Your big sister used to tease us about it. And I mean all the time. Sally was such a know-it-all when we were kids. I was never sure which position she thought was better—hare or tortoise."

"Definitely tortoise," he supplied, "for all the obvious reasons. A tortoise doesn't leap into the fray without thinking."

"Because of short legs."

"What?"

"A tortoise has short legs—they aren't made for leaping." She scanned his tall frame. Rae stood five foot ten, but he had four inches on her. "Metaphorically speaking," she added, "I'm sure *your* legs can leap just fine."

With frustration, Griffin palmed his forehead. "For ten seconds, would you ditch the play-by-play? Let me finish."

"Sure."

"When we were in high school—long before the White Hurricane—I knew I was in love with you. I'm a tortoise. I think things through. I knew what I felt was real, clear back when we started our freshman year. I kept up the best-buddy routine because I knew your feelings weren't the same . . . at least not until our last months of high school. From ninth grade on, there's not much else I thought about, other than sealing the deal."

"I was a girl, not a business transaction." Her brow arched. She darted a glance at the door. "I really do need your help with something. Actually, I need a favor. A big one. Can we hash out the other stuff some other time?"

"No."

"What?"

"Rae, let me get this out."

Impatience leaped in her gaze, but she tamped it down. "Fine . . . but I have no idea where you're going with this."

"I spent high school tortured by one obsession—making love to you," he clarified, picking up the pace, needing for her to understand before the emotion thundering through him brought him to a standstill. "I was convinced that if we were intimate, you'd be mine forever. Sex would give me the guarantee I was seeking. I never entertained a minute's doubt. I was sure of it. From an adult perspective, I realize how dewy-eyed that sounds. People get laid all the time. It doesn't mean anything."

"For *some* people." Rae withered him with a look. "Take me off the roster, pal. I'm of the opinion that jumping into bed with your lover *should* mean something."

"I agree—and stop pulling me off track," he snapped, getting to the heart of the matter. "I had lust on the brain—and my sister knew I was going to do something stupid. Sally read me the riot act in about ten different ways. Then she made me promise not to put the moves on you until I was . . ."

Why didn't I give Rae the shorter version?

"Until you were . . . what?" She was going to make him say it aloud. Fine. He was a tortoise. But he knew how to leap.

"Until I was old enough to pop the question."

Merriment played with Rae's lips, but her eyes were sad. She wanted to make light of his snap confession. Fluff it off. She didn't quite succeed.

"If you'd gone down on bended knee, Everett would've pitched a fit. I can't even imagine. Your father would've grounded you permanently."

A thoughtful expression eclipsed the merriment. She was listening to him fully now.

It helped Griffin plow through the difficult parts. "My father's opinion didn't matter—not after the White Hurricane, and Hester died. When you lost your mother, I threw my common sense out the window. My decency too, Rae. I became the guy who only cared about scoring with his girlfriend."

"That's *all* you thought about?" The hurt she tried to contain bloomed quickly across her face.

"I should've been your stand-up guy," he said hoarsely. "The one you could lean on. I should've been your friend, and—"

"All right, Griffin. Stop."

But he couldn't, not yet. Not until he'd laid his emotions bare. "When you broke up with me, I knew I'd pushed you past your limits." Swallowing down his pride, he added, "I knew I deserved to lose you."

"Stop." Pain fissured across her mouth. "I get it."

Eyes lowered, Rae stepped back, retreating to the picture window. The snow was coming down harder now. Sheets of white burying the landscape until nothing was discernable.

"It's all right," she murmured. "All things considered, I suppose we're even. I never explained *why* I broke up."

"I'm not asking. It doesn't matter now."

"I *can* tell you that I blamed you. Like you'd betrayed me."

"I did."

"No, Griffin. That's not what I mean. Everything that happened . . . it wasn't your fault."

Lost in her own counsel, Rae pressed her nose to the glass. As if she was searching the night for answers she'd never find. Answers that Griffin, in his private agony, knew they'd lost years ago.

"I'm such a dope." From over her shoulder, she regarded him. "I spent years believing you were responsible. Griffin, I wasn't an angel. I wanted you too. That night when we were supposed to meet behind the post office . . . it was supposed to be our first night. I was ready to sleep with you too."

"You were?" He'd never been sure. Assumed she'd changed her mind.

She nodded. "Why didn't you show up?"

The question startled him. "I did. You weren't there, Rae. I drove around the parking lot for half an hour, wondering if you'd driven to the wrong place."

"No, I was there . . . *you* were late."

"You were waiting for me?" Confused, he sensed an undercurrent. Something Rae wasn't telling him.

Had decided *not* to tell him.

What right did he have to press? He'd said his piece. Getting the confession off his chest didn't make him feel better, especially with the undercurrent rushing faster now between them.

Letting it go, he asked, "What did you need to discuss?"

Chapter 28

Griffin listened to her suppositions with growing unease. Midway through, he left Rae pacing in the living room and went into the kitchen to make her a cup of chamomile tea. He poured himself a glass of water. When he returned, he asked if she'd like to sit down.

Taking the cup, she gratefully sat on the couch. "Your niece is the key," she repeated, as if she hadn't already driven home what she needed him to do. "Will you talk to Jackie?"

"Of course."

"I don't want to believe one of the girls pushed my daughter into the pool. Not intentionally."

"No one would want to believe that. They're just kids."

"If another girl *did* push my daughter, she probably didn't realize Lark was standing close to the pool's edge. And it was icy outside. None of the girls should've been allowed to go into the pool area in the first place. It's just so stupid. Why didn't Katherine tell the girls to stay in the house?"

"Rae, slow down." He nudged the cup toward her lips. "Drink."

She was becoming overwrought. It was another aspect of her personality he'd never before witnessed. It occurred to Griffin that his expectations were framed around the Rae he'd known in high school. An illusion. The seventeen-year-old girl he'd known had matured into the woman seated beside him. This version—the true version of

Rae—was a woman who'd lost her daughter only months ago and now feared a heartbreaking accident was something more.

No wonder she'd assumed the worst from Quinn's story.

Griffin said, "Quinn was hanging around outside the Thomersons' hoping to see Lark?"

"But not for the reasons you think. They were just friends. He went over to lend moral support even though he knew he probably wouldn't see her."

"Support via text message. Sounds like a typical kid's behavior."

"It is." Rae took another sip of tea, set the mug down. When she turned slightly, their knees almost touched. "Quinn's parents get drunk just about every night. Whether they stay home, or come back from the bars drunk, they fight. And I mean, knock-down-drag-outs."

"They've been doing that for as long as they've known each other." Griffin recalled the many times his mother had tried to intercede in the Galeckis' wretched lives. He suddenly understood what Rae meant. "Was Quinn also hanging around Thomersons' to avoid going home because of the fighting?"

"Probably. At least he'd learned how to avoid being collateral damage."

"How?"

"From Lark. She came up with a plan to keep him safe," Rae said, clearly taking pride in her daughter's ingenuity. "She'd sneak him into her bedroom whenever Mik and Penny were out of control. Have him stay until the coast was clear. Then he'd drive home around midnight. By then, his parents were too drunk to drag him into one of their battles. They thought he was in his bedroom the whole time."

"He'd lock the door and leave music playing?" Griffin had used that ploy a few times himself in high school.

Rae nodded. "Then he'd climb out his bedroom window. Good thing he and my daughter both had bedrooms on the ground floor.

Lark's strategic planning would've been harder to pull off if either of them lived in a two-story home."

"You didn't know about any of this?"

"Not a clue. Anyway, I'm sure Quinn was texting Lark from outside Thomersons'. Earlier that night, she'd told me she didn't want to go to the slumber party. A change of heart."

"Because of her falling-out with one of the other girls." Only a theory, but Griffin knew Rae was convinced of its veracity.

"Right. Once she'd gone to Stella's house, Quinn probably hoped she'd change her mind. Call me to pick her up. Then he'd have somewhere safe to stay until midnight." A faint tremor went across Rae's shoulders. "Pacing outside the brick wall, Quinn heard everything. He's sure he heard two girls arguing."

"Thanks. I'm clear on everything now."

"You'll talk to your niece?"

"Absolutely. I'll take care of it tomorrow. Rae, do you mind if I share this with my sister? Sally will want to know what I'm discussing with Jackie." He grimaced. "Lately I haven't been on the best terms with my sister. Bringing her in on this will smooth the way."

"It's fine. In fact, why not ask Sally to join you? It'll make the conversation easier for Jackie, having her mother there."

"I'm sure it will." Hesitating, Griffin chose his next words carefully. "There is one thing. Before you get too far out on a limb with conjecture, I want you to keep Occam's razor in mind."

"What's that?"

"The simplest explanation is more likely the right one. Which is . . . ?"

With visible relief, she blew out a breath. "My daughter slipped and fell."

"Right. No one pushed her."

"What about Quinn's version of the events? He's not making it up."

"I'm sure he's telling the truth," Griffin agreed, his tone soothing. He was calling into play all his verbal powers of persuasion to calm Rae, because he couldn't embrace her. He couldn't offer physical comfort. "Rae, here's what I believe happened. Lark and one of the girls were arguing about something."

"About *you*," she cut in, faintly chagrined and insistent, all in the same moment.

"Sure, that's possible. But it could've been something else. A remark one of them made at school that embarrassed the other. A boy they both had a crush on. Whatever it was, Quinn overheard the debate. Then the other girl went back into the house. Perhaps Lark was about to follow her inside and slipped. Or she began pacing—"

"And then slipped." Rae covered her face with her hands.

She looked broken.

Pain lanced Griffin, sure and swift. "Either way, there was nothing sinister at play."

"It was an accident."

"That never should've happened. Rae, I'm so sorry that it did."

He rested his hand on her curved spine. But only for a moment. Touching her brought a different sort of distress.

Sexual longing is a form of muscle memory. Their bodies, he mused, were automatically primed from years earlier. All those breathless hours of foreplay. If he had any sense, he'd get off the couch. Finish the conversation at a sensible distance.

She looked at him suddenly. "How is Jackie?"

"Not great. I suppose it's the same for all the girls." He frowned. "More importantly, how are *you* doing?"

"Before tonight, I would've said I'm managing. Quinn's revelation didn't help." She regarded him, her eyes lingering for too long. "Grief is hard. It hits you like a hammer. You can't prepare for those moments. They just come. In one respect, it does get easier. You learn to expect the blows."

"Do you exercise?"

The practical suggestion cleared her gaze of some of the pain. "Not as much as you do, obviously," she said lightly. "You look good. Really great. The term 'beefcake' comes to mind."

"I'll take that as a compliment."

"As it was intended."

Without warning, she lifted affectionate fingers. Slowly she feathered the lightest caresses across his brow. Taking her time as she traced curious fingers across his receding hairline, her attention delving, thorough, as she altered the atmosphere between them.

Her touch pinioned Griffin between agony and bliss.

"Griffin Marks, your worst fear is coming true," she teased, and her breathing hitched. Touching him was affecting her too.

She meant his biggest worry, their last year of high school. "It is," he agreed.

The power of her tenderness brought him a fraction closer, and she smiled. "Your hairline is receding. I doubt you'll believe this, but . . . it looks good on you. You've always had a great forehead. Wide, sturdy. With your hair moving out of the way, you look distinguished. You'll look even more distinguished in your forties."

"Rae."

"Hmm?" She was toying with his ears now, her eyes sparking when he shivered.

"Either stop what you're doing," he said, his resolve slipping, "or let two play this game."

"What game?"

Tired of her teasing, he captured her mouth in a hungry kiss. Cupping her face, he took his sweet time, his head swimming; when Rae whimpered with need, he brought her fully into his arms. Then he dragged his mouth across her cheek, savoring the taste of her skin, before he kissed her again.

He allowed them both a few minutes of bliss. No more. If they were taking their relationship in a new direction, they weren't doing so tonight. Not after the disturbing conversation they'd shared. Not while Rae—still in mourning and fearful about the circumstances surrounding Lark's death—was too fragile to make a life-altering decision.

There were mistakes a wise man didn't repeat.

The snow had let up. Only a smattering of white flitted through the night air.

"Would you like another cup of tea?" Griffin asked. He was hoping to keep her near for another hour or two, just to talk.

"That would be great."

Deciding to have some himself, Griffin made two cups. By the time he returned to the living room, Rae had smoothed down her wild hair. Her posture—straight, nearly rigid—slowed his pace.

When he set the cups down, Rae pulled in a breath. "I want to tell you something." She inhaled another breath, clearly steadying herself. "Griffin, I've never told anyone what I'm about to share. I sure didn't think I'd discuss this with you. Before Quinn came into my life, I'd done a good job forgetting. Oh, that's not the right word. Not forgetting—burying it. One of those memories you resist, because it tears you up too much. With everything that's happened—between you and Lark, and with Quinn, his parents—I think you need to know. In case what happened back then has more bearing on the present than I'd like to believe."

Protectively, Griffin placed his hand on her knee. The reassuring gesture eased the tension on her features. Lowering her hand on top, she held his fingers tight. Seeking assurance that he'd anchor them both before she carried them out to rough seas.

The silence wound out.

Then Rae led him into the past.

Chapter 29

MARKET

MARCH
Two months after the White Hurricane

Red ink blazed across the envelope: FINAL NOTICE.

Rae dropped her book bag to the floor. Snatching the envelope from the kitchen table, she read quickly.

According to the notice, her father hadn't paid the electric bill since December—one month *before* her mother's death in January. By nature, her father was forgetful. But this was negligent. Was she supposed to do homework by candlelight?

A more distressing thought surfaced. If the electric bill had gone unpaid for months on end, what other bills were past due? Connor no longer visited the grocery store with any frequency. He left Rae to fend for herself. For weeks she'd been doing all the laundry and the general housekeeping, tackling the chores in the evenings before digging into homework. Keeping up with housework was exhausting for a high school senior preparing for her final exams, and Rae had begun to give up on the effort. How to manage household bills was even more daunting. She had only the slimmest understanding of home mortgages, health insurance, and similar obligations that adults were supposed to manage. She'd been accepted to Ohio University in Athens. Her college career would begin soon.

Rae's stomach lurched. *Has Dad paid my tuition?*

With dismay, she scanned the countertops. Dirty dishes were everywhere. The mess had gone unnoticed because she'd begun avoiding the house. Lately Rae was practically living with Griffin and his family. She stayed there most evenings until after dinner. Clinging to the normalcy of the Marks household. A better alternative than dealing with her father's erratic behavior and inscrutable silences. Sometimes he talked to himself in mumbled, disjointed sentences. One day in February, she came home from school to discover the farm's livestock missing. The chickens, the goats—even the dairy cow was gone from the barn. Her father had sold them all. Then he'd closed himself inside her mother's art studio for long hours and refused to answer when Rae knocked.

The house resembled a psychiatric ward, with Connor the only patient.

And Rae—left without a functioning parent to guide her through the crushing loss—was beginning to despise him.

Her temper flaring, she spied a heap of bills stuffed behind the toaster. A messy stack of neglected responsibility.

"Dad!"

Grabbing a handful, she stalked down the hallway. His bedroom was dark. On the side of the bed, his silhouette was a curved bow.

Rae turned on a lamp. "When did you last pay the bills?" She waved the envelopes before him. "Dad, you have to snap out of it! I'm sad too, but I'm not shirking my duties. Mom wouldn't want that. My heart's broken just like yours, but I never skip classes."

Silence.

"What's next? A final notice from the bank? Do you expect us to live on the street?"

Still no reaction. A pungent, unclean odor rose from Connor's rumpled clothes.

Disgusted, Rae stepped away. "I'm ashamed of you. The least you can do is clean yourself up. Where's your self-respect?"

The difference between typical grief and serious depression is canyon-wide. Rae didn't understand. Until the White Hurricane, she'd been reared in a stable home with two loving parents. The sorrow engulfing her father was incomprehensible.

"Are you even listening to me? What's the matter with you?"

Her attention swept the room, taking in the tangle of clothes strewn across the carpeting and Hester's pitiful funeral wreath propped against the wall. When had he taken it from the cemetery? The roses had gone limp, blackened from frost. Withered petals were scattered beneath.

"Fine. Just sit there." Her voice breaking, she latched on to her anger. "Where's the damn checkbook?"

Her father blinked, yet his eyes remained unfocused. "Language."

"Go to hell, Dad. If you won't take care of us, I don't have much choice."

In a fury, Rae approached the dresser to search for the checkbook. She cracked open drawers, then slammed them shut. The checkbook wasn't hidden amid the rumpled clothes, and she expelled a frustrated growl. At the sound of her anger her father crawled into bed, shoes and all. When he pulled the blanket over his head, tears scalded her eyes.

Stalking out, she brushed them away. Anger was safer. She refused to fall apart like her dad. Instead she dredged up the pithy nuggets of wisdom Griffin's mother offered on a daily basis.

Hester isn't gone. She'll always live inside you, Rae. Even when it's difficult, find the joy in living. Prepare for college. Don't fall behind in your studies. Your mother would expect nothing less from you.

Her homework forgotten, Rae stepped into the art studio. The tang of paint clung to the air. She found the checkbook beneath a sheaf of bank statements on the table before the studio's wall of glass. There were also three checks from art galleries—a tidy sum. The money from Hester's life insurance policy was already deposited in a savings account in Rae's name. Hester, ever prudent, had set up the policy years earlier.

Clearing a space, Rae paid the bills. She filled out deposit slips and made a note to transfer funds from her savings account. By the time the last envelope was sealed, a headache pounded at her temples.

Lonely and frustrated, she picked up the phone.

Sally answered. "Hi, Rae. Hold on. I'll get my brother."

The phone clattered down. The sounds of soft music and adult laughter drifted through the line. Griffin's parents entertaining guests. This afternoon Winnie had been preparing canapés when Rae and Griffin walked in from school.

"Hey, babe. What's up?" Surprise laced the greeting; it was after nine o'clock.

"Griffin, I know it's late. Can I come over for a little while? My dad's being weird. I need to get out of here."

"Sure." Happiness replaced the surprise in Griffin's voice. "I'll be at the door waiting."

When she arrived, the foyer chandelier threw sparkles of light across the walls. Frank Sinatra warbled from the living room. Griffin's parents were drinking martinis with their guests.

The intrusion went unnoticed, and Griffin led her through the kitchen. They hurried down the stairwell to the basement.

Dust swirled in the air. An old couch sat against the concrete wall. A wooden crate stood in as a side table, with a CD player on top. There was also a beanbag chair that Sally had picked up somewhere, and the mini fridge Rae had given Griffin at Christmas, before the White Hurricane upended their lives. Although Winnie Marks had decorated every inch of the main living areas, her two children preferred the jumbled crash pad they'd created together.

"Do you want a Coke?" Griffin asked.

"No, thanks." Rae flopped down on the couch. "I just need a breather. Twenty minutes, and I'll let you get back to your studies."

"Stay as long as you'd like."

"Can I move in?" She let her head fall back on the cushion. "Commandeer one of the guest rooms?"

"It'll get my dad's vote." Griffin sat down beside her. "He loves having the sharpshooter around."

"I wish he'd stop calling me that."

Griffin flicked her nose. "Me too. It makes me think twice whenever I say something that pisses you off."

Despite her gloom, Rae laughed. "Then don't piss me off."

"Hey, I don't do it on purpose. Your temper is unpredictable." Griffin wrinkled his wide, oversize nose. Rae loved his nose, how the sheer heft was nearly as expressive as his eyes. She was about to tell him that when he added, "Sally's convinced Dad loves you more than me. Her too."

"Stop it. The great Everett Marks loves you best. That's why he criticizes you, Griffin. He's determined to mold you in his image."

"Fat chance. I can't wait until we leave for college and I get away from him. I hate working at the dealership. Gas fumes and picky customers. He can dream all he wants. I'm never taking the place over."

A common complaint, and Rae kicked off her shoes. Her eyes were still burning. "Well, I'm glad I get along with *both* of your parents." Blinking away the dampness, she reached for humor. "If they'll let me move in, I'll clean Everett's rifles to earn my keep."

The humor failed, and Griffin noticed her lower lip wobbling. "You're not thinking about it, are you?"

A dumb question, as usual. "I can't stop that day from popping into my head. It just does." Vivid, jarring, like a film replaying nonstop. A crushing remembrance of the worst moments of her life.

"Everything's okay," he whispered, moving closer. Providing solace wasn't a skill set normally honed by a teenage boy, but he made the attempt. "The White Hurricane's over. The way Hester died . . . no one should go like that. It makes me sick too, thinking about your mom caught outside in the blizzard. I know you're hurting a lot more than I am. It will get easier. Not today or tomorrow, but someday."

"I can't stop seeing it in my head. Spotting my mother under the tree, believing she was okay and then—"

"Rae, don't do this to yourself. We've covered this ground a million times. Think about the future, not the past. *Our* future."

Breaking off, Griffin searched her gaze for confirmation she wouldn't give up. That she believed their future together would heal the grief she was only beginning to feel, the bottomless heartache of losing the mother she'd adored.

He rested his fingers on her chin. His pupils dilated, like windows opening to his soul.

Lately, his touch made Rae breathless. Even when her heart was crumbling.

Their gazes tangled. Searching, probing, as Griffin's fingers trailed fire around her mouth.

This new, intensely physical aspect of their relationship perplexed them both. As kids, they'd tussled in the grass. Played sports together in the summer heat. During a disgusting phase in ninth grade, they'd lobbed spitballs at each other whenever they met in the school cafeteria. Their chosen form of greeting, and Rae had prided herself on grossing out the other girls.

Everyone at the high school assumed they'd been dating since freshman year. But it wasn't until the end of their junior year that they'd traded a few lip-smacks. Out of curiosity. The experiment left them both feeling silly. After a decade of friendship, they seemed incapable of viewing each other in a sexual way. Which suited them fine. They were content being two unremarkable teenagers who'd skirted the self-confidence killers of dating, or vying to fit into the popular crowd, because they had each other.

The White Hurricane changed everything.

As Rae mourned and her father slipped further away, she often found herself nuzzling in Griffin's arms. She'd never been prone to tears—Rae gravitated toward physical activity or wisecracks if she felt low—but the changes overtaking her life were frightening. Hester, buried. Connor, drifting away. At times, before Rae became aware of the sorrow bubbling up, Griffin would draw her into his arms. He'd rock her slowly, until her emotions settled.

It was here, in the privacy of his crash pad, that the hugging had led to kissing.

Griffin kissed her now, his lips moving slowly over hers. For a boy with no dating experience, he'd become an expert.

Pausing, he cradled her face. "Don't be sad—everything will get better. We don't have to wait until August to move down to Athens. We can get summer jobs near the campus. We'll find somewhere to stay until we move into our dorms. When we come home for winter break, your dad will be better. He'll pull himself together."

"What if he doesn't?"

"Then move in here. My parents won't mind."

"Don't tease."

"I'm serious. Rae, I don't want you living anywhere you're not comfortable." The embers in his gaze leaped higher. "I'll always protect you. You know that, right?"

Words escaped her. She was acutely focused on Griffin's hands, lowering now, toying with the hem of her shirt. Testing the limits of his self-control—and hers. When his palms slid underneath, they both gasped. It was a revelation, how easily they were able to pleasure each other.

Throwing off her own reservations, Rae dipped her hands beneath his T-shirt. Griffin's breath hitched. The reaction was more thrilling than the downward plunge on a roller coaster. Boldly now, she ranged over the hard muscle girding his waist with curiosity and the sudden, dizzying awareness that she could give pleasure as well as receive.

Griffin's skin felt like fire.

One moment they were trading the lightest caresses. The next, their hands were everywhere, touching, exploring. Griffin's kisses became more urgent, demanding. When they fell back together on the couch and he rolled on top, Rae marveled at how well they fit together.

Breaking off, he lifted up onto his palms. "Not here." He was panting, his mouth quirking into a grin. "It'd be our luck for Sally to come down."

Rae scrambled upright. "I'm not sneaking upstairs to your bedroom. It's too big a risk. Everyone's home."

"That's not what I mean." He brushed his lips beneath her ear, and she quivered.

She angled her neck back. *What do you mean?* The glint in his eyes was mesmerizing.

With a start, she understood. Excitement bubbled through her.

He pulled her to her feet. "Give me ten minutes," he said, deciding for them. Which was astonishing—most of the time, she took the lead. "My parents won't notice I'm gone. They're too busy partying with their friends. Let's meet in the parking lot behind the post office."

"Which post office? Griffin, there are three in town." To her consternation, Rae couldn't mask the eagerness in her voice.

"The one with the big parking lot and no one around. We'll have the place to ourselves." He brushed his mouth across hers. Frowning, he cleared his throat. "Unless you'd rather go home. Totally your call."

The decision was easy. On tiptoe, she nipped at his ear.

On the way to the foyer, Griffin made a detour away from his parents and their guests, who were laughing in the living room. She stayed close behind as he walked through the family room in a beeline to the liquor cabinet. They'd only sneaked into his father's booze twice before and weren't sure what they liked. Scanning the options, Griffin chose a bottle of whiskey.

"To celebrate," he said.

"Great thinking." Rae hid the bottle under her coat. She smiled mischievously. "Don't keep me waiting. If you do, I'm drinking this bad boy alone."

~

Security lights illuminated the empty post office.

Driving around back, Rae frowned. Griffin couldn't have meant she should park near the lights. Far to the left, a row of small businesses in a long brick building were closed for the night. They were tucked far enough back from Cherry Street to lend privacy. Griffin would have no trouble spotting her car in the empty lot.

For a night in March, the temps were surprisingly warm. Rae opened the driver-side window. In the glare of headlights, she could see that the strip of grass before the shuttered businesses was already greening, as if, two months ago, the freak blizzard hadn't covered Chardon in heavy drifts of snow.

The minutes ticked by. Rae cut the engine and doused the headlights. Where was Griffin? Unzipping her coat, she glanced at the bottle they'd taken from Everett's liquor cabinet. Knob Creek. Opening it, she took a swig. The alcohol burned going down her throat, and she coughed.

She took another swig, pleased at how quickly the booze relaxed her. The bitter taste was no picnic, but the lazy sensation flowing through her veins was fantastic. The frisson of anxiety she'd carried around since the White Hurricane miraculously began to dissolve.

Griffin, hurry up.

Taking a third, larger gulp, Rae pondered the reasons for the delay. Had Griffin meant that they should meet behind the drugstore on Cherry Street? Now she wasn't sure. Or maybe he was having trouble sneaking out of the house. A possibility if Winnie returned to the kitchen to prepare more snacks for her guests. Or Sally, catching him on the stairwell, was interrogating him about going out at ten o'clock on a school night.

Sally was only two years older than Griffin; a minor detail. Sometimes she gave him a hard time.

Then Rae hit upon the reason for the delay: Griffin was stopping at the twenty-four-hour drugstore at the other end of town. He was buying condoms. The prospect made her both anxious and excited.

The liquor was already making her feel loose and free, and another swig seemed unwise. She took one anyway. Then she got out to sit on the hood of her car. From somewhere far off, the wail of guitars reached her ears. From a bar nearby? She didn't know, or care. Mostly because the moon drew her attention; it was a bobblehead in the sky. It wouldn't sit still. Lying back, she laughed.

Time slowed to a luxurious crawl. She'd nearly dozed off when two voices—angry—came out of nowhere.

"This is my night out with the guys, Penny. Did you leave Quinn alone in the apartment?"

"Stop yelling at me!"

"How many times are you going to pull this stunt? You're my wife, and I'm telling you to go home."

"I'm going back to the tavern. Quinn's fine. I dropped him with the neighbors."

"You're lying. Do you want my boss's wife to keep nosing around in our business? If another complaint goes in to those damn social workers, Winnie Marks will be back to hinting I should put my son up for adoption."

"Tell your boss and his high-and-mighty wife to stay out of our business. I told you I left Quinn with friends, and he's fine."

Rae lolled her head to the side. "Both of you, shut up! Can't you see I'm sleeping here?"

As she sat up, a sickening rush of stars cascaded across her vision. *Whoa.* When they cleared, she managed to focus on the approaching couple. Late twenties or early thirties. A beefy man with a woman who barely reached his shoulders. The woman's close-cropped hair was dyed a freakish shade of blonde that was nearly white. In the moonlight, it was hard to make out the tattoo on her neck. A pitchfork?

The man seemed familiar. Blinking slowly, Rae couldn't recall why.

The woman was faster on the uptake. "Mik, look who it is. Isn't she the girl who's dating your boss's son?"

"Her name's Rae. She hangs around the service desk whenever Daddy makes the little shit work. The boss treats her like his favorite pet. Weird, if you ask me."

The woman neared. She chuckled as Rae, scrambling off the hood, nearly lost her balance.

"Are you a princess, Rae?"

"Of course not." The words slurred, and she clamped her mouth shut.

The woman smirked. "Why does the boss man like you? You're not much to look at."

The insult stung. "Because I'm a perfect marksman," she tossed back, taking care to enunciate every syllable. A stupid thing to say, but nothing else came to mind.

"You're . . . what?"

"A perfect shot," Rae said, dimly aware that the whiskey was giving her confidence. Although she was dizzy, she managed to point at the post office. "See over there? From where you're standing, I can hit a target that far away."

"Bullshit."

Griffin, where are you?

"I don't care if you believe me. I'm the best marksman in the county."

The man—she remembered now, he was a mechanic at Marks Auto—strode past his wife.

"Marks*man*? You're no man. Not with those bodacious titties." He laughed at his own joke. "You've sure got a bod."

His wife whacked him on the chest. "Shut up, Mik." The sexual innuendo didn't sit well with her, and she backed Rae up against the car. "What are you doing out this late, little girl? Is Griffin on his way to meet you?" Chuckling, the woman surveyed the empty lot. "I guess if you're a kid in high school, anyplace will do."

Humiliation collided with Rae's bravado. "Lady, why don't you listen to your husband and get home to your kid?"

Through her drunken haze, Rae sensed she'd gone too far. The woman—Penny—was no one to mess with. Rae hadn't meant to provoke her.

Penny was, she now realized, also drunk. So was her husband. A sliver of fear dove through Rae. She was woefully unprepared to deal with grown-ups who were under the influence. Griffin's parents only drank socially. Her father hardly drank at all. Before her mother's death, her parents drank a glass of Scotch on special occasions, but that was about it.

"Where do you get off, telling me what to do?" Penny demanded. "You're worried about my kid? *You* go home and take care of him."

"I don't even know him."

"Yeah? Well, he's more work than he's worth. The little brat can't do anything for himself." She pivoted suddenly, toward her husband. "Why don't you go home and deal with Quinn? I sure didn't want a kid."

The remark shivered anger down her husband's spine.

"I'm going back to the tavern," she added. "I need to have some fun."

The anger put something fierce in Mik's eyes. "You said Quinn's staying with a neighbor. Did you leave my son alone in the apartment?"

"Who cares if I did?"

"I care, you lazy bitch!"

"He's in bed. He's asleep."

A fearsome charge passed between the couple. The electricity snapping between them was veering toward overload. Rae wanted to get away before the argument went too far. After too many swigs of whiskey, she didn't trust her feet.

The world spun as she sank onto the hood of her car.

"Get home, Penny. Now. If you don't, I swear I'll beat you to within an inch of your life."

"I'm not scared of you."

For a woman fifty pounds lighter than her husband, Penny *did* seem fearless. A metallic taste coated Rae's mouth, and she couldn't look away.

"I'm not telling you again."

"Good. Because you're not the boss of me."

For proof, Penny swung a fist at Mik's jaw. Nimble and quick, she landed the punch.

Before he could react, she'd sprinted away into the night.

Blood oozed from the corner of his mouth. Blinking slowly, he held his jaw. He looked comical then, swaying on his feet.

Rae found herself grinning. *He really doesn't know what hit him.*

The thought, combined with the shock of physical violence, brought laughter gurgling up her throat. An inappropriate reaction.

A terrible miscalculation. For the rest of her life, she'd question why she didn't scramble inside the car instead.

She blurted, "I guess wifey got in the last word."

Anger surged across Mik's face. "Who gave you permission to disrespect my wife?" Catching Rae by the shoulders, he stripped off her coat. She was about to scream when he clamped a hand across her mouth.

He shoved her into the car.

Chapter 30

Sharing the grim secret brought no relief.

Mostly, the telling brought shame. A black tide impossible for Rae to outrun. She let it rush over her.

Beside her on the couch, Griffin stared straight ahead. He gave no reaction.

When it seemed he'd never break the silence, she rushed into the void. Rae wasn't sure which was worse. The telling, or the consternation turning Griffin's features to stone.

"That night . . . I never should've opened the bottle of whiskey. Why did we even take it from your father's liquor cabinet? Teenagers do the stupidest things." Rae got to her feet. She needed to escape the black tide threatening to drown her. "It's not like I'd ever been drunk before. That March after the White Hurricane, we'd only just started sneaking into your dad's liquor cabinet—believing we were old enough to imbibe, which we weren't. I guess I was getting bored, waiting for you to show up. Downing all those shots of whiskey was my first mistake."

Nervously she cast a glance. Was Griffin listening? His eyes were glazed.

"My next mistake was sticking around. Once Mik and Penny came into the parking lot shouting at each other . . . I should've got back in the car. Right then, before everything spun out of control."

Slowly Griffin lowered his elbows to his knees. He clasped his hands like a man seeking the solace of prayer.

Dragging her attention away, Rae looked out the window. "I didn't have my cell phone—I was so upset with my dad that night, I'd stormed out without grabbing it. Even after I got to your house, I didn't realize I didn't have it. A typical Rae move, leaping without thinking. Anyway, I should've left the parking lot once the Galeckis showed up. Driven to the nearest house and banged on the door. It's not like I could've driven home. I was too drunk."

For a moment, she was angry at her younger self. Furious at the inexperienced girl whose actions led to terrible, unforeseen consequences. With effort she resisted the sinking sensation gelling inside her. The destructive thought had plagued her throughout her early twenties. As if she'd been responsible for her own rape.

It wasn't my fault. I know that.

She knew the self-reproach was falsehood. Those corrosive thoughts only made the healing more difficult.

Rape is an act of violence. I'm not to blame.

"The last mistake I made that night? It was the biggest one of all."

She leaned against the window's glass, welcoming the chill. Welcoming the cold understanding. There was only one path forward. Live with the scars from that act of violence.

She was still learning.

"After Penny struck Mik, I should've kept my mouth shut. Griffin, I can't explain it . . . it was terrifying and funny at the same time." Miserable, she pressed her face fully to the glass. Pinpricks of pain chilled her skin. "No—that's not accurate. That's what I believed at the time. Probably believed for a long time afterward. Here's the truth: I was so frightened, I automatically mouthed off. Went into my comfort zone of cracking jokes. As if I'd bring the situation under control by taking charge in the most asinine way. My stupid, impulsive habits. I always leap before I—"

Startled, she lifted her face from the glass. Soft, nearly imperceptible sobs reached her ears.

Griffin was crying.

He'd buried his face in his hands. His shoulders heaved as he tried in vain to muffle his despair. Apparently to keep himself together until she finished rambling. Rae swallowed down a sob. His grief was tangible, more powerful than incense.

Sensing her appraisal, Griffin dragged his hands from his face. In a flash, his gaze turned to steel.

"I'll kill him for what he's done to you."

"Wait. Griffin, no." She took a step closer, hesitated. "I didn't tell you so you'd take revenge."

"He's a dead man."

"Griffin!" Stunned, she wrapped her arms around herself. "Do you hear yourself? You're not being rational. Stop talking like a crazy man."

"Mik has to pay for this. *I* want him to pay. Barring that, I'll settle for seeing him do a long stint in jail."

"No."

"Now, hold on. Rae, we can't let him get away—"

"No!" Lifting a hand, she thwarted further protest. "You're forgetting about Quinn. What will it do to him, if I drag his father through the courts? Assuming I even can." She had no idea of the statute of limitations on rape. Nor did she care. "It's over, Griffin. You're behaving as if this happened tonight. Deal with it—I have. I've made my peace with the past. You must do the same."

"How can I, after what he's put you through?"

"Because I'm asking you to."

Surrendering to her decision, he rose. This time when he approached, he didn't wait for an invitation. He bundled her into his arms. Griffin was a large man, but he'd always been uncommonly gentle. With the lightest touch, he steered her cheek to his chest. Held her against the uneven thump of his heart as grief shuddered down his spine.

Never before had Rae witnessed his tears—his ability to display strength and vulnerability, all in the same instant. It was moving, heartening. The sensation of safety spilled through her.

Leaning fully against him, she closed her eyes.

They stood holding each other for long minutes. After Griffin had brought his emotions under control, he brushed his cheek against the crown of her head, asking, "Does Mik know he was Lark's father?"

"I'm not sure."

Sensing the evasion, he tightened his hold. But his tone remained level.

"You don't know for certain."

"Griffin, I think Mik suspects Lark was his child."

"Based on . . . ?"

"When I was seven months pregnant, I saw him on Chardon Square. He made a wisecrack."

"What did he say?"

"I can't recall. Something about my condition. I had a major baby bump by then, swollen ankles—the works. The way he looked at me . . . I knew he'd put it all together." On Griffin's sturdy back, Rae let her hands cling fiercely. She dispelled the memory. "Don't ask me to dredge up the details. I can't."

"Forgive me." He tipped up her chin, rubbed his nose against hers. "You're right. It doesn't matter." Then his eyes widened. "Quinn is Lark's half brother."

"That's right."

"And you're—"

"Raising Quinn now. He's eighteen, Griffin, but he's missed a lot. Kids raised in negligent homes rarely mature on time. I plan to remedy that. This may sound strange, but I feel closer to my daughter now. Knowing I'm giving her half brother safe harbor. Knowing I'm giving Quinn a chance to develop and mature, because he's a great kid. He's becoming such a sweet young man—I'm so grateful he's come into my life." Rae's eyes were misty, her nose runny. Without thinking, she dried her nose on Griffin's shirt. Which was gross, but the gesture put soft lights in his eyes. Then she added, "On the outside, Quinn seems incredibly different from my daughter. On the inside? There are lots of similarities. The patience with complicated tasks. The ability to focus on one thing with single-minded purpose. Lark used that focus to create art and do complicated puzzles. Quinn can follow a detailed French recipe without missing a beat."

"Mik has the same focus," Griffin conceded, "but manifested in a different way. He can tear apart a vintage car's engine and put it back together again. The other mechanics at the dealership stand in awe of him. I suppose Mik's an artist, in his own way."

"He is."

Griffin tensed. "Pity the rest of his character is less admirable."

"We're all children of light *and* darkness," she said. "It's up to us to choose which side wins out."

The comment relaxed Griffin the slightest degree. Then he dipped his face into her hair.

"Rae," he murmured, "you're growing a mystical side."

"Strange, isn't it?"

"Kind of like you're growing a second brain. One nothing like the original. Who knew?" Playfully, he nipped at her ear as he steered the conversation in a new direction. "Your parents' cow in the way-back-then. Didn't Butter have two stomachs?"

"A cow has four stomachs."

"Maybe you'll grow four brains. It'll be interesting to watch."

"Ha-ha."

Usually she dominated in the teasing department. It was nice that Griffin was catching up. Maybe *he* was growing new aspects to his personality too.

After a moment, she said, "I've been through some hard times. They either tear you up, or compel you to find a deeper meaning."

"Good point."

Griffin seemed about to kiss her. Instead, he smoothed the hair from her brow. Setting her aside, he strode out of the room.

"Where are you going?" She felt adrift without the warmth of his arms.

The feeling dropped away when he returned.

He placed a handgun on the table. A semiautomatic. It would fire one shot each time the trigger was pulled.

"Griffin, why do you have a gun? You hate guns."

"As much as you do," he agreed. "If Mik comes to the farm looking for Quinn, it takes time to call the police. I'll sleep better knowing you have protection."

"He won't go that far," she said, aware she wasn't sure. Would Mik dare?

Griffin asked, "Do you remember the basics? Don't load a weapon until you're ready to use it. Wash your hands afterward—bullets contain lead. Keep the ammo separate from the firearm."

"Stop. I remember the basics—mostly of using a rifle. Your father only gave me a few lessons with handguns. They weren't Everett's preferred weapon to pick off wildlife." She wrinkled her nose in disgust, adding, "I hardly remember those lessons."

"We'll visit a shooting range next week, for practice."

A strip of ribbon encased the bullets. "Is this a gift from Everett?"

"Presented to me at my housewarming party."

Meaning the weapon had been stuffed in a drawer for the last two years. "What did Winnie give you?" she asked, picking it up.

"Stoneware and a gift certificate to a kitchen store."

"God bless your mother. She's elegance personified." The gun felt heavy in Rae's hands. A device made for one purpose only—to kill. Quickly, she set it back down. "My dad thought we should buy a gun, after my first confrontation with Penny. I vetoed the idea."

"I'm overriding your veto. You've given me a lot to digest, Rae. I need to think. And I need you to keep the gun until I get everything worked out."

"If Everett refuses to fire his favorite mechanic, I don't see what you can do. Further, you don't have my permission to tell your dad what I shared with you in strict confidence."

"I wouldn't discuss this with my father under any circumstance. As for Mik, he's already lost his job. It took some doing, but I finally got my father to fire him."

She geared up to ask how he'd managed the feat. The look in Griffin's eyes quelled her.

Anxiety pinged through her. "What are you planning?" Griffin *was* a tortoise. Careful, sure to analyze the problem of Mik Galecki from every angle. There was no telling what he was mapping out.

Her phone buzzed.

"I pried Quinn from his bedroom," Connor announced in a voice loud enough for Griffin to overhear. "Now he's beating me at poker."

The lighthearted disclosure made the moment feel surreal. Dragging her attention from the gun, she cleared her throat.

"How's your tummy, Dad? Are you still regretting the double doses of Italian food?"

"I'm better. The ginger tea helped. I've had three cups. What's keeping you? Me and Quinn need a third for our poker tournament."

"I'll be home soon."

A grin lifted the corner of Griffin's mouth. Then he gave her a look: *Just tell your dad where you are.*

On cue, Connor asked, "What sort of errand are you running? You've been gone for two hours."

"Dad, I'm at Griffin's house." The silence was deafening. Foolishly, she added, "You remember Griffin Marks. Don't you, Dad? Well, I'm at his house. Just talking."

Griffin rolled his eyes.

Connor said, "Should I break out the chocolates or the party hats?" He knew she overdid the chocolate whenever she was sad.

"Definitely the latter."

"Yeehaw. I might break out the Scotch too."

"No! Your stomach doesn't need more excitement tonight."

"Rae, I hate when you're bossy."

As she was hanging up, Griffin fetched her coat. He placed the gun in one pocket and the bullets in the other.

"No arguing." He guided her arms into the sleeves. "Go home, get some rest. We both need it. I'll call you tomorrow after I talk to my niece."

"That would be great. Thank you."

"You don't need to thank me, Rae. I'm happy to help." He brushed a kiss across her lips. "Try not to worry."

Chapter 31

Snow pattered against the windshield as Rae turned onto the farm's long, winding driveway.

In the distance, the house was a flickering dot. Behind the snow-crusted dwelling, colorful lights glowed.

Rae's heart lifted. *Mom, are you looking down from heaven? Is Lark with you? Your twinkly lights . . . Dad turned them on for poker night.*

The headlights bobbed. Gently, she eased off the gas. In the wet snow, she noticed a new set of tire tracks.

Had Quinn run out for snacks? If he and Connor planned on late-night poker with midnight tacos, she was begging off. Like Griffin, she had a lot to think about. Where to store a gun in the house. Whether or not to share Griffin's concerns with her father.

Whether she'd have a future with Griffin. Much had changed in two short hours. She needed a good night's sleep to sort herself out.

She was reaching for the garage door opener when her heart lurched.

Tire tracks rutted the lawn. Rammed against the maple tree, a blue truck glinted in the moonlight.

The door to the house hung open.

The car fishtailed as she slammed on the brakes. It came to a halt. Rae was out and through the living room in seconds.

In the kitchen, playing cards were scattered across the floor. A chair was on its side by the wall. Whoever'd jumped out of their seat, they'd done so in a hurry.

Lying prone near the sink, her father tried to get up.

"Dad!"

A thread of blood ran down his chin. As she heaved him into a sitting position, he winced.

"Dad, are you hurt? Is anything broken?" She wasn't sure if he could stand.

He pushed her away. "Rae, they're out back. We heard a racket outside, then Mik stormed into the house—I forgot to lock the door when you left. He beat Quinn awfully bad. I don't know how the boy got away."

Frantic, she glanced toward the living room. Her purse was in the car. She'd dropped her phone into her purse.

Teeth chattering, she fell back on her bottom. Dug inside her coat pocket, found the weapon.

Her father paled. "Where'd you get a gun?"

On autopilot, she filled the clip. Snapped it into place, and Connor flinched.

The dog was scrabbling at the mudroom door. Barking and then scrabbling some more, determined to get outside to protect her master. Rae pushed Shelby back. The last thing she needed was a dog injured during the fray.

Beneath Hester's lights, the snow glistened. There were footprints everywhere. Proof of a struggle, with no obvious winner. Rae's stomach overturned at the speckling of blood visible beneath the first tree. The area near the barn was also lit brightly. The center acreage lay in darkness. Mik was approaching the shadows.

Dragging his unconscious son. Quinn's legs cut grooves in the snow as they moved forward.

Dread ran hot in her veins. "Mik—stop where you are!" Rae willed her pulse to slow.

A tense moment. His fist was tight on the collar of his son's sweatshirt. Pivoting, Mik spotted her. He swayed slightly.

Then he began dragging Quinn back in her direction.

"I'm warning you—stop where you are. Let Quinn go."

"Don't tell me what to do," he shouted back.

His retort was slurred. Rae trembled. How to deal with a man under the influence? He'd never listen to reason. Not in the state he was in.

Willing herself forward, she paused beneath the fourth tree. The lights were brighter here. The glaring ribbons of gold and green fell across her. With her right hand, Rae lifted the gun into view. To ensure Mik understood.

Incredibly, the danger incensed him. He advanced, faster now. Fast enough for Rae to glimpse the damage to Quinn's face—the beating that had rendered him unconscious. The blood oozing from his slackened lips. Wisps of fury ran through her.

Mik roared, "You can't disrespect me. Put it down, or I'll teach you a lesson."

Fear caught Rae in a desperate hold. The instinct to run was nearly overpowering.

No.

If she gave in to the fear, there was no telling what Mik would do next. She could flee the danger he represented. But what about Quinn? His life rested in her hands.

Near the sixth tree, Mik let the boy go. And came faster. There wasn't much time now, and Rae stood transfixed. Between fear and anger, her pulse beating out of rhythm.

Griffin's words ricocheted through her.

I'll kill him.

In a two-fisted hold, she aimed the gun at Mik's chest. At the center, where his cold heart was beating. Mik was a feral animal. Rabid and deadly. She didn't need Griffin to take him down.

She'd do the job.

Beneath Hester's twinkling lights, Quinn's head lifted from the snow. Vomit heaved from his lips. His father was still advancing, nearing Rae, when the boy's frightened gaze found hers.

Rae's mind suddenly cooled. Went placid like the river-water gray of Griffin's eyes.

With the skill of a born marksman, she moved her aim a fraction higher. Slightly to the left. Away from the center of Mik's chest.

Guns are killing machines. Even the desire to bring injury can result in death. A person can bleed out from a gunshot wound quickly. For a fleeting second, Rae lifted her gaze heavenward. *Mama, help me.* Rae knew there were no guarantees.

Moving fast, Mik raised his fists.

She pulled the trigger.

The bullet found his flesh, threw him backward. His arms flailed out. Snow exploded around him as he fell onto his back.

"Rae!"

Her father limped out the mudroom door. Had he called the police? Rae perked her ears, desperate to detect the shrill call of sirens—and heard nothing.

She didn't know if Mik still posed a danger. "Dad, stay back," she roared.

Her command froze Connor in place.

Racing to Mik's side, she cried out with relief. He wasn't moving. Dread lowered her to her knees. Beneath his shoulder, the pool of blood was growing.

Tearing off her coat, Rae staunched the bleeding. Quinn was sitting up now, his eyes wild with terror.

She darted a quick glance. "Quinn, I need you to be brave." She colored her voice with affection, hoping to steady him.

He began trembling uncontrollably. On a whimper, he swiped at the blood on his face.

"Quinn! Look at me. It's okay, baby. I'm here. You're safe. Where's your phone?"

His eyes found the pool of blood inking the snow. With understanding, he searched his pockets. Rae's hands were sticky with blood. Mik's eyes were closed; his lips were bluish.

Quinn held up his phone.

"Dial 911. Now." Turning, she located her father, still awaiting her signal to approach.

"Dad, can you help Quinn to the house? Can you walk?"

He nodded.

As they limped away together, she pressed harder on Mik's shoulder. He groaned. She'd hit him somewhere in the upper chest, near the shoulder.

"Mik, wake up! Damn it—do it now!"

His eyelids fluttered.

～

Police and paramedics converged on the farm. Mik was taken to the county's Mercy Hospital in grave condition. The ambulance sped away from the property, the sirens screaming into the night.

The sheriff was in the kitchen with Connor, listening to the account. An officer took notes. Thankfully her father had suffered only minor injuries, allowing Rae to concentrate her efforts on calming down Quinn.

His eyes bruised and his lips swelling, he'd begun shaking again.

On the couch, Rae slowly rocked him. He was curled up at her side, his bloodied face tucked into the crook of her arm. For a boy nearly her height, he seemed much smaller.

An officer with salt-and-pepper hair approached. He seemed hesitant to disturb them.

"He should go to Mercy's ER," the officer told her. "The sheriff called in for a second ambulance." His pitying gaze skipped across Quinn's huddled form and back to her. "Would you rather I drive you in?"

"There's no need. But thanks." She watched headlights arc across the yard. "We have a ride."

She heard someone crash through the door. With relief, her gaze caught Griffin's.

~

The sun was rising on a chilly Saturday morning by the time the ER docs finished checking Quinn. During a facial X-ray and tests, Rae stuck by his side. The cuts and bruises on his face were many, but he'd suffered no permanent damage.

Griffin had thoughtfully tossed a blanket into the back seat of his car. They left the ER a slow-moving, exhausted trio. Griffin helped the silent youth into the back seat, then tucked the blanket around him. Quinn murmured his thanks.

Griffin steered onto the two-lane highway. "I'm sleeping on your couch," he announced.

Rae's eyes began to close. She forced them open. "I'm sleeping until noon."

Behind her, the blanket rippled. Clasping the edge, Quinn pulled the fluffy material over his head.

From beneath, his muffled voice: "Can I sleep all day?"

"Sleep until Sunday, if you'd like." Rae stifled a yawn. "Totally your call."

"Great. I'm sleeping until Sunday."

The idea *was* tempting. "Maybe I will too." Rae let her eyes drift shut.

Griffin chuckled. "Not happening." Bringing the car to a halt at a stoplight, he glanced behind. "Hey, sport. You're not the only one who knows how to cook. How does roasted chicken and garlic mashed potatoes sound? I'm cooking when I wake up. The grocery delivery's already set up for this afternoon. The bird and the spuds will be on the table by six o'clock."

The blanket shifted. "I guess I'll wake up then."

Chapter 32

On Sunday afternoon, Quinn was still holed up in his room.

Rae checked the time—one o'clock. She took a last sip of her coffee. They'd all slept in ridiculously late, but she was beginning to worry. She'd expected Quinn to make an appearance by now. It seemed he planned to stay in his room like a hermit.

I have to get him moving. Whether he wanted to discuss Friday's traumatic events or not, she needed to give him time to prepare. His special visitor would arrive soon. He *was* a teenager—he'd want to clean up, make himself presentable.

At the sink, Connor began stacking the breakfast dishes in the dishwasher. The dog, tired of her master's self-confinement, stuck close to Connor's legs. If a stray bit of toast fell off the counter, Shelby wouldn't miss it.

An hour ago, they'd left a tray outside Quinn's bedroom. After long minutes, he slid it inside. Good thing too. If he'd declined the meal, the eager Shelby would've gladly chowed down on scrambled eggs, hash browns, and a double helping of sausage links.

Shutting the dishwasher, Connor shooed the dog away from his legs. "Ticktock, Rae." He frowned at her.

"Dad, I can read a clock."

"Plus you should give him an update," he said, "about Mik."

"I know."

"He may need to talk first. About everything or nothing at all. Give him space to sort through his feelings out loud. It might take some time."

"Dad—I know." Rae sent a peevish glance. "This isn't my first lap on the parenting highway."

"Right." Connor picked up a kitchen towel, dried his hands. His weathered brow creased. "I'll do the man-to-man talking later this week. For now, the boy needs tender loving."

"He does," she agreed. Not that she was sure what to say.

Was it worth mentioning that Penny hadn't even called? That the authorities believed she'd left town? *Quinn's had enough shocks this weekend. The news about Penny can hold until next week.*

Rae doubted he'd welcome the other news. Regardless of Friday night's events, Mik was Quinn's father. The youth deserved an update on his condition. She wouldn't feel right dodging that news until later.

On Mercy Hospital's sixth floor, Mik wasn't doing great. Under normal circumstances, the sheriff—who was the son of one of Connor's friends on the geezer squad—wouldn't run afoul of HIPAA rules. But with Penny missing, Quinn *was* next of kin. It hadn't seemed out of place to share the details with Rae and Connor—in case Quinn wanted them.

The bullet had caused extensive damage to the bones in Mik's right shoulder. He'd gone into surgery Friday night, within minutes of reaching the hospital. Another surgery was scheduled for tomorrow.

"Rae, what are you waiting for?" Connor speared her with a look. "You're a mother. Go act like one."

"Go pop a chocolate, Dad. You're sassy when your sugar's low."

He chuckled. "You first."

Rising, she went out. There was nothing to gain by stalling any longer. Holding her breath, she rapped on Quinn's door.

Silence. She rapped again. "May I come in?"

More silence. She rested her forehead against the door's cool wood, certain she shouldn't just walk away. She heard a shuffling inside.

"You can come in."

Quinn was seated on the floor—the T-shirt he'd just pulled on visibly inside out. A circle of opened textbooks surrounded him. Every last one from his book bag. He didn't appear to be studying; more like he was skimming through the photos and the various diagrams.

Closing the door for privacy, she asked, "Do you want to talk about it?"

"No."

"Talking helps. Better than keeping your emotions bottled up."

A foot away, the book bag sat like a gaping mouth. Grabbing it, Quinn turned it upside down. Shook out two pens and a packet of gum.

With care, he lined them up beside the textbooks. "Would my dad have killed me?"

Rae's heart knocked around her ribcage. "I don't know."

"Why do people drink?"

"Not everyone does, Quinn. At least not to excess."

"You don't."

"Not anymore."

The remark took him aback. "You were a drinker?"

"That's not what I meant," she said, aware there was much she'd never tell him.

Which hurt: she'd love for him to know that Lark was more than his good friend. More than the guardian angel who'd swooped into his world last summer and stayed long enough to offer protection. Lark was in heaven now, but Rae had no doubt her sweet girl—Quinn's little sister—would continue to look out for him.

Quinn waited for her to continue. At length, Rae said, "Listen, I only drank to excess once. I was your age. It's not a mistake I'd ever repeat. Now that I'm older, I have a drink once in a while. Not often—it's just not my thing."

"I'm glad it's not."

"Want my advice?"

"Sure."

"Consider staying away from booze. Your parents are alcoholics. It's a disease that often runs in families. I'm not trying to scare you. If you imbibe—in the future, I mean—you might have the tendency to overindulge. It's something to keep in mind."

"You're not scaring me." Quinn shrugged. "I doubt I'll ever drink."

"Good choice."

"Yeah."

Rae hesitated. "Oh, I nearly forgot," she lied. "Your friend Ava, from school? She's coming over. Just to say hello."

Quinn's brows climbed his forehead. "She is?" Beneath the purplish bruises, spots of red warmed his cheeks.

The entire town knew about the incident. "Griffin's bringing her over," Rae explained. "They'll be here soon."

During Friday night's melee of PD and paramedics descending on the farm, Quinn had lost his phone. Griffin and Connor had both scoured the acreage between the house and the barn, to no avail. When Quinn didn't pick up calls yesterday, the resourceful Ava remembered that Rae worked for the woman living next door to her on North Street—Evelyn Witt.

Evelyn gave her Rae's number.

Suddenly Quinn appeared crestfallen. "Rae, I don't want Ava to see me like this. All banged up. I look really bad."

Concealing all the cuts and bruises was an impossibility. That didn't mean they couldn't mask some of the damage.

"There's something we can try, if you're feeling adventurous." Rae tipped her head to the side. "I have liquid foundation, the kind women put on their skin to conceal things like blemishes. Want to try it?"

~

"Is there any dinner left?" With newfound energy, Quinn scraped back his chair and went to the counter. "I could go for seconds."

After the visit with Ava, he was definitely feeling better. He wasn't going to school tomorrow, but Rae doubted he'd spend the day hiding in his room either.

He lifted the slow cooker's glass lid. "Mind if I finish the stew?"

Connor glanced at Rae and Griffin. Then at the boy. "We have a guest, Quinn. Shouldn't we ask if he wants the last of the stew? Especially since he made the great eats?"

"Oh."

Griffin wiped his mouth, then tossed the napkin into his bowl. "Chow down, kid. It's all yours."

"Thanks!"

Rae savored a last spoonful and pushed her bowl away. "We have a guest *and* another great cook. Who knows? Maybe I'll get out of kitchen duty the rest of my natural-born life. Why learn, when I'll never catch up?" Thinking of something else, she gave Griffin a curious look. "Walk me through how you pulled off a great meal with everything else you accomplished today. You met your parents for church services this morning, put in an hour at work, then picked up Quinn's girlfriend—"

The slow cooker's glass lid clattered down. "My *friend*. Don't jinx me, Rae. I'm not sure Ava likes me that way."

Connor snorted. "There were enough pheromones spiking the living room to knock me out cold. Trust me. That girl likes you."

Quinn went red.

Rae shushed her father. "May I finish? I'm trying to ask when our talented guest had time to make dinner. Which was fantastic." She let her eyes linger on Griffin too long.

He took the steamy appraisal as an invitation to play footsie beneath the table. Again.

"No mystery," he told her. "I threw everything in the slow cooker before I met my parents at services this morning."

"You're amazing."

"I know." He slid his empty bowl toward hers. "I cooked. You clean up." He turned to her father. "What are your thoughts on watching the Cavs? Game's on soon."

"Sounds like a plan."

Carrying the bowls to the sink, Rae darted a glance. "Griffin, it's starting to feel like you've moved in permanently. What if I *don't* want to watch the Cavs? You have your own house—I've seen it. A nice, cozy place right next door to Yuna's. Feel free to visit your home if I'm in the mood for a movie."

"I think I'll put my place up for sale," he teased.

"Hey. Totally *not* a tortoise response. Slow down!"

His eyes flashed. "Make me," he murmured in a way that made her breathless.

Quinn flipped open the dishwasher. "I don't mind if Griffin moves in." Clearly, he wasn't well versed in adult flirtation. He thought Griffin was serious. "Can we vote?" he added, lifting his hand. "What do you say, Connor? Are you with me?"

"Well, son . . . responsible adults don't move in with each other willy-nilly. If they're in love, they get married first." Clearing his throat, Connor grinned with pure mischief. "Now, don't get me wrong. I hope there's an election soon on the matter, because I'll gladly cast my vote."

Playing along, Griffin raised his hand. Then he leveled Rae with a heated glance. She caught herself sighing.

The doorbell rang.

Embarrassed, she pivoted away. "I'll get it," she said.

On the front stoop, Griffin's sister and his niece both looked nervous.

Sally offered an apologetic smile. "We're sorry to barge in like this."

"It's fine," Rae assured her.

Relief crested in Sally's eyes. "My brother mentioned you wanted to speak with Jackie later this week and, well, my daughter wanted to drop by anyway. She insisted, in fact. Not to stay, of course. We don't want to intrude." The relief melted beneath the anxiety bringing her nervous hands to her waist. "There's something else, however. I hope you don't mind if we take care of that first."

Turning, Sally cast a pointed look at the driver of the other car. A silver BMW that Rae hadn't noticed.

Katherine.

Startled, Rae glanced at the passenger side. Katherine had arrived by herself—her daughter, Stella, wasn't in the car.

Chapter 33

Katherine cut the engine and got out. Rae wondered at Sally's stern gaze, still trained on her best friend as Katherine wavered beside the BMW in her elegant coat. She clutched a Kate Spade bag. The breeze fluttered a tendril of her brown coif.

Sally's eyes continued to throw darts.

With an air of disbelief, Rae watched the interplay between the two women. Then with anger, rippling through her so quickly she feared she couldn't contain it.

The impulse to slam the door shut nearly took hold. *I can't deal with Katherine.* For a terrible instant, her thoughts wheeled back to the night of Lark's death. *Nothing good will come from talking to her.* Then Rae's attention returned to young Jackie, shivering on the front stoop beside her mother; biting the side of her lip, Jackie rocked from foot to foot. Her eyes leaped from the driveway to the house and then back again.

Jackie was also watching the three women, sensing every current snapping and sparking between them.

Something other than sorrow carried Rae outside. She wasn't sure how to define the emotion as she swept past Sally and her daughter and started across the icy, snow-crusted lawn. A beeline toward Katherine, forgoing the front walk or the pretense of congeniality—or shoes, for that matter. She'd left them beneath the kitchen table while enjoying Griffin's superb meal.

Smart, Rae. Stalking outside in your bare feet. It'll be just your luck if you lose your balance and—

Ten paces from the driveway, the treacherous ice took hold. Rae fell hard on her side.

Beside the car, Katherine dropped her purse. At an impressive speed for a woman in three-inch heels, she raced across the grass.

"Rae! Are you hurt?" Falling to her knees, she helped Rae into a sitting position.

"Don't touch me!"

Rae shoved her back. Shoved her hard enough, in fact, to push her onto her bottom. Mud rained down on them both. For painful seconds, they sat staring at each other. Rae felt sick, and embarrassed, and still angry as Katherine heaved in a breath.

On the exhale, Katherine began to sob.

"It's the migraines," she blurted, clutching the sodden grass. "They started again, right after my divorce. They're blinding. I've tried everything from yoga to meditation, but they still come. Unpredictably. I knew it was foolish not to fill the scrip earlier in the week, but Stella kept insisting we needed Halloween decorations for the slumber party. I forgot to fill the scrip. After the girls arrived, I shouldn't have left . . . I was only gone for thirty minutes, but that's no excuse. It's my fault you lost your daughter."

A buzzing started in Rae's ears. "Yes, it is."

"I know. I'd give anything to bring her back."

Another sob broke from her throat, stirring Rae's pity. Katherine appeared broken, her fingers lifting from the grass to swipe the tears away, unaware that she was leaving dabs of mud on her cheeks. She was more distraught over Rae's unbearable loss than would've been imaginable a scant five minutes ago.

Quickly she took hold of Rae's hand.

"I can't begin to guess what you're going through, Rae. None of us will ever truly understand. I'm not asking for your forgiveness—I don't deserve it—but I am grateful you're allowing Sally to bring Jackie to talk it out. She's begun seeing a child psychologist. It's helping, reliving that night. I want my daughter to begin therapy too. She needs the help . . . all the girls do. Losing your daughter has taken them out of childhood too soon."

Abruptly, Katherine halted the monologue. Covered her face as her shoulders quaked.

Rae struggled to her feet. The cold wind batted her hair in every direction. For a long moment, she stood there feeling nothing at all. As if Katherine's surprising disclosures had hollowed her out.

Aren't you worried what Jackie will tell me about Stella? With the thought came a jolt of pain, burning in Rae's chest. She reminded herself that a parent couldn't control her child. Not at the age of fourteen. If Stella had done something unthinkable, Katherine wasn't responsible. A minor point: broken, distraught, she'd carry her daughter's burdens like any good mother.

"Katherine."

The quaking of her shoulders bent her forward. It was terrible to witness.

"Katherine, let me help you up."

Which Rae did, gingerly. Holding on until Katherine's feet were steady and she'd stopped crying. Taking Katherine by the elbow, Rae steered her to her car.

"Can you drive? If you can't, let me call for a ride."

"No, I'm fine. Thanks for hearing me out."

"Of course."

A tiny thread of civility, enough to stop Katherine in her tracks. "Truly. I'm grateful you listened. I'm so very sorry."

"Thank you," Rae heard herself say. "The apology means a lot." Emotion clogged her throat.

And then, without thinking it through, she hugged Katherine. Without reservation—with only the need to impart comfort. To heal some small portion of the pain they were both feeling. Just as swiftly, she let Katherine go.

Eyes blurring, Rae walked away.

Chapter 34

Wordlessly, Rae ushered the others into the house. The soft click of a purse; fishing around inside, Sally withdrew a handful of tissues. Without asking permission, she knelt to mop up the worst of the mud on Rae's feet.

"Do you want us to give you a moment, to change?" Rising, she took a gander at Rae's shirt.

"We don't mind," Jackie added.

"No, I'm all right."

Opening the foyer closet, Rae grabbed a sweatshirt hanging in back. She pulled it over her head. Whatever Jackie was here to tell her, she couldn't bear to wait.

Sally placed a protective hand around her daughter's shoulder. "Honey? Do you want to ask Rae?"

The question was barely out when Griffin's voice came from the hallway.

"Rae! What are you doing out there? I thought we agreed you'd handle the dishes!"

Tossing a dish towel from hand to hand, Griffin waltzed into the room. "Sis." He grinned. "Fancy meeting you here."

Surprise competed with the mild delight on Sally's features. "Griffin. Hi."

Whatever the details of his falling-out with his sister, Griffin hadn't revealed them. Rae *did* know they hadn't spoken in some time. A situation he apparently planned to mend, from the look on his face.

Sally beat him to it. As he helped her out of her coat, she said, "I owe you an apology, little brother." She cast a curious glance at Rae. "Maybe more than one."

"Save it. I owe you about twenty apologies."

"For what?"

"All the stuffed animals I took from your closet in high school."

"You didn't!"

"Oh yes I did. Rae used them for target practice when Dad took us hunting. No way would she aim at the *real* furry critters." He feigned confusion. "Wait. Rae owes you those apologies."

A moment of levity in the middle of a tense situation. Totally Griffin's style. It was enough to banish the jitters pinging through Rae's body.

"Hey, don't look at me," she said. "I thought they were *your* stuffed animals. Castoffs from childhood."

Jackie, studying her feet until now, hugged a large paper bag close. A bag Rae hadn't noticed until now.

The girl asked, "Uncle Griffin, what are you talking about?"

He gave her a peck on the forehead. "Antics I pulled on your mother in the long-ago. Never mind, kiddo." He took her coat. "Are you here to ask Rae?"

"Ask me *what*?"

"Guys! The women need the house! Let's watch the Cavs at my place."

Like buffalo, the men stampeded from the house.

Sally closed the door behind them. "Why do I have the feeling my brother knew we were coming over?"

A feeling Rae shared. *Tortoise.* A slow-moving creature with superb planning abilities.

Jackie volunteered, "Uncle Griffin asked me to come around now. Didn't I tell you, Mom?"

Sally released a sigh. "You did not." Nervously, she assessed the living room. "There's not enough room here. Rae, I hate to be a bother. Is there somewhere we can spread out?"

They went into Hester's studio. Anxiety trailed Jackie as she caught sight of the wooden desk—the one Lark had used when working on her crafts. Recently, Connor and Quinn had moved the desk back to where it stood before Lark's death, near the wall of glass. Beside it, the row of houseplants on Kameko's much smaller, kid-size table gave the studio a cheery feel.

From the bag, the girl hefted out a large photo album. New, white leather. Next came a large manila envelope, stuffed full. Opening it, Jackie spilled out a host of photos—of Lark.

As a baby, during her toddler years and beyond. Lark cartwheeling across the lawn before Jackie's house with a group of girls. A snap Connor took last summer, when they walked the farm together. And more photos of Rae hugging her daughter or tickling her—lifting her from a bubble bath. Rimming Lark's mouth with that first tube of lip gloss in sixth grade. More images of Rae with her daughter than she could count.

Joy and grief tangled inside her. Rae pressed her hand to her heart. As she did, she felt another hand come to rest on her back. Sally's.

Steadying her, one mother to another, as Jackie bent over her work.

"Uncle Griffin asked your dad for the photos." Shuffling through the images, Jackie began sorting them into groups. She ran a nervous palm across her short, jagged hair. "Is it okay that I'm making an album for you?" She looked worried then, her eyes darting to Rae's. "I wanted to make it as a surprise gift, but it's better this way. I'm making an album for everyone in my family—they get to help. Pick out the photos, how they want them ordered."

"I'd love to help. Thank you, Jackie. This is the sweetest gift ever."

"Do you have a chair? It's easier if we sit down."

"Of course!"

Sally drifted toward the door. Peered out. "Is the kitchen that way?" She gestured to the left.

"You can't miss it."

"Should I make coffee?"

She was leaving them alone. The project, Rae understood, was a light to help a distressed child navigate a dark journey. The retelling of the night when Lark died.

"That would be great," Rae said. "Jackie, would you like tea? I have ginger, peppermint, and chamomile."

"Chamomile, please."

After Sally left, Rae grabbed two chairs. Together they sat down. She asked, "Can we do this chronologically? Start when Lark was a baby?"

"I was hoping you would say that. Can I show you my favorites? It'll only take a minute. Then you can decide if they're the ones you want in the album."

"Sure."

The girl slid the grouping of photos near, of Lark from infancy to age three. Pushing the album aside, she began lining them up in neat rows. Keeping her hands busy as she steered herself back to the night of the slumber party.

"Stella was mad at Lark all week long. Uncle Griffin didn't like Stella's mom anymore. I don't think he ever liked her much to begin with . . . they weren't dating very long."

"You're close to Stella. That must've been awkward for you."

"It was. Big-time. Me and Stella . . . we thought it would be cool if they ended up together. Then we'd be related, like new cousins. And Stella doesn't get along with her dad. She's hardly talked to him, since her parents got divorced. He lives in Shaker Heights now."

"Stella wanted a new dad?" What child wouldn't want Griffin? He was patient and kind, perfect father material. "She was angry because Lark was bragging that Griffin was *her* father?"

Jackie nodded. "It made Stella really mad. She didn't want Lark to come to the slumber party, but I'd already asked her to go." Her fingers paused on a photo of Lark as a chubby toddler. She wore a bright-yellow swimsuit with a design of watermelons embroidered on the fluttery skirt. "Rae, is it my fault Lark died? She wouldn't have come if I hadn't encouraged her."

Briefly Rae hugged her. She knew not to pull the child off task. It was clear this was difficult for Jackie.

"No, sweetie. It's not your fault. I encouraged Lark too. I knew she was fighting with someone, but I didn't want her to miss the party."

"Stella and Lark went outside together," Jackie said, "right after Mrs. Thomerson left for the drugstore. The other girls were in the basement, watching the movie. I told them to come back inside. I could see it was icy—they didn't even have their coats on."

"They wouldn't listen to you?"

"Stella did—finally. She came back inside. She went down to watch the movie."

A tear plopped down on the desk, startling Rae. The urge to offer solace was strong; she didn't dare. Now that Jackie had begun the awful tale, it was best to let her finish.

Her hands fluttered like butterflies, hovering above the final photographs in the group. Sorting quickly, organizing with efficiency.

"I went back out, to reason with Lark. She told me to go away. That she only needed a minute to herself. To cool down. Or decide to leave. She was sending a text. She was by herself, Rae. I'm positive. She was sending a text and pacing near the pool."

Grief welled inside Rae.

Should've stayed home.

The grief threatened to pull her into the watery depths of despair, but she focused on what Jackie had revealed instead. The glimmer of light at the center of a tragic story.

No one had caused Lark's death. It *was* a terrible accident. *How could I lose my precious child this way? My beautiful, perfect girl—taken in the most banal way.* There was no sense to it, no reason. If any number of things had been different—if Rae had agreed that Lark should stay home, if the girls hadn't argued, or if Chardon hadn't experienced a freak snowstorm in October and Lark hadn't gone outside and slipped on the ice—she'd be alive today. She'd be painting her toenails three shades of green and leaving butterscotch candies on Connor's books whenever she'd worn through his patience.

She'd be here, in Hester's studio, making it her own. *Mom, what do you think of this?* Holding her latest artistic creation aloft, leaving paints and brushes scattered about for Rae to clean up.

I love you, baby girl.

Eyes closed, Rae swallowed down a sob. The heartache nearly overwhelmed her, but she clung to the other part of Jackie's story: Quinn overheard the sharp words between Stella and Lark, but Stella, thankfully, had gone back inside. She'd done no harm.

Sorrow is contagious like a virus. When Rae sensed Jackie's close appraisal, she pushed the grief aside. She gave Jackie's hand a quick squeeze. The relief trembling across the girl's mouth was the sweetest reward.

Rae brightened her voice, saying, "Are we ready? May I choose my favorites now?"

"Go ahead." Jackie paused, the soft skin between her brows puckering. "My mom says I shouldn't ask those questions. The ones bugging me. She says it's not polite."

The unspoken questions hung between them: *Was Lark telling the truth? Was my uncle her father?*

Leaving the questions floating between them, Rae selected the chubby-baby-in-swimsuit pic. A definite keeper for the first page of the album. Which photo of Lark as a newborn was her favorite? She couldn't decide.

With a cryptic smile, Rae made another selection. "Your mother's right," she said at last. "It's best not to ask."

Chapter 35

Near dusk on a warm Sunday in April, Rae literally stumbled over the talented Hester Langdon's final surprise. The two large boxes of lights were hidden beneath a rumpled drop cloth in the basement, near a hodgepodge of paint rollers and brushes.

The lighting wasn't from Germany, like the rest. The shipping label read Mexico City. Wedging off the lid on the first box, Rae gasped. The errand that had brought her into the basement was forgotten. Hoisting both boxes in her arms, she hurried out of the basement.

"I thought you went downstairs to grab paintbrushes for the trim work," Yuna said. "What is that?"

After the day's work, no one had the energy to make dinner; Yuna was throwing together sandwiches and bowls of chopped carrot sticks. Griffin, Connor, Quinn, and Kipp were taking turns scraping the barn and pressure washing the surface. Griffin had rented industrial sprayers to add a new coat of red paint.

Rae set the boxes on the counter. "Forget about the paintbrushes. You've got to see this." She rustled through the tissue to withdraw a large globe of thin azure glass. Then another, in a sea-green hue. Doing a quick calculation, Rae guessed there were twenty globes in each box.

"They're part of your late mother's project?" Yuna lifted out a gorgeous purple light. "Why weren't they with the others?"

"I'm not sure. Maybe they were a last-minute addition to Mom's design. Somehow, the boxes got separated from the others. Maybe when my dad packed everything away, after the White Hurricane."

The sound of their excitement brought Kameko into the kitchen. Shelby, aware the five-year-old kept treats in her pockets, was hot on her tail.

"Mommy, let me see!" In big-girl fashion, the child pushed a chair to the counter. She climbed on top. "Can I hold one?"

"Better not, sweetheart. They're fragile. Here. You can look while I hold one. Isn't it pretty?"

"It is!"

At Kameko's feet, the dog gave an elaborate sigh. Lowering her head to the chair's seat, she trained her eager canine attention on her biggest admirer. A familiar signal, and Kameko withdrew a biscuit from her pocket.

Rae arched a brow. "How many treats have you given her today?" With all the activity surrounding the barn refurb, none of the adults had been keeping count.

"Oh, I don't know. A lot?"

"Why don't you cut her off now?"

"But this one's blueberry and salmon. It's her favorite!"

Stacking the sandwiches on a paper plate, Yuna sighed. "My bad."

Rae chuckled. "Don't worry about it."

Recently Yuna had discovered a doggie bakery in Beachwood where she'd spend "girl time" with her daughter, letting her choose new taste sensations for Shelby.

Rae tousled the child's glossy black hair. "Kameko, this is similar to your juice box obsession—Shelby doesn't know how to refuse the goodies. Keep it up, and we'll never get her to eat dinner." Thanks to constant loving, the once-starving dog was beginning to pack on too much pudge around her middle.

"Oh, all right." The rest of the biscuits clattered onto the counter. Then she pointed at the nearest box. "What's that, Auntie Rae?"

A neatly folded sheet nested beside the wads of tissue paper. A schematic.

With excitement, Rae drew it out. Her mother's neat cursive ran across a sketch of the trees nearest the house. From the looks of it, the globes were meant to attach to the lighting already in place. With her finger, Rae traced a smudged line of writing near the bottom of the page. Impossible to make out, except for three words in the middle of the sentence.

With a start, she read them. *Griffin to hang . . .*

"Be right back." Hoisting the boxes into her arms, she hurried out back.

"Rae—wait! What is it?"

She was too excited to explain. During the last months, why hadn't it once occurred to her that Griffin knew as much about Hester's grand design as anyone? He and Rae had been tight in high school, best buds during the summer before their senior year—before they'd discovered the passion that would alter their relationship. Griffin had been over at the house constantly. He'd been fascinated by Hester's new project, discussing the design with her whenever he and Rae stopped goofing off outside, or spent blistering-hot afternoons inside playing board games. And he'd been the one most excited about getting started on the project, overriding Hester's objections that she'd hire a man in town to hang the lights. At seventeen, he'd needed absolutely no encouragement to climb the highest trees to handle the task.

Remembering, she quickened her pace. She peered at the barn, where her father stood discussing something with Yuna's husband. Quinn was on a ladder, a steel hand scraper in his fist.

Rae spotted Griffin ambling toward her.

"Where's the eats?" he called out. He joined her beside the third tree from the house. "I thought you and Yuna were bringing something out. We're starving." Frowning, he took the top box from her arms. "What's all this?"

Together, they opened the boxes on the grass. "Griffin, look at this." Unfolding the schematic, she pointed to her mother's handwriting. "'Griffin to hang'—do you remember this? It looks like my mother wanted you to put these up."

"She did." With a casual shrug, he pointed to the label. "These are the lights from Mexico—she ordered them after the ones from Germany. About two weeks later. It was right in the middle of all those doctor visits. Right around when we finished eleventh grade at Chardon High."

"What doctor visits?" she demanded, misunderstanding him. "I was perfectly healthy in eleventh grade."

He flicked her nose. "Not you," he said, "your mother's visits." He studied her closely, nodding with satisfaction when she released a sudden breath. As her eyes began to blur, he kissed her lightly on the forehead. "It's no big deal, Rae. You went through so much the year of the White Hurricane, some stuff got lost in your memories. It happens. Besides, everything was fine in the end."

Slowly Rae came to her feet. She had forgotten—completely. *What's wrong with me?*

Griffin nodded at the back deck. "Go on—turn on the lights. I know how these fit into place. Hester showed me."

"You remember?" she asked, her voice catching. She swiped at her eyes.

"Like it was yesterday. And don't cry. You should feel happy—your mother is thrilled we found the last parts of her design." He teasingly glanced at the clouds racing across the sky. "Right, Hester?"

"Well, don't keep me waiting," Rae said, pulling herself together. "I'm eager to see the final result."

Starting toward the deck, she wondered how she could've forgotten Hester's breast cancer scare. It had seemed inconsequential to a teenager;

her mother hadn't even mentioned the tests until receiving an assurance from her gynecologist that the tumor was benign. The same night she'd told Rae, she'd gone into all-out creative mode, staying up late in the studio to begin plotting out the lighting design.

Griffin had just screwed the final globe into place as Rae returned to his side. The effect was beautiful, the larger bursts of illumination spilling color across the grass. A rainbow of hues, a celebration of light.

Considering, Griffin slung an arm across her shoulder. "Your mom had a saying, after the doctor gave her the all clear and she got excited about this project. Not a saying, come to think of it—it's what she called this project, whenever we talked about it that summer. I can't remember what it was."

"I do," Rae murmured, her heart lifting. "Hope lights the way."

At last, she knew it was true.

Chapter 36

At eight o'clock, Night on the Square was about to begin. In Chardon Square's center green, a large dance floor was set up near the courthouse. On the dais, the live band tuned their instruments. At the other end of the green, white table linens fluttered. Tables were set up across the expanse, as well as in the gazebo and the maple shack at the other end.

Rae asked, "How are you holding up?" She was standing alone with Yuna near the courthouse, away from the general commotion.

Yuna patted her baby bump. "The morning sickness hasn't bothered me for weeks. Over and done with." She looked down, past her shimmery teal dress, to her feet. "The swollen ankles are no picnic."

"Once Kenji arrives, it'll all be worth it." The happy couple would welcome their new son into the world later that summer. "Is Kameko still referring to her brother as the 'mean baby'?"

"Not lately."

"Wow. Talk about a turnaround. I assumed she'd keep up the nonsense until she *met* her baby brother."

A sudden grin took Yuna's lips hostage. "Okay, you got me. She probably would've. One of those bad habits a kid picks up, and it's hard to break."

Now Rae was intrigued. "How did you cure her of the 'mean baby' habit?"

"Through negotiation. We narrowed down our son's potential name to three options. We let Kameko pick her favorite. When he's old enough, she can tease Kenji about being allowed to pick his name. I'm sure he'll find ways to tease her back. The story of siblings, right?"

Rae didn't know; she'd grown up as an only child. But the thought was surprisingly sweet. Yuna's two younger sisters both lived nearer to Cleveland. Kipp's older brother was in Columbus, but they were also close.

"Griffin and Sally still tease each other," Rae said, "even though they're in their thirties. I'm glad they're still close."

"Where is Griffin?" Yuna checked her watch. Kipp was already at the table the foursome would share with another couple.

"Go on—sit down with Kipp. Stand here much longer, and you'll need to pee. Griffin's just running a little late. Some hang-up at work."

"I *always* have to pee." With a wave, Yuna hurried to their table.

Near the gazebo, Rae spotted him. Griffin had stopped to chat with Quinn—who looked agitated. Last night, Griffin had come out to the farm. He'd presented the youth with a fancy, space age–looking razor. They'd spent long minutes alone in the guest bathroom as an eighteen-year-old boy received his first lesson in proper shaving.

Dressed in a new blazer, Quinn swept the crowd with his gaze. The petite Ava, her brown hair swishing across her back, appeared at his side. They were grinning at each other foolishly as Griffin, taking his cue, ducked into the crowd. He was shaking hands and pausing for brief conversations as he wended his way toward the courthouse, where they'd agreed to meet.

Mik was in a minimum-security prison near Dayton. Probably for another two years. He was participating daily in the prison's anger-man-agement sessions. He'd also volunteered to help younger inmates learn the basics of mechanics in the facility's workshop. Small steps, but for a man with a deplorable history of abusing others, they meant something.

Penny was long gone, their house sold. No one knew where she'd gone; Quinn didn't care. Nor was he interested in visiting Mik—only Rae had made the trip, once.

She went alone.

She doubted she'd ever find the means to forgive what he'd done to Quinn—or to her, so many years ago. She was only human, and that level of forgiveness seemed beyond anything she was capable of achieving. But she wanted to make peace with the past—to confront it, then let it go. She was no longer satisfied with burying the worst secrets or allowing them to fester inside her.

Rae only stayed long enough at the correctional facility to get the facts: what Mik had done to her, he'd never done to another woman. There was no way to know for certain that he'd told her the truth. But she believed that he had.

In September, Quinn would begin commuting to culinary classes at Tri-C. The discussion of when Quinn would move out was off the table. Not for several more years, Rae hoped. He wasn't done growing up just yet.

Griffin appeared at her side. "Sorry I'm late." He kissed her.

"Were you trying to glad-hand everyone here? If you're planning to unseat Kipp as Chardon's mayor, we should give him fair warning."

"Nope. Just making connections." Spotting his sister and Trenton on the other side of the dance floor, he waved. Then he motioned toward a middle-aged woman in a flowered dress. "Is she the owner of the new printing shop? Maybe I should wander over, say hello."

"Griffin, sell design services on your own time. You don't see me hitting people up about their insurance policies. Stop working. We're on a date."

"Right."

His glance skipped over her hip-hugging silk dress. She'd spent hours at the store, pushing off suggestions as Yuna—practically waddling and complaining about needing to pee—made her try on dozens of styles. Apparently, the effort was in vain.

Griffin said, "Thank you."

"For what?"

He threaded his fingers through her long, untamable hair. "For not getting your hair done. I was afraid Yuna would talk you into going overboard. Styling your hair and putting it up on your head. I like it the way it is."

"I need a trim. My hair's getting too long."

"I love your long hair."

For proof, Griffin dipped his face near. He pressed a lingering kiss beneath her ear. Rae trembled. Drawing back, he smiled triumphantly.

They were at risk of their gazes tangling. Whenever it happened, Rae experienced the intensity of a July heat wave. Griffin, she knew, did too.

He cleared his throat.

Donning a reserved expression, he gestured at the festivities. "You did a great job." His gaze was still fiery. He managed to drag his eyes from her face. "You've added lots of younger people to the mix. Young and old—a good blend. Night on the Square is becoming the city's hottest event."

"Don't give me credit. Two of the men on the planning committee came to a truce. They'd been battling over a DJ versus the five-piece ensemble we've used in the past. They settled on a wedding band that plays modern *and* the classics."

Griffin's expression shifted. "I wish Lark were here to join us." Sadness darted across his features.

The sky was turning from reddish gold to midnight blue. The evening's first stars winked bright.

"I'm sure she is."

"I loved her, Rae. In the brief months I knew Lark, I tattooed her on my heart."

The admission touched her deeply. "Even though she wasn't your child?"

"She was *our* child, Rae—in all the ways that count. Lark is stubborn, like her mother. Bright. And funny, when you least expect it."

Now Rae's eyes were misting.

"You're talking as if she's still here," she managed.

"Because she is, in our hearts. Perhaps she's watching over us too. Hanging out with Hester, somewhere past those stars over there."

"Are you growing a mystical side?"

"I suppose." A contemplative silence, then he said, "Like I was saying, Lark is stubborn like you. She intended to come into the world that night, and she did. The circumstances don't matter. Lark arrived when she'd planned. I'll always be grateful I got to know her."

He reached for her hand. Rae clung tight.

"I'm glad too," she murmured.

"I'm looking forward to getting to know her better, someday." Griffin studied the darkening sky and the stars winking on in silvery threads. "Rae, during our last year of high school . . . we picked out four names. Remember? We wanted two girls, two boys. The perfect combination."

"Lark, Sophie, Adam, and Penn."

"Do you think our other kids are with Lark, waiting to make a grand entrance?"

The sweet question nearly closed Rae's throat. Letting go of his hand, she trailed her fingers up Griffin's sturdy arm, past his wide shoulder. She rested her palm against his cheek.

Then amusement—unbidden—melted the emotion tightening her throat.

"Reality check," she said. "In our relationship, who's the hare and who's the tortoise?"

Griffin smiled. "I don't recall."

AUTHOR'S NOTE

On January 25, 1978, residents in northeastern Ohio went to bed unaware that two low-pressure systems converging over the state would build into a blizzard for the record books.

The Ohio Turnpike shut down for the first time in its history, and ten-foot snowdrifts pummeled houses and buried cars. A major general of the Ohio National Guard described the White Hurricane's effect on transportation as comparable to a nuclear attack. Windchills plummeted to forty degrees below zero Fahrenheit; fifty-one Ohioans died during the blizzard, many as they huddled trapped in their cars, or as they tried to walk to safety in whiteout conditions.

Geauga County—where this novel takes place and where my parents and three younger sisters resided in 1978—is snowbelt country in the best of times. During the White Hurricane, the city of Chardon came to a standstill for days.

At the time of the blizzard, I was a college student safely ensconced in the Cleveland suburb of Shaker Heights, renting a room from one of my father's old fraternity brothers. And while I didn't experience the worst effects of the White Hurricane, the frightening stories my parents and younger sisters told for years to come were destined, one day, to find their way into one of my books.

For readers who lived through the real White Hurricane, I hope you won't mind that I moved the historic storm to present day for the purposes of my story. None of the characters depicted here are based on real people, and I took artistic license by creating fictional establishments on and near Chardon Square. Any errors in fact made to describe Ohio's storm of the century rest solely with me.

ACKNOWLEDGMENTS

To my wonderful editor, Christopher Werner, for his brilliant suggestions and for taking the time from his busy schedule to read early drafts; to my developmental editor, Krista Stroever, for all her fabulous insights and keen eye; and to Lake Union's editorial director, Danielle Marshall, for the opportunity to write *The Passing Storm* for Amazon Publishing.

To my agent, Pamela Harty, for her generous advice and friendship.

To my copyeditor, Sarah Engel; my production editor, Nicole Burns-Ascue; and my proofreader, Claire Caterer, for both their patience and their careful edits. Heartfelt thanks to Caroline Teagle Johnson for the beautiful cover design.

And to Barry, for reading every review throughout the years and believing even when I entertained doubts. I love you, always.

BOOK CLUB QUESTIONS

1. Discuss how the White Hurricane alters Rae's life as she begins to keep secrets from the people she loves. Would she have kept those secrets if she had lost Connor during the blizzard instead of Hester?
2. Has a significant life event—good or bad—ever led you to keep a secret from someone you loved? Why?
3. Other characters—Connor, Quinn, Yuna, and Griffin—also keep secrets. What are those secrets? Why are they kept?
4. How do the characters Yuna, Sally, and Connor serve to deepen the reader's understanding of Rae? Of Griffin?
5. How does the White Hurricane symbolize the novel's theme of drawing up courage and self-love to face uncomfortable truths?
6. How does weather alter the mood of a given scene? Cite examples.
7. Lark does not appear in the novel. Yet her presence is strongly felt. Discuss her impact on the character or characters of your choice: Rae, Quinn, Griffin, Connor, Jackie, and Katherine.

8. Early in the book, the reader learns that Rae had refused to give Lark information about her father. Later, Rae chooses not to tell Quinn of his biological connection to her daughter. Do you agree with Rae's decision? Are some secrets too damaging to share with a child or a young adult?

9. The special nature of the relationship between siblings is explored through Griffin's interactions with Sally. Would the story's events have been different if Griffin had an older brother instead? In what way?

10. Discuss your favorite character in the book. What did you find most appealing about him or her?

If your book club would like to discuss *The Passing Storm* with the author, please contact her at christine@christinenolfi.com with BOOK CLUB DISCUSSION in the subject line. Christine is usually able to schedule several online meetings per month through Zoom, Skype, or Facebook.

ABOUT THE AUTHOR

Christine Nolfi is the proud mother of six adult children. She is the author of *The Road She Left Behind*, a top book-club pick by *Working Mother* and *Parade* magazines; the award-winning Sweet Lake series, which includes *Sweet Lake*, *The Comfort of Secrets*, and *The Season of Silver Linings*; and the Liberty series and the Heavenscribe trilogy. A native of Ohio, Christine now resides in South Carolina with her husband and their crazy wheaten terrier, Lucy. For the latest information about her releases and future books, visit www.christinenolfi.com.